# A Stallion to Die For

## An Equestrian Suspense

# A STALLION TO DIE FOR:
# AN EQUESTRIAN SUSPENSE

Library of Congress Control Number 2012914260
Casebound: 978-1-938756-00-9
Trade: 978-1-938756-01-6
Kindle: 978-1-938756-02-3
EPUB: 978-1-938756-03-0

Publisher's Cataloging-in-Publication Data

Stanton, Judith.
    A Stallion to die for : an equestrian suspense / Judith Stanton.
    p. cm.
    ISBN 978-1-938756-01-6
    1. Horses –Fiction. 2. Eventing (Horsemanship) –Fiction. 3. Three-day event (Horsemanship) –Fiction. 4. Competition horses – Training –Fiction. 5. Suspense Fiction. 6. Love Stories. I. Title.
PS3619.T3668 S83 2012
813.6 –dc23
        2012914260

Design by Frogtown Bookmaker
Front cover photo copyright © 2012 by Samantha L. Clark
Back cover art copyright © 1988 by J.L. Osborne (1923-2006)


Published by Cat Crossing Press
www.catcrossing.com

# A Stallion
## to
# Die For

## Judith Stanton

Cat Crossing Press

Also by Judith Stanton

Fiction

*The Kissing Gate*

*The Mad Marquis*

*His Stolen Bride* (RITA Finalist)

*Wild Indigo*

Non-fiction

*The Collected Letters of Charlotte Smith*

Judith is donating some of this novel's proceeds to Old Friends equine retirement facility, and you can too. Read about them at www.oldfriendsequine.org. And you can follow Little Silver Charm, Old Friends' soccer-playing miniature horse, on Facebook.

*For Carol,*
*who brings the same integrity,*
*loyalty and laughter*
*to her horses and her friends*

# Part One. Hawks Nest Stallion

## *August*

Three-day eventing, once called the Military
Games, was a contest for cavalry men and their
mounts. America first sent a team of three
horse and rider pairs to the 1912 Olympics. It
has been the Triathlon for horses ever since.

On the first day, dressage tests the horse's
obedience while executing school figures on the
flat. On the second, a grueling cross-country
gallop over solid obstacles tests the courage,
stamina, and boldness of horse and rider. On
the third, a short stadium jumping round proves
the horse is fit and sound.

Competitors can be sixteen to over sixty,
and men and women compete equally. The risk and
thrill of cross-country attracts bold, fearless
equestrians. Even today, riders and horses die
competing. The faint of heart need not apply.

> *A History of the U. S. Army Olympic*
> *Equestrian Team (1912-1948)*
> Colonel Jacob McRae, USA Maj. Ret.

# One

At the McRae Center sign, Lexy Imbriani turned onto a dirt lane, feeling miserable and conspicuous in her flaming red Neon Rent-a-Wreck. Driving on the wrong side of the road had been hard enough. But halfway between the Raleigh-Durham airport and Southern Pines, NC, the air conditioning on her dinged and dented rental had conked out. She'd rolled the windows down, and the superheated air had lashed tendrils of her light brown hair around her face.

She'd jiggled the AC lever again, and again no luck. Another ten minutes of this, and she'd pass out. It was so bloody hot. Not that she could fix the weather, the car, or her life. The dead lump that had lodged in her chest for a month now had left her numb to heat and ratty cars and foreign roads that led to people she barely knew. Except Hamp Gambrell, her last hope.

On either side of the rutted lane, posh black four-board horse fencing marked off paddock after paddock, but not a horse in sight. They'd probably retreated to their run-in sheds to escape the flies.

Hamp's directions said to keep driving until she saw the barns, so she nudged the car ahead, feeling its tires slip and bounce on the sandy drive. Slowing, she passed a gabled mansion, quite new, a five-car garage, a big regulation dressage arena, and a stadium jumping arena four times as large. Its bright multicolored jumps sparkled in the sun. Looked like the owners had the new synthetic footing too.

And money. Buckets of it.

But where was Hamp?

She squinted into the glare, the heat siphoning off her last bits of energy. It even sounded hot, cicadas whirring from the trees and crickets chirping in the straggly grass. A yellow early-morning sun shot arrows of light through tall long-needled pines, and she adjusted the sun visor so she could see.

Already she missed trees heavy with leaves, and the cool green Yorkshire heaths she'd left behind—three days ago? Four? It had been the worst month of her life, her mother dead in a car accident, her father learning he was not her father, then kicking her out, pulling strings and getting her stripped of her EU citizenship. And now this, exiled to the United States, which she hadn't visited since she was three. But she'd been born here, so was a citizen, and they had to take her in.

She rounded the corner of the farm's white steel-clad stables and saw Hamp, his back to her, hosing his lanky chestnut at a washstand in the sun, tall and lean and looking easy in his skin. Relief trickled through her. Super that he was an Olympic prospect, but far better that they were lovers. Pulling under the scant shade of a skinny pine, she cut off the engine, got out of the sauna that was her car, and walked toward him, shoes crunching across the sand.

"Hamp," she said quietly, approaching him and his horse from the side, mindful of spooking the big gelding. "I made it."

Hamp turned, and his green eyes searched hers. "Lexy, thank God. I thought you said yesterday." And he shut off the water and took her in his arms.

Exhausted as she was, her heart skipped a beat. His cropped black hair spiked in all directions, trendy and wildly out of keeping with who he really was—a thirty-year-old half-Navajo old soul from a sheep ranch in New Mexico. Last winter he'd come to England to campaign Axiom to compete at Badminton, and they'd fallen for each other hard, horses and hot sex their bond. In May when he'd left, her mother had been alive.

Lexy fought a wash of grief and gave her best shrug. "Got held up at JFK. Homeland Security took exception to my under-used American passport and lack of a permanent address."

"Damn." He shook his head in sympathy. "You must be bushed."

"I'm okay." But tears sprang to her eyes.

He drew her close and murmured in her ear, "I am so sorry about your mother."

Mortified, she cried onto his shirt, wracking sobs she'd held back for days. He tightened his arms around her as if he could absorb her grief, cancel her mother's lie. He waited until she calmed, then pulled away to look at her again.

"Bad news here too—barn fire last night, farm next door, Chip's cousin, you know. Jordan McRae."

"God," she said, fearing disaster had followed her. Then she realized Hamp smelled like smoke. "You were there. You all right?"

"Singed, spooked. We got the horses out, but it was Jordan's third weird accident this year."

Lexy blew her nose, too drained to find the right words. "Anybody hurt?"

"Luckily, no. A wing of one of the barns collapsed, coupla empty stalls used for shavings, storage, hay."

She pressed her lips together, trying to hold back another bout of tears, but he seemed to see right through her.

"Hey," he said gently. "I've got great news. That job. Ben Holt needs a rider."

"For what?"

"To keep his horses in work."

"He's hurt?"

"No, Ed Faraday's out of commission, and they tapped Ben to coach the U.S. three-day team for the next Olympics. He's got the travel schedule from hell, no time for his horses. But if he hadn't been driving past Hawks Nest last night coming home from the airport, nobody would have seen the fire."

Lexy shuddered against Hamp. "What luck."

"Anyway, I told him about you. He said he'd give you a try."

She blinked, trying to wrap her fried brain around such news—a barn fire where no one had died, an unhoped-for opportunity for her. She'd come to Chip McRae's farm to live with Hamp. But Ben Holt, four-time Olympic eventer, was icing on the cake. He'd coached her in England a couple of years ago. He'd been the best.

"Or Deirdre Fleming needs a trainer," Hamp added judiciously, "if you want to move to Virginia. She's just found out she's having twins. So you have a choice."

Amazing. She hadn't been able to choose between peanuts and pretzels on the plane—planes. Birmingham to JFK, JFK to Dulles, Dulles to RDU. Limp pasta, soggy bread. She'd had a stale bun before the no-frills red-eye flight, and nothing since. She felt weak but hated the thought of food.

"Yeah," he went on, "between living with me and working for the Olympic coach, or one of the top trainers on the East Coast."

She fought her way to a response. "I can't thank you enough. I'm down to my last pound. Euro. Dollar. Whatever."

He gave her a wry smile of sympathy—he was an outsider too—and touched her face with the gentle fingers that worked magic on his horses. And on her last spring. Given how hot they'd been for each other, she marveled at his restraint. If he'd pushed for a kiss, she felt so frazzled she'd have detonated.

"You're gonna be fine," he said earnestly. "It's America. Anything can happen."

For her, it already had. And she hadn't told him what her father had done with her horses.

An oversized rig with too many wheels at its rear axle rumbled up the drive, pulling what looked like a six-horse box, its aluminum skin glinting under the midday sun. From inside, a horse's hooves thudded against its padded walls in protest, the sound carrying over the truck's roar fifty yards away.

A shiver passed through her, a jolt of dread.

"Shit, gotta run." Hamp unhooked Axiom, trotted him into a stall, and returned to her. "You wait. I'll be back."

But Lexy never stood by when a horse was in trouble.

Despite her fatigue, she caught up to Hamp. "Who is it?"

"Jordan's stallion, Nobilo. Bo. You saw him in France at Pau."

Yes, she'd been younger when she'd seen Jordan McRae and her big dark bay thunder around the cross-country course. Later they'd won the Pan Am Games, and he'd been her top Olympic prospect before her accident.

"I thought she sold him," Lexy said.

"She did. Bought him back last month. Ben helped her put together a syndicate, bought a share himself."

"But they're practically sworn ene—"

She broke off as Ben Holt came up from the barn, clothes smeared with dirt and ashes. She noted his whipcord frame and the tanned, lined skin of a lifelong horseman who spent his days outdoors. He was older than Lexy by at least two decades, but he moved like Hamp, light on his feet and alert to everything.

He held up a hand and closed his fist, signaling *Stop. Here.* The driver eased the big rig to a halt as if it carried royalty.

Nobilo landed a volley of kicks on the inside wall, and the whole rig rocked.

"Oh my God, he'll ruin himself," Lexy cried.

Ben's head jerked around to her. "And you are—" He frowned, his iceberg eyes taking in her unkempt state.

She opened her mouth, but Hamp cut in in his mild way. "This is the rider from England I recommended. Lexy Imbriani. She came in first for riders under twenty-five at Badminton last May," he added with pride.

Ben scrutinized her, tapped his brow. "I've seen you ride—"

"At a clinic at Bishop Burton, a couple of years ago."

"Yes, right. You want to be useful, go stand at the window by Bo's head and talk to him. Hamp, get some extra ropes."

"I'm hired?" Her head whirled.

"Provisionally. You have references? On top of Hamp's."

"In the mail."

"Visa? Papers?"

"Passport. I'm an American citizen."

"Okay. I gotta check this guy's legs for injuries." He looked calm and confident, like Ulrich Dichter, the horse whisperer she'd studied under in Spain, and she felt a spurt of hope that he could calm the stallion.

Hamp sprinted off, and Lexy hurried to the side of the horse box, leaving Ben behind the stallion. But she knew horses could see almost 360 degrees around them, except their own tails and the ground beneath their noses, and this one didn't miss a trick. Furious, he kicked the wall, *thud, thud, blamblamblam,* as if to beat it down and kill the man behind it.

She'd seen horses rage like this and knew some idiot owner was behind it. Working with Ulrich, she'd learned she had a gift for helping troubled horses. On her side of the horse box, the windows were bolted open to let in air, but the hot morning sun slanted in opposite, leaving Nobilo in shadows on her side. She stepped closer. He bared his teeth and chomped at the horizontal bars that protected her.

*You don't scare me,* she thought, adrenalin masking her fatigue.

When she'd seen Jordan McRae compete him at Pau in France, he'd been brilliant, sane. So what had happened? Releasing her tension, Lexy let out a breath and ducked her head, saying with her body, *I'm not your enemy.*

He didn't lunge at her.

She made the calming noise Ulrich used to settle a distressed horse—*chrrrr, chrrrr,* trilling her *r's* softly. He called it mare-speak, used to comfort foals.

She moved nearer, squinting to see inside.

Bo flicked one ear forward then flattened both ears against his head.

Freezing, she let him inspect her through the barred window, his eyes flashing with hostility.

She stole a glance at him, and gasped.

Above the noseband of his halter, she saw a hole in his face as big as a golf ball. Pus drained down to his nostrils. Nausea rose in her throat, and pangs of sympathy washed her thighs. The wound screamed of abuse and stupidity. His coat had the hard stare coats took on when owners neglected feeding, grooming, basic exercise. They hadn't put a head guard on him either or boots to protect his legs if he scrambled for balance or, like now, kicked.

He looked as if they'd hauled him out of some filthy stall and driven him onto the trailer, good riddance. She could feel his hurt and his hatred of human beings, and clenched her fists to hide her shaking hands.

Behind the box, Hamp had returned, and Ben was unlatching the rear door, preparing to lower the ramp.

She hurried to him. "You need to see this."

Ben lifted a sandy brow. "See what?"

"His head. He's hurt."

He clicked the latch in place and came to check. Interesting. He'd hired her in a snap, and now he was taking her at her word. No fuss, no hesitation. He saw the wound from a couple of steps out, swore, and then appeared to relax as he closed in.

Bo squealed and reared, banging the unprotected top of his head, his poll, against the trailer's metal roof. Flecks of his blood splattered through the window.

"That's coming from his poll," Lexy blurted.

Ben nodded and opened a side door that gave him access to the horse. "I'm gonna see how bad it is. At least, get a head guard on him..."

Lexy wanted to reach out and stop him. She'd have gone about it differently, taken more time, given the horse a chance to smell her, trust her, settle. But Ben was far more experienced than she, and he was, after all, part owner of the horse.

Scared for the horse and him, she watched him ease into the trailer, calm and cool in the close heat.

# Two

The stallion screamed and bared his teeth and lunged. Ben backed out in a flash, holding his forearm, blood oozing between his fingers. "My fault, damn it. I know better."

Lexy scowled, amazed he blamed himself.

Hamp, whose concern for man and horse showed in his clenched jaw, dove into the tack compartment and whipped out a first aid kit.

"Later," Ben said, wrapping a bandana around his injury. "He's okay, I think. The wounds on his face, though—Ah, crap. What am I going to tell her?"

He stepped aside and speed-dialed someone.

"Jordan. Ben," he said. "Bo's here. He's hurt."

He listened.

"Nope, Ty just got here... No, no colic... Yes, he's on his feet."

A longer silence while he listened again.

"It's his face, a suppurated wound. Big as a silver dollar. They didn't tell you?"

Evidently not. Lexy could almost hear the woman's anger spitting through the air.

"A. Hole. In. His. Head," Ben said. "Nasal cavity. Infection, sinus drainage." Pause. "No, I don't know what happened. Call your buddy Roger. This horse needs his services."

A pause. "No way. I'm bringing him home."

Lexy felt like an eavesdropper, but Hamp could hear him, too.

Ben pressed his lips together, then said into his cell, "Look, I'm slammed. Your cousin Chip doesn't run an equine hospital here. Which is what Bo needs."

More listening. Lexy could feel her repugnance for discord twisting in her gut.

"I'm *not* welching on a deal," Ben said, his jaw muscles working. "The deal was for me to get a healthy horse up to speed for competition. I'd have squeezed that into my crazy schedule to get you back in the saddle." He chewed his lower lip, listened a little longer, then said calmly, "Open the gate, Jordan, and call your vet. We'll be there in ten."

He pocketed his cell and gestured Hamp into the truck.

In a pinch, it would seat five grown men, two in the captain's chairs and three on the rear bench. There was room for Lexy, but they didn't invite her. So she stood, dismayed. Bo had suddenly become the most important creature in her world, and they were hauling him away.

Ben stepped on the truck's running board.

"Camera on, Tyrone?" he asked the driver. An on-board camera would let them monitor the horse from the cab.

"Nope, busted." Tyrone looked up from making entries in a log. He was a compact black man with big, good-looking features, bunched muscles under a tight denim shirt and jeans, and a surly attitude.

"Hamp," Ben said. "You got your cell?"

Hamp checked his waistband and nodded.

"You ride in the trailer, and call me if the horse goes down or wigs out."

It wasn't an English horsebox, Lexy realized, but the old, well-kept trailer had a ten-foot tack and dressing room in front partitioned from the horses' quarters. From it, a person could safely watch the horse through a high oblong Plexiglas window.

"Right." Hamp stepped inside and slid the window open.

Bo exploded, slamming his shoulder against the partition as if to crush the man on the other side.

Damn, Lexy thought. Bo hated men.

Ben scrubbed his hand over his mouth, taking his time with a distraught horse as any good horseman would. Lexy waited too, her heart in her throat. She approved that Ben hadn't punished Bo but approved his determination more. It spoke to some deep part of her, the part that had fallen for Mind the Gap, the mare who'd become her beloved Mindy, when she'd first seen her huddled in that slaughter wagon. Today Lexy was falling headlong in love again with a damaged creature who was beautiful and wild.

Not hers, but she had to help him.

Tense, noisy minutes passed, and Bo kept fighting.

Hamp poked his head out. "Not working, Ben."

"No shit," Ben said.

From a distance, a horse whinnied. Bo let out a piercing neigh, unlike the well-behaved cross-country machine Lexy had first seen in France. Mares in heat—in estrus—now answered him urgently from barns and paddocks. Nearer, a stallion put in his two cents with a lower, angry cry. Bo blasted out a challenge, more whinnies back and forth, more challenging for them, more worrying for her.

Bo's previous owners clearly hadn't known how to manage a stallion.

"It's the mares," Hamp said. "He's losing it."

"We better pull out," Tyrone put in. "He'll settle on the road."

"It's not far enough for him to settle," Hamp said.

"I agree," Ben said. "He's got the scent of the mares, and he wants at them."

"I'd like to try with him, Mr. Holt," Lexy butted in, surprising herself.

"Ben," he corrected. His eyes were as blue as Arctic ice, and they bore into hers, assessing her more keenly than at that clinic where she hadn't been able to make her elbows or her back do what he'd asked.

"I mean, maybe it's men," she said. "He didn't kick at me."

"So he didn't," Ben said. "Your cell working?"

"Don't know," she said, taken aback by his directness. "It's in my bags."

"Use mine," Hamp said. "Punch memory three for Ben."

Ben answered, and she slid into the dressing room. Before he could click off, she reported softly, "His eyes look wild, but he only flicked an ear at me."

"Okay, good call," Ben said. "He gets in trouble, call me and we'll stop."

Then Ben and Hamp went to the truck's cab, leaving her on her own. Inside, the air was close and hot and smelled of anxiety and muck and an ungroomed, sweaty horse. Outside, she heard the truck doors bang shut and felt the vibration of the engine as Tyrone powered up the diesel and rolled down the sandy drive and onto the county asphalt in such a slow and steady arc Lexy couldn't feel the turn.

But Bo felt it, and lowered his head and spraddled his legs for balance, scrambling. The rig straightened onto the paved lane. As best she could see, expensive four-board horse fencing and a fringe of tall lean pines lined either side. The rig picked up speed, and Bo fidgeted.

"Easy..." she crooned. "Easy."

He pawed, ignoring her. Shortly, the rig turned onto a driveway lined with ancient oaks. Jordan McRae's farm was the Southern plantation of Lexy's imagination, from her mother's annual screenings of *Gone with the Wind*. Except this plantation had fenced-off areas with big, cheerfully colored jumps and a large, new, covered arena. Part posh and part shabby chic. The rig rolled to a stop in front of the warren of buildings that made up Hawks Nest stables. To Lexy's surprise, most of the three wings were still standing, only the far end of one still smoldering.

She opened the tack compartment's door, stepped out, and gagged on the acrid odor of charred wood and burnt hay. One fire truck remained. A county sheriff's cruiser arrived, another left, and another sheriff's bright white SUV sat in the middle of the parking area. Then she saw a woman running up from the skeletal remains, bracing one leg on a cane.

Had to be the celebrated Jordan McRae, tall and slender with short thick chestnut hair. As she neared, Lexy could see her matching chestnut eyes. They were blazing.

Ben met her halfway, taking her free hand to slow her down.

She retracted it, her face gray as ashes. "What the hell happened to my horse?"

And in that moment, Jordan's Southern accent sounded so like Lexy's mother's she thought her heart would break.

# Three

**H**e's hurt," Lexy explained.

Jordan looked past her to Ben. "I need to see this. Get him out."

Ben steadied her shoulders with his hands. "Not here, Jordan, not in the open. We don't know what we've got."

She jabbed her fingers into her close-cropped hair in dismay. Bo whinnied again, and anxious answers echoed from the pastures. Then he was kicking, going down, thrashing, and Lexy heard a frantic scramble.

It would be suicide to enter.

Despite a doubting look from Jordan, Lexy slipped into the dressing room and *chrrred* at him again. The trailer tie had held, and he clambered to his feet, head down in defeat, eyes glazed. *Chrrr,* she said over and over like a lullaby. He flicked an ear at her and took a shuddering breath.

Outside, Lexy could see Jordan hacking her lungs out. Ben patted her back. "That cough sounds serious," he said.

"I need to see Bo. You're scaring me."

"He's got issues, but he's not fighting now. Lexy's pretty good with him." Ben glanced at Lexy then turned back to Jordan. "You, however, are in denial."

"No, I'm on auto-pilot." Another coughing fit took over.

Ben stood by until she stopped. "Smoke inhalation, right? You seen a doctor?"

"When?" She nodded at the patrol car she'd just hobbled away from.

"Gwen's still here?"

Jordan shrugged. "You know my sister—always has her sheriff hat on. She's not leaving till her arson man finishes."

"Crap. You don't suspect arson."

"Absolutely not. Barn fires happen. Mice chew up the wiring. A mower throws a spark. Some dumb fuck lights a cigarette."

Lexy shuddered.

"Hey," Ben said to Jordan. "Your horses are safe. Let Gwen do what she's gotta do. And let's unload Bo. It was hearing those other stallions that sent him over the edge."

"Is there an arena we could unload him into?" Lexy blurted, knowing she was out of line.

Jordan McRae cut her a look, as if seeing her for the first time.

"And you are—?

"Lexy, ma'am."

"My new hire," Ben put in. "She's going to work my horses when I'm on the road. Highly recommended, just got in from England."

Jordan gave Ben a withering scowl. "And you brought her along because—?"

"She's the only one he hasn't tried to kill."

"*Kill?* My Bo?"

"Not kill, exactly." Ben held out his bandaged arm. Blood had seeped through the bandana, and Jordan gasped. "Jesus, Ben."

Lexy thought she saw the start of tears, but Jordan blinked them away.

"We can use the covered arena, Jordan," Ben said. "Out of the sun. Give him water, space, some privacy, a chance to settle down."

Jordan gave a tense nod of assent.

Lexy helped Hamp roll back the arena doors. Tyrone executed an expert Y-turn and backed the trailer to the opening. Bo's iron shoes thudded on the rubber matting, as if to say, *Get me out. Out, out. Out, out.*

The end of the trailer jutted into the arena, leaving the truck's cab in the sun. Under the vaulted metal roof, it wasn't so brutally hot, and Lexy's eyes adjusted to the shade. Between the top of the fence and the bottom of the eaves was some open space. Giant industrial fans mounted at either end pushed the sticky air around.

A big brown-haired bear of a man hurried up. "Afternoon, Ben," he said in a genial, silky Southern accent.

"Roger," Ben said, barely courteous.

"Jordan called. Said Bo needed me."

"He's got to settle down before we get to the vet part."

Ben sent Tyrone to round up hay and fresh water, then talked everyone through his plan for leading Bo off the trailer. He had the most fastidious safety standards, Lexy was pleased to hear.

When he finished, she headed for the trailer's access door.

"Lexy, wait," he called out.

She reached for the latch, puzzled. "He's responding to me now. I can handle him."

"Wait," he repeated. "Let me get him off. Then we'll see."

Lexy stiffened but gave way, and Ben reached for the latch.

"I'll do it," Jordan said. "He's my horse, and nobody knows him better."

"He's the syndicate's horse, and I've got a share. I'll get him," Ben said.

"I can handle my own horse, damn it," Jordan said.

Lexy sympathized with Jordan. She'd loved her own horses and couldn't forget the helpless sense of loss when she'd discovered her father had taken them from her. Getting either of them back in Bo's condition would break her heart.

Roger's gaze dropped to Jordan's cane. "Let them do it, Jordan. I want you safe. In fact, my best advice is to ship him out before you or somebody gets hurt."

"Not an option," she shot back.

Ben's brows snapped down. "Hate to admit it, but Roger's right. I'll find Bo a good trainer. We'll still have control."

"Look," Jordan said. "Your quick thinking saved my barn, and I couldn't be more grateful. But Bo stays here. After this fire, I need him more than ever."

Lexy felt a tangle of loyalties, but she was on Jordan's side.

Ben let out an exasperated sigh. "And he needs water. You latch the doors open and get out of the way. Lexy and Hamp can do the ramp."

Yielding, Jordan stepped back. Lexy and Hamp drew the arena doors tight to the trailer's sides so Bo couldn't escape. Ben climbed inside the trailer through the access door, lead line in hand, and snapped it onto Bo's halter in a seamless gesture before the stallion could bite him a second time. With Hamp, Lexy lifted the latch and lowered the ramp. Hamp unhooked the butt bar and quickly moved aside. Bo struck out at him anyway, then reared and banged his poll against the trailer's roof again. Tearing the lead from Ben's grip, Bo scrambled to escape, his equine brain imagining predators coming from all sides. Careening backwards down the sloped ramp, Bo flung himself from the trailer, his massive hindquarters pumping, his shod hooves scrabbling over the pebbled rubber matting. His hind legs buckled, and he landed on his butt and tumbled backwards tail over head.

Lexy's stomach clutched. He could have fractured his back or neck or skull. A few feet away from her, he powered to his feet, spraddled his legs and shook himself violently. Grit and sand spewed off him like ash from a volcano. Lines of sweat streaked his unkempt mahogany coat.

He lifted his muzzle and curled his upper lip in a Flehmen response as he caught the scent of the mares in distant paddocks. Beyond the bitter scent of smoke, the smell of their estrus called to him. He raised his dark head and trumpeted to his new herd.

All Lexy saw was the oozing wound in his face. Mentally she was setting out gauze pads and Betadine to clean and treat it and Vet Wrap to cover it. Jordan's vet would have antibiotics on his truck.

Hands outspread, Ben motioned everyone behind him, then averted his eyes and hunched his shoulders, inviting the horse to trust him.

Bo would have none of it. With a furious bellow, he tore down the right side of the arena, then snaked his neck out like a wild stallion patrolling its edges to protect his mares. Bears could be out there, or wolves, or robber stallions. Once, twice, he cruised the ring in a ground-swallowing trot.

Awed, Lexy couldn't tear her gaze from his raw power. No one else moved either, everyone feeling her selfsame awe. Hamp gave a soft whistle of admiration, and Jordan's face shone.

Bo picked up a gallop toward the far end, the lead line whipping his side, driving him on. His matted mane flapped against his neck, but his long tail streamed behind him like a flagship's semaphore. Bearing down on the far end at full speed, he bounced to a harrowing halt inches before he'd have hit the metal gate and snapped a leg.

"Sweet Mary," Lexy gasped, standing by Hamp and Ben and Jordan. There was nothing they could do.

Bo called to the mares so hard his sides pumped like bellows. Then he reared to his full height and struck the air. Landing, he pivoted off his hindquarters and trotted toward them, his stride floating and head held high as if to say, *I'm back. You got a problem with that?*

*No, no problem,* Lexy thought.

"He had a bad trip," Jordan said hopefully to Ben. "Give him a few days at home, he'll settle in. He knows me."

Ben moved toward her, hands low, fingers wide. "With a stallion, it's not going to be that simple."

"I'm sure I can bring him back."

He sighed and leaned against the trailer, hands flat behind him. "You don't get it, Jordan. Didn't we have him vetted?"

"Of course, *we* had him vetted. Roger, tell him," she said, looking over her shoulder.

Roger pushed off the arena's railing and loomed over them. "I called in a favor from a buddy in Ocala, Ben. Said he checked out fine."

Ben crossed his arms. "Evidently not."

"Doug Willis and I go way back," Roger reassured Ben in his rugged Southern drawl. "The horse checked out fine, just like Jordan said."

Ben turned to her. "How did he look to you?"

"He looked great on video."

"You didn't go see him."

"Florida's a long haul, and we're short staffed."

"You could have sent me," Ben said gently, as if talking down a freaked-out horse.

She averted her eyes. "I've leaned on you enough."

"Seriously, Jordan. Sell your share. The syndicate's got some flexibility, and I can find him a proper trainer."

"I can do the ground work. I just can't ride."

Ben looked at the horse, then her. "You don't have a rider or a trainer with a prayer of reclaiming a horse that's this far gone."

*I could,* Lexy thought. She'd brought Mindy from the brink and Caravaggio, and trained with the best.

Jordan shook her head emphatically. "He stays here. He needs me."

"You keep him here, he's going to hurt somebody."

Roger put an arm around her. "And that somebody could be you, my dear."

Jordan slid from Roger's grasp and turned to Ben. "He's still brilliant, Ben. He's got the moves, the depth, the drive."

"Jordan, please. Let me tell you what I'd tell any of my clients."

"Okay, shoot," Jordan said grimly.

"I would tell them not to break their heart over a beautiful ruined horse they can't even ride."

"Thank you for your professional opinion, Ben."

He met her gaze, then said to the vet, "Your services are premature until we get that horse to settle down."

"Fine," Roger said to Jordan. "Y'all call me." And he left.

Lexy could have sworn Ben's eyes twinkled with satisfaction, but he said only, "Hamp, move the truck. Key's in the ignition."

Hamp answered something Lexy couldn't hear then pulled himself into the truck's high cab.

"We have to open the arena doors," Jordan reminded Ben, refusing to leave. Lexy couldn't leave if her life depended on it. No, that wasn't quite right, she thought as her plan blossomed. Her life, her future, depended somehow on staying with this stallion, never mind how desperately unmanageable he seemed.

Ben sighed. "Lexy, help Jordan on the left. I'll get the right door."

Lexy went to Jordan's side and put her hand on the door, saying, "I can handle it."

Jordan glared at her. "What part of this embarrassing argument did you miss? I'm not incapacitated."

"Of course, you're not," Lexy said in her British best. But the sliding door's rollers jammed overhead, and Jordan had to let her help.

The truck's engine grumbled to life, and Hamp drove it a few yards forward, clear of the gate. Together, Lexy and Jordan closed the heavy door while Lexy grappled for words to offer this angry, injured stranger.

"Ms. McRae, you're right. Don't give up on Bo."

"Give up on Bo? Not me."

"Me either," Lexy said with all the conviction she could muster. Then she waited until Jordan had to look at her. "I believe I can help your horse."

"That won't be necessary. Contrary to what Ben thinks, I do have people who can work with him. Tyrone, for starters."

"Tyrone?" The *driver?*

"My barn manager. He drove Bo up from Florida. He always handles Bo in the breeding shed."

"You mean before these last owners messed him up?"

Jordan McRae bit her lower lip, her chin trembling.

"Perhaps—" Lexy glanced at Jordan's cane "—I can do what you're not able to just yet."

Jordan's chin steadied, then lifted in pride. Which might be all she had left, Lexy realized. Crippled, her barn burned, and her stallion-of-a-lifetime ruined.

"I have staff," she said. "Not just Tyrone." And she turned seemingly to resume her argument with Ben.

"Please," Lexy said, stalking after her. With a zeal she thought she'd lost in England, she played what felt like her last card. "I studied with Ulrich Dichter in Spain and Denmark, salvaging whack jobs headed for the knackers. Worse off than Bo. Far worse. I know I can help him."

Jordan stopped and faced her. "Well, damn. I saw Ulrich work with stallions in France. That's one hell of a credential." She jabbed her cane in the arena's groomed, forgiving surface. "I'll give you a shot."

"Really? Super," Lexy babbled, her exhaustion vanishing. "You don't know what this means to me. I'm thrilled to bits."

"We'll see how it goes," Jordan said. "I'm sorry. I didn't get your whole name."

"Imbriani. Lexy Imbriani."

*"Caroline's* daughter?"

"You knew my mother?" Lexy's heart thudded, raced.

"When we were young." Jordan braced on her cane as if needing support. "She was a working student for my father when—gosh, she must have been your age."

"You were friends?"

"Pals, yes. How's she doing?"

Lexy's throat closed, but she forced words. "Mom was killed in a car accident a few weeks ago, driving down to groom for me at Bramham. She was speeding, they said, but I don't know. Ran off the road into Lake Windermere. The water there. It comes right up to the pavement."

The facts. She did not believe them. Her mother was alive somewhere in England, in a barn, brush in hand, grooming Reggie to a sheen. Lying to her out of love.

Jordan's eyes softened. "I can't tell you how very sorry I am for your loss."

"I miss her awfully," Lexy confessed, loyalty and betrayal colliding inside her once again. How could Enrico Imbriani not have been her real father? And who could that man be? "But she'd have wanted me to go on, keep busy, live the dream."

"The dream?"

"The Olympics, you know. She gave hers up for me."

Jordan's warm expression closed. "That's too bad. I had that dream too."

"But *you* made it. So did Ben."

"Yep," she said, as if their success had been inevitable. "It's a lot of work. Lot of sacrifice. Lot of luck. And a lot of money."

"I understand that."

Jordan gave her a slight smile. "We can help you with the work part. Sacrifice too. The luck and money, not so much."

# Four

Lexy took heart. She wasn't afraid of work. The money, the horses—her father had given and taken away, but the luck part had just happened. She had a new horse to work with. A fabulous horse. At a fabulous farm. With fabulous ULRs, upper level riders. And perhaps, in Jordan, a coach who was Ben Holt's equal and wouldn't be forever on the road.

At the end of the arena, Bo wheeled on his hocks and trotted, flinging his legs out in the lofty extensions that made him look as if he were flying above the ground, all power and majesty. Lexy couldn't breathe for the beauty of him, and her exhausted body tingled in a new wild way.

Whatever the stallion had suffered, his spirit was unbroken, and he had the look of eagles she'd been seeking all her life.

Ben walked up to her. "You ready to go?"

Oh, dear. He didn't have a clue.

"Actually, Jordan invited me to stay and work with Bo."

"Did she now?" Ben said, betraying nothing in his tone. Tyrone came in, still surly, with a hay bag over his shoulder and a five-gallon bucket in each hand, water slopping over the sides. Ben took the buckets, carried them as near to the stallion as looked safe, and set them down. Tyrone followed with the bagged hay and tied its cords to one of the steel girders that arched up to support the roof. Not far from Lexy, Hamp crossed his arms and propped a booted heel against the gate, taking in the scene.

Ben walked over to Jordan, and Lexy heard him say, "If you're determined to keep that horse, send him to DeLacey Stone in Charlotte. She takes on the worst cases and always turns them around."

Jordan drew a line in the sand with the tip of her cane. "No. I let him go once, and see what happened. He's back, he stays with me."

Ben crossed the line and angled his body to hers. "Danny. This is a bad idea."

Lexy bit her lip, uncomfortable to be eavesdropping but fascinated. Sworn enemies did not use pet names.

"He's my horse," said Jordan. "Fifty-two percent gives me the final say."

Ben let out a breath between clenched teeth. "You have to get well before you take on a risk like this. Even then..."

"I'd like to see what Lexy can do with him," Jordan said.

Ben turned to Lexy. "I can't hold my offer more than a couple of days."

Lexy lifted a brow at Jordan.

Jordan nodded. "May take longer than that."

Ben stepped away. His eyes were on the stallion, but his fingers drummed his thigh. Lexy couldn't help thinking that the unflappable Ben Holt, who had beaten the best eventers in the known universe, would be thwacking a crop against the calf of his brown boot right now, if he had one in his hand.

He came back to Lexy. "Okay, a week."

"I'm honored at your offer, truly," Lexy began as politely as she could. Still, enthusiasm crept into her voice. "But this is what I do best."

"Take wild risks?" He shook his head. "You could get hurt. Badly. I don't recommend this for you any more than for Jordan."

"Thank you, Ben," Jordan said to him, softer this time. "You know I can coach her. Daddy will help too."

He turned to Lexy, his lined outdoorsman's face unreadable. "You stay here over a week, I can't hold your spot."

Lexy was torn. Ben Holt wanted her to ride his horses. The very idea that he thought she was good enough tempted her. He could teach her so much, and she had much to learn. She'd had big dreams for the Games next summer, dreams destroyed when her father had taken her horses back.

But Bo was here, and with him, she had a hope of redeeming a soul as hurt as hers. "With respect," she said finally, "I'll take that chance."

"Well then, be careful," he said, then zeroed in on Jordan. "She micromanages her horse on cross-country. Don't let her get away with that."

Lexy felt stunned. Two years ago, she'd ridden for him at Bishop Burton in Durham, and he remembered the exact bad habit that still got her into trouble? Damn. Now he was the U. S. Olympic coach. If anyone could help her fulfill her dream, he could. Oh God, what would her mother say? Trust your intuition? Be true to yourself? As she had not been to her own daughter? Lexy winced at her betrayal, not sure what her mother would have thought.

But she was making a big mistake, a stupid mistake—in front of Ben, Hamp, and Tyrone, for everyone had gathered now. Tyrone, however, didn't seem to care. His gaze locked on someone entering the arena. A uniformed woman in a gray shirt with a dark tie and darker pants strode toward them, her lips set in a thin line.

"Looks like the sheriff has something to report," said Hamp with an edge.

As the woman neared, Lexy could see epaulets and a gold badge above her left breast. Stitched-down creases made her trousers look neat, but mud and ashes marred the shine on what looked like regulation oxfords.

"So did ya find anything, Sis?" Jordan asked. In challenge, Lexy thought, puzzled by the dynamics between people so new to her.

"Yes. We did." The sheriff, evidently Jordan's sister, touched a fist to her pursed lips then lowered her hand. "Bad news. Very bad."

"Oh, come on. Not arson."

Arson? Lexy's heart clutched. In Southern Pines? Historic horse center of the U.S., which Hamp had called horse heaven.

"No, Danny. Not yet anyway. Worse." The sister-sheriff seemed to fight emotion. "It's a body."

"Good God, no," Jordan gasped, and Lexy gasped too.

"Accident, or murder. Depends on what my arson guy turns up."

Jordan's tanned face blanched. "Who in the name of all that's—"

"We don't know yet, but I got a hunch." The sheriff turned to the barn manager. "Do you know where Winslow is?"

Tyrone's dark eyes flashed. "Sleeping it off somewhere, fucking drunk."

"Ty, Winslow Dawson is your mother's husband—"

"Ex-husband. Ruth kicked the bastard out."

Jordan's sister, the sheriff, glared at Tyrone. "Well, whatever started that fire, a black man died in it. Could be Winslow. Can't be sure. But I'm sure as hell not going to ask your mother to identify that body when you're right here and can do it for her."

Tyrone's fists knotted, and defiance fired his coal black eyes.

"How can this be?" Jordan asked Gwen. "This morning I thought we'd accounted for everybody."

"Everybody you thought had a reason to be here," Gwen said.

"Yeah, well, he always had a reason," Tyrone said bitterly. "Restraining orders never stopped him from hitchhiking out here to hit on my mother. He was so soused, he probably went off like a Roman candle."

"For God's sake, Tyrone, have some respect for the man," Jordan said.

Lexy watched, blindsided by tension on the farm.

"This may have been his last ride, Ty," Jordan said. "Go help Gwen, please. I'll warn Ruth and Daddy, all right?" She touched Tyrone's broad shoulder with a gentle hand.

Tyrone shook it off. "Don't suppose I get a choice."

"No, you don't," Gwen said, and linked her arm in his. "Put your big boy britches on, and let's get this over with."

Silenced, Tyrone marched off with her, and Jordan turned to Ben, looking stunned. "I can't believe this is happening."

"You want me to get the cart and drive you to the house?" he asked.

"God, yes, would you?" Her eyes filmed with tears. "I left it by the barn, by the wing that burned."

Ben strode out of the arena when, to Lexy's astonishment, Jordan hobbled toward Bo, jabbing her cane into the sand with every other step.

"Ms. McRae, wait!" Lexy cried, loud as she dared without inciting another equine rampage. Jordan set her shoulders and kept walking, her limp making her look vulnerable. Bo wouldn't be the only wounded creature Lexy would have to work with.

"Ms. McRae, please." She jogged to catch up and touched the hand that didn't clutch the cane. Despite the heat, the hand felt cold. After her mother died, Lexy had been a block of ice for weeks. "I'll watch him. You have more important things to do."

"Jordan," her new employer corrected her. "If you're going to have a front row seat watching my life fall apart, call me by my first name."

"Jordan," Lexy repeated. It was a nice name, very masculine, American. British girls still got names like Lucy, Olivia and Pippa.

"And don't ever try to keep me from my horse."

"Of course," Lexy said, taken aback by her sharp tone. "I wouldn't dream of it. But today, he could explode, and you might not get out of his way fast enough."

"And you will?"

Jordan McRae sounded like she could lead troops into battle but looked on the edge of tears.

"Absolutely. Positively." Lexy touched her hand again. "Don't worry. I'll handle him like he was my own, and come get you if he needs you."

"I'll be at the house, or the barn, or the sheriff's office— God, what a nightmare."

The low drone of an electric engine signaled Ben's return in Jordan's crimson golf cart. Between the headlights on its stubby nose, it sported a black emblem of a hawk dropping on its prey. For Hawks Nest Farm, competing. Ben stopped where Jordan could step easily into the passenger's seat. Which was on the wrong side, and Lexy felt another blip of dislocation. She was not in England anymore. And neither was her mother.

Lexy's grief kicked in again. Would she ever stop missing her? Or worrying about her mother's confession in that letter to dear Pookie?

Bereft, she looked at the stallion, the one living being in the world who needed her. He was miserable too.

Jordan got in the cart, and it whirred off, its wide tires scoring the deep sand. Lexy glanced at Hamp, a boot heel still propped on a girder, looking solid like the rock monuments in the desert he'd grown up in.

He pushed off and came to her side, his black brows frowning. "Ben's right, Lexy. This isn't a good idea, landing here in the middle of an arson investigation."

"You think?" She wished he'd said something before she'd made her decision.

"To say nothing of that horse. I'd hate to see you get hurt."

"I'm not worried about that. Mindy and Caravaggio started out lost causes, and I spent weeks with Ulrich. I can handle him."

"That's what every quadriplegic in our business said to themselves while they were still walking on both legs. No call to court disaster."

"Hamp, I'm saving a horse, using what I know."

"The fire, the body—they're disasters. Not even counting them, you're walking into an unhappy situation work-wise. Professionally, Jordan's under suspension. Sure, you can ride her horses, but you can't compete them till her suspension's lifted."

"Which will be when?"

"Dunno. A month or so, at least. But more. Tyrone's a tough nut. And Jordan's brother Parker—he's the black sheep of the family. They're a troubled bunch."

Up till now, Hamp had been such a private person, Lexy was touched he would confide in her. Still, he knew her story. "Worse than my ex-father?"

"Maybe not worse. But if you work for Ben with me at Chip's, I can watch your back."

As her mother had always done.

As Enrico Imbriani hadn't.

She swallowed against the lump of gratitude that clogged her throat, and stammered, "I—Thanks. But I'm hooked on that horse. I saw him at his best at Pau. It's obvious Jordan can't ride him. I can—not just save him, but put him in work, maybe compete, a three-star, maybe a—"

"Whoa, Nellie." Hamp's green eyes bored into hers. "You're talking about taking him to the top. That's crazy."

"Crazy would be giving up my dream."

"You like roses? Lilies? Mums?"

She blinked, confused.

"For your funeral."

"Hey. Give me a little credit."

"My mistake." His cell must have rung. He checked the number and jammed it in its leather case. "So. You have a plan?"

"I'd like to give him some room first, see if he'll stop worrying about the mares, drink some water, eat some hay. Catch his breath, you know."

"And then?"

"I need a soft lunge line and ropes or fencing tape long enough to partition the far end of the arena. Oh, and a whip—not to whip him," she added, "a whip to—"

"To communicate, I know."

"Carriage length is best. Know where can I get one?"

"I'll see what I can round up." Hamp flipped open his cell, called the barn, spoke to someone in Spanish, and left to meet them. Lexy was fluent in English and Italian and could get by in French and German. But though she'd studied in Spain with Ulrich, he'd spoken English so she'd acquired only a smattering of Spanish. But still, Hamp sounded native.

In a few moments, Bo ambled over to the buckets, took hasty gulps of water, and tore out a mouthful of hay. Then he wheeled and went back to his anxious patrol. Lexy, alone now, leaned on the fence where Hamp had been, feeling far away from home. Ten, fifteen minutes passed, and Hamp returned with coils of white woven fencing tape draped off his shoulder. A short, bandy-legged man wearing jeans and a work-smudged T-shirt walked beside him carrying fiberglass fence posts.

Hamp introduced Eduardo, head groom.

"Ees all we find. Look everywhere."

"Super," Lexy said. "We need to partition off only a small area, thirty-five feet square. Ulrich called it a *picadero*."

"A leetle riding school?" Eduardo translated.

"Exactly," Lexy said. Drained though she was, the work revived her. Eduardo set three stakes. With Hamp's help, she laid the inch-wide white tapes on the ground end to end, making sure she had enough to pull two lengths across the width of the arena. They slip-knotted each pair together, and then with the two men at the walls and Lexy in the middle, they quietly dragged the jerry-rigged fence down the enclosure.

Bo watched with wide, suspicious eyes. Several yards away from him, Hamp secured his ends through perforations in the girder. Lexy tightened the ropes on her side and helped Eduardo fasten them, leaving Bo no place to run.

"You going to work him now?" Hamp asked.

"In a while."

"Be careful." He squeezed her hand, concerned, and left, asking Eduardo to keep an eye on her.

She upended an empty bucket and sat, watching Bo pick at his hay. From before she could remember, she'd been mesmerized by horses and could no more imagine life without them than life without her right arm. They'd given her friendship and adventures, been beings she could love and trust. Been her refuge from her father's anger.

After a few minutes, she took the lunge line and carriage whip in hand and slipped under the makeshift fence. Ulrich lived to rescue horses everyone had given up on. She'd seen him reclaim a dozen. But she'd never faced one this far gone alone. In three strides, she closed in on Bo's space, out of kicking range but well aware he could charge her as fast as he'd charged Ben.

She held the whip out to the stallion, signaling him to move away.

Giving an angry bellow, he reared, struck out with a foreleg, and landed with a heavy thud. Wheeling, he lunged at her and struck out with the other leg, missing her head by inches. Raw fear gripped her. What if Ben was right, and Bo turned vicious?

Nostrils flaring, eyes flashing with anger, the horse swept past her again.

No! she thought. She had to make this work.

So she stood her ground, the lunge line draped lightly in her left hand and the carriage whip in her right.

He circled her, guttural bellows rising from deep in his chest, warning her of his rage. For an awful moment, his fury shook her, though she'd seen Ulrich stand up to horses just as rank. Breathing into the center of her being, she entered Bo's world, moving as he moved, swinging her whip in lazy rhythm, never striking at him, simply watching him rear and buck and lunge. She kept an always equal distance from him, watching for the slightest sign his fury was ebbing.

Finally, he came down on all fours and lowered his head, his protest now reduced to snorting at the dirt and pawing with his left front leg. He was filthy and unkempt, but beneath the crusted dirt and anxious sweat, she saw only majesty.

Hope soared. Legs slightly apart, she balanced lightly on her feet, breathing softly, in and out, and gave him her stillness.

He lifted his head and turned to face her, legs planted on the ground. Not fighting now. She took the whip in both hands and held it on her fingertips, parallel to the ground.

This is not the snake that strikes your legs.

He waited, deep distrust and vigilance flashing in his eyes.

Taking her time, she poked the whip's shaft into the ground, then held it upright, casually, as if it were a friend. His ears flicked forward with guarded interest and then flattened against his head. He was ready to explode—or yield, her fervent hope, if she was patient. Holding her free hand low, she snapped her fingers and gestured him to move around the tiny makeshift *picadero*.

He picked up his lofty springing trot.

Silently, she free-lunged him, asking him to trot round her in a circle, shadowing his movements. His strong, airy way of going dazzled her, and the compliance he now freely gave her bowled her over. He remembered his training, but she wanted more. She dropped her hands and leaned back in an exaggerated stop, and he bounced to a square halt, eyes large, ears forward with attention. He did not hate all humans.

He did not hate her.

In fact, he was curious. She walked up to him face to face, the most dominant position she could take, but made little of it. He stood, and his compliance took her breath away.

He had let her in. She extended her hand for him to check.

Arching his neck, he lowered his head, sniffed her palm with his velvet muzzle, and her heart lifted with a joy she thought she'd lost forever.

# Five

A couple of hours later in the thick midday heat, Bo raised his head, whirled and trumpeted. Lexy whirled too, taking in trouble at a glance. A helmeted blonde was trotting a gorgeous gray smartly into the arena, its legs done up in white protective bandages. It whinnied back, stopped, lifted its tail and peed a stream of thick cloudy yellow urine. A mare in heat.

What Bo coveted.

The blonde jerked the heavy hardware in the mare's mouth and smacked her shoulder with a long dressage whip, forcing her to trot to the far end. On the ground, a man in a black polo shirt, black boots, and dark gray riding breeches followed.

Bo thundered up and down the flimsy white-taped *picadero* fence, bellowing, neck arched, tail flagged, legs thrashing.

Lexy ditched her whip and lunge line and streaked across the arena. "Are you out of your mind?"

The woman's shoulders squared with sublime confidence as she brought the mare to a perfect halt in front of Lexy and looked down a sculpted nose. "I beg your pardon," she said, her glossy lips pressed tight.

"That mare's in season. Get her out of here!" Lexy heard her voice shake with anger. To the man in black she yelled, "You! Close that arena door behind her."

The woman shot a contemptuous look at Bo and headed out.

At the gate, Jordan arrived, took in what had happened, and leaped from her cart. "Damn it, Marina. Lexy was just getting through to him."

"I didn't know he was in here," Marina said, all innocence which Lexy didn't believe for a minute.

"But you know to be extra careful when Tosca comes in season."

"We have an agreement. This hour in the arena is reserved for me."

"It's not safe right now." Then Jordan turned on the man. "Damn it, Parker. Quit gawking and close the gate." Parker—he must be the brother, the black sheep Hamp had warned of.

Parker grinned. "Say, 'Welcome home, bro. And when did you get back?'"

"Today, obviously," Jordan sputtered. Lexy winced at the anger sparking off her.

"And who's the babe?" he asked, eying Lexy up and down.

"Ben's new assistant, Hamp's friend," Jordan said with a warning emphasis on Hamp. "Help Marina out." Then, to Marina, "After you put her away, come back and we'll reschedule."

Parker whispered to Marina at the main door of the arena, and started to close the gate after her, only to admit a grizzled older man. He rode a chunky ATV, painted in Hawks Nest's black and crimson. He putt-putted across the arena, leaving Lexy, Jordan, and Parker in the dust raised by his bike.

"What's going on here, Jordan?" the old man growled when they caught up. His thick hair was white, and decades outdoors had carved deep lines in his craggy face.

"Looks like Bo's back in training," Parker offered helpfully.

The mare gone, Bo paced less anxiously, showing off his Olympic form.

"This isn't training, Daddy. It's rehab," Jordan said defensively.

Daddy? Ohmigod. It was Colonel McRae, eventing legend. Lexy had known of him since her Pony Club days. As a young officer, he'd represented the U. S. in the 1948 Olympics. Then he'd written the book on how to do it. She'd memorized it.

"Right," Parker said, grinning still. "You're going to tame the savage beast, and I can campaign him for the Olympics."

"No way in holy hell," said Colonel. He had a honeyed Southern accent like Jordan's, and chestnut eyes, the color of hers, twinkled under steel gray brows.

"What's to lose, Pop?" Parker said breezily, but Lexy detected belligerence beneath his façade. "I finished Rolex." In Lexington, Kentucky. The only four-star event in the States. Good on you, mate.

"By the seat of your pants," Colonel said bluntly. "Like you do everything."

"Besides, Parker," Jordan said, "Lexy may be riding him."

Colonel turned on Lexy. "You, a girl, ride Bo? Absolutely not."

"I didn't mean today, Daddy."

Colonel's eyes narrowed over his hawk's beak of a nose, still accessing Lexy. She eyed him back, not sure what to say. "Then when? Next week? Next month? What are you planning this time behind my back?"

"It's not behind your back," Jordan said, as if Lexy weren't there. "He just got here. You just got here."

"I forbid it."

"If and when he's ready for her to ride, I'll decide," Jordan said stiffly.

"Without consulting me," Colonel stated.

"I don't make big decisions without consulting you."

"You took over the books, my checking account, the works."

Jordan looked like she wanted to shrivel up and die. Parker's eyebrows waggled. Lexy felt her breath go shallow.

"That was an act of desperation," Jordan said. "Not your fault, not my choice."

"Bringing this horse home is an act of desperation too. And it won't work."

"Aw, Pop," Parker broke in. "Give her a break. You're not the only magician in the family."

"And you think you are? Listen, son. You want to win something, you've got to earn it."

Lexy froze, fascinated, horrified, ghosts from family clashes taunting her.

A slow deep burn climbed up Parker's throat and cheeks and ears. "Son of a bitch. You're never going to forgive me, are you?"

"Forgiveness is a two-way street."

"Parker, Daddy, please," Jordan said. "The past is past."

"No," said Parker. "The past is here and now. That's why you've got the farm, the only competition stallion in eventing, and you're still our daddy's favorite."

"I ran this farm the last twenty years. You have no idea how hard it is. Want to trade places?" she asked.

"Yes," he said, and then to Colonel. "Yes, Pop. For the umpteenth time, I would like to run the farm. And now's the time, with Jordan hobbling around, pretending she can manage."

"I am managing," Jordan said.

"Sorry, Sis, but you aren't, not since you killed Rosie, got suspended, burned down your barn."

Heaven help me, Lexy thought. What had she gotten into?

"She did not burn our barn or kill that mare." Colonel went nose to nose with him, his military posture imposing. "I think somebody's out to get her."

"Stand up for her. Like always."

"Because she does things by the book."

"Your book."

Lexy fled back to Bo's end of the arena, their argument not ended. Rivulets of sweat streamed down her ribcage.

Someone out to get who? Shades of her ex-father.

# Six

Hours later, Lexy checked Bo for signs of distress, but he stood in the shadows, sorting through his hay with quick businesslike twitches of his upper lip to get to the choice bits, and then the tranquil munching. After the dysfunctional family from hell had disbanded, Jordan had rushed off to meet her insurance appraiser. Lexy's afternoon had gone by in a steamy blur. The heat, thank God, had broken half an hour ago, but the designer jeans and long-sleeved silk shirt she'd been traveling in since Friday felt like a wool blanket.

Now, Jordan's red-and-black golf cart jounced toward her across the hoof-pocked sand. Late afternoon sun speared in through the far door and the open space above. The light was soft, golden.

"You okay?" Jordan asked.

Yes. No. Yes. Lexy turned to her, blinking.

Jordan gave a guarded smile. "That wasn't a trick question."

"I'm thirsty, that's for sure."

"This will hit the spot."

Jordan passed her a small wicker basket. Lexy dusted off her hands and lifted the lid. Neatly stacked were a thick plaid cotton napkin, a sandwich in crisp white paper, a blushing fuzzy peach cold from the refrigerator, and a thermos. She unfastened its cap, poured a pale yellow liquid with crushed ice into it, and took a sip.

"Lemonade!" she cried, and drank it down. She unwrapped the sandwich, peeked inside, and her lost appetite came growling back. "And white-meat chicken salad? With grapes! Blimey."

"Made from scratch. Compliments of Ruth Gantt, our housekeeper, chef, and backbone of the farm."

"But the man who died in the fire—wasn't he her husband?"

"Ex-. After we got home from making the funeral arrangements, she couldn't just sit there," Jordan said, and turned her attention to Bo. "How's he?"

"Calmer. Dried off. Bored. Needs a bath." Lexy took another draft of lemonade and bit into the sandwich. The homemade white bread was precisely sliced, the chicken tender, gently seasoned with flecks of herbs she didn't recognize. Such caring, she'd known only from her mother. Not that Caroline Imbriani cooked. They'd been lucky to have time for Indian take-out, but she'd been Lexy's coach, groom, driver, and best fan.

Lexy blinked against hot tears, missing her.

Jordan noticed and looked away, as if embarrassed.

Lexy forced down her next bites, and the words of that letter to dear Pookie, the one she'd secreted away, muddled her again. Enrico Imbriani was not her father. *Don't go there,* she told herself for the hundredth time.

But she'd deserved to know who her father was.

"And you? Need anything?" Jordan asked, studying her stallion worriedly, but not a word about the family fight.

"No, I'm fine. Hamp's taking care of me."

"We like Hamp. Glad he's on your side."

So was she. "Your brother stayed after that first bunch left. Does he event?"

"Yep, foxhunts too, plays polo cross in his spare time. Trains and sells mid-level prospects, but events Advanced if he can keep one long enough to make it to that level."

She choked down the last of her sandwich. "Don't think I saw him in England."

"Never made it there. He's talented, frustrated."

Lexy had to smile. "There's a lot of that going around."

"No kidding," Jordan said, and trailed off, as if she wasn't used to sitting around having idle conversation. Neither was Lexy. Horse people stayed on their feet, grooming, watering, feeding, cleaning tack. Riding. Putting horses first. "Did you run into any new problems?" she asked. "I mean, with Bo."

"Not Bo, no. Just that blonde again, asking for your brother. Her name didn't register."

"Marina Sterling," Jordan said in a neutral tone.

"The whisky heiress? She finished ahead of me at Badminton. She's here too?"

"Yep," Jordan said, and sighed. "And her four horses, Preliminary to four-star, full-time groom, manager, accountant. Look, I'll introduce you properly. She helps pay the bills."

Lexy wadded the paper from her sandwich, feeling awkward. "Sorry. Didn't know that when I ordered her out."

"Yes, well. She doesn't own the place." Jordan turned her head at the hum of a light engine. "Oh dear, Daddy's back."

Colonel McRae wheeled into the arena and parked by Jordan's cart. Lean, erect, beak-nosed, he wore a khaki safari shirt, tan riding breeches, and brown field boots. Looked ready to lead a cavalry charge, but had to be in his eighties. He dismounted his steel horse with the ease of a younger man, glanced at Jordan, then studied Lexy.

"You remember Lexy, Daddy?" Jordan said.

"I'm old, not senile. Course, I remember her." He stuck out his hand to Lexy. "Colonel McRae."

"It's really Major McRae, retired," Jordan explained. "Colonel is his given name."

"Call me Colonel," he drawled amiably.

"Colonel, sir," Lexy managed.

"Just Colonel, darlin'."

"Lexy finished top rider under twenty-five at Badminton in May," Jordan said. Behind Marina, who was older.

"Did you now?" he grunted, as if unimpressed, then his eyes narrowed on the scruffy stallion. "How'd Bo make it through the afternoon?"

Not waiting for an answer, he marched toward Bo. The stallion's nostrils flared. Well before Colonel got to him, Bo struck out at him, then burst into a show, bucking and rearing angrily as when they'd first confined him to the small *picadero*.

"What the devil?" Colonel yelled, stubbornly striding into danger. "There's not a mare in sight."

Lexy shook off her stupefaction and darted after him, grabbing his arm. "Not so fast, if you don't mind, sir—I mean, Colonel. He's hair-trigger—"

"I see what he is," he bit off, shaking off her hand, but stopping. "He was never like this. Never." He pivoted, looking for Jordan, who almost crashed into him. "What the hell were you thinking, bringing him home?"

She visibly braced. "We need the money."

"Money, baloney. What happened to his face? Son of a bitch looks like something the dogs drug up."

"I know he looks bad today," Jordan said. "But if we can just get him to his stall, clean him up, and treat his injuries— that's the main thing. Tyrone and Eduardo are coming to lead him to the stallion wing."

"No," Lexy protested. Both heads swung toward her. It felt like flinging herself into the fire to disagree with two of the most renowned equestrians in eventing. "We have to start over, and it has to be me."

"You? This is men's work, darlin'."

Jordan glanced heavenward in exasperation, and Lexy looked from one to the other, confused. Was Jordan her boss? Or Colonel? But Jordan had hired her, and she wasn't going to let the old man *un*hire her.

"I'm twenty-three, Colonel, four years older than you when you rode in the Olympics, and I've been riding since I was three."

"Stallions?"

"No, not often," she said. Stallions could rarely handle the three diverse phases of an event. Geldings had the temperament for it. "But I trained with Ulrich Dichter in Spain, so I know how to work with cases like Bo."

Colonel huffed. "This better not be more of that horse whisperer bullroar."

"I promise not to whisper one word."

Colonel turned to his daughter. "I don't like it."

"But Lexy's—" Jordan started.

"I don't like it either," Lexy broke in before her boss could change her mind. "Bo's in trouble, but he's coming around for me. I can bring him back."

Colonel leveled a fiery look at her. "I don't sign off on suicide missions on my farm."

She met his gaze. "I plan to live to be at least as old as you are. Sir."

He pressed his lips together, but his eyes glimmered.

"You need a helmet," he muttered.

"Ulrich doesn't wear one."

"Ulrich's a goddamn fool. Jordan, get this girl a helmet!"

Lexy covered her mouth with her hand to hide a grin of victory.

# Seven

Bo worked well in front of Colonel, and an hour later, the evening sun slanted through the arena. It was almost dusk, but the air seemed only marginally cooler. Outside, Lexy saw Parker drive off with the Whiskey Queen, doubtless headed home to air-conditioning and tall iced drinks. The farm was quiet. The mares must be eating their grain before evening turnout.

Halfway down the ring, Jordan's cart and Colonel's ATV sat nose to nose. Jordan stood apart from her father, talking into her cell, tension in the cast of her shoulders, probably still dealing with the fire's aftermath.

"Jordan," Lexy called out when she put her phone away. "Can you let those tapes down? He's ready to go to the barn."

She felt uncomfortable giving orders to her new boss, but Jordan hobbled over to the *picadero*, untied the tapes, and dragged them aside. Lexy glimpsed Colonel sitting on his ATV. He gave her a thumbs-up, and she felt as if she'd ridden double-clear over her first four-star cross-country course, no time faults, no refusals. It surprised her how much his approval mattered. All she'd aspired to today had been to make this horse feel safe.

But she could tell Bo did not feel safe yet. Walking well ahead of him, she made a circle where the *picadero* had been, then led him past the coiled tapes. He cocked his head and pricked his ears at the scary white snakes writhing in the sand, then planted his hooves, refusing to take another step.

*Snakes are dangerous, lady,* he was warning her.

*Not these ones,* she told him, marching past to show him he could too. He snorted, shied, but followed, taking a couple of fancy sidesteps. Baby steps, to be sure, but pride trickled through her.

Then he went rigid again. What now?

Tyrone and Eduardo trudged toward them, carrying thick rope lead lines. "Ready, boss," Tyrone said to Jordan. He was a big man, though no taller than Lexy, and Lexy hadn't seen him crack a smile.

Jordan lifted a hand—in consent?

"Ready for what?" Lexy butted in, not happy to see chains.

"To take him to the stallion barn like I always do," Tyrone said.

"He's doing fine with me." She lifted the lunge line to show Tyrone she was controlling him with only two fingers, but inside she was flaming.

Jordan pushed off the fender of her father's ATV and stuck her cane in the sand. "You got off to a great start, Lexy, but I saw Bo scramble off that trailer. He's not himself. Tyrone's handled him for years. We can't risk Bo getting loose. Or you getting hurt."

Lexy felt sucker punched, set up by Tyrone who didn't want her on his turf and shot down by her boss who ran hot and cold. She should have listened to Hamp's warning. But no way would she abandon Bo.

Lexy cast a look at Colonel, hoping for his support. He sat, soldier straight, plainly waiting to see if she had guts.

Guts? Eventers jumped solid obstacles bigger than her rental car.

"Jordan, Tyrone, look at him," she called, turning to them. "He's coming along for me."

Tyrone shrugged. "Very impressive."

"Lexy," Jordan began earnestly, no trace of Tyrone's sarcasm. "We put a man on either side, two ropes. It's their job."

"No disrespect to you or your staff, my way's working fine."

"Yeah, in the arena," Tyrone said, annoyed.

To hell with him, Lexy thought. He hadn't seen half of their good work, and he was dismissing Bo's huge progress out of hand.

So show them.

She led Bo on a winding serpentine, leaving a track of hoof prints in a big loopy *S*. The changes of direction focused him on her, and he grew lighter in her hand. The blinding setting sun angled in, lighting his injury. She stopped to see what they'd be up against and lifted her open palm to his muzzle. He lowered his head in simple trust, and her heart expanded. Then she noticed something sparkling on his ears and above his eyes.

*Metal bits?* Holding her breath, she drew as close to his head as she dared and examined it. Staples—ordinary *staples*— were embedded in the flesh above his eyes, along his ears, and in the bridle path at the top of his neck. A cringe of pain washed down her thighs. *Jesu Cristo! Madonna mia,* she swore, oaths she'd learned as a schoolgirl, whispered behind nuns' backs. How had she missed this outrage?

The shadowed arena must have hidden it, or his neglected coat.

She gestured for Jordan, who limped over, motioning the others to stay behind.

"There's more," Lexy said when Jordan got to her. "Look at his eyes, his ears, his poll."

Frowning, Jordan studied Bo's head and neck, and her eyes grew wide. "Dear God. They tortured him. Fuck them," she said, her face flush with fury. "Fuck Chip. He'll hear from me."

"Chip McRae?" Lexy asked. "Hamp's boss?"

"Yes, my own cousin acted as my agent. He was in with Rupert Klein, who sold Bo to the Proctors as an Advanced horse to take their kid up the levels. He was cocky, too aggressive. Chip and Rupert flipped Bo for a profit, like he was a house. I'd bet the farm Chip got a nice percentage on that second sale, too, the slimy toad."

She whipped out her cell and speed dialed. "Roger. It's Jordan. Bo has other injuries. I need you."

She listened intently, then said crisply, "The sooner the better," then blew out a breath, waiting for his response. "No, you'll have to see it to believe it." She clicked off, then held her hand out to her horse's muzzle. Horses have long memories. Most forgive, but none forget.

Bo nuzzled Jordan's palm, as if certain of a treat, and tears rimmed her eyes.

"Oh my God, my poor, poor baby," she cried, her voice breaking. "*Damn* them." She looked from ear to poll to eyebrow, staples everywhere. "What did I do to you?"

"You couldn't have known," Lexy said, moved by Jordan's dismay.

"No, I should have suspected when my beloved cousin turned solicitous. He's never helped himself to anything but other people's pockets and other men's wives." She put her fist to her mouth and looked away. "Sorry. I shouldn't—I'm just so tired."

And in shock and pain. Lexy was appalled at this further glimpse inside the famous family. If only their betrayals didn't feel so damn familiar, but all she could do to help was divert Jordan's attention to Bo.

"Bo's ready to be moved, if you'll ask everyone to leave."

Jordan gave her a bleak look. "It's not safe. You could get hurt, or him."

"You saw him on the serpentine just now. He did fine. Better than fine."

"That was in here. With both gates closed."

"I don't know the layout of your farm, but if he got away from me, could he escape?"

"The gate to the road is locked, and the entire yard is fenced."

"Then please, let me try. His belly's full of tried and true old ways."

Jordan hesitated. "What if—"

"Give me a chance, give him a chance. If I can lead him across the arena, I can get him to his stall."

"You'd better. This horse means everything to me."

Lexy was touched. She'd felt that way about Caravaggio and Mind the Gap. Still did. She shuddered, horrified to think they'd ended up with incompetents as Bo had done.

# Eight

Outside in the fading light, the acrid smell of the burned barn assaulted Lexy and made Bo snort, but their walk across Hawks Nest's yard was uneventful. Eduardo went ahead to show the way. Tyrone, against her wishes, walked beside her, but Bo seemed not to notice him or the burst of sound when Colonel revved up his ATV.

No, the stallion simply walked with her, vibrantly alert to the sights.

There was a *barn!* He lifted his head, then craned it in the other direction.

There was a *tree!* And merciful heavens, running towards him, a *dog*.

A trim golden retriever waggled up, eager to adore him. Bo lowered his muzzle and blew into its face.

Silly endearments for her killer stallion like *honey bunny* and *lambie pie* flitted through her. Her mother would have used them too, Lexy thought, and her throat closed. If only they could have shared this moment. Her mother would have understood. Somewhere between Bo's biting Ben's arm, then accepting Lexy's touch, she'd fallen irrevocably for the most troubled horse she'd ever met.

Jordan and Colonel met them at the barn, leaving their vehicles at the railroad ties that marked off a parking area. They strolled in together, Jordan leaning on her father's arm, limping worse than Lexy had seen all day.

Lexy ushered Bo down the aisle, his iron shoes making muffled footfalls on a rubberized brick surface. Farther down, a stallion whickered, curious. Bo whickered back, more interested than antagonistic. Jordan directed them into a large airy stall. It looked fourteen-by-fourteen, big, and Lexy could see it was built of polished oak with metal grilling at the front. Overhead, its metal trusses rose so high a horse could rear and sport about without crashing his head. The Dutch door on the far side must lead to a private paddock. The stall was bedded with fresh, fragrant pine shavings, a sweeter smell to Lexy than coffee in the morning.

They must have smelled wonderful to Bo, too. With a satisfied grunt, he buckled onto his knees, sank into the bedding, then flopped on his side and rolled, exuberantly claiming his new space. Everyone's eyes were on the stallion's steel-strong yet fragile-looking legs as he rolled to the other side, then powered up to stand.

"Looks sound," said Colonel from the aisle.

Jordan sighed. "Yes, thank God, but filthy."

"He needs a bath, and elbow grease," Lexy said. "I'll take care of that."

"Not without somebody watching," Colonel ordered.

"For crying out loud, Daddy, I'll be here," Jordan exclaimed.

Lexy glanced between them, still unsure who was in charge.

Colonel looked at Jordan's leg. "You make sure Tyrone's near. Tyrone, if I'm not here, you keep an eye on her."

Tyrone grunted assent and left, claiming Eduardo to finish evening chores, which went on in the face of barn fires, dead ex-husbands, and crazy stallions.

Jordan gave her father what Lexy thought must be an evil eye, the *mal'occhio* the nuns once warned her of.

Colonel lifted his hands in defense. "Let Tyrone help, darlin', for safety's sake. This isn't our old Bo. We don't know what he's going to do."

Lexy backed away and studied the barn's rafters to give them privacy. They must have been going at each other for ages.

Jordan joined her and pointed to an enclosed portion of the loft. "Your room's over the tack and feed rooms. Bed, chair, dorm fridge, hot plate, toilet—pretty basic. You'll have to use the boarders' shower in the tack room. Best we can do for now."

For the chance to work with this magnificent stallion, she'd have camped out in her sleeping bag. "Sounds palatial."

"You do have stuff?"

"Clothes and things, in my rental car. Hamp promised to drive it over soon. Had to ship my tack."

"Good luck with that," said Jordan, mustering a tired smile.

"Welcome aboard," Colonel added in a genial tone. "Of course, you know, you still have to prove yourself."

Yes. Wasn't that the story of her life?

The hot sun flared then dipped below the pines. Twin beams from headlights pierced the twilight gloom. The vet drove up and parked a big gray Hummer beside Jordan's cart.

"Smartest thing he ever bought, he says," Colonel volunteered to Lexy, no doubt admiring the vehicle's military pedigree. "Has a full-sized custom Portavet mobile veterinary clinic with a tap for filtered water, and a refrigerator for temperature-sensitive drugs. Plus locked cabinets for the hard stuff—painkillers, tranquilizers, enough, if necessary, to kill a horse. Not a field emergency he can't get to, except a rock face in the Smokies. Even then he's got a winch."

The bear-like vet hadn't noticed Lexy earlier, but Jordan introduced her now. He gave a perfunctory nod and put a consoling arm around Jordan's shoulders.

"So sorry, my dear," he said in his deep drawl, "to hear 'bout something else on top of everything. What's up?"

"Look," Jordan said, her face grim.

In the stall, under the barn's bright fluorescents, Tillinghast took in the horse's face. "Dang," he said, then let out a low whistle. "Staples. Man." Dragged out as *may-yun,* Lexy noted. "What the dickens happened, Jordan? Colonel?"

"Don't know," said Colonel, and Jordan added, "No idea."

Tillinghast scrubbed a hand over his mouth, muttering ominous *hmm, hmms.* "I'd swear those look like acupuncture points, but this beats all."

Another *hmmm,* and then a *humph.*

"Doug Willis?" Jordan asked. She looked small next to her vet's reassuring bulk. "He did the pre-purchase exam and failed to mention a face wound. He had to know."

Tillinghast swiveled his big head at her. "No way, honey. Not Doug. I called in that exam for you early in July, then you had to round up the money which took you until now. Anything can happen to horses in a month, a kick, a bite, they run into a fence, they fall playing in a paddock. Plus, it's summertime, and swampy humid Florida is worse than us. Wounds go bad fast, you know."

Pressing her lips together, Jordan shook her head.

"You want me to call Doug, he may know who did it."

"Probably some yahoo from the boonies," Colonel said.

"Or the owners could have done it," Roger said. "Some of them'll try anything to save a nickel." He blew out a long-suffering sigh. "Horse people, ya gotta love 'em. Look, I'll get some Xylazine and sedate him," he went on. "You got a weight on him?"

"Used to be thirteen seventy-five, but he's dropped a hundred, maybe one twenty-five."

Lexy worried. She wanted Jordan's vet to work a miracle, but after what she'd seen, she hated turning Bo over to yet another man. Perhaps, under sedation, he wouldn't care. Tillinghast came back with syringes and a road kit stuffed with instruments and ointments. "Weight loss notwithstanding, he's a big boy, but let's try one bolus first. Rather underdose than overdose him."

Colonel rolled back the heavy stall door, and Tillinghast stepped in, agile for such a big man. He moved correctly to the horse's shoulder, found the jugular on Bo's throat, slid in the needle, then the plunger, and emptied the tranquilizer into him with no fuss.

"Good boy," he said with his rumbling voice. He rubbed the spot to disperse the medication and picked out another syringe.

"What's that?" Lexy asked.

He blinked as if he'd forgotten her. "Some antibiotic while we're at it," he said. With the syringe between his fingers, he stroked the center of Bo's neck, the usual spot for intramuscular injections. On his third stroke, he flipped his hand and popped the needle in. Bo didn't seem to notice.

"He took that well," Jordan said.

Tillinghast showed his too-white teeth. "It's all in the wrist, my dear."

Outside in the aisle, they waited for the drug to take effect. Colonel and the vet set about planning an outing to a gun show at the state fairgrounds in Raleigh. In minutes, Bo's head drooped toward the shavings, and the vet took out a stainless-steel cannula, much like a pair of needle-nosed pliers.

"Somebody ought to hold him." He sized up his options, an elderly man, a crippled woman, and stopped at Lexy. "Think you can prop his head up?"

Bo's eyes were flat from the Xylazine, and he seemed to notice nothing.

"Of course," Lexy said. She'd aced her horse husbandry course at Bishop Burton and then spent vacations apprenticed to an equine vet with a frantically busy practice. She lifted the stallion's head and tucked her shoulder under his jaw. His sharp jawbones cut into her.

"Gotta start somewhere," Tillinghast said, humming a deep but toneless tune as he inspected the cruel staples.

"How bad are they?" Lexy whispered, and shifted Bo's head to give him more support. He was zonked, eyelids fluttering shut, breath whistling in his throat. The stench of his wound curled into her nostrils.

"Don't see infection, except for that hole on his schnozz. Probably ought to clean it while he's under." He set about doing that, his big, blunt fingers surprisingly effective, Bo surprisingly indifferent. With horses, one never knew. Tillinghast cleaned the wound, dropping one medicated gauze pad after another into the shavings, and pronounced his work a success. Then he leaned in to see the staples.

He kicked shavings off his barn boots and turned to Jordan. "Must be thirty, forty staples. But I don't see infection, m'dear."

"Still, they have to hurt," Lexy said to him privately when he turned back to the horse.

"Prob'ly feel like fly bites, nothing worse."

She didn't want to second guess Jordan's vet, but fly bites hurt like hell.

"None of them touch any large nerves, and the ones over his eyes are well above the occipital aperture. So, not interfering with his vision, boneheaded as it was for somebody to do this to him. Not to worry."

"But the pain..." Lexy persisted, not buying his assessment.

Tillinghast shook his massive head. "No sign of pain, my dear."

"Then why's he trying to kill people who come within ten feet of him? Men, in particular."

He scowled at her where no one else could see. "Maybe he's ticked about that trip. I don't see any indication they're hurting him. In time, they'll work their way out."

Lexy forced courtesy. "Pardon me, but I don't see it that way. Jordan and Colonel say he's changed, and pain changes animals. So why can't we start on those staples while you've got him under?"

"All right, fine. Shouldn't take but seconds," he said curtly. "Brace yourself, young lady, and let's get this over with."

*Wait*, she thought. She hadn't meant hurry. That couldn't be safe or smart, but Tillinghast worked fast, clamp jerk flinch, clamp jerk flinch, harder, faster, three staples, four. Suddenly,

Bo reared straight up then came down on all fours, swinging his head like a truncheon.

In a blink, Lexy was sprawling in deep shavings, but she glimpsed Tillinghast's khakied butt as he headed for the door.

She picked herself up slowly. Tyrone was back and peering through the bars. So were Jordan, Colonel, Eduardo, and Hamp. Hamp must have brought her car, and she couldn't wait to see him. His dark brow furrowed with concern.

*I'm okay,* she mouthed at him.

*Good work,* he mouthed back.

"Tyrone," Tillinghast's big bass rumbled. "You get a twitch and get your ass in here."

Lexy hated twitches, two short sticks like bobbies' truncheons linked by a rope or chain. Their users wrapped the rope around the horse's tender muzzle and twisted it tight until he submitted. Her mare Mindy broke out in a sweat at the sight of one.

Lexy caught Jordan's gaze and shook her head in disapproval.

"We never twitch him, Roger," Jordan said, as if on cue. "He fights it."

"There's always a first time, my dear," Tillinghast said, gently condescending.

"But on drugs, he could go ballistic," Jordan protested weakly. Her face looked gray from exhaustion. It was night now, and she'd been hobbling on that bad leg since before dawn. Damn. If Lexy was going to be of use to her new boss, she should bloody well stand up for her and her horse.

"Jordan's right," Lexy said. "I've been with him all day, and he only just now quieted down. Anything could set him off."

Jordan gave Lexy a grateful glance. "So, no twitching, Roger. We'll take the slow route."

"Ah, give him a shot at it, darlin'," Colonel interrupted. "You've mollycoddled that horse since he was in short pants."

Lexy stifled a snort of disapproval and saw Jordan's face flush red. "On your head then," Jordan said and stalked to the far end of the aisle.

Lexy sucked in a breath. She'd been warming up to the crusty old chap and wished to hell the way he treated Jordan didn't remind her of her control-freak father.

Bear-like, Tillinghast entered the stall with another syringe. For what? To put the horse on the ground if he failed with the twitch?—which she was convinced he'd do. The cannula poked from a pocket of his vest. Tyrone followed, shorter but brawny too.

Lexy's heart hammered. They had to know how wildly unpredictable a drugged horse could be.

Tyrone held the twitch behind him, as if Bo wouldn't instinctively feel they were ganging up on him. They stepped up confidently, a man on either side of his drooping head, and Tyrone knotted the rope over Bo's muzzle. Tillinghast leaned over Bo's subdued head, set his pliers above the orbit of his eye, and wrenched a staple out.

Bo flung his head and leapt across the stall in a single bound, shouldering past what must have been five hundred pounds of muscled men. His force drove Tillinghast against the oak wall, and his forehead hit with a bone-crunching crack. As dazed as the horse he'd drugged, he staggered toward the door.

Tyrone got up off his hands and knees. "Son of a bitch," he gritted out, scrubbing horse shit off his hands and jeans with fistfuls of clean shavings. Bo watched with dull eyes, but now the sedation had to be wearing off. To her astonishment, Tillinghast picked up his tools and ordered Tyrone to get the twitch.

No way in hell. Bo was her charge, hers. She opened the stall door enough to slip inside and block the vet's way.

"You need to step aside, young lady," he said.

"Doctor, Jordan warned you he'd act up, and this proves her right. She said no twitch, and she doesn't want you to try it again."

"You're new here, am I correct?" Tillinghast gave her a bland non-smile no one else could see. "You need to know this is one of the premier farms, run by a couple of the most respected horsemen, and women, on the East Coast. And this is as good as it gets." He put an arm around her shoulders, not gently as with Jordan, and push-pulled Lexy to the back of the stall, his easy Southern accent turning hard. "Don't mess with me, Miss Imbriani. Like I said, those staples will work their way out in time, no danger to the horse."

"Just the pain," she reminded him.

He snorted. "Whether you'll work out here, my dear— that's the question."

Lexy's fight smarts, tempered by her father's rages, had taught her not to cross a big, angry man. But she could make sure everyone heard. "Jordan's wishes and her stallion's well-being are all that matter here. I'll get those staples out without twitches, fights, or further injury. Starting tomorrow."

To her surprise, her stand spurred Jordan into action. She limped into the stall and put a hand on her vet's burly forearm. "Lexy's right, Roger. It's late, and we're whipped. The horse is coming off a fourteen-hour haul. To say nothing of Tyrone, who can't have slept a wink. Let's call it a day, unless you can do more without the twitch."

Tillinghast shifted to the smooth smile he seemed to reserve for Jordan. "He's got enough antibiotics in him for twenty-four hours. You know how to inject the next round."

"Can do, and I can keep that wound clean." She patted his paw as a tamer might pat an irritable circus bear. "Daddy and I appreciate your coming out. It's good you started the antibiotics, and I'm relieved you saw no infection."

He collected his tools and rumbled off. Lexy knew she hadn't made a friend.

Thank God for Hamp, standing there, holding up a set of keys, beckoning. "Oh right, my car. My things. I need to—" she started.

"Go." Jordan waved her off. "I'll stand watch. I've got a few more minutes in me before I collapse."

Hamp had parked her Rent-a-Wreck under a low-branched tree. Joining him there, Lexy began to wilt under the load of the day's events. The sultry air stank of the burned barn and for an instant, she feared, of human flesh, but a light breeze shifted—from the west? Oh God, she wouldn't know which way was west until she saw the sun rise. The breeze stirred up a too-sweet scent from a nearby bush she did not know the name of, and she was wobbly from exhaustion.

Hamp caught her up to him. "You okay?"

"I'm... I'm..." Sad. Scared. *Lost.*

"Glad you're here," he murmured, and kissed her, reassuring her that he was there for her and she was home. He tasted of Coke and peanut butter, a cheap protein favored by eventers who were always broke. "Proud of you," he murmured, coming up for air. "Standing up to that old windbag."

"Who does he think he is, anyway?"

"Powerhouse around here. Colonel's best friend too. Highly regarded."

"Sloppy. Arrogant."

"Ben Holt thinks he cuts corners too, but don't worry about him. Worry about me." Hamp grinned and returned to their kiss. This one was longer, deeper, and her sad heart lifted. Clutched. She could enjoy this. Shouldn't. She still had work to do. As if sensing her reluctance, he pulled back but held her fingers, keeping their connection.

"So..." he said, as if they had hours to chat "...what do you do now?"

"Just the basics for Bo." All day she'd studied him, thinking how best to bring him back. Too tired to stand another minute, she scooted onto the still warm fender of her car.

Hamp stepped into the space between her parted knees. "Yeah?"

"Keep everyone out. Make him depend on me alone for feed, water, grooming, twenty-four seven. No one else touches him until he's eating out of my palm. Then, whatever it takes to get those staples out. But no force." Anger at Roger bubbled up again. "What a disaster. Did you see Bo leap across the stall from a dead standstill? Imagine him cross-country."

"That's my girl," Hamp said, and drew her to him.

She settled her legs around his hips. She was tired to the bone and grimy too, but she so needed this comfort. This love.

"I meant," he said with a quiet chuckle, "what are you going to do with me?"

She laughed but felt the danger of loving him too much, too soon. Still, he'd given her space to talk. "How about another kiss?"

"How about let's go home, start getting you settled in." He rented a nearby huntbox—a stable below with living quarters on top.

She'd been looking forward to it, but now, she grasped the magnitude of her commitment. "The twenty-four/ seven part, with Bo. That clock's already started."

"Ah, damn. That sucks—"

"—rocks," she finished for him, then nuzzled him, seeking the reassurance of his lean, fit body. "I want us together more than anything."

"Except Bo."

"It's a career-changing opportunity."

"So was working for Ben Holt."

"But Bo and Jordan and Colonel—all together." She bumped him with her forehead, seeking the right words. "When my mother died, I lost everything."

"Except me."

"I'll be next door. I want to see you every day. Promise."

He rubbed his thumb along her lower lip, a promise of desire.

"All right, lovebirds, that's enough." A man's voice she didn't recognize drawled through the night air.

"Hey, Chip," Hamp said, his gentle hold on her never slackening.

Must be Chip McRae, Hamp's boss, Jordan's cousin. The one who'd talked her into selling Bo. How long had he been there—sizing her up like a filly on the auction block?

"We got a situation, son," he said to Hamp, emerging from the shadows. Lexy had a sense of bulk but couldn't see the man's face. Hamp stepped between them as if to shield her from Chip's gaze. "What's the matter?"

"That new warmblood got turned out with the two-year-olds and got chewed up."

"Roger coming? He was just here."

"One of your herbal concoctions may be all he needs."

"Be with you in a sec," Hamp said. He dug in his pocket and pulled out the keys to her car, and a cell phone. "For you. Homecoming present. All programmed, prepaid. You got a hundred minutes."

"Thanks," she choked up, too moved by his caring to say more.

Then he climbed into Chip's big Escalade, rolled down his window, and made the phone sign with his hand. *Call me.* "I'm memory one. Got it? Memory number one."

She nodded. But she wanted to howl at the white hot rising moon. Not only had she messed up with Hamp, she'd turned down a job offer with the U. S. Olympic coach to work with the top stallion in eventing. Who he thought could kill her.

# Nine

Lexy pressed the knob on her travel alarm and sat up on the hay bales where she'd slept. It was dawn, and flocks of American birds whose songs she didn't recognize were chirping their brains out. The sun turned the sky deep fuchsia behind the tall pines. Her stomach felt like it was stapled to her backbone. She'd slept deeply, but not enough, setting the alarm to get up every hour to check on Bo.

She pushed to her feet, tore off a generous handful of timothy hay and entered his stall. He cocked his ears, still wary of the devil cannula.

*You want food, you come through me,* she thought, and stretched out her bribe, prepared to wait all morning.

After a moment, he snatched a mouthful and stepped back, pleased to play the thief, she could see it in his eyes. Whatever he'd suffered, his ordeal hadn't destroyed a quirky sense of humor. When she hand-fed him to gain his trust, he made a game of it, one he could win. As long as he didn't crowd her, she'd let him get away with it because she loved his testing, questing spirit.

He chomped the hay, winding in long strands of it.

After he finished, she held out the rest.

He snorted at a rustle in the aisle and refused another bite.

"Try gingersnaps," a man's voice drawled behind her.

Bo sidled into the shadows, and she turned. It was Parker, Jordan's brother, in the same high-fashion black and charcoal, nothing out of place. Feeling filthy and rumpled, she stalked into the aisle and closed the stall door behind her. "This horse doesn't need more help from men."

"Sorry." He flashed a crooked smile and held out his hand.

She took it unwillingly. Yesterday he'd set Bo's progress back a notch.

"We didn't exactly meet. I'm Parker."

"I can tell." He had Jordan's whiskey-colored eyes and hair, and an air of privilege. He offered a paper sack. "Breakfast, compliments of Ruth, mother to us all."

"Thanks." Lexy set the sack on her bed of hay and rolled up her sleeping bag. She felt his eyes on her but refused to stop what she was doing or how she went about it. She sat on a bale and opened the sack. It held a thermos of coffee. Grateful, she took a sip and unwrapped another white-bread sandwich. In the morning? "What's this?"

"Fried egg special," he said helpfully. "With bacon, lots of butter. Ruth believes in fat and protein."

Ruth, who'd lost her ex-husband yesterday. Stifling that dark thought, Lexy sank her teeth into the sandwich and closed her eyes in pleasure. "Umm."

"I didn't get your name."

"Lexy Imbriani."

"Umm," he said, using her same tone. "Sexy Lexy."

"Just Lexy." She glared at him. "It's early to be hitting on a stranger."

He took her left hand and turned it over, blatantly looking for a wedding band, then switched to a Frenchman's British accent. "*Mademoiselle* Lexy. Is that Alexa? Alexis? Alexandria? Wheech-ever, eet has a certain *je ne sais quoi*."

She shook her head, charmed against her will by his playful French and relentless flirting. "I'll bet you speak French to all the girls."

"So many girls, so little time." In eventing women outnumbered men three to one, more at the lower levels.

"Not a bad gig for a bloke."

"You figured that out."

"Getting a date—" she was thinking, *getting laid,* but wasn't about to trot that out "—must be like shooting fish in a barrel."

"Better," he drawled, and his eyes glittered. "Nobody dies."

"Very funny."

"Hey," he said, his McRae chestnut eyes obliging as a spaniel's. "It's easy. All you gotta do is pick one and ask. For starters, how 'bout supper tonight at Ashten's?"

Obviously someplace local, and she was supposed to be impressed. "No, thanks."

"The Belltree, Wednesday? The local eventing crowd goes there."

"That's good to know, but no."

"O'Donnell's Pub, lighter fare, taste of home." His cocky grin told her he wasn't used to being turned down.

She glanced at Bo in the shadows. "I'm married to my horse. He needs me more than anything right now."

Parker's smile vanished. "Yeah, I saw him yesterday. Tough luck for my sister. How's he doing?"

"He'd be doing better if people would stop spooking him."

"No, seriously."

"He needs to feel safe again. From everyone. Including you."

At that instant, Bo poked his nose against the stall's bars and belted out a searching whinny. Parker lifted his hands as if surrendering and backed away. Moments later, the outline of a horse and rider broke through the rays of sunlight spearing through the barn door, and Lexy's heart skipped a beat. It was Hamp, as he had promised, riding his four-star gelding Axiom, out for a hack in the relative cool of early morning.

Silent as a cat, he slid off Ax, snapped him into crossties, and loosened his girth. Hamp once said his big red horse seemed to want nothing more than to take off his shoes and join the guys for a beer in front of the TV. Hamp nodded at Parker but spoke to her. "Morning, Lexy. Last night go okay?"

"Quiet. He's a born sneak thief, but off and on, he's eating out of my hand."

"Good for you," he said, and reached into a pocket. "Carrot, buddy boy?"

Bo pressed his muzzle against the bars, begging for the carrot which pleased Lexy inordinately. He did not think all men were bad. Hamp held it on the flat of his palm, and Bo wolfed it, munching contentedly.

Hamp turned to Parker. "Have a good trip?"

Parker gave an easy smile, unlike the sexually loaded messages he'd fired at her. "Ireland's great. Just flew in from Ocala. Left my new guys there in quarantine."

"Yeah? What'd you get?"

"Irish Sport horses, from the national stud. Already started, ready to move up."

"Need any help?" Hamp asked. Lexy was surprised to detect eagerness in his voice.

"Sorry." Parker turned a pocket of his breeches inside out. "Broke the bank on the three of them, plus flying them over, and the quarantine. Sis is on my case. I'll have to train 'em on the cheap—myself."

"Yeah, I know how that goes."

There was an awkward pause. Lexy read it to mean the two men weren't best mates and their apparent camaraderie was some subtle sparring for her attention.

*I'm the good guy. No, I am.*

"Lexy..." Hamp started, and Parker too.

A hot blush fired her cheeks.

Parker raised an eyebrow. "Thought you were married to your horse."

"I am. Jordan hired me. My personal life is my affair."

"Obviously," he said with a grin to her. "Round one to you."

Shit, shit, shit.

Hamp clenched his jaw, and Lexy's stomach knotted. Hawks Nest might be the center of the eventing universe, but the tensions here felt to her like seismic shifts.

"Remember. Gingersnaps," Parker said, still grinning, and strolled down the clean-swept aisle. "You might try some on yourself."

"What was that about?" Hamp asked after Parker disappeared.

"He asked me out."

"Jerk. He runs through women like he runs through horses."

"I turned him down."

"You better had." Hamp stripped his gloves and jammed them under his belt.

"I'm sure he spent more time vetting his new horses," she said, worried Hamp might make more of this than there was to it.

"He's got a great eye, great instincts, and is as talented as they get. But when it comes to training, his work ethic is slack."

Lexy hated gossip but had to learn more about this insistent Don Juan. "Where does he get the money?"

"Computers. Some kind of consulting. Also does the websites and keeps the computers up and running at the Center, and here. I'm guessing the McRae siblings have trust funds."

"A great deal if you can get it."

"And Colonel's a soft touch," Hamp said, then hugged her to him. "Wish you were at my place."

She hugged him back. "Me too," she murmured at his ear. He smelled of a pine-scented soap from his morning shower. He tilted her face up for a kiss, and made it deep and hot. "Ah," he said, breaking away. "Coffee and bacon and you." He was silent for a long moment, as if content to simply be with her, then sighed. "Gotta get home. Anything I can do before I go?"

"Yes, as a matter of fact there is, now that Bo's standing quietly." She got a scoop of grain and poured it in a bucket. "I'd like to see if he'll let me groom him while he's eating. You know, make an end run round his fears."

"And you want me to...?"

"Come in and scrape me off the wall if he slams me against it like he did the vet last night."

He grimaced. "Colonel was right. You should wear a helmet, and that vest."

"Don't wimp out on me now." She put on Jordan's helmet. "They ganged up on him, and Roger moved too fast. And I am not a man."

"No shit, Sherlock," Hamp said with a playful leer, then crossed his arms and settled in to watch.

As she'd hoped, Bo buried his face in his feed trough and didn't look up until she'd brushed him hard all over, except around the staples. She came out sweating, breathing hard, tumbled the tools into the tack tote, and bumped Hamp's shoulder. "See. He's going to be fine."

"Promise me you'll be careful," Hamp answered. "Every minute, careful."

"Cross my heart and hope to die." She marked a cross on her chest.

"Don't even think that thought." He shuddered, and the concern in his eyes bowled her over.

"Sorry," she said.

"Not every death in eventing happens on cross-country."

"Yes, sir. I know that, sir. Barn safety rules are posted on that sign."

"Memorize them," he ordered. "Again."

"Like I didn't do that years ago," she shot back. But she couldn't help grinning she was so pleased he cared, and then the sadness gripped her. Only her mother had looked out for her like that.

Hamp tightened the Ax-man's girth, released him from the crossties, and put on his own helmet. Outside the sun had cleared the tops of the pines, the sky was blue without a cloud, and the heat was rising.

He mounted in one smooth movement, legged the big gelding into a swinging trot, and headed for the Center. She turned to the barn with a lump in her throat.

She was happy and sad, eager and scared, glad she was here and sorry she'd left England. But she'd fallen for Hamp Gambrell, which didn't feel right with her mother just dead, or safe with Parker McRae angling for her right in front of him.

Bo would be her refuge. Horses always had been.

*Coward's way out.* Imbriani's taunts echoed in her head. *Get a real job, get married, have babies.*

*No way,* she backtalked him, then and now.

Horses could kill you, but they didn't lie, cheat, steal, or sell off your best friends.

# Part Two. Fatal Plus

## *September*

Dressage means simply schooling. Its principles were first described by Xenophon, fourth century B.C. Greek soldier and historian. His non-violent ideas about training horses were restored by European military equestrians in the fifteenth century.

In dressage, the horse is schooled on the flat to move forward with balance and impulsion in all three gaits when given subtle cues from the rider. The goal of this training is to produce an equine athlete that is supple, athletic, responsive, submissive, and happy.

> *A History of the U. S. Army Olympic*
> *Equestrian Team (1912-1948)*
> By Colonel Jacob McRae, USA Maj. Ret.

# Ten

A couple of days later, Bo was coming around, Lexy thought, so she left him to check the action in the arena. At one end, she saw Ann Voss and Rachel White, boarders and Jordan's students, warming up. At the other, Jordan was coaching her eleven-year-old niece Brianna whose mother, Gwen Settlemyre the sheriff, was watching. Poor Bree froze.

"Do windmills with your arms," Jordan urged. "And breathe. Remember to breathe."

"Thank you." Bree picked up her reins and executed a spiral-in on the twenty-meter circle as good as Lexy had done at Brianna's age. Her boss was a super coach, Lexy realized.

The mother walked over in her sheriff's uniform. "Let's get going, honey. I gotta be at the county commissioners' meeting at six-thirty."

Brianna's hopeful face fell, and Lexy's heart squeezed as she remembered her father dismissing her like that.

"Nice lesson, honey," Jordan said kindly, then with an edge to Gwen, "She's a hard worker, like you."

"She'd better be—" Gwen's head swiveled toward the sound of horses bellowing in the stallions' wing. Lexy heard them too. Bree, Ann, and Rachel fought to control their mounts as they pitched and sidled underneath them.

"Horse fight," Gwen said grimly, one hand on her pistol and the other on her taser, as if compelled by training to go on alert.

Lexy sprinted to the barn, the sickening sound of outraged horses growing louder. There, in the first stall, Marcus—Jordan's six-year-old eventer—twirled frantically, snorting and trumpeting to the fighting stallions. She ran on. Bo's stall was empty. Her heart plummeted. Someone had fucked up royally.

Orsino's stall was next, and empty too, but the back door to his paddock was wide open. Looking through it, she saw the stallions, one mahogany, one gray, jockeying for position, heads flashing as they struck each other's haunches. Neck snaking down, Bo bit at Orsino's hocks. Orsino lashed back at Bo's. Then to her horror, they reared and locked their chests in battle, forelegs pumping, teeth bared and tearing at each other's necks.

Orsino was too old for this, and Bo too valuable to risk.

Frantic to stop them, Lexy opened the faucet, dove for the hose, dragged it into the battle zone, water her only weapon. Under assault from a stallion in his prime, the grand old gray toppled to his knees then valiantly lunged up to meet his foe. With a cry of desperation, she marched into the high-fenced paddock and blasted water in their faces. The shock broke the lock-holds they had on each other's necks, and they parted like prizefighters. Blood oozed from bites and poured from gashes on their necks, legs, and shoulders.

"Tyrone, Parker! Round up ropes, blankets!" She heard Jordan yell, then, "Damn it, Lexy. Get out of there. Help's on the way."

Tyrone came flying in with Parker, ropes dangling and big blankets flapping.

Lexy backed to the doorway. Only then did she release her grip, shutting off the spray but still aiming the nozzle at the stallions.

They circled each other, great threatening snorts rising from deep within their chests. As one, they shook water from their heads and streaming manes, then clashed again, fury swelling.

The hell with Jordan's orders. Lexy had to stop them.

She dove into the paddock, astonished to see Hamp heading for her.

"No no no!" she shouted, waving her arm and pointing at the Dutch door into the stall. It was the stallions' one way out. "You go back. I drive Bo in, you close the door."

Striding toward the flashing hooves, Lexy trained the nozzle at Bo's head, using the spray to force him from Orsino and chase him into the stall. He lunged through the open door, kicking out.

His shod hoof caught her thigh. A blinding pain flashed through her. She dropped the hose, staggered through the door, and crumpled to the shavings, grasping her leg in agony. But she could still see Bo, high on a toxic mix of adrenalin and testosterone, patrolling his territory. Then Hamp flung himself between them, onto her.

"Let me go." She pushed him away and struggled to her feet. "They need me."

"They could kill you. Parker!" Hamp called. The two men bridged their arms and carried her, protesting, to her hay bed. She batted them away and struggled to her feet to see.

Tyrone pulled the tattered bandage off Bo's nose and slipped a halter over his head, humming. She watched in disbelief as he led the wild-eyed stallion in small circles to calm him, then down the aisle to his stall next door. Could Tyrone have put Bo in Orsino's paddock? Or Parker? He was always around.

"How bad's he hurt?" she called, seeing ruddy blood smeared over Bo's mahogany coat. Behind her, Jordan turned the water off and dragged the hose into the aisle.

She and Tyrone went in to inspect him. "Bite marks," Lexy heard him say. "Scrapes and scratches. Looks like all the blood's Orsino's."

"Ah shit," Jordan said. "Daddy will be pissed. Orsino's his last, best campaigner." She left Tyrone with Bo and came to check the older stallion.

Limping, eyes peeled for any clue, Lexy followed her. In the paddock, they found the old fellow, winded and defeated. He let Lexy rest her hand on the crest of his bloody neck.

"I was slow and late. Useless," Jordan said.

Lexy felt hot tears of shame and frustration. She'd been useless too. "Let's move him to his stall and treat his wounds."

Blood trickled from flesh wounds on his haunches. Jordan touched her fingers to his jaw and led him forward. He took a hopping step on his right hind leg, barely touching a toe to the drought-stricken grass, and stopped.

Lexy's heart sank, and she saw Jordan shudder. Her boss knelt stiffly and ran her fingers down his hindquarters, hock, cannon bone. She pressed her fingers to the fetlock he wouldn't put his weight on, and he flinched.

With an anguished shake of her head at Lexy, she took her cell in a trembling hand, speed-dialed a number, explained in two short sentences, and hung up.

"Thank God," she said to Lexy. "Roger's in the north pasture following up on a filly from yesterday. Says he'll be here in five."

Which was a good thing, Lexy thought, as she patted the fine old stallion, hoping to comfort him.

But an awful omen.

# Eleven

Everyone gathered around the old stallion—Parker, Tyrone, and Hamp who brought Lexy a plastic chair. She refused it, digging her fingers into her palms against the pain of standing. "How the hell did Bo get into Orsino's paddock?"

"Through Orsino's stall," Parker deadpanned, leaning against the fence.

"She means," Hamp ground out, "who put him there, asshole."

Parker blinked, all innocence. "Dunno."

Tyrone glared at her. "*Somebody* let him in."

"Not her," Hamp said, standing by her like a rock. "She risked her life to save them."

Tyrone snorted. "I'd of risked mine too if I'd put my horse in the wrong place."

"Jesus, man, she didn't do it," Hamp shot back. His bronzed skin flushed with anger, and the old jumpy panic fired in Lexy's veins. Horse fights she could handle, but men's anger drove knives of fear into her.

"Somebody done it," Tyrone went on. "Plus, she got here first."

"You look to your own staff," Hamp said, the cords of his neck taut as new wire fencing.

Parker stepped between them. "Gentlemen, let's not argue," he drawled. "Coulda been an honest mistake."

"It could have been on purpose," Lexy spurted, then wished she'd had the sense to hang back.

"Hell, luv, if you're looking for a culprit, even Hamp here could have done it. He has more to gain by disabling Jordan's best Olympic prospect than Tyrone. And he had the opportunity."

Hamp's hold on Lexy's elbow tightened.

"That's absurd," she blurted, panicking at Hamp's quick anger. Her father used to go from calm to lethal too, but perhaps she could forestall an outright eruption. "Hamp—he was just bringing me—"

"Come to think of it—" Parker cut in, his eyes glinting. "What *are* you doing here, sneaking around after our new employee like some thieving Indian?"

That hit Lexy like a slap, and Hamp slammed a fist into Parker's gut.

Parker crumpled, doubling over. "Fuck," he gasped. "Cancha—take a—joke?" Then slowly, rising like a broken puppet pulling itself together, he straightened his left shoulder then the right, stretched out a leg, planted a foot, did a half circle with his head, adjusted it with both hands. Once erect, he gave a lopsided grin and charged Hamp, head down, like a bull. Hamp stumbled backwards across the aisle and crashed against the wash stall wall, only his athlete's balance keeping him on his feet. Parker met him there, fists flying.

"Do something!" Lexy yelled at Tyrone.

"Let 'em fight," he said hoarsely. "It'll do 'em good."

Hamp caught Parker's shirttails and yanked them over Parker's head, pinning his arms and blinding him. With a roar, Parker staggered around, ripped off the shirt then launched himself on Hamp. Hamp crashed on the rubber pavers with a grunt, Parker on top of him. In the moments it took Hamp to catch his breath, Parker stripped off the remnants of the shirt, straddled Hamp, and battered his chest and face.

Frantic to help Hamp, Lexy grabbed the hose and blasted its jet spray on Parker, his face, belly, privates, but the deluge sprayed Hamp too. He sprang up, drenched and sputtering. Parker lurched to his feet, naked from the waist up, water dripping from him. Unrelenting, Hamp pulled Parker to him, and they rolled on the floor like tomcats out for blood.

"Break it up, you bozos," a deep male voice rang down the aisle.

Lexy twisted to see Colonel leap off his ATV, his lifelong habit of command sparking off him like bullets. He collared Hamp, grabbed Parker by the hair, shook his head in disgust.

"No fighting on my farm—not in my barn, and not in front of ladies."

"Sorry, sir," Parker muttered, and spit blood from his mouth. "We were just—"

"No excuses, damn your hide," Colonel said fiercely. "What the devil's going on? And you." He looked at Hamp as if it were his fault. "Don't you live somewhere else?"

"I'm next door. Chip's trainer," Hamp said.

"Your mother would be ashamed of you, young man."

At thirty-something, Hamp didn't answer to his mother, but bowed his head to Colonel, water sparkling in his spiked black hair. "Yes, sir."

Colonel gave a crisp nod, and his hawk-like gaze took in two drenched and sullen men, an upset woman, water flooding the barn's aisle, and a stall door gaping open.

"Where's my daughter?"

"In there," Lexy said. "With Orsino."

"Somebody, anybody, tell me what happened."

"Bo got into Orsino's paddock, and they had a fight," Parker said. There was a hang-dog look about his face, as if he had a lot of practice at confessing. "We were trying to figure out how he got in there."

Colonel glowered. "With your *fists?*"

"Coulda been Tyrone, Hamp, some groom," Parker said. "Coulda been me. Hell, it could have been this little lady," he added smoothly, and put an arm around her, further provoking Hamp, and her. "You haven't been here two whole days, luv. It's an understandable mistake, right horse, wrong stall."

Lexy picked up the hand and dropped it to his side. "I know which horse goes where."

"May be," he said, undaunted. "But you're so green you barged in between two fighting stallions and got kicked. Thank God, your leg's not broken."

"You're hurt?" Colonel asked her.

"Bruised. Nothing compared to Orsino." She described the stallions' battle. "Roger's on his way."

"Good," Colonel said, then turned to Parker. "Lexy needs ice, lots of it."

Parker headed for the tack room, double time. "And the first aid kit for Bo," Lexy called after him.

Hamp took Lexy's hand. "You get off that leg. You did what you could, you stopped the fight."

"But how did he get in there?"

"How indeed?" Jordan asked, emerging from Orsino's stall. Again, her face was gray as ashes, but she turned to Lexy, her voice raspy with outrage. "As for you, I didn't hire you to take a risk like that."

"I had to do something."

"Which didn't work."

"But he's all right, isn't he?"

"No, he's not," Jordan said, her voice breaking, and went to her father. "I'm sorry, Daddy. I'm afraid he's not going to make it."

"That bad?" Colonel said evenly. But he looked shocked and sad, the lines in his craggy face deeper than this morning, and Lexy realized a death watch had begun.

"He's still on his feet," Jordan said. "But he's three-footed lame. I'm pretty sure the right hind's broken."

Unfixable at his age, if ever, Lexy knew. Jordan took her father by the elbow as gently as a funeral home director and ushered him into Orsino's paddock. Lexy sat on the hay, Hamp beside her, her leg throbbing so bad that she felt like throwing up.

Worse, her heart was breaking for the old campaigners—Orsino and Colonel.

After a while, Parker came back with ice and the first aid kit. He set them down and offered Hamp his hand. "No offense, man."

Hamp looked at the hand as if it were a cold dead fish but shook it. "Yeah. Heat of the moment. None taken."

Lexy was not convinced, but she watched Parker join his father and sister at Orsino's side. Hamp settled the ice pack on Lexy's bruise, grabbed his kit, and started for Bo's stall.

"That's my job," she said, holding the ice pack to her thigh as she tried to stand.

"You sit." Gently, he pressed her down.

She pushed up at him. "Bo doesn't like men, but he likes me."

"Stay. He'll like me too." He carried the kit into Bo's stall.

Long minutes passed, and she was alone. Ice numbed the bruise, but her pulse throbbed. First the stallions, then the men, and worst, Hamp's flashpoint temper, too like Imbriani's.

"Terrible about Orsino," Hamp said when he returned. "But Bo should be okay. Welts, bruises. Coupla bites broke skin. I cleaned 'em up. I'll come back after dark with a poultice for his bruises, and for yours."

Hamp had recovered the quiet manner she loved in him, but when he shook the bag to make it conform to her injured leg, the rattling cubes made a harrowing racket in the too-still barn. Finally Tyrone came out with Jordan, not talking, leaving Parker and Colonel standing sentry for Orsino.

Roger's big truck rumbled into the silence, and he walked straight to Jordan, his heartiness subdued. With his big arm around her shoulder, they went to his new patient, Tyrone following them, hands clasped behind his back. The day's heat had not yet broken, but Lexy shivered as she strained to hear. Their words were few and muffled. Roger came out alone, his face set, and rummaged through his Portavet.

"This looks bad," she said to Hamp.

He nodded and meticulously adjusted the ice bag on her leg, nothing to say, nothing else do.

Roger came back carrying three full syringes, one clear and two cobalt blue.

"What's that?" Jordan asked.

Tillinghast looked grim. "The blue stuff... Fatal Plus, it's new. Quick. They're dead before they hit the ground."

"But what—?" Lexy started, her throat dry.

"Fetlock's broken, honey. Whether from kicking, being kicked, or landing on it wrong, there's no way to tell," he said, and disappeared into the paddock.

"Oh my God," she whispered. Hot tears splashed down her face, but she couldn't stop shivering. Hamp pulled her to him, and she laid her head on his shoulder.

A few moments later she heard a thud, a familiar sound when a healthy horse drops to its knees to take a roll. Then she heard the flop of half a ton of horseflesh hitting the ground, never to roll again, and she knew the fatal dose had worked as fast as the vet said it would.

Suddenly she was swept back to her mother's memorial service where people had murmured condolences at her, words she'd barely heard and hardly believed although they'd been kindly meant. Her mother was dead and gone, and Lexy would never understand that letter. Even so, now, today, she couldn't bear to sit still while any creature in the universe was dying, especially that fine old gentleman she'd only just met and failed to save. Overcome, she turned her head into Hamp's chest and wept.

He pressed his lips to the crown of her head, then said, "I'm so sorry, sweetheart." He didn't ask if she was crying about her mother or the horse, but she felt he knew. She was crying because life was short and fragile, and good people and good horses breathed it in one minute and died the next, but she had to go on living.

By the time everyone reassembled in the aisle, she'd dried her tears, looked up, and realized they were staring at her. She absolutely had not put Bo in Orsino's paddock, but how to prove it to a band of strangers?

# Twelve

L ong after dark, Colonel wandered to the barn, his square shoulders slumped in defeat. Lexy felt miserable. Hamp had stopped by after supper and wrapped the bruise on her thigh with a poultice of herbs and hot peppers, a recipe he said his Navajo grandfather had taught him. Then he'd left for the Center to school the horses he'd missed riding because of the day's emergency.

She laid the poultice aside and limped behind Colonel into Orsino's paddock. A heavy green tarp covered the massive corpse, its belly the highest point of the mound, distorting what had been the stallion's awesome symmetry while standing, walking, leaping. A stiff hind leg stuck out under the tarp, its hoof protected by an iron shoe he would never take another step on.

"You don't get used to this," Colonel said. He tucked the tarp's edges under the exposed hoof, making the cover Army-regulation neat. "Tyrone took the backhoe and dug a grave in the meadow where Orby used to—"

The old soldier broke off, but didn't shed a tear.

"I'm truly sorry," she said.

"Could have been worse. That horse was never sick a day in his life, and he didn't suffer long," he started bravely, but his voice cracked. "Better this way."

"I don't see anything better about it."

He glanced at her, as if surprised. "No. You're right. I'll miss him. He was my best friend. You got any idea about that mix-up?"

"No, sir, none." Lexy found herself saying *sir* because of the gravity of the situation. "I was at the arena watching Jordan give a lesson when the fight started. I came running, got here first, then Jordan. The barn had been deserted, and—I know it looks bad. I'm in charge of Bo. But I know which stall is his, and I left him in it."

"I'm sure you did." He led her to the aisle, started to leave, but turned back. "I don't ordinarily approve of women getting into brawls, darlin'."

She hung her head. "I apologize."

"You held your own. Are you all right?"

"Very well, thank you."

"From Bo's kick, I mean."

"Hamp's bringing me another poultice in the morning."

"That hothead?"

"He's not like that."

"I hope you're right. Get a good night's sleep."

But she couldn't sleep. The air was thick and hot. Outside, crickets chirped and tree frogs croaked, but Orsino's stall was silent. She'd only just met him but still felt the void of loss that such a magnificent creature had been put down.

If only she'd not left Bo alone. Or found someone to attend him. That was it. Someone accountable, responsible, but who? She didn't know who to trust. She should have double-checked the stall door's latch. Or padlocked it. No, ridiculous. She'd suspected nothing. No one had. She fluffed her flattened sleeping pad, and the new cell vibrated.

Hamp, she thought, and her spirits lifted. The cell felt small and unfamiliar in her hand. Under the barn's bright fluorescents, a text message glowed on her screen.

**Fatal Plus**
**when death's a must**
**works on people 2**

What the hell? Was this some kind of sick joke, a taunt—a threat?

She read it again. God.

She sucked in a breath to control the fear rising in her. Could this be aimed at her? No, she'd been here only two days and knew hardly anyone.

So who in the world could have sent it?

Not Hamp. He couldn't have been more disturbed by Orsino's loss or done more to protect her. But his violent temper gnawed at her, reminding her of Imbriani's.

She checked the caller's number. It was one she'd never seen. She pocketed the cell and paced the aisle, guarding her horse and thinking.

Anyone could have put Bo in that stall. Not Colonel or Jordan, of course. Parker had pointed at Tyrone, Hamp, even himself facetiously. Marina had shown up later, blonde and bronzed and brittle, full of questions for Jordan, but Parker had shielded his sister from her nosy friend and then told Marina everything. Roger Tillinghast could have been in the barn as well, come to think of it, before going out to check the filly. And what about that groom Tyrone had fired after the barn fire? She hadn't met him, didn't know his name.

More to the point, why would anyone want to hurt Jordan's top stallion? Or scare his new handler away? Unless—

If someone intended to sabotage Jordan's breeding program, Lexy realized with a jolt, they could get to Bo through her. She reread the message: *Fatal Plus when death's a must works on people 2.* Then it dawned on her.

Hamp was the only one who had her number.

A shiver iced her spine.

No, no way, not remotely possible. He was her lover, friend. He'd persuaded her to move to Southern Pines, to live with him. He'd lined up jobs for her, treated her bruise.

Bought her the phone. Programmed it himself.

She wrapped her arms around her ribcage, panic spreading through her, worse than when she used to hide from her father's fists. Hands shaking, she switched off the lights, plunging the barn in darkness, which had always been her friend, in closets, under beds, while her mother had taken the blows for her. Had her father suspected something then? And what could that possibly matter now?

Because her mother was dead. And she still did not feel safe.

Horses had been safe, barns too. She and her mother had escaped to them. But Lexy was on her own as she had never been. Should she tell Jordan, who owned the horse? Or Colonel, who owned the farm? Or run, or hide, or leave?

Not again. Years ago, she and her mother had fled her father's villa in Italy for England. Just this month, Lexy had been exiled from England and come here as a last resort. Her only resort. She would not run. She would find safety in this barn, in this blessed darkness. Slowly, her eyes adjusted to the faint light of a quarter moon. For a moment, the din of crickets and tree frogs seemed to fade. Marcus, Jordan's up-and-coming stallion, blew out a peaceful nighttime sigh. Bo snuffled through his hay bag, the brutal fight forgotten.

Then in the hot night, she heard footsteps padding up the sandy drive.

Her heart thundered. Had Tyrone come back to finish things? Or the fired groom? She dove into Orsino's empty stall, fear scalding her. She could hide, but she had to stay. She had to learn everything she could.

"Lexy?" It was Hamp. "I brought you another poultice."

*Works on people 2.*

Feeling like an abject coward, she scrabbled over the pine shavings to the front corner of the stall and crouched under Orsino's feed trough, the cell clamped in her sweaty palm.

She couldn't face Hamp yet.

She didn't know what to say.

"Lexy?" he called louder, with concern, but his footsteps sounded calm, unhurried. A light clicked on, the one in the open wash stall, not the banks of blaring fluorescents. She heard him slide Bo's stall door open. "You in here?" Hamp asked. He murmured to the horse, words in Navajo she didn't understand. The door slid closed. The bolt clanged into place.

"Damn," Hamp muttered as if puzzled not to find her, then said louder, "I called Grandpop in Chelley. Gave me a recipe for a stronger poultice. Lexy? Are you here?"

He was so close he should hear her heart drumming, but she couldn't move a muscle.

Then his shadow crossed the doorway of Orsino's stall, and suddenly he was kneeling in the fragrant shavings, pulling her to him. "Hey, sweetheart, you all right?" His voice was quiet, no trace of the man who'd bludgeoned Parker, but she stiffened, full of fear. He pulled away by inches and tipped her chin up with his fingers. She couldn't meet his gaze.

"You're scaring me," he said, sounding confused, or angry. She couldn't tell, she couldn't speak, the message on her cell blazing in her brain.

She brought it up and stuck it out for him to read.

He scanned it and frowned, his hand tightening on her jaw. She flinched away, and he spat out something vehement in Navajo, it must have been. A curse?

"That's fucking sick."

"You should know," she blurted.

"Me?" His green eyes narrowed. "You can't think I—" He shot up, jammed his hands in his hip pockets and stalked the aisle, his footfalls faint as if he were wearing slippers. Moccasins, she thought, ashamed to think like Parker, and that sobered her so she found the nerve to run after Hamp and catch his arm. It was rigid.

Which proved her right, or proved her wrong, or didn't prove a thing.

"You're the only one who has this number," she said.

He stopped, turned, set his jaw. "That's not strictly true."

"I haven't had time to give it out to anyone."

"I have," he said evenly but with guarded eyes.

"You what? To who?"

"To Jordan. We were watching you work Bo. She was worried about keeping tabs on you. I was too. I gave her your new number."

"Without asking me?"

"You wanted to hide your number from your boss?"

"No, but—"

"No, but what? First, you thought I sent that message? Now you think Jordan did?"

"Of course she wouldn't. She has no reason."

"And I have?" He flicked his hand by his side in anger, and she flinched. "I probably saved your life this afternoon."

At risk to his own. Shame swept her, and she wanted to apologize, but *sorry* seemed so inadequate.

"You were the only one who had my number, except for Jordan."

"And you never set your phone down in the barn? People coming and going. Crazy horses. Horse fights. My fight. You sleeping in the aisle."

"I left it with my things a time or two when I went in with Bo."

"That's all it would take."

"No. No one was here."

"And you have eyes in the back of your head? Damn it, Lexy." He whipped out his cell and dialed a number.

"Who are you calling?"

"Jordan's sister, Gwen."

The sheriff, who'd been here when the fight broke out.

"Don't. It's the middle of the night."

He rang her up. "She'll be here in five minutes," he said from across the aisle. She had a house on the far corner of the Hawks Nest property and would come straightaway.

Mortified that she'd hurt Hamp, Lexy sat on the hay, no comfort anywhere.

Gwen Settlemyre strode in. Up close, she was clearly a McRae with her father's beaky nose and military posture, and her sister's thick chestnut hair. A badge flashed on her khaki shorts, and a gun sat in the holster strapped at her hips. And Lexy again felt a shock of dislocation not to be in England anymore where even the police didn't carry guns. Hamp made introductions and told Gwen what had happened with the stallions after she had left—the euthanasia and the taunt Lexy had received.

Hesitating, Lexy handed the sheriff her cell with its glowing message.

"Interesting," Gwen said, showing no surprise. "Any idea who sent it?"

"None whatsoever," Lexy said. Hamp came to stand beside her, still as a stone.

"Any idea why?" Gwen asked tonelessly.

"It would be the sheerest speculation," Lexy said.

"Speculate."

Lexy looked at Hamp. "Maybe to get at Jordan?"

"Or to get at you," he said. "To stop you working with the horse."

"Care to elaborate on that," Gwen said. She had, Lexy realized, Colonel's military air.

"You know eventers," Hamp said. "Everybody supports everybody to their faces. Behind their backs, not so much."

"Yeah. Anything specific, like a lead?" Her keen gaze fixed on Hamp. "Anything like that nasty little fistfight this afternoon?"

"You must have talked to Colonel," he said evenly.

"Nope, my brother. Parker loves to fight." Her brief smile only showed her teeth. "Had a smash bang up good time."

Lexy winced. "Parker pointed at everybody. According to him, anybody could have put Bo in old Orsino's stall and left the door open to his paddock. Even me."

"Did you?" Gwen asked bluntly.

"No!" Lexy said. "Absolutely not."

"Easy. It's okay."

"I mean, anyone could have sent that message."

"Anyone who had access to your number," Hamp reminded her, then said to Gwen, "That would be me and Jordan, that we know of. If Lexy or Jordan left their phones out, anybody who knew their way around a cell could have lifted the number. Boarders. Staff."

"Family," Gwen said wryly, and studied the message. "Sorry, folks. This is nasty. But for it to be actionable as a harassing phone call, it's got to meet some specific criteria. Offer a direct threat, happen repeatedly, interrupt your phone service, make false statements. I don't see any of that. Do you?"

"No," said Lexy.

"It's a threat," said Hamp.

"Or a statement. Or a joke. Plus, it's a text message. We don't have a voice to go on. So, no suspect."

"Can't you trace the number?" Hamp asked.

"That may work on *Law and Order*, but no. These pre-paid dealies are easy to falsify."

"So that's it?" Hamp persisted.

"Pretty much. I can see your concern." She turned to Lexy. "Sorry I can't do more."

"Sorry we bothered you," Lexy said.

"No bother," Gwen replied, but her tone had stayed flat, and Lexy felt she must be bored. "These things happen all the time. Hard to trace, harder to prosecute. Fact of modern life. Look, you get another message like that, you call me."

"Whatever for?" Lexy asked.

"Paper trail. Starts with me." She started to leave but turned and said to Lexy, "And welcome to North Carolina." Then she walked off, looking like she bench-pressed three hundred pounds.

Lexy shrugged at Hamp. "What you want to bet, we got her out of bed."

"You did the right thing. And now you should tell Jordan."

"No way."

"She needs to know."

"I'm too new. She'll think I'm a magnet for disaster. Bad enough we wasted Gwen's time. She'll tell Jordan anyway."

"Nope, she can't. And now you know what she needs from you."

"You think?"

He nodded.

A sense of futility washed through her. "I haven't been here two days, and I've managed to alienate everybody on two farms, including you. And now I'm persona non grata with the local sheriff."

"Hey," he said, and chucked her chin with a gentle fist. Then he drew her to him for a quick sweet kiss, and her stomach dipped with desire. She could have this all the time, she thought, his love, if she wasn't so set on redeeming Bo.

Then as if to give her space, he pulled away. "You still think I did it?" he asked quietly, a hint of uncertainty in his eyes.

"No, of course not. You couldn't have."

But then who did? Tyrone, Parker, Marina? That groom? Roger the two-faced vet?

*Hard to trace. Harder to prosecute.*

# Thirteen

Mid-afternoon on Thursday, four days after she'd arrived, Lexy couldn't free herself from Orsino's tragedy or the creepy message. The stench of the fire still hovered over the farm, made more intense by the afternoon sun. Next to Bo's stall, Orsino's seemed cavernously empty. Her cell was mockingly blank. The staff and boarders talked in whispers around her, but the messenger had gone silent, leaving her in limbo, dreading more, or nothing.

She turned to dump another forkful in the wheelbarrow, but Bo sneaked in and tipped it over. Ten minutes' work spilled on the rubber pavers. "Bugger, Bo!" she swore, but his big brown eyes twinkled. He sniffed at the mess he'd made, the game he'd played, the power he had to make her yell in the middle of a dull day in his stall. She refilled the wheelbarrow, blocking him from dumping it again, laughing. Without him, her constant companion and new best friend, she'd never laugh again.

"You making progress with our guy?" Jordan asked, just back from taking Ruth and Colonel to Winslow Dawson's funeral.

"Some." Lexy averted her eyes, not wanting to betray her worries. "His injuries from the fight are closing fast. I cleaned the wound on his face and packed it like yesterday."

"I wish you'd waited. I'd like to have seen."

"Sorry, but he was so willing. Seems to understand we're on his side," Lexy added. "The flesh is scabbing over, so I picked off the scabs."

"Roger wants wounds exposed to air to keep abreast of infection," Jordan said. "Daddy leaves them to protect the tender new flesh beneath them."

Just then Tillinghast's big truck rumbled up. He ambled down the aisle, a purple bruise running from his cheekbone to his shadowed jaw. "Afternoon, ladies. I was in the neighborhood and thought I'd check on Bo." Clucking and hmm-ing, he pressed his face against the bars, examining the horse but not offering to go in. "Nice bandage."

"He's settling in," Jordan said. "But I worry about those staples."

"They'll work their way out. They're not hurting anything."

Lexy bristled. "I'm sure they hurt him all along, and the ones left still do."

For a second, Tillinghast's eyes flashed with resentment, but he turned to Jordan and said smoothly, "If you insist on those staples coming out, my dear, there's only one safe way. I tranq him again, deeper this time, and I'll have them out in minutes."

"Let's not, Roger," Jordan said to Lexy's surprise. "Lexy's got a bond with him. Slow may be better, especially as we're seeing no infection. If he backslides, we'll call you."

He cupped her elbow with a bear-like paw and steered her down the aisle for privacy, it seemed, but his sultry Southern voice still carried.

"What do you know about this gal, my dear? She just drifted into your life. How do you know she's who she says she is?"

"Lexy came to us well-recommended."

"You've seen the recommendations then."

Lexy tensed. Maybe she was right to suspect Colonel's best friend and Jordan's ex-fiancé. Nothing she could put her finger on, but he obviously wanted her out of there.

"I trust Ben and Hamp implicitly," Jordan said.

"You haven't seen the paperwork." Roger wagged his head, clucking in concern. "First, you don't go see the horse, now this girl. You're getting careless, my dear."

"She's handling Bo just fine, Roger. She loves the horse—"

"Shoot, honey, I'd love him too. He's worth what? Five hundred K?"

"Not now," she said. "But he will be. I'm counting on Lexy to bring him back."

"Women." Roger heaved a sigh, jammed on his baseball cap with *Sandhills Equine Specialists* embroidered above the bill in hunter green, and gazed out across the barnyard at the drought-dried paddocks, then looked down at Jordan.

"You're a dreamer, my dear, always were. Guess that's why I love you."

Lexy saw him bend his big form down and brush a kiss across her mouth. Eww.

"See you tomorrow," Roger said. "Gotta keep tabs on that filly."

And he left. Lexy shuddered. What the hell just happened?

Were Roger and her boss an item? What about the vibes Lexy thought she'd sensed between Jordan and Ben Holt? And suddenly, there was Colonel, swinging in on his ATV. He nabbed Roger before he could get to his truck. She could hear the die-hard sportsmen planning a fishing trip. Finishing, Colonel came to Jordan, erect and proud, but Lexy could see a hitch in his stride. He was taking these latest losses hard.

"You shouldn't have broken your engagement, Jordan."

"Daddy!" she spurted.

Lexy's gut roiled. Would a spurned fiancé be more or less likely to make trouble with a new employee? More, perhaps.

But why? She ducked into Bo's stall. She'd rather not hear their fight but couldn't help it.

"A vet on the farm would be a godsend," Colonel went on. "I won't last forever, and I hate to think of you alone."

"It's my life."

"I'm thinking of Bo too," he added.

"So am I. Lexy's the one who can help him, not Roger."

Lexy looked up from picking through the shavings, pitchfork in hand.

Jordan limped into the stall, her father muttering after her.

"Thanks for taking up for me with Roger," Lexy said to her.

"Thanks for taking such good care of my horse."

"My pleasure. When I finish, shall we go after a couple more staples?"

Jordan shot her father a glance that shouted, *Don't you dare butt in,* and said, "Suits me fine. Just don't tell Roger."

Lexy finished the stall and pushed the wheelbarrow to the muck pile, appalled by Colonel's meddling in Jordan's life, confused by Jordan's way with Roger. By the time Lexy had emptied the load and gotten back, Jordan was headed for Bo's stall with a bucket of chopped alfalfa. Horses crave the protein-rich hay like chocoholics crave chocolate.

"Whoa, ladies. Helmets required," Colonel ordered.

Lexy popped into the tack room, got two helmets, and they strapped them on.

"The best light's by the door," Jordan said.

Lexy agreed. This newest-looking wing of Hawks Nest's stables gave its stallions every amenity. Huge stalls had sliding doors that opened to the aisle and Dutch doors opposite that opened into private paddocks, allowing maximum cross-ventilation in the Sandhills' oppressive heat.

"Where do you want me?" she asked her boss.

"I'll take the left, and you go after the staples in his right ear."

Jordan put the bucket in front of Bo, and he buried his nose in it. Aware of Colonel's skeptical gaze, Lexy massaged the long muscles of Bo's arched neck, pressing the heel of her hand closer to his ear with each new stroke. Bo accepted her ministrations like a monarch and munched greedily. Lexy worked her fingers lightly over his head.

"Trying to desensitize him to my touch before I get to his ear," she said, and took out the needle-nosed cannula. Humming a soothing love song, she zeroed in on a staple and extracted it. Jordan held the bucket, and Bo would not be parted from his alfalfa.

"That's my man," she crooned, then said to Lexy, "Wow. He couldn't care less."

Lexy studied his ear and selected another staple. "Let's go for the next one then."

"Don't press your luck, ladies," Colonel coached from outside the stall.

"Doesn't look like luck to me," Jordan said. "You let Lexy work."

Preferring work to worry, Lexy extracted five more from the outside edge of Bo's right ear and dropped them one by one into Jordan's free hand, stopping before Bo emptied the bucket.

"Magic drug, alfalfa," Lexy said, feeling a great weight lift. "Magic horse," she added, whispering in his ear and nuzzling his neck.

"God, I'm glad he's back," Jordan said. "Let's give him some time in his paddock."

"Super," Lexy said, her breath catching with anticipation.

Jordan opened the Dutch doors and showed her how to bolt them to the outside wall. "Handy to pop the guys in their paddock when you're mucking out," Jordan told her. She opened the top and bottom halves and stood aside.

With a snort, Bo forged onto the sandy surface, lowering his head and sniffing the perimeter as if still in the arena, but no longer desperate. Satisfied the space was his, he rolled vigorously in the sand, got up, shook, then ambled over for more hay, confident he'd get it.

"Oh my word, he's gorgeous," Lexy said, her pulse zinging with awe for this special animal. "Filthy again, but gorgeous. I'd love to work him."

"Nope, he's not ready." Colonel walked in, and Jordan closed the bottom half of the Dutch door. Colonel leaned on it, assessing Bo with his decades of experience.

"Don't be an old coot," Jordan said. "*You* may not be ready, but Lexy's doing great. Not in the paddock though. It's his private space."

"We'll need more room anyway," Lexy put in quietly.

"How about the arena after the heat breaks? Everybody will have left, and nobody can interrupt."

"You mean tonight?" She was eager to put Bo back in work if only at leading and lunging, the building blocks for all that was to come. But what if Colonel was right?

"It'll be cooler too," Jordan said.

"That's super," Lexy said. "I'm ready."

"The question is, of course," Colonel said, "is he?"

"Why don't you join us, and find out?" Lexy challenged him.

"B'lieve I will," he said, and mounted his ATV and putt-putted back to the house as if he were satisfied. But Lexy suspected he was never satisfied with himself or others. At least he'd be there in the dark, and she'd have not one but two people to watch her back. An old man and a crippled woman.

# Fourteen

"Good, Lexy. That will be all," Jordan called out from the center of the indoor arena where she stood with Colonel after breakfast. "Walk Jazz a few minutes, and trade off with Tyrone."

*About damn time,* Lexy thought. In the two weeks since she'd taken charge of Bo, Jordan had drilled her in dressage on her older eventer Jasmine. Colonel shadowed them. Despite impressive workouts on the mare, Jordan kept postponing Lexy's riding Bo. Was it the whispered suspicions about her role in Orsino's death? Thank God, she hadn't told Jordan about the message. It made it look like she attracted trouble.

She nodded and loosened Jazz's reins.

The brilliant mare stretched her nose toward the ground and took up her easy, swinging walk. It was a little after nine a.m., and the heat was suffocating. Jazz was drenched with sweat from their half-hour workout, Lexy too. She hopped off, paddock boots digging in soft sand. Tyrone, unsmiling, led Bo in, swapped reins with her and led Jazz out. Lexy couldn't figure out why he was such a dark cloud, but with no new evidence, his brooding kept him on her list of suspects.

Bo's mahogany coat gleamed from her daily grooming, and he looked smart in his black tack, tall, bright-eyed. She might be on Tyrone's shit list, but she was proud of her work with Bo.

The first week, she'd cleaned the wound and changed its dressing twice a day. It was closing nicely. He'd let her pluck more staples with no one to help. He trusted her now in his stall, his paddock, and the makeshift *picadero* she roped off for him whenever she took him to the arena. Under Jordan's critical eye, she'd lunged him in it several days, then moved to the larger arena, adding a lightweight bareback pad the first two times as if he were a green horse, then graduating to a saddle.

He'd taken both in stride. Hence, today's lesson, their first ride.

She'd asked Hamp to come watch, and he held Bo while she adjusted tack. Thank God, he was speaking to her after the text message fiasco. They had a date tonight. The boarders Ann and Rachel strolled through the big door to watch too. Ann looked Jordan's age, Rachel older. She'd never seen one without the other, but they hadn't spoken to her since Orsino had been put down.

Parker joined them and said something, and they laughed out loud. Bo tensed, fidgeting under saddle, and Hamp shot them a dark look. "Hey, guys. Button it. We've got a powder-keg here." Quieting, they moved outside the arena door.

"What are they doing here?" she asked.

"Probably spying for Marina." Just then the perfectly dressed and coifed blonde strolled up with Minx, her opinionated little Jack Russell, trotting merrily alongside.

"Oops, wrong," Hamp said. "There's the Whiskey Queen, doing her own recon."

"Whatever for?" Lexy asked.

"She hates being left out of the loop. And Parker—" Hamp kicked the sand. "You know what I think of him."

"King of the barn scuttlebutt," she said. And another suspect, along with Marina. She checked the bridle, tightened the girth, and let down the stirrups. "Ready."

"You sure you're up to this?"

"I worked my whole life to ride a horse like Bo."

Hamp gave her a leg up, and suddenly, finally, she was mounted on the scariest, most gifted horse she'd ever met. She double-checked the stirrups' length, took up the reins, and settled into the saddle. He turned his head and sniffed the toe of her left boot, as if to make sure she was his barn buddy, the human who cleaned his wounds and brought his feed and groomed him. She patted his neck, walked him round the outer edge of the arena, then asked him for a trot to warm up. And her awareness of anything but him receded.

His stride was bigger than Jasmine's, huge in fact, but like the mare, he seemed happy to be at work. After a couple of uneventful laps, Jordan asked her to ride him on a twenty-meter circle. Once they were on it, Jordan became more exacting, tweaking the position of Lexy's hands, the length of her reins, the flat of her thigh against the saddle—a little more, a little less, higher, lower, longer—*millimeters*. And then his back lifted under her. Jordan knew exactly how to tell her to ride him. With every stride Lexy felt his power underneath her, dazzling her. There was more horse in front of her, behind her, and beneath her than any she'd ever ridden, all pure athlete, all stallion.

"Come off the circle next time around," Jordan said, her tone still quiet, "and ask him to lengthen across the diagonal. Just a smidge, he's got a huge extension."

Lexy's heart clutched. His huge extended trot was what she wanted most in the world to feel at this moment, but once she'd released it, how could she control such power? "Ride like Anky," she whispered, and felt her breath move all the way down into her feet. They rounded the corner, and she squeezed ever so lightly at his girth and relaxed her elbows to let him lengthen into her hands.

His first stride almost catapulted her from the dressage saddle's deep seat. Instantly she adjusted her balance, exhilarated to feel his scope and passion for his work. At the far corner, he came back to her easily, slowing, and she followed Jordan's instructions for the next... *oh!*... It seemed like only minutes, but time flew, and she flew on her horse, collecting him on the short ends of the arena and then extending across the diagonal. Jordan asked her to trot down the center line and halt. Bo tucked his hindquarters beneath Lexy and bounced to a perfect light square halt.

Then he lifted his head and trumpeted for the mares, losing focus.

Minx scooted out of Marina's arms and took after Bo, yapping shrilly. Spooked, Bo lunged sideways, and Parker and his groupies erupted into peals of laughter.

Bo's head shot down and heels kicked back, stripping the reins from Lexy's hands and pitching her inches above the saddle. Before she could think, she was on a bucking bronco. She came down hard and sat deeply into the saddle. He bucked thirty meters down the center line, reins flapping. She caught them with one hand, balanced herself, and found the rhythm. A few more lunges, and her weight slowed him. Crow-hopping to the wall, he came down to a walk, and she caught her breath, only to see to her dismay Hamp squaring off with Parker.

*No!* Furious and fearful of a reprise, she galloped Bo straight at them. They parted ways, Hamp to the right, Parker and crew scrambling to the left. "I'll fight my own fights," she bent over in the saddle and hissed at Hamp, then straightened and spoke down to Parker and Marina, shaking with anger. "This horse is a powder keg, and you just messed up days of work. Get out. Just get out of this arena."

Chastened, Hamp took Bo's reins and stood at her side, both of them watching as Colonel followed the troublemakers to the giant door, reaming them out in words too low for her to hear. Then he stalked back to her and Hamp.

"My daughter did not ask you for airs above the ground, Miss Imbriani," he said. But when she glanced down, she saw a twinkle in his eyes.

"No, sir." He did not protest the *sir.*

Jordan caught up, took Bo's reins, and stopped them, looking disgusted. "Let's try for five minutes of submission, then call it a day. Pick up a working trot circle at C, then spiral in on the circle and back out. Finish on a loose rein at the walk. Make as if those yahoos hadn't been here. My mistake. They're banned for the foreseeable future."

"We're not done," Hamp said to Lexy sternly, but stepped out of the way. Bo executed the spirals fluidly, and Lexy brought him down to his long-strided walk. She let the reins slide through her fingers, a cue to him that they were done. Like Jasmine, he stretched his nose down almost to the sand. Jordan put this stamp on all her horses with the sublime equitation Lexy had seen at Pau. Now, under Lexy's legs, Bo's back felt long and relaxed, and there was trust and something she'd not seen in him, tranquility.

Hamp met them at the door, and she dismounted.

"Good way to get yourself killed, cowgirl."

Incensed, she dug into a pocket for a peppermint. Bo lipped her palm and wolfed the treat, cracking it with his massive molars, as if nothing had happened.

"You're telling me to quit?"

"You said it yourself," Hamp said. "He's a powder keg. Anything could spook him, anywhere."

"I stayed on."

"Right, Velcro on your britches. Some days it helps, some day it won't."

She wanted to smash something. "I need you on my side."

"I need you alive. Look, I can't make it tonight. I'll call."

"Fine." But it wasn't. Tears of frustration burned behind her eyes. Her first ride on this fabulous horse had been a disaster. She wanted to ride him today, tomorrow, every day for the rest of his working life. Jasmine was a dear, a pro, rock solid, but Bo was genius, even bucking. He could have dumped her in a heartbeat if he'd been serious.

Outside, the heat was rising, so she walked Bo to cool him down, wishing Hamp could control his temper. Near the barn, a striped barn cat darted in front of Bo. He snorted, still full of beans.

"Proud of yourself, eh, lad?" she murmured. In the wash stall, she filled a bucket with cool water and added minty liniment, so strong it tickled her nose. She swabbed it into his coat and was hosing it off when Parker strolled up, an equestrian fashion plate in charcoal breeches and black polo shirt. He ducked his head sheepishly.

"Sorry about the hijinks in there, luv."

An apology was a start, but she still suspected him. "We survived."

"I mean, I know I shouldn't have laughed. Sometimes I get carried away."

She picked up a rubber-edged scraper and sluiced the excess water off Bo, anger ratcheting through her. "If he'd tossed me, I could have been crippled. Can't make a living in a wheelchair. Who the hell's side are you on anyway?"

"Yours, luv."

"No way. You know horses. I'd swear you wanted to see me fail."

"Hey. You did great. Even Colonel was impressed. And I can tell you that's one tough gig." Parker unfolded his arms and pushed off the wash stall's wall. "Look, gotta run, horses to work. Sorry, but don't hold that dust-up in the arena against me, okay?" he added, looking at her until she had to meet his gaze. It forced her to notice his long sun-bleached lashes, high cheekbones, strong nose, honey brown eyes which were puppy-dog sincere.

She moved him down the list. "Thanks for the apology, Parker."

He made a small arc with his hand, like a bow. "You're welcome."

"I won't hold it against you, but I'm not going out with you either."

He blinked, surprised, then drew a line in the air between them. "Score one, Imbriani. My serve next." And he strolled down the barn aisle, whistling. He knew his world-class athlete's body was a marvel women threw themselves on.

But she was in love with Hamp. What she loved most about him was his Navajo creed of finding harmony with nature and his horseman's code of doing right by every horse. He was darker and more complicated than she'd realized during their affair in England in the spring. And he respected her, unlike the blokes in England who'd looked at her the way water spaniels looked at ducks. She wished he didn't have such a temper, and she wished she could live with him, but he seemed to understand. Her career, like his, came first.

She pressed her forehead to Bo's wet shoulder. He craned his head around and nudged her. She wished she hadn't stumbled and jumped to the conclusion that Hamp had sent that message. He'd been guarded since then, and it was her own stupid fault.

But try as she might, she couldn't throw off being Imbriani's daughter. Distrust was second nature to her. Being suspicious of everyone around her, however, was new.

# Fifteen

A hand touched Lexy's shoulder and she lurched up, starkly jolted from a night dream of misty England. "Who? What?"

In dark shadows, Jordan bent over her. "Lexy, honey, it's me."

She blinked and forced herself back to Southern Pines, Hawks Nest, hay bales she slept on in the aisle. Her heartbeat slowed from the speed of an automatic handgun to the marching beat of a big bass drum, but she couldn't hide her shaking hands.

"Sorry, didn't mean to scare you," Jordan said solicitously. "You worried about this weekend?"

No-o-o. Not this weekend. After their rocky start, Bo had come round amazingly fast. For Lexy, there'd been no question of going back to work for Ben. Then Jordan had surprised her by signing her up to compete Bo first time at the nearby Horse Park, but...

"I hear footsteps at odd hours, outside the barn, behind it."

"And you told no one, not even Daddy?"

"I thought I was being hyper—neurotic—after Orsino and the fire."

After the message.

"Sweetie, it's time you started sleeping upstairs. And locking the door."

"But Bo—"

"That's an order. Bo will be fine. He knows he's home. That's huge."

"Thank you," she said, and pulled the horse cooler around her despite the evening's warmth. "But you woke me because—"

"I'm going over your entry," she said. "Everything's set, except your medical card. You had one in Britain?"

"Yes, of course." Eventers all over the world were required to wear medical cards sealed in a plastic envelope on their left upper arms in case of a fall or other emergency—heat exhaustion, heart attack, insulin shock. Forget the card, and be disqualified.

"You need it here too."

"Now?"

"No, no. Tomorrow's fine."

"It's with my stuff." She dashed to her apartment, taking the steps two at a time, hoping to make things right. She returned in moments with her British health card and took it out of its clear plastic envelope. She unfolded the paper, worrying. "Will this do?"

Jordan glanced at it. "Let's make sure it has everything the USEA requires."

"Super. Thanks," Lexy said.

"We can go over this inside."

Lexy followed her into her office across the aisle.

Jordan sat in the desk chair. "Pull up a—"

Lexy looked around. The floor was littered with evidence that Jordan had been prepping for the event—checking equipment trunks, bridles, breastplates, girths, and galloping boots Bo would need for every phase, the show tack custom made for him—the reliable old Stubben for dressage, a Devoucoux for cross-country, and a new Butet for stadium jumping—that had fit Lexy perfectly.

Lexy dragged a bucket over and turned it upside down. "Seems early to pack."

"It's almost a year since I competed him. Sold him." Jordan pressed her lips together, studied the form, then said, "The medical and contact information has to be current."

Lexy scanned the page in Jordan's hand. It was folded in half, then thirds. Its small print and narrow lines held tons of information—height, weight, date of birth, glasses or contacts, dentures, allergies, current medical conditions and medications, past fractures, metal plates—anything the EMTs might need to know to care for an unconscious rider.

"Nothing new on the medical side," she said. "I've been lucky. Fractured my wrist when I was eleven. Greenstick fracture. Hurt like heck."

"Yeah? Me too," Jordan said with a rare grin. "That's two things in common. We fractured our wrists, and we love Bo."

Lexy smiled back, feeling forgiven, and then saw the name of the emergency contact person. Tears sprang to her eyes. She handed the card to Jordan, and her brow furrowed.

"Lexy, honey?"

"The emergency contact listed here—" Lexy's voice broke. "It was my mother. I haven't updated it."

"Oh, honey—" Jordan's voice broke too.

"I need another contact." Lexy swallowed hard. "Would you—?"

"Of course," Jordan said warmly, then her gaze dropped to the open card.

Weirdly, watching her scan it, Lexy could have sworn blood drained from her face.

Jordan pored over it as if it were a legal document, which in a manner of speaking it was, then repeated, "Of course," sounding numb and turning back to her computer.

The screen was empty. Jordan goosed the mouse. The weather map popped up, bright and factual. Outside it was eighty-two degrees at ten forty-eight p.m., humidity seventy-eight percent, no rain in the forecast. So the drought continued.

"Let's check the USEA website," Jordan said woodenly. "I'm pretty sure we can sign you up tonight and print off the medical form. You can fill it out tomorrow."

"Super," Lexy said, off balance and put off. "If it's not too late."

"Not at all." Same flat voice. Jordan navigated to the website and the application form, gave Lexy her chair, and excused herself to the bathroom, leaving Lexy lost. Strange woman, who ran hot and cold. Fighting doubt, Lexy keyed in her personal data, and Jordan came back.

"Finished," Lexy told her. "I'll run up and get my credit card."

"No need," Jordan said automatically. "I'm sponsoring you. I pay."

"Really? Thanks." Lexy smiled, grateful. It wasn't as if they had a contract, which her mother would have insisted on. But hadn't Jordan been pals with Lexy's mother? Or had they been more than pals, even confidants? What if Jordan had been Pookie?

No. Impossible. She'd have said something from the first.

# Sixteen

A couple of evenings later after night feed, Lexy walked outside to clear her head. A breeze whispered through the needled pines, and unshed autumn leaves crackled on tree branches. A cat, possum or raccoon scurried through dry leaves on the ground. An owl hooted from the woods, and another, deeper, answered.

But the nearer she got to the Five Points Horse Trials, the tenser she became. Competition nerves she never used to have had started firing days ago.

Jordan had changed, had become more and more exacting. Colonel was more exacting too, but where Lexy could satisfy him, Jordan kept correcting her impulsion, collection, the flying change, the canter depart, the not-perfectly-square halt.

As if Lexy never got them right.

Perhaps she should confront Bo's owner, straight up. And say what?

Do you blame me for Orsino's death?

Can't you bear for someone else to ride your horse?

Or what did you see on my medical card?

Every line on it was absolutely valid. Perplexed, she walked on, crossing the stream she and Bo now forded a couple of times a week to get to the cross-country practice course.

Water splashed over rocks, tumbling and frothing as if roiled by the wind. Nearby, something crashed across the trail. A falling limb? A dog in chase? A fleeing deer?

She was not scared of the creatures of the night.

And yet she felt a sinister presence and wished she'd brought a torch. She turned toward the barn, hurrying back, no answer, no relief in sight.

A hand clamped her mouth, and a powerful arm gripped her torso and pressed her to a solid body.

"Bloody hell," she yelped, struggling against his hold. But the hand tightened, and fingers pinched her nose. Furious and frantic, she kicked back at his legs, missed, threw her body sideways. Her captor crushed her breasts with a tight, cruel hold and whispered in her ear, "Your rich father bought your success. He can't protect you here."

He'd never protected her.

"Fuck you!" She bucked against his bulk and heat, kicking back, spiking the heel of her paddock boot into his shin.

"Stupid bitch," he grunted, and shoved her to the ground.

Her left knee and hand jammed onto the hard-packed trail. Pain shot through her wrist, the one she'd broken years ago. She shrieked, furious, and sprang up in time to see his lean outline sprinting toward the barn. Shaking inside out, she ran after him, desperate to catch a glimpse of his face. But he disappeared around the far corner of the stables.

Then silence. No more steps, no engine roared to life, no tires squealed as a car tore out of the driveway. Fricking bloody coward.

He'd disappeared as noiselessly as Hamp materialized for their rides in the mornings. Not that it was Hamp. No. She'd just talked with him. He was home. She'd heard his dogs play-fighting in the background, then was mortified she'd felt compelled to rule him out.

But she hadn't recognized the gruff voice whispering in her ear.

It hadn't had Parker's drawl, Tyrone's sulkiness, or Eduardo's soft flow. Had it been Italian? Because it struck her that a stealth attack had earmarks of her ex-father's underworld connections, never mind his respectable public image as a member of the Italian Olympic selection committee.

*Bought your success* swept her like a curse. All he'd bought her was loss and exile.

No, the threat had to come from nearer home. At least one, and perhaps three, of her fellow competitors at Hawks Nest wanted to win at any cost. Wanted her too rattled to compete and didn't care if they hurt her or she got hurt. They'd scared her, no doubt about it, and her wrist hurt like hell. Bugger all, had she broken it again? She flexed it up and down, left to right, and winced. If broken, she couldn't move it, could she? Ice packs would help.

Ice packs would have to wait. She scrambled to the barn, pulse pounding in her ears, and grabbed a torch and scissors, the closest she could come to weapons if he was hiding out there, waiting. She swept the yard and woods with the powerful halogen beam.

From beyond the stream, iridescent eyes gleamed red in the bright light—a homely possum, an American creature new to her. The poor dumb thing froze in its tracks.

Retracing her steps, she went back to the stream and shone the torch across the trail. There were faint smudged footprints where her attacker had fled, but the packed dirt trail was hard and dry and her untrained eye could not make out a trace of tread.

Okay, call Gwen now before the morning dew obscured everything.

But Gwen would talk to Jordan and Jordan to Colonel, and the family might put their heads together and decide there was too much risk for her to ride their horse next week. She would put body and soul on the line to reclaim Bo for Jordan, and he deserved his day in the sun. She could watch her own back.

# Seventeen

**B**ut no way could she tell Hamp, she thought, jolting awake before dawn, the feel of her attacker's grip slimy on her body. She'd paced the aisle for hours before collapsing on her bed. God knew how she'd gotten any sleep.

Hamp would go ballistic if she told him. She'd rather show up for dinner at his place tonight as if nothing had gone wrong. Dinner would lead to exactly what she needed, to get lost with him, to stop the shaking she still felt inside, not knowing who'd attacked, or why.

So mid-afternoon, she showered, polished her toenails, and took out her only pair of sandals. Her jammed wrist had ached all day, but she'd wrapped it tight and done her chores and ridden. She'd go without the wrap tonight. She could ice it when she got back, every night, all night until the competition two days from now. Conquer some discomfort, and Hamp didn't have to know. She dug into the tiny closet and pulled out one of her two summer dresses, the floral sundress with a flirty skirt.

The Rent-a-Wreck's AC was now repaired and she'd bought the car with some of her dwindling inheritance from her mother. She drove the mile down Youngs Road past Chip's to Hamp's.

She'd been to his hunt box, a barn below with a small house on top, set amidst tall pines. She loved the way paddocks fanned around it, and pine needles carpeted the modest front yard. Roses like the ones on her dress wound up trellises on either side of the big open door to the barn aisle. Outside, a bright red chestnut poked his nose over his paddock gate and whickered. It was Ax, expecting treats. In the next paddock, Cody trotted up, his flea-bitten gray coat making him look older than his six years. From the aisle, a dog barked, a mellow baying, and the big black-and-tan hound came up to sniff her knees, all wags. Yahzi, Hamp's reservation dog, possibly part wolf. She put out a hand, and he snuffled it, friends.

She took the stairs. Yahzi bounded ahead, more doorman than guard dog. At the top, she could see Hamp had left his door and windows open to catch the evening breeze. Succulent aromas of meat and vegetables filtered through the screen, and something sizzled in a pan. She walked in. She'd been in blokes' apartments, but never one that looked like a home. Indian pots and baskets were artfully arranged beside an end table and a reading chair. God, how she wanted life to be this normal, no messages, no muggings, no looking sideways at everyone she met.

Hamp set the pan off the flames and met her with a checkered dishtowel flung over his shoulder. His gaze took in her done-up hair, her summer dress and red-tipped toes.

"Wow. I hope Yahzi didn't mow you down. Come on in," he said, his tone strained. He gave her a hard, searching kiss. As a lover he was sometimes measured, rhythmic, like riding dressage, at other times full-gallop daring, like driving to leap a giant obstacle. She was breathless when he drew away, covered his pots, turned off the flames, and led her to his bedroom—a Spartan affair with four-poster bed, ladder-back chair, rough-hewn dresser and bedside table, lamp with ten-point antlers for a base. Very old West.

He shucked off his neat dark-wash jeans and button-up short-sleeve shirt, helped her from her sundress and pulled her down beside him. His bare skin was dark and spiked hair black, and his green gaze smoldered, worried. "Last night I dreamed you were attacked. Like a spirit vision, like Parker hitting you when you tried to stop our fight. I can't get it out of my head."

She shivered he was so near the mark. "That's over, I'm okay."

His brow creased. "I want you to move in with me now. I need to know you're safe, need to keep you safe."

"We talk about this every time we're together."

"Yep, and we're going to talk about it again. Bo's on track, I saw him. You don't need to be his keeper. He doesn't need babysitting anymore."

"I don't know that absolutely. He's not out of the woods. And I promised Jordan."

"She'll understand."

"Right, and pretend she's better. She needs me too."

He didn't look convinced. Lexy reached her arms back to prop up and face him squarely, forgetting her jammed wrist. She yelped.

"Jesus, sweetheart. I didn't mean to hurt you. What's wrong?"

"My wrist," she blurted, mortified her secret was out.

He took her cool hands in his warm ones and inspected both wrists. "The left one's swollen."

"Only a little."

"What the devil did you do?"

She felt a hot blush rise and scrambled for an alibi. "I was shifting a bag of feed into a bin but picked it up wrong."

"Bummer." He tracked across the room to the kitchen, his lean naked body a dark shadow in the dwindling light, and she could hear him in the refrigerator's freezer, chipping ice.

She scrambled after him, in only her bra and panties. "No, that's all right. Don't bother. It's getting better."

He chipped away. "If you can't even rest your weight on it, how can you handle Bo this weekend?"

"I've ridden injured. Everybody has. I'll be fine."

He cut her a critical look. "You gotta be one hundred and ten percent to mess with any event horse worth his salt, but a stallion—"

He chucked splinters of silver ice into a pack and secured it to her wrist with a dishtowel. "There, that's a start." He gave her a warm smile. He had a bow-shaped mouth, almost too pretty for a man. "Where were we?"

She smiled back, eager to stop talking before she had to tell another lie. "Snogging. Can we go finish?"

He scooped her up, deposited her on the bed, and gave her another kiss. Finally, he broke off and unhooked the only lacy, girly bra she had in her collection of sports bras and halters. He gave a low hum of appreciation, then let down her hair. "Do you know how beautiful you are?"

"I'm tall, thin, gangly, and white as a sheep."

"Delusional, too." He planted kisses from her mouth to her throat and down her tall, thin, pale white-woman's body. She was shivering with guilt and memory of her attacker, when his fingers peeled off her thong. Her ash brown pubic curls had half grown in since she'd last waxed them.

"Amazing." His eyes shone with the sensual intensity that had bowled her over last February in England.

"No faking I'm blonde," she murmured. Just faking everything else.

"I never understood the waxing thing with women. Doesn't it hurt?"

"Not with Lidocaine, but I can't afford it."

"I like real."

Words stuck in her throat. *Not getting it from me.*

He made love to her slowly, carefully, teasing her that he could get a second dishtowel and strap her to the bed. Bondage with a twist. The thought was almost titillating, but she couldn't forget her lie. Hamp's temper might distress her, but she was violating the love he'd shown her and the trust he'd put in her. Unlocking her fingers, she determinedly ran them through the black hair that dusted his pecs, with an arrow trailing down to jet black pubic hair and erect bronze cock, waiting for her touch.

She touched him there then gave an exploratory lick, hoping he couldn't tell how compromised she felt, her lie and her attacker lodged in her mind, intruding on their moment.

"Don't, or I'll explode," he said through gritted teeth. He groaned and took her in his arms and she hugged him back, angry she couldn't surrender to him the way she'd imagined. As if not sensing her inner turmoil, he made slow sweet love to her, his hands mindful of every sensitive place on her. His fingers came to rest on her aching nub, and his eyes took her in as if she were a rare desert flower. Then he cupped her with his palm and watched for her reaction. As she had to do on cross-country, she commandeered her mind and body to be fully in the moment. She was at the brink of orgasm when he entered her, then to her relief and exquisite pleasure, it grew and spread and widened in her, and doubled in intensity when he came with her.

Afterwards he helped her find her clothes, threw on his jeans, and the weight of her deception settled in to shroud her evening.

He'd cooked for her before but not with a secret hovering between them. He signaled Yahzi to lie on a dog bed in the corner, washed his hands, and got two dark brown bottles of beer from the refrigerator. Then he set heavy earthenware plates on a glass-topped wagon wheel that made a coffee table and served the food.

He sat cross-legged on the floor, and she sat too, the ice pack slumping off her wrist. She untied it and took a bite of food. "Yummm. What is it?"

"Fry bread and mutton stew. Mom taught me. Grandpop says the recipe is authentic, but she showed me how to make it in a slo-cooker. The electric kind, not hot rocks. We don't use them anymore except for ceremonial food."

She laughed, but he had little more to say. They'd learned so much about each other in the spring. Still she loved the pride she heard when he talked about his family. His mother was a weaver, and one of her rugs hung on the wall. It was a handsome primitive scene of reservation life with horses, cows, homes and hogans, an ancient blue truck, and sheep. His father was an anthropology professor at one of the tribal colleges. He helped Hamp's grandfather with the sheep.

Afterwards, she helped Hamp wash dishes, the hot soapy water soothing to her wrist. Barefoot, he walked her to her car, no longer questioning that she had to go.

"Let's do this again," he said.

She made herself smile. "I'd offer to cook, but I'm hopeless."

His eyes widened in mock shock, but a grin tugged at the corners of his mouth. He kissed her tenderly, and she shivered. "I love making love to you," he said, and opened her car door. "Be careful driving. Deer, foxes, possums, and raccoons—it's prowling time. Meet you at the barn six-thirty in the morning?"

"Super," she said, and sped back to Hawks Nest in the cooling night, chilled to the bone to leave him so under such a cloud, to be alone with her lie. The moon was bright enough to read by, and it shafted through the pines, marking the road like prison bars.

Then it struck her. His hands on her body had been erotic, but rough and callused from years of handling horses, ropes and hay, and cleaning stalls and tack.

The hand that had ground across her mouth was smooth, like a woman's or a city boy's. Not one in a hundred people at an active competition barn would have soft hands. But Parker spent too much time at his computer to do chores, and Marina foisted everything off on the hired help. Was it Parker? Could it have been Marina? Enough of sitting back and waiting for the next assault. She'd find out for herself what was going on.

# Eighteen

That night, Lexy camped out in the aisle again, guarding Bo, Hamp's earthy smell of pine and herbs still clinging to her. When her alarm went off at three a.m., she left her post. Upstairs, she stepped into her darkest pair of jeans and sneakers, pulled on a long-sleeved black tee, and twisted her hair into a bun, feeling ridiculous. She topped off her new do with a brown bug-repellant baseball cap, bill backwards, American style, then put the keys to the boarders' lounge and the family's tack room in her jeans' pocket.

If she had to pick locks to get into their tack boxes, she was screwed, but eventers were trusting folk, or had been in England, and rarely locked their stuff. If a box was locked, would that be a clue? Downstairs, the stallion wing was ghostly quiet, the horses sleeping standing up. In the wild, prey animals like horses slept three hours or less in twenty-four, napping in open fields in safe company, usually standing. A locking mechanism in their hind legs kept them on their feet.

She crept down the dark aisle with the tiny light she always carried to check on Bo. But at the sound of her padding softly on the bricks, the hyper-alert stallion whickered. "Hey, buddy boy," she murmured, and shone the light so he could see her, then aimed the beam on their surroundings. Nothing to worry him but her. She offered a peppermint. He took it as his god-given right and let her blow into his nose.

"I'll be back," she said.

She hoped. Marina and the other boarders first. Yesterday Marina had come to say that Jordan had banned Minx from the arena, so she should feel safe. Her forced smile and non-apology secured her spot on Lexy's list. Both the family tack room and the boarders' lounge were locked after hours, but Jordan had entrusted Lexy with a key to the former for access to medicine, supplies, and the shower as well as a key to the lounge where she stored her tack box. It had arrived from Bishop Burton yesterday. She hadn't gone through it yet, dreading the sweet memories of her mother that it held. Dreading the letter that didn't name her father.

She unlocked the boarders' lounge—a tack room with a sofa and a couple of comfy chairs—and slithered in, feeling like a snake on a mongoose farm, with all eyes on her and every creature ready to pounce. Saddles were ranged six wide, three high on saddle trees that stuck out from an inside wall. Their shadows shifted as she moved a narrow cone of light over them, then over a dozen well-cleaned bridles classically tied up and hung on practical wooden brackets.

Beneath them sat large plastic storage boxes and a handsome mahogany tack trunk on wheels. Her mouth dry, Lexy opened the first box on the right, identified by magic marker as Rachel White's, feeling like a criminal. Inside, it was bandbox neat with a medicine kit, bell boots, leg wraps, everything she would expect to see in easy reach, nothing she did not. It had an expenses log and another log of lessons that included a conditioning schedule for her horse, slavishly following the program Colonel had laid out in his strategy for cross-country riding, Lexy noted as she flipped through it by flashlight. Ditto, Ann Voss's box, but it was messier. Rags dank with leather cleaner and conditioner were crumpled in a corner and smelled faintly of mold.

Then a couple of other boarders' storage boxes, none as obsessively neat as Rachel's. Lexy had never had a take on her. She and Ann always arrived together, put in their time and left. They competed at Preliminary, well below her, so neither had a compelling reason to go after her. She riffled through three more boxes, the smells of liniment and ointments, hoof preparations, poultices, standing bandages, some clean and tightly rolled up for their next use, some not—rising up around her, but not a single clue.

Marina's expensive trunk at the end of the row stood out from the rest with its big diamond monogram MSS in a contrasting light wood inlaid on its front and top.

A lock, surprisingly open, dangled from its clasp. Lexy's heart jigged triple time. She took it as a stroke of luck, but Greta, Marina's long-suffering groom, would catch hell if Marina found out. Lexy checked her watch: Three twenty-eight a.m. No one was competing this weekend so no early risers at this ungodly hour.

Still, she poked her head outside the door and scanned the boarders' aisle, lit softly by the moon. A tail swished, and a hoof stamped on the rubber mats that lined the stalls' floors. A picky eater nibbled at some unfinished hay.

She shut the door behind her and lifted the top of the mahogany box. Light bounced off its mirrored underside where Marina could check her stock, tie pin, snood, and diamond studs. Inside were boxes within boxes, everything freshly washed or brushed, folded and put away. She kept conditioning logs for Tosca, Savannah, and her two younger horses, filled out faithfully in an elegant backhand with a flourish of lower loops, the kind of script ladies cultivated for writing thank-you notes on fine linen cards. One thick leather-bound three-ring notebook had a section for each horse with additional pages on its supplements, feed, vet visits, injuries and outcomes alternating in the upright script and a studied lettering that Lexy recognized as European. Greta.

On her knees, Lexy dug to the bottom of the trunk, noting where each box or book had been and hastily putting each one back. Not only did nothing suggest misdeeds, everything was Pony Club neat. Holding the torch between her teeth, she flipped to the end of the three-ring binder. Its final page was a print-out of Lexy's competition record—Badminton last but going back two years—Gatcombe, Bramham, Hartpury, Blenheim Palace. Every event.

She gasped. What kind of competitor tracked someone else's every win, place, lose, retirement or elimination—hers and hers alone? And why? To psych her out? She kept up with where she stood against others in the points standings. But she hadn't printed out their records and stored them in her trunk.

She banged the notebook shut and put it where she'd found it, under the conditioning logs, her heart drumming as she locked up and crept toward the family's tack room. Parker, Jordan and Colonel had trunks there. Her stomach turned at the thought of breaking into theirs.

Because she'd never done anything illegal in her life. Well, sure, she'd driven a bazillion kilometers over the speed limit in Italy, France, and England. Everyone did that. But snooping into other people's stuff was both scary and repugnant. She didn't want to know who was messy and who wasn't. Who was keeping creepy records. She didn't want to find her tormenter, man or woman, living under her nose. Or did she? She rounded the corner to the stallion wing. Holding her light low, she slid her key into the lock then, through the half-light door, saw the computer's monitor in the corner of the room.

Someone's head and shoulders partially blocked its glow.

Too late to turn back. Feeling ridiculous in her baseball cap, she chucked it in the aisle, strode in, and flicked on the light.

Parker swiveled his seat and faced her with bloodshot eyes, crumpled clothes, his chestnut hair smashed to one side of his head and sticking out on top.

"Damn," she said boldly. "Are you okay?

He swung his head around and bared his teeth in a grin that made him look like Batman's Joker. "I'm always okay. Haven't you figured that out?"

"Frankly, no. There's a lot here I haven't figured out."

"You mean, like Colonel?" She tried to gauge the blank look that replaced the fake grin.

"Colonel McRae's my hero."

"Yeah, well, lucky you. He's my father. Didn't ask to be born, ya know? You don't get a choice."

"No, shit, Sherlock," she said, thinking of Enrico Imbriani.

Parker raised a brow not quite of interest. "Yours too, eh?"

She shrugged. She didn't want to go there now. Parker didn't seem to care.

Everything she'd come to think of as essentially him was stripped away—the charm, the sexy drawl, the astonishing male beauty. The glow from the monitor cast ghoulish shadows under his eyes and made his cheeks look sunken.

She didn't understand. Her mission was a bust, but a blast of sympathy for him overrode her suspicions. "Is something wrong between you and Colonel?"

His fingers tapped the keyboard in what looked like secret code. She knew just enough about computers to send an email, clear her inbox, and enter competitions.

"The Lord giveth, and the Lord taketh away," he said.

"That's illuminating."

"Moneybags, the greedy old goat. Won't help out with the new horses."

"I thought you bought them."

"It was a loan. Used to be, he'd stake me till I sold one and could pay him back. Waive my board, loan me entry fees, stuff like that."

Horse people, horse poor. She got that. "Sorry."

"You'd think a man would do something for his only son."

"Didn't work for my father's only daughter," she said, reminded too sharply of Imbriani's vengeful disposal of her horses.

"I gotta put Brad up for sale in three months—well before he peaks. You know—moves up to Advanced, *wins* something. Kiss of death to sell a horse not in the winnings. Takes off ten, twenty thousand in value, and I have to pay Colonel back right away. I'm working double shifts. And schooling those guys takes a back seat."

"That's rough," she said, feeling not so much puzzled as yanked around. Parker was pulling double shifts at work? And schooling three horses on the side? That had not been her impression of how he operated, not according to what she'd seen and Hamp had said. Parker swanned around the universe, attention deficit disorder on steroids except when it came to getting into women's pants. There, he was obsessive-compulsive.

Parker jabbed the keys, the fastest hunt-and-peck typist she'd ever seen. Was he drunk? Or high? On the screen, a background frame changed patterns around a stunning picture of him on Brad clearing the big ditch and brush.

"Gorgeous photo," she offered.

"Whereas—" he didn't look up from the keyboard "—my fucking lame and lame-brained sister is Daddy's girl. Anything she wants."

Lexy bridled. "She works from dawn to dusk and then some."

Parker gave her a stark glance. "You know what they say it takes to get to the top?"

Her head spun at his sudden shift, but she shot back, "Total focus, one great horse, and a bottomless checking account."

"Not bad, Imbriani. But no. It takes talent, perseverance, luck. It helps to have all three, but you can't get there on talent alone, or perseverance, or just plain luck."

"Oh. And you've got—?"

"Talent and perseverance. My sister got the luck. The money. *His* support."

Parker's upper lip twitched in anger, which swamped her, then convinced her of his sincerity. "I'm sorry you feel that way. Must be hell."

"Hell is me being better than her, and her getting more of everything." Then he looked Lexy over, seeming to step outside the cage of his self-consuming anger. "You're up late." His gaze dropped to the light in her hand. "What's that about?"

"My torch—I mean *flashlight*—I came to use the toilet."

"There's a toilet in your room."

"I'm sleeping downstairs again. To be double sure Bo doesn't get into more trouble." Get *put* into more trouble.

"You weren't there when I came in."

Suddenly her heart was in her throat, and he was the Inquisition. "I, um, heard something outside. Went to check."

"Yeah?"

"Deer, a couple of spikers, still in velvet."

"Ah. Night grazing." He gave an ironic nod, a glimpse of charm returning. "Seriously criminal activity. You must have been scared stiff."

"I don't scare easily." She forced a smile and lied. "They were dining on Ruth's roses."

"Lexy Imbriani, deer stalker."

"Um. Still need to use the bathroom," she said, extending her little lie into a whopper. She needed to stop him asking questions.

"Be my guest." He hunched over his keyboard and resumed typing, shutting her out. Clipped to his belt—which usually sported a monogrammed leather holster for a cell and a BlackBerry like Marina's two or however many she had—was a chunky prepaid like the one Hamp had given Lexy when she'd arrived.

In the bathroom, she gulped in ragged breaths and opened the cold water faucet to cover up the fact that she couldn't pee now if her life depended on it.

Bloody hell. Parker had a prepaid cell, activated and in use. He hadn't tossed it. Hadn't bothered. Because he was innocent? Or the cockiest wanker on the planet?

She dried her hands. She had to get a closer look at his cell, his car, his hands.

She stepped behind him, peered at his computer's screen, and bumped his shoulder with the side of her fist. "Sorry you're down, mate."

"Comes with the territory."

"How about I take you up on that dinner offer, my treat?"

He pivoted in his chair, his tormented eyes bright. "On you? I'm not that broke."

"Me either." For now.

"What about your boyfriend?" He found his lost grin.

She grinned back. "He'll probably cut your balls off if he finds out." Then really tie her to that bed.

But changeable Parker gave a shout of laughter, suddenly so upbeat that offending Hamp seemed worth the risk. And she would learn what Parker was up to, if anything.

# Nineteen

Jesus. What had she been thinking? Madly in love with Hamp, and she'd invited his worst enemy to dinner. Stupid, stupid, stupid.

Bo, however, didn't mind. He'd given her an exhilarating dressage workout, and she was walking him on a long rein, done for the day, but pumped. Her cell vibrated at her waist. She checked the display, expecting Hamp.

It was Parker. Crap.

"We on for dinner?"

"You betcha," she said, trying to sound enthusiastic, but last night's bright idea looked crazy after sleeping on it. She wasn't afraid of Parker. If he'd been her attacker, she'd fought him off, but now she was risking her relationship with Hamp.

"You up for a trip to Cabin Branch first?" Parker asked. "Best tack shop in Southern Pines. Gotta pick up a cross-country saddle they're reflocking to fit Timmy." Timbuktu, one of his new imported geldings. Quarantine over, the three had been shipped from Florida and were now stabled with the stallions.

"Cabin Branch? Super. I need repellent wipes."

"Pick you up at five," he said flatly and clicked off.

*No, wait,* she thought. *My invite, my call.*

She'd fight over that when he got here. She dressed in her good raw silk slacks topped by a designer tee and linen blazer—her go-to uniform for Trot Up in FEI competitions, country chic, the reverse of the sexy sundress she'd worn for Hamp.

"I drive," she said when Parker pulled up in his battered 'seventies-something red Porsche.

"Scarlett, m'dear," he said in his thickest drawl yet, "I'd eat kudzu before I'd let my friends see me disrespecting a lady I asked on a date."

"I asked you, and it's not a date. It's a mental health rescue operation."

His full lower lip poked out. "Then it's not good for my mental health to be seen driven around town by a woman."

He looked so down she submitted, then second-guessed her decision every turn he took. Downtown in the old historic district, he arrowed the old Porsche into a slanted spot in front of Cabin Branch. Don, the tack shop's owner, kept it open late so Parker could meet with George, master saddler, in his repair shop in the basement.

Upstairs, Lexy took in the crowded coziness of the place. Hundreds of riding jackets were squeezed on rods, stacks and stacks of crisp show shirts and leather full-seat breeches lay on counters, and model boots, saddles, bridles, bits and stirrups were neatly arrayed on walls. She breathed in the smells of oil and soap and leather not yet broken in. She should feel at home, but watching Parker drive here in a funk had been unsettling. What did his grim mood mean? Her attacker had run off after she'd resisted, almost as if he hadn't been serious. But if it had been Parker, was he serious now? And how much danger was she in?

Not that much. She reminded herself she ran four miles three times a week, worked out with weights, and pitted herself against horses almost ten times Parker's size, with instincts a hundred times sharper. Parker had to be fit too, but tonight they were going to dinner in a public place.

With him driving.

Her chest tightened. She should have insisted.

Back upstairs, he conferred with Don about a more severe bit for Brad, another of his new geldings. As part of her job, she grained them and mucked out their stalls. Parker paid for Timmy's saddle and Brad's bit and, outside in the Porsche, settled the saddle in her lap. "Sorry about this, mate. Nowhere else to put it."

Better, she thought, to be treated like a mate than lusted after like a hot date.

A late afternoon Amtrak train rumbled down the center of Main Street's old historic district. Parker backed the Porsche out of their slanted parking space, as expertly as the Grand Prix driver she'd dated a couple of times last year. A few blocks farther on, he wheeled into a slot in front of a building with tall, wide windows and a quaint pocked-brick façade. Ashten's.

She slid the saddle onto the console and hauled herself up from the low seat.

He came round, frowning. She was near his height—almost tall for a woman, and he was just right for eventing. Just right for her attacker, and a chill skated down her spine. Buck up, she told herself. He wouldn't attack here. Then she'd go home.

He slapped his hand on the roof of the car and leaned in on her. "You got a problem with chivalry?"

She hid her discomfort with a bright smile. "Eventer. Women compete against men equal-equal, remember?"

"Yes, ma'am," he drawled, recovering his jaunty grin. "But this is the South."

Escorting her in, he touched the sleeve of her linen jacket with his fingers. Bloody hell. She couldn't tell if they were soft or callused, the whole purpose of this risky trip. Inside, she peeled the jacket off to make sure she felt him next time. His gaze blatantly checked her endowments beneath the tee. Not much there, but she gritted her teeth. She couldn't duck out on an opportunity to get to know him, even accept another touch.

The maitre d' seated them upstairs. It was light and bright with abstract paintings on silvered walls. The late day sun glared in her eyes. Parker swapped seats so it wouldn't blind her, not the act of an assailant. So she was back at square one, only edgier.

He ordered lamb tenderloin and recommended wild Scottish salmon to her.

"For a taste of home." Recovering slightly from his funk, he scanned the wine list with an expert eye and ordered a nice Riesling to go with their appetizer and an American red she'd never heard of for their entrées. He said it would bridge the mellowness of his lamb and the gaminess of her salmon.

No wonder on his good days, he swept women off their feet—a speedster in a vintage sports car who mastered wine lists at a glance. Their shared appetizer came, and she watched him dip crusty bread in a fruity olive oil that took her back to Italy. He had masculine hands with blunt-tipped fingers, chewed nails, but she couldn't see his palms to check for calluses.

He polished off his wine and rallied, gossiping about boarders, doling out secrets like prized truffles. Nikki, Hamp's student, wore falsies under her sports bra. Marina had been fat as a little girl. Ann and Rachel were growing a private crop of marijuana at a location he was sworn not disclose.

"But I can get you some." He winked, and Parker the irreverent was back. "It's only illegal if you get caught."

His mantra, no doubt. But she laughed, entertained. She sipped the Riesling he'd selected, and he asked her about Bo with what seemed like genuine concern. Disarmed, she rattled on about how well Bo was doing, healed and happy to be in work. Then it struck her like a stone. He didn't want her riding Bo, and he was setting the tone, picking her brain about her horse when she'd meant to be grilling him by now, hoping for a slip, a clue.

The lamb and salmon came, and a pinot noir from Oregon.

Between bites of tender fish and sips of berry-rich wine, she turned the tables on him, praising his geldings until he had to talk about his training program and his plans for them. Self-absorbed blighter that he was, it wasn't hard to get him talking about himself. She needed his version of who he was, not just Hamp's. Parker confessed he'd been in and out of trouble as a kid. After a series of joy rides, wrecks, and fire alarms set off in school, he'd put a harmless garter snake in the car of a teacher who was baiting him. She'd had a wreck. The principal had called his father in. Outraged, Colonel had shipped Parker off to military school which he'd secretly liked because he'd learned to shoot better than his sisters. But then he'd flunked out of the Citadel, Colonel's college, his real attention on the girls at a local stable. Colonel had never forgiven him.

Parker's cell jingled, and he reached to turn it off. Lexy could see it was his BlackBerry, not the pre-paid he'd had last night, and not what she needed to see.

Bugger. She twisted in her seat. She hadn't seen his hands, wasn't learning what she came for, and had jeopardizing her relationship with Hamp.

"But you finished college?" she pressed.

"Computer science at State. Slide-by grades, my specialty," he said with pride.

"Ever married?"

He widened his eyes. "*Moi? Mais non,* mam'selle. *Jamais.* Never."

"I know French, Parker," she said frostily.

"Le mah-reh-ahzh, eet would ruin my reputation." He was heavy on the accent, teasing, but the disconnect between his gloom last night and this growing cheer jarred her. He acted as if his pranks and failures were normal, and had no remorse for anything.

They finished their entrées, and he lay his knife and fork on his plate tines down, then leaned back in his seat, cracking knuckles.

"So…You and ol' Hamp have a fight, or what?"

She put down her utensils, chugged the dregs of the pinot noir. "If we did, you'd be the last to know."

"Why else take me up on my offer?"

*Your rich father can't protect you here.* Her attacker's raspy threat buzzed in her ears. But she was safe here, the restaurant filling with early diners.

"I'm looking into you."

He flashed her a smug grin. "I can tell you up front I'm amazing in the sack."

"That is so not where I'm headed." She leaned forward and said frankly, "I've been wondering if you put Bo in Orsino's stall."

He gave her his spaniel face. "Why would I do that?"

"To get me fired."

"And I would do that because—"

"What you said. You want the ride on Bo."

He waved the hand she still had not examined. "Mam'selle. I have all the horses I can handle."

"You could sell them. Isn't that your plan?"

"Too soon." He grew serious again. "Selling one now, I wouldn't break even. Is that what you recommend?"

"You're working me."

His gaze returned to her chest. "I'd like to."

"Sheesh, Parker. Knock if off."

"In the presence of your nubile pulchritude?"

She should have left her jacket on.

"Dammit, you're so full of it. But I think you're capable of anything."

"Anything?" He lifted a finger as if to test the non-existent wind. "Do I detect a change of heart? Can we go to bed now?"

"I'm not going to bed with you. Ever." She caught their passing waiter's eye and mouthed *dessert*. He came, and she ordered the crème brûlée, Parker the chocolate molten lava cake.

"Pity about sex," Parker went on, not to be put off. "We'd be good."

"Or a disaster."

"Avec moi? Impossible." *Ahm-pah-see-blah.*

"Wretched accent too, with that drawl."

He blinked, all innocence. He was so damn handsome with his warm spaniel eyes, full lower lip, and hawks' beak nose. She had to put him down.

"Problem with you is, you always have an answer."

"That would be incorrect." The smile slipped from his face, and the bitter man from last night's wolfing hour was back. "I don't know what you see in Hamp. I don't know why Colonel won't let me run the farm or why Jordan gave that horse to you, not me. I don't know why I have such fucking rotten luck."

Oh my God, what just happened? His brain was like the Porsche, turning on a dime, then zero to sixty miles per hour in ten seconds flat. Or was this the ploy of a great deceiver and she was in over her head? He *was* working her. Call him on it.

"We make our own luck, Parker," she corrected.

For a second his spaniel eyes flashed resentment the way they'd done with Colonel, then their waiter set dessert before them. Needing the break, she spooned a taste of the crème brûlée into her mouth, but its crust tasted more bitterly burnt than caramelized. Across the suddenly too small table, Parker picked at his lava cake, his mood dark as the molten mousse.

"The only sonabitch with more rotten luck than me's Tyrone."

Caught off guard, she paused with another spoonful halfway to her mouth. "Tyrone?"

"Yeah. For me, there's cachet to being *known* as Colonel's son."

"Pardon me?"

"Tyrone's the dark skeleton in the family closet."

"Tyrone? Ruth's son?"

"By Colonel."

Blindsided, she shoved the pudding into her mouth, shocked to learn from Parker that her esteemed mentor's family life might be as sordid as her own. "That can't be."

"Everybody idolizes my father. He's not what he seems. I'm the bastard son he doesn't support and Ty's the bastard son who slaves for him as the hired help."

"You're bitter and he's surly."

"Yeah. Fueling his surliness is about forty-three years of being used and abused. Which makes him a much better candidate for your suspicions than me."

Another dodge. "Why would he go after me?"

"To get Colonel's goat, Jordan's too. He's angry."

"You're angry too."

"He works his fingers to the bone, but I have fun." He waggled his brows.

Dessert done, he flashed a credit card before she realized the waiter was coming with the bill. "My treat," she reminded.

"You can get it next time," he said.

"There isn't going to be a next time."

He helped her into her jacket so efficiently she missed her chance to tell if his hands were rough or smooth. Bummer. At the car, he edged her out, opening the door before she could. Annoyed, she pulled the saddle onto her lap, freeing his seat so he could drive.

And so she could collect her thoughts. He was cleverer than she'd realized, less predictable, more in control. More dangerous. So far, nothing had gone as planned, and she wanted to be free of Parker's slippery talk and shifting moods.

Was he acting? Or unbalanced? Or messing with her mind?

He steered the old Porsche out of town, hand-shifting up to speed, the high sexy whine above its throaty roar rolling into her open window. Then he took a left where she remembered right. Where was he taking her? A quarter, half mile farther on, the wide, four-lane street curved through residential Southern

Pines, past posh estates of multi-millionaire retirees from the frozen North who'd moved here for year-round golf.

This was west. Hawks Nest was north.

Her blood froze.

She saw her body floating to the shore of some deserted pond.

"This isn't the way home."

"Little detour, trust me." His hand reached down and squeezed her knee.

Shit oh shit. Was that the hand that had clamped her mouth? She couldn't tell through silk pants. Was he her attacker or was he trying to seduce her?

She should have accused him of the attack outright in the restaurant, gauged his reaction, and grabbed a cab for home. If they had cabs in Southern Pines.

She didn't think he had a weapon other than his strength. Thank God for the hours she spent in weight rooms, but was her sprained wrist ready for a fight?

It was a gated community with no one at the gate. He waved a pass card before a reader. "What, no guard?" she asked, trying not to show concern.

"Daytime, it's open. The condo association decided guards cost too much for nights which are quiet with everybody home, so we put up cameras."

An ornate, wrought-iron barricade swung open, and he drove past hulking new homes, the wretched American excess she'd already seen at Jordan's cousin Chip's, to rows of semi-attached homes, narrow, three stories high, each with a different façade, fancy, new.

Dinner clumped in her stomach. "Coming to your place wasn't the deal."

He grinned, sexual allure oozing from his pores. "Before you commit to ol' Hamp, you ought to see what you'd be missing."

Reluctant to get out, she waited for Parker to open her door, her pulse jittery. She knew the danger. Men pounced on women who came to their flats, assumed they were primed for sex. But she couldn't let a chance to spy on him pass by. He escorted her in with his new bit in a bag, the saddle on one arm and a hand at her waist.

Again no skin on skin. Bugger.

Inside, she'd expected a man cave or bordello. She got countrified estate, a decorator's warm palette of tree tan, earth brown, sky blue, leaf green. Old masters repro oils of horses covered the walls, elegant and orderly, suggesting old family class whether or not he had money.

"Blimey. Very posh."

*Prrrrr-meyowr.* A huge fluff of cat jumped from a bookcase and wound around her legs, its big brush of a tail leaving long white hairs on her good slacks.

"Troll loves horse women," Parker said.

She would not be the latest in a parade of them. "What kind of name is Troll?"

"He came here wild, hid out under my deck like a troll under a bridge. Here, buddy." He picked him up and draped him over his neck. Troll purred madly as Parker led her through the condo. Kitchen here, wine cooler, upscale stove. Office there, floor-to-ceiling books, electronics, banks of monitors, computers, phones, a pricey ergonomic office chair. More horse prints lined the stairwell wall, leading no doubt to his bedroom.

He put down the cat, looked up the stairs, and inclined his head in invitation. How many women had succumbed to his cocky sensuality? "C'mon, luv. Troll doesn't care, and ol' Hamp wouldn't have to know."

*Jesus.* "Read my lips. Not bloody interested."

He flashed a leering grin. "Stubborn's good. You'll be worth the wait."

"There'll be no wait. Not happening tonight, next week, next year."

"Then what did you come here for?"

"*You* brought *me.*"

"Coulda said no."

"Would you believe, I wanted to check out your flat."

"For what?" he said, the spaniel look again.

"Cell phones. Because I also got a threatening message on my cell."

"Yeah? What did it say?"

She told him, alert to any twinge of shame or even recognition.

"Honey, that's mean," he said, instant sympathy on cue.

"Gwen thinks they used a prepaid. You had one last night."

"And so you're searching my apartment?" he asked, hurt. Or miming hurt? Making her feel crazy. "I'd put my money on Marina there. She's a bitch. I got nothing to hide."

He opened a drawer in his bedside table, took out a prepaid, shoved it in front of her and flipped through its memory. Nothing, nada. Zilch.

"What are you doing with a prepaid anyway?" she asked, floundering to get him to say something.

"One of my client's got a suspicious husband."

"A client?" She was suspicious too.

"Hey. I have women clients," he said easily, but his innocence felt fake.

"You could have used another phone. Gwen says people toss them after."

He blanked his face. "Piece of work, my sister."

She wanted him to quit dodging everything she said. "And then someone, a man, I'm sure, grabbed me outside the barn the other night, threatened me, and threw me to the ground." But she sure as hell wasn't going to ask him to pull his pants down so she could look for bruises on his shins.

"Asshole," he said with Hamp-like vehemence.

"I think you were behind it all—Orsino, the message, the attack."

"I'm flattered you think I could be that demonic."

"Everybody knows you're a devil, Parker."

"With *women*, luv. Get that part right." Troll leapt from his perch on a little table, rubbed her leg again with the scent glands at his nose, then glided from the room. "Get lucky tonight, buddy," Parker called out. Not for the cat to hear, she thought, but her.

"You let him wander around in town?"

"Balcony's open. He comes and goes."

Suddenly, Parker swooped in on her with a silky knowing kiss, warm lips, no tongue, but hard desire. She wrenched her mouth away, her heart beating a tattoo of warning.

Hamp would kill him. Dump her. "No, Parker. No. Take me home now."

"Don't worry, luv. I wouldn't hurt you. I just want to make love to you."

Oh God, he was crazy and unpredictable, and using the words of a really bad song. He clenched her jaws with the soft skin of his palms, and she knew.

No calluses. It had been him. She steeled herself to smash his nose into his skull if he did not back off. "I love Hamp."

His spaniel eyes went slightly hard. "You don't know what you're missing."

Oh but she did. Mischief, mayhem, calculation and evasion from a man with the morals of a Bic lighter.

# Twenty

And finally it was Saturday, cross-country day, her first full-fledged big-time event with Bo, and Lexy was jazzed. On Thursday, they'd aced dressage, coming in a respectable third behind Hamp and a rider she didn't know. Hamp had placed first on Travertine, aka Trapper, the Intermediate horse he was riding for Ben Holt.

Under a flat gray sky, a ghostly fog swirled up from a holding pond nearby and blanketed the ten-acre warm-up field. She could see the tops of the jumps, but horses and riders looked like they were emerging from the mists of time, armored for battle in helmets and brightly colored safety vests.

"And what's your first responsibility?" Colonel asked in warm-up.

*Keeping tabs on Parker.*

Because he'd *assaulted* her. The soft skin of his hands had preyed on her since that night at his condo. Earlier this morning, he'd finished with his three horses in Preliminary. Now he was free to be on course, lurking. Refusing to give in to that worry, she checked her sore wrist, the tape hidden under the cuff of her long-sleeved shirt, and wrenched her thoughts to Colonel's question.

Which *first* responsibility had he meant? "Get around clean?"

He bit his lips and crossed his arms.

"Use the first four fences to establish my speed and rhythm?"

He huffed. Wrong. "And...?"

He'd stressed everything equally. She made a stab. "Stop obsessing over distances? Let him take the initiative?"

"No. And no." He jabbed his index finger in the air. "First. Never forget you're riding the only stallion on the grounds. Plenty of folks don't want him here. Be alert. Know where the mares are. All the time."

"Got it."

"Prove it. How many mares in warm-up right this minute?"

*How many places could Parker be?*

But she surveyed the field, forcing her attention to Colonel's question.

Hamp and Marina galloped the flat ten-acre field, warming up their Intermediate contenders. Geldings. So were the other three horses entered whose riders she'd met at last night's party for competitors, though their names and faces were a blur, and which horse went with who—a mystery. But she'd studied the entry status list, practically memorizing everyone's times in her division, and knew who went before and after.

"None."

"On course?"

*Parker?* "One."

"Are you sure?"

"No, sir." She was only sure she needed to know where Parker was.

"Then listen up. There are two mares in your division. One's finishing the course this minute, and she could walk right past Bo. Probably won't, but she could be in season. When she finishes over there, you make sure he's here. The other mare doesn't start until you're well back at the barn."

"Yes, sir."

"And don't *sir* me. Be smart. Be good. Be forward."

Lexy nodded and gritted her teeth. Competing had been easier with her mother. Would be easier today if Jordan wasn't so formal and remote. If Lexy wasn't convinced that Parker, diabolical charmer that he was, had been lying through his teeth on their dinner date and was now bent on bringing her down.

Colonel put a paternal hand on her bent knee, unaware of her dilemma or his son's duplicity.

"Darlin', my greatest fear has always been that Bo would get loose, and then where would he go? He'd head straight for the nearest mare in season and start doin' what comes naturally to any self-respecting stallion, rider be damned, mare be screwed. Everybody hurt. You give him everything you got, every second. Now get back to your routine, Ninety Eight," he said sharply.

She trotted off, nerves jangled, but Colonel's lecture had jerked her back to competition mode, and she could see the swirling fog, the dull gray sky, the orderly jumble of half-a-dozen competitors popping over practice fences, their coaches calling out tips, reminders, corrections. *Normal*, she told herself. No one, nothing out of line. Another voice, upbeat and resonant over a PA system that carried across the course, announced the starters by number, bringing her time ever nearer.

She passed Ben Holt standing near the jumps, coaching his Olympic prospects. He tipped his cap at her and smiled. Somehow, with Colonel on her case and Parker somewhere out there, Ben's notice gave her courage.

"Six minutes, and you're up, Ninety Eight," the warm-up steward said from beside the officials' pavilion, a ten-foot square canopy on wobbly aluminum poles.

Ninety Six, a tall woman on a big black-and-white Clydesdale cross, galumphed out of the start box nestled under a spreading elm beside the holding pond.

Ninety Seven was Hamp on Trapper, Ben's seven-year-old *wunderkind* from England, the handy bay she'd have been riding if she'd not jumped ship to work with Bo. Hamp was walking the gelding on a long rein, relaxed as if they'd finished a morning hack at home.

One last go at warm-up. She cleared a vertical, a simple three-rail fence, and then circled to an oxer—two verticals set a few feet apart and jumped as one fence—and circled again to a solid, round but inviting coop. Bo was fit, forward, jazzed, and knew what was coming. She reported back to Colonel. Jordan stood beside him, hands propped on her cane.

"Don't worry about making the time, Lexy." She was courteous and professional, but as remote as she'd been since— when?

Did she think they weren't ready? Or was she pissed she couldn't ride?

"But you don't mean crank him down?" Lexy asked.

A shadow crossed Jordan's face. "No, but rate him. And don't let him run away."

The opposite of Colonel's plan. *Let the fence be the bit,* he'd said, devoted to her cross-country training. She was doing it his way.

"Three minutes, Ninety Eight," the steward said.

And in that instant, Hamp's big bay catapulted out of the start box and was up to speed in three strides, powerful, efficient. Lexy grouped her forces to go next, but she remembered Jordan's accident on Rosie on this very course. Fear slammed her. Parker could be on course, behind a tree, beyond a jump, around a bend at distant corners out of sight of the scattered spectators, no one the wiser.

Three minutes felt like ten. She nodded at the tall thin steward who, like Jordan, had a limp, probably from riding horses. Or rather, falling off them.

*Don't go there.*

She closed her eyes, and a map of the winding course flashed on the big screen inside her mind. The course wove in and out over the Horse Park's two hundred acres, never crossing itself, like the outline of a giant five-leaf clover sketched by a drunken mapmaker.

Yesterday she'd walked the two-and-a-quarter miles five times, twice with Hamp, who'd splashed barefoot through the water complex and invited her to follow suit. She'd put in a toe and shrieked at the chilly water, excruciatingly aware he didn't know about her date with Parker. Hamp had laughed at her, and she'd waded in after him, determined to show him she trusted him.

A third time, Colonel had gone round with her, riding a scooter, by permission, over the access lanes that paralleled the course. It was the one concession event management made to his age and reputation. He'd had her explain her line of approach to every obstacle, then tweaked her idea or given her a better one.

Finally, she'd gone round twice alone, struggling to put Parker out of her mind as she'd touched the obstacles, clambered over them, owned them. Twenty-eight obstacles, thirty-four jumping efforts counting the combinations. An early downhill jump into a shallow pond looked friendly. Near the end of the course, a water complex looked fierce.

*Horse and rider down at the Coffin,* the announcer called, his tone showing none of the alarm that seized her. The Coffin was a three-jump effort near the end—a log then a stride to a wide deep ditch and a second stride to a log beyond. On this course, it came two jumps before the water complex and asked tough questions of a tiring horse. Riders hurtled at it down a dipping hill, and the distances from log to ditch to log were tricky. Jordan's mare had died there, and she'd been all but crippled, but the three jumping efforts, though tough, looked fair. Colonel had spent more time with Lexy analyzing that obstacle than any other, unnerving her with his argument that Jordan's accident had been sabotage. She'd walked back twice to study it alone.

Could Hamp have approached it wrong? Lexy agonized, imagining EMTs rushing to him at the scene, the Safety Director at hand.

Fifty yards across the warm-up field, a competitor she'd met last night plunged across the finish line and raised a fist in triumph. Must have ridden a double clear—no time or jumping faults. That left two or three horses on course ahead of her, she was no longer sure—Hamp, and the colored Clydesdale cross she'd seen start. Was there a third? Whoever had fallen would be eliminated, even if horse and rider seemed fine.

*Horse up, folks,* the announcer said two, three minutes later. *Rider's on her feet, walking off.* "Her" feet—*She* could not be Hamp. But Lexy felt no relief. *Hold on course while we fix the fence,* the announcer went on. *Start Box, wait for my word.*

Lexy checked in with the starter who stood by the start box—a sixteen-foot-square post-and-rails affair—holding a large flat stopwatch. She could enter the box from the side. The front opened onto the course.

"Don't worry, we won't start without you, Lexy," said the jovial red-faced fellow.

"Yes, sir," she said, taken aback that he knew her name.

"Your first time here?"

"How d'you know that?"

"Honey, I know everything." Then sweetly in that drawl, "You want me to count down the minute when we get to it?"

"Tell me the thirty-second mark, then the last ten, thanks."

She walked Bo on a loose rein, as Hamp had done with Trapper, but competition butterflies kicked in, rioting. *Butterflies are fine,* her mother used to say, *as long as they're marching in formation.* Like geese, Lexy imagined, and marshaled them into a vee, and then to her surprise, she felt her mother's presence, bathing her in love and confidence. Lexy blinked back tears the feeling was so brief, so sweet, so opposite the searing grief and scalding fear and doubt that had pursued her.

*Riders, the course is clear. Start box, next competitor.*

"One minute okay, Lexy?" the starter asked.

Lexy nodded and kept Bo walking. He was calmer than she was but hadn't been waylaid in the night. Where would Parker be?

"And remember," the starter said. "Shiny side down, fuzzy side up."

"Pardon me?"

He grinned and waited.

"Oh!" She got the joke. Shiny horseshoes, fuzzy manes and tails. *Keep your horse on his feet.* "You bet." Her focus returned, and the butterflies poised, wings up.

"Ten," he began, seconds later. She legged Bo into the box. Some horses reared, many fidgeted. All knew what the count meant. Bo gathered underneath her, a rocket on a launch pad. "Three. Two. One. Go, and good luck."

Bo sprang from the box and instantly found his speed.

The first four jumps were set in an easy loop that ran through a mile-round, regulation steeplechase track. Bo thundered over the dried grass and sandy surface. Lexy saw and felt a dozen things a second—Bo's pace, the distance to each fence, the reins in her hands, the balls of her feet in the stirrups, the galloping lanes, a blur of spectators, a judge at every jump.

*Now on course, Ninety-Eight, Lexy Imbriani fresh from England on Nobilo, twelve-year-old Thoroughbred stallion home-bred by home folks, Hawks Nest Farm. Welcome back, Bo. And welcome to North Carolina, Lexy.*

Surprised she'd even heard the announcer, she charged into the fourth jump, a small barn it took two strides to gallop through and then clear a gate. It made for a dramatic change from sunlight into shadow and back into bright light. Then they veered right into a sparsely wooded patch where spectators stood in clumps, a blurred kaleidoscope of colors, backpacks, wide-brimmed hats, drinks, and dogs on leashes, yapping. In a flash, she saw a clear path through, and then a clutch of late-comers stumbled into her path.

"Heads up!" someone yelled, and a judge's whistle shrilled a warning. *"Horse on course!"* the woman cried when they did not move fast enough.

Bo motored past them, and fifty feet away, Lexy centered on the spot she'd picked out yesterday. Two giant mushroom skinnies, their narrow, gaily-painted tops asking two hard questions. Will the horse jump something funny looking? Something only six feet wide?

Yes! And yes! Bo popped the first one, stride, stride, stride, and cleared the second effortlessly, in rhythm. Then he plunged down the steepest hill on course, ears pricked with enthusiasm, and cleared a rounded coop, dropped six feet, landed solidly on the ground below, and descended the hill toward the turtle pond where Hamp had teased her yesterday. Bo splashed into water a foot deep, which spooked some horses awfully. But he cantered through, happy as a kid in puddles, and jumped the giant carved wooden turtle in the middle, spraying water up around them. Then out and onwards, through a doorway, past warm-up with horses and riders milling, down into woods again over a tricky couple of corners, a hedge, a table, then up a bank and down the other side.

Bo loved his work. He made her work easy. She clamped down on her excitement and galloped on. Onto a trail cut into pines, down a big hill dotted with miniature cabins, big as any obstacle on course. Halfway down, they dropped three feet into a sunken road and popped out again, and at the bottom, soared over a trakehner—a huge log suspended above a deep ditch, dry from drought. They were two-thirds through the course, flying up a hill, and she checked her stopwatch.

Bugger. In her obsession with Parker, she'd not set it, so had lost track of time.

But their pace was good and forward, and she remembered Jordan's injunction. *Don't try to make time. Just get around clean.*

They were clean, and she could feel Bo breathing in the efficient rhythm of an athlete in top form. She was too. He pounded up a long hill, and she aimed him for the wide stone wall before them. He soared over it, the *wheee!* factor kicking in. He took the kennels next and then plunged downhill for the coffin, but ugly images assailed her. Not a spectator in sight, only the jump judge behind the darkened windows of her SUV. Lexy tried to shake off thoughts of Jordan's fall and Colonel's sabotage theory—of Parker—but the jump was isolated, and she felt utterly vulnerable.

Bo cleared the first log, took a short stride to the ditch, and bounced over the bigger log on the other side. She yelped with joy. *Go, Bo! Good boy.*

The next, a high, wide pile of cordwood, asked for scope, but Bo felt strong, and it was well within his range. She balanced to marshal him through the challenge afterwards, a six-foot drop into water a good foot deep, two strides to a large log and two long strides to a bank with a log on top. Approaching the complex, he surged beneath her, heading in too fast, and she asked him with her seat and reins to rate himself. She felt his jaw clamp on the bit, resisting her, and her heart clutched.

*Not now,* she thought, after they'd come this far. But Colonel's voice rang in her ears. *Let the fence be the bit.* So she gave Bo his head, and he hurtled over the first log and dropped into the water with a defining splash, then powered through and over the middle log and up the bank at the speed he'd taken everything so far, forward, sure.

"Well done, my man!" She slapped his neck with pride. He was hyped on endorphins too. Then she gathered her reins and piloted him over the final obstacles, an overturned canoe and an enormous final table, built like a farm wagon. Then home. At the finish line, he came down to his big trot then big walk immediately, a pro who knew his day's work was done.

She vaulted off, tension leaching from her. Beyond the finish line, Hamp was cooling Trapper, and he gave her a war whoop of victory.

"Double clear, cowgirl. Way to go."

"You saw?" she asked, loosening the girth and hiding near tears of relief to have gotten back alive. If her nausea was a measure, Parker had won the day.

But Bo had conquered the course—she came back to that. He was slick with sweat, and veins distended beneath his clipped coat. His flanks heaved, but he was far from winded. In fact, the pride in his arched neck and the confidence in his big brown eyes told her he could run another longer, higher course.

"The last bit, yeah," Hamp said. "He's a cross-country machine."

Colonel put a veined hand on Bo's bridle. "Any problems we didn't hear about?"

"He was awesome," she said. Omitting the fear of Colonel's son that had made her ride so difficult, she gave him the blow by blow her mother always insisted on. What they'd done well, what they could have done better, what to work on when they got home, a never-ending thread of self-scrutiny and striving for improvement. "He got strong coming into the water complex and clamped down on the bit. So I let him do it his way. It worked."

"No, it didn't," said Jordan, now at Colonel's side. She looked dark as the storm clouds overhead. "You should have rated him. Did you see your time?"

"Oh shit. I'm so sorry," Lexy blurted. "You said not to worry, so I let him find his rhythm. How slow were we?"

"Slow? You came in almost two minutes under optimum. Didn't you work with her on speed, Daddy?"

"Not particularly, darlin'. Just wanted her to come in safe. You know?"

"Damn it, Daddy. Nobody knows better. My suspension just ended. So the powers that be are watching us. You. Me. Bo. And now Lexy. Riding too fast is dangerous. The Technical Director can slap her on the Watch List if she tears around another course like that."

Lexy's heart had stopped pounding, but Jordan's anger ratcheted it back up, and her temper. "He was never out of control, not for one single, solitary moment. This course was chicken feed for him. You trained him. You rode him. You *know* him. Isn't this what he always gave you?"

By then, the next horse and rider had crossed the finish line, and family and grooms surrounded them in a flurry of stopping, dismounting, loosening the girth, swapping out the bridle for a halter, and celebrating. Another double clear, no doubt.

Jordan glanced at them, then gave Lexy a look so hostile and untrusting it chilled her to the bone. "Take him back to the stables, hose him down, cool him off, load up. We'll talk about this at home," she said and walked away, not using her cane.

# Twenty-one

Lexy led Bo back to the permanent stables. He was still jazzed, but she was ripped with doubt. On course she'd learned he had the speed and scope to go Advanced, with her in the saddle. But Jordan was right. She'd ridden him too fast, endangering the love of their lives and Hawks Nest's future.

She needed Hamp. He would help her sort things. She spotted him cooling Ax, walking away from Shed Row D. She waved but he ducked his head. Puzzled, she led Bo toward him. Bo needed cooling too, but Hamp glanced away as she got near, his face a mask.

"Are you and Ax OK?" she asked. "That hold on course, I was terrified for you."

He walked on. "We're fine." *Don't mess with me.*

She fell in beside him, no patience for a prima donna mood with so much pressing on her. "Jordan says I could get charged for dangerous riding."

"Hah, a redundant notion if there ever was one," Hamp said, still not meeting her gaze. "Because we're riding half-ton animals whose natural imperative is self-preservation by means of flight."

"Seriously," she said, puzzled by Hamp's distance. "She'll take him away from me."

"What if she does? He'll do fine with Parker," Hamp growled, angry as he'd been when he'd tackled Parker.

"Jordan's not passing him off to her brother!"

"Whatever." Hamp's tone was bitter and still he wouldn't look at her.

Desperate to connect with the man she loved, she asked quietly, "Do you know something you're not telling?"

He shocked her with a withering glance. "Do you?"

"I—No." Nothing she could tell.

He stopped Ax and Bo stopped too, both horses thrusting their noses into the grass and ripping up great mouthfuls.

Hamp turned on her, his bow-and-arrow lips pressed in a thin line.

"Look, cowgirl. You want to go out with Parker, fine by me. But I'm outta here."

Ohmigod, he was ditching her. "Who told you that?"

"Does it matter?"

What mattered was Hamp's anger. "I didn't *go out* with him."

"Dinner then his condo counts with me." The pain in Hamp's face shredded her. "Did you sleep with him?"

"God no," she blurted. "What do you think I am?"

"Another piece of Euro-trash, high-fiving it with a jet-setting trust fund ne'er-do-well who buys three horses in Ireland and flies them home?"

Blasted by his insult, she searched for a measured tone. "You got it wrong."

"Shoe fits, wear it."

"All right. I was investigating him. I can't prove it, but I think he let Bo loose in Orsino's paddock. I think he texted me that message."

Hamp's high brow knotted. "Come again?"

"Orsino's death. The message. Parker's at the top of my list of suspects."

"And you didn't tell me?"

She gulped in air, his rage too like her father's. "You fought him once. I couldn't take a chance you'd go after him again."

"So—" he jerked with anger, accusation "—*you* were going to tackle him?"

"No-o," she said with exaggerated patience. "I hoped to trip him, catch him lying."

"And how'd that work?"

"Talking to him's like herding cats. I'd shut one door and he'd squirt out a window, slither through the cracks."

Hamp crossed his arms, still skeptical. "Example."

"Crazy things." She pressed her fingers to her forehead to remember. "I'd say, 'I got a threatening text message, and I think you sent it.' And he'd say, 'Man, that's sick.'"

"He didn't deny it."

"Or when we got to his condo, I told him Gwen thought they'd used a prepaid, and I was looking for his. He said, 'I'd put my money on Marina. She's a bitch.'"

Hamp whistled as if impressed. "That's a non-denial denial if I ever heard one. You honestly think it's him?"

"Perhaps. Yes."

Hamp put his hand on her shoulder in sympathy, and she melted in relief.

"Somebody attacked me, too, his size," she admitted, caught off guard.

He went hard on her again. "Attacked you? When?"

God, she couldn't tell. He'd kill Parker.

"Lexy, you're not helping here."

She tugged Bo's head up from the grass, sprigs with roots dangling from his mouth. "Can we walk?"

"If you'll talk," he snapped, pulling Ax alongside.

But what to say? So much was at stake.

"Promise me—" She faced his angry gaze "—you won't do anything rash. I don't know who did it, or why, or what it means."

"Pretty clear to me. Parker wants the horse. He will stop at nothing. Tell. Me. What. He. Did."

"I can't know it was him, not for sure. Several nights ago, I stepped out to get some air, heard a noise, and headed back to the barn for safety. Someone grabbed me from behind, and a voice I didn't recognize told me my father's money wouldn't keep me safe here."

Hamp swore in Navaho.

"Well, it won't," she went on. "I fought his hold and kicked his shins and he threw me to the ground."

"Which is when you sprained your wrist."

"Yes."

"You shouldn't have lied to me."

"He bolted. He was gone. He hasn't been back. I'm fine."

Hamp undid a kink in Ax's lead line, scowling. "Hate secrets."

"Hate fighting."

"If you say so. Look, I got students warming up."

"Okay. Don't tell anyone, all right? You know how things get around."

"Of course I won't," he said, then, "What do you take me for?" He put Ax up and went back to his students.

She turned a cooled Bo into his stall, shaken. Owing to her ex-father's machinations she'd lost everything in Europe and risked all to rebuild her life here.

Success with Bo was her last hope.

If Jordan still supported her.

If she could nail down Parker.

If she could keep Hamp on her side.

Heading for the Hawks Nest trailer, she ducked into a Portapotty, no different from the ones in England, Europe, the stench beneath the antiseptic smell. She peeled her breeches down and perched her bum above the plastic seat, idly scanning the adverts on the door.

*Board with paddocks, turnout, exercise,* said one.

*Beloved eventer for sale, owner off to college,* said another.

*Clinic. Jordan McRae, Olympic medalist coaching.*

*HORSE KILLER* slashed across her name in blaring red.

Lip gloss? Parker?

Why not? How many women's purses did he have access to?

She jerked up her breeches, zipped the fly, snapped the waist, and ripped the flyer down, crumpling it in her fist. Rosie's death had been an accident. Had broken Jordan's heart, to say nothing of her body.

But Jordan would want to put up a clean copy.

Lexy found her in her 350 Ford Club Cab, windows sealed, her forehead resting on the steering wheel. Lexy gulped, wondering if Jordan had seen the defaced flyer.

She tapped the window with her fingernails.

Jordan jerked and looked up, her eyes moist.

Was this about the flyer? Or was she furious about Lexy's dangerously fast cross-country ride on Bo? Remorse pierced Lexy. She'd never meant to add to her boss's pain and problems, so perhaps she should forget about the flyer.

Jordan frowned, pressed a lever, and the window glided down.

"I'll learn to rate him," Lexy blurted, clutching the window frame. "No excuses, but he felt so happy, going round."

Jordan's expression went blank. "You and Bo are having a brilliant weekend, which is what we've been working for. Do stadium tomorrow. No rails down, and you've got a lock on third."

So she wasn't being fired. "He's a packer over knock-down jumps."

Jordan's smile looked forced. "I know."

If Jordan shared Lexy's suspicions about her brother, there'd be no smile at all.

# Twenty-two

*No rails down, and you've got a lock on third.*

And a chance at second, even first, if she could put Hamp's anger behind her long enough to ride her horse. She'd hurt him by going out with Parker, no matter her motive, and betrayed him by keeping it a secret. Now in warm-up for stadium, a short course in a manicured sand arena over colorful knock-down jumps, Hamp cantered around on Trapper, fiercely focused, along with the last half dozen competitors in Open Intermediate, taking practice jumps.

Overhead, thick clouds banded the sky, gunmetal to pearly gray, and thunder rumbled in the distance. Lexy stopped by the fence to speak with Colonel.

"Sounds like rain," she said. Good news in this awful drought.

"No such luck, darlin'. That's cluster bombs from the artillery range at Bragg."

"At nine a.m. on Sunday morning?"

"The Army shoots whenever it wants to," he said, assessing Bo. "How's your horse?"

"Ready."

"And you?"

She let go of the reins and laced her fingers, jamming her gloves to a perfect fit. "Totally. For him, yesterday was a walk in the park."

"Today won't be. That's a true Intermediate stadium course. Big, fast, twisty."

She knew. At seven-thirty before the first division started at eight, he'd walked her through it with Parker and Marina, being especially hard on Marina whose Intermediate gelding was notorious for dropping rails. The horse's fault, of course, not hers.

"Remember—" Colonel had turned to Lexy. "Don't lean in over fences. And watch your time. Nobody's making it."

But, Lexy had thought, the competitors went in reverse order of yesterday's finish, the weaker competitors first. They were the ones not making time. Parker and Marina, both in the running, had walked off together, heads inclined toward one another, talking.

"Mare count?" Colonel drummed his fingers on the fence.

She yanked her thoughts around to his question. "All at the stables."

Two mares and fifteen geldings had finished the final stadium jumping phase in Open Intermediate, leaving five riders yet to go. The draft cross was fifth, Parker unexpectedly fourth, Lexy third, Marina second, and Hamp first on Ben's horse Trapper. Fewer than four points separated them, so time faults or rails down could turn the final standings upside down.

Parker reined in beside them on Brad, one of his new imports, a striking blood bay gelding. Brad had sailed through the three-day quarantine for geldings in Florida, so Parker had had a month with him. Lexy thought his work ethic had been slack. He'd ridden George, his twelfth-place horse, first thing in the morning, a concession given to riders with more than one horse in a division to allow them time to prepare their next ride.

He looked unruffled. He unbuttoned his immaculately tailored riding jacket for air, flashing its red silk damask lining.

"Brad likes the new bit, Pop." The severe but legal one he'd bought with her at Cabin Branch. Brad was sweating in the humid morning, his chest flecked with foam from chewing at his new bit.

Colonel grunted. "Told you, son, I'd rather you take him Preliminary first time out, and in a snaffle." Lexy agreed but held her tongue. Bo went in a snaffle. Parker was using the bit for a quick fix with a hot horse.

"Nah," Parker said easily. "He'll attract more attention at Intermediate."

"A quicker sale, and at a higher price, no doubt," Lexy said.

Parker flashed her a smile. "Especially after I win this division."

"You'll have to go through me first."

"I thought of that." His gaze drifted to the center of her aging jacket.

"Down, boy," she ordered, wishing she could button it tighter.

"Offer's always on the table."

"I'm not interested."

"Ah. But you have the right to change your mind."

She just changed direction, showing him her back as she angled Bo toward warm-up, squashing Parker's image from her thoughts. But his number came over the loudspeaker as fourth in the order of go, and she couldn't escape him. She couldn't let him put her off her game again.

Like Parker on George, Hamp had gone early on Artemis, his other horse in this division. Now he was warming up Trapper, Ben's horse, the horse he had the lead on, She hadn't talked with Hamp last night, pride on her part and anger, she guessed, on his. Was he done with her?

Bo took three warm-up jumps in a fluid, forward rhythm. At least *his* mind was on their work. She rode over to Hamp, determined to mend fences. She couldn't see who he was chatting with until she pulled alongside. It was Marina, who cantered off without a word.

"'Lo," he said stiffly. He looked rumpled, frazzled. Last night, she'd made a showing at the competitors' wine and cheese party, but afterwards gone back to Hawks Nest alone and gone to sleep.

"You okay?" she asked.

"Yeah. Fine."

She was not convinced. "I'm so sorry about everything."

He took that in with a sad, measured gaze and nodded. "Let's go see how the course is riding."

"I—Sure," she said. She wanted more. It was a start. They turned toward the arena, Hamp's lanky gelding taller by an inch than Bo. "What was wrong with Marina back there? It's not like I've got the plague."

"Competition superstition."

"Be rude to your fellow riders?"

He snorted, not amused. "She's got her game face on. Talks only to her coaches before her round."

"You're coaching her?" So he kept secrets too. She tried not to care.

"As of last night. She's—um—questioning Colonel's method," he said neutrally.

Which meant, Lexy surmised, that Marina blamed her loss on Colonel and latched onto Hamp, the nearest hot-shot coach, never mind that she was competing against him.

For stadium, a dozen elaborate jumps rose up across a manicured sand arena. Cheerful plastic flowers decorated the standards and marked ground lines. But the jumps' painted poles rested on shallow cups, waiting for the merest rub to knock them down: penalty, four points. The tall Valkyrie of a woman on the Clydesdale cross was putting in a solid round, the ground shaking beneath hooves big as dinner plates.

"How'd Artemis go for you this morning? I was tacking up."

Hamp let out a breath of disgust. "Two rails down, three time faults. I blew it."

She winced in sympathy. "What happened?"

The big Clydesdale cross cleared the final combination and thundered past the stop clock at the finish line.

*Double clear, Miss Vallainecourt on The Devil You Know,* the announcer said. A couple of friends yelped in approval. A smattering of applause rippled through the early morning spectators—a couple of dozen people clumped in twos and threes on half a dozen four-tiered portable bleachers. As in England, outsiders were welcome at events, but in the U.S., few came—family and friends, students, instructors. Colonel, Roger, and Hamp's boss Chip. Parker trotted Brad into the arena, nodding at the Valkyrie as she left the ring.

"That second combination rides short, is all," Hamp explained. "But it dropped me out of the ribbons on him."

"Sorry," she said, meaning it.

"Thought I had my act together, bringing six horses. Yesterday was bad. Today got bad faster."

"What happened?"

"At the last minute Chip decided to rescind the courtesy of my using his groom, even for Ben's horses. I told him to go to hell, I'd do it myself. Dumb move."

"So you need help."

"Huh. I need an army."

It was her opportunity to make up with him. "Let me finish here, and I'm your man."

"Thanks, but I kinda like you as a woman," he said, still sober, but her gnawing worry she'd ruined their relationship lifted like a morning fog. With Hamp at her side, she studied Parker's round as if he were merely a competitor.

Brad was a neat, accurate jumper, snapping his knees to his nose to clear a jump. Lexy could see Parker lengthening and shortening him to manage the tricky distances, a good preview of the course for her as the gelding was near Bo's size and style. But a few jumps from the end, he spooked at the Liverpool— two vertical fences over shallow water in a rectangular blue plastic wading pool. Then the gelding fell apart, tossing his head to evade the bit, pushing against Parker's hands, then crashing through the last four fences, wooden rails clattering in his wake. With five fences demolished and twenty points lost, Parker finished well down in the standings.

Leaving the ring, he shrugged at her and Hamp.

"Bad luck," she said, and Hamp threw in a sportsmanlike, "Tough break."

An indomitable grin spread across Parker's face. "Yep. Brad's gonna have to learn to love blue water."

Ring stewards reset the fallen poles, and she fought to focus on the task at hand: twelve jumps, tight course, with tricky bends and testing distances. Brain in gear. Breathe.

The announcer called her name.

"Go for it, cowgirl," Hamp said, almost himself again. "You know you got the best horse here."

"I do, don't I?" she said with a flush of adrenalin, and trotted Bo into the arena. A bell rang, which gave her forty-five seconds to show him the course before she crossed the start line. She aimed him for it, passing the Olympic coach standing by the rail, watching her beneath the bill of an official USEF cap. He gave her a thumbs up.

Her butterflies flocked into formation.

Ears pricked, Bo soared over the first three jumps, an inviting solid yellow oxer, a vertical with its rails fanned, a Swedish oxer with rails crossed, a dozen or so bending strides between each one. Thank God, he was a pro, forgiving her ragged nerves. She gathered him for the triple combination, three jumps in a row with two strides between the first two and one between the second and third. Jump, stride, stride and jump and stride, and jump—blimey, he took the fences like a machine.

The next two jumps—a gate and a fake stone wall painted on wood sections that would fall if touched—had tight striding. Colonel had warned her they were tricky, demanding that the horse lengthen and then shorten, the opposite of what came naturally, but Bo came back to her like an accordion. She could have sworn he'd sized up the distance for himself.

Another long bending line took her to the two giant oxers that had given Hamp such trouble. It asked more of the horses than the triple. Both jumps were big efforts with two short controlled strides in between.

Bo, the accordion man, extended over the first oxer, came back to her for the two short strides in between, then powered up over the second element. He was flying, and she was flying on him, but she stifled her elation and bore down on the Liverpool that had tripped Parker up.

*Come back to me,* she signaled Bo with a flutter on the reins.

*No big deal,* he responded, lofting over.

A triple bar was next, and then a final vertical, and she let loose the reins and nudged him with her legs to speed past the automatic timer at the finish line.

They were done. Clear. And under time, she was positive.

She patted Bo's neck, knuckling the spot above his withers where mares nibble their foals. *Brave lad,* she murmured. From a distance, she heard scattered applause and hearty male cheers.

Hamp and Parker met her at the gate, Colonel, too, wreathed in smiles and offering congratulations. Chip was watching Hamp, not her, and Roger was watching Jordan, who came up, her smile restrained. "You did good, great," she said, then propped against the fence to watch Marina who was in second. Marina executed a careful round, no rails down, but three time faults.

Which placed Lexy one-point-two points ahead of the Whiskey Queen.

And advanced her into second place.

After his stellar round cross-country, Hamp had a lock on first and so went last, needing a perfect round to hold his lead. To beat her. He started strong, smoother and more effortless than anyone before him. She couldn't outride this man, but she loved his style, so quiet and in harmony with his horse. Two-thirds through, over the second oxer of the double combination, Trapper's left hind rubbed a back rail. A groan rose from the crowd.

For breathless moments, the rail rocked in its cups then toppled on the sand with a soft thud. *Oh Hamp,* Lexy thought. *You lost.* Then, *Oh my God.*

Incredibly, she'd won.

She covered her mouth with a gloved hand, holding back sobs of amazement and relief. She'd worked so hard. Been so lucky, so alone. But her nerves had held, and so far, this weekend Parker hadn't tormented her about anything but sex.

The officials checked the standings. After a delay, the announcer called the top six finishers into the arena. Lexy first, a gracious Hamp in second, the grinning Valkyrie in third, a pinch-faced Marina in fourth, and a couple of women Lexy had met at last night's party and quite liked because they'd talked on and on about their horses.

Outside the arena, Parker had stuck around on Brad. Bottle blondes in tight white breeches hung out with him, worshipful, as if he were a rock star, win or lose.

In the arena, officials doled out awards, sixth-place, fifth-place ribbons. Fourth. Third. Hamp's. Lexy got a perpetual trophy named for a local someone she'd never heard of, a silver bowl she could keep for a year and do what with it?—stash her car keys and her change? Then came her winner's ribbon. Its satin sash ended in a fancy crenellated blue rosette. She draped the sash across her chest. The rosette fell at her hip, and two feet of streamers fanned over her thigh. She'd won sashed rosettes going back to her Gymkhana days, but nothing represented the battle she'd fought for this one, in America, on her own. Bo had been awesome all weekend, but—her breath lodged in her throat—her mother wasn't there to share their victory. Jordan had deserted her, Parker had been a hound dog, and she'd hurt Hamp.

"Damned fine showing, cowgirl," he said, sounding more himself. "Be proud."

From the PA system, tinny, patriotic music blared across the grounds for the victory gallop, but Hamp's injunction was exactly what she needed to keep the tears at bay. Lexy nudged Bo into a forward gallop. It felt so damned good, the next five finishers galloping behind her like knights of old, ribbons whipping as they sped around.

The applause lasted a few strides only. Hardly anyone had stayed to watch, and outside Hawks Nest and the McRae Center, hardly anyone knew her.

"And the crowd goes wild," Hamp called out over the thundering hoof beats.

Some spectators laughed, and she laughed too, a real laugh, for the first time in months. Back at the trailers, she hosed Bo and loaded him in the trailer. Jordan okayed her staying to help Hamp. Colonel urged her to get a handle on the Advanced competitors, her future rivals, and went home with Bo and Jordan. Lexy slaved for Hamp late into the afternoon, no time to watch other rides. Together they fed, brushed, braided, tacked up, untacked, hosed off, hand walked his half-dozen horses, and then mucked out. She'd done what any competent groom would do for her rider. Each time he tackled the stadium course with one of his four remaining mounts, Lexy wiped the last trace of dust off his boots. When her mother had done that for her, it had been an act of love.

Now, doing it for Hamp, Lexy was scared it was love too.

Hamp won Advanced on Ax and placed in the ribbons with both of Chip's Intermediate horses, not quite beating her, but she was thrilled for him.

The day that had started before dawn rushed by. The sun came out. As hour had piled on hour, it sank in how brutally hard it was to compete a string of horses all on one weekend and keep up with his students, not just Marina but lower-level ones like the adorable Nikki from Chip's barn. Lexy kept referring to the chart he'd scotch-taped inside the tack stall to track which horse needed what and when and where, the least she could do after all he'd done for her.

He was set to go last on Code Talker, an off-the-track Thoroughbred in need of Hamp's special touch that he'd bought and started before she'd arrived. He'd just bumped Cody up to Preliminary. They won their first time out.

From across the yard, Marina strolled up groomed to the nines in leather full-seat riding breeches from Germany and waterproof boots from Ireland. The pricey boots had brown horizontal strips of cowhide alternating with pebbled pigskin. They were the rage with eventers here and in England too. Up against her immaculate turn-out, Lexy felt sweaty and grimy, her decidedly less posh clothes smeared with dirt and bits of hay.

Marina's gaze skipped past her as if she were the hired help.

"Don't forget, Hamp," Marina drawled. "Dinner with me at Ashten's, seven o'clock tonight."

Lexy's heart twisted in confusion, pain.

Hamp pointed a finger at her rival, cocking an imaginary gun, the first faked thing Lexy had ever seen him do. "You betcha. I'll be there."

Lexy watched Marina walk toward the air-ride six-horse trailer with luxury custom living quarters she kept parked at Hawks Nest. A quarter million dollars, at least, or whatever quids or Euros translated into. Needles of jealousy stabbed her, not for the money, clothes, or horses, but for the access Marina had to Hamp, who she hadn't lifted a finger to help today. Now she was taking him to dinner, at Ashten's of all places.

Lexy's long hard weeks of striving to please her bosses, of barely seeing Hamp, of Parker's nasty sabotage came to a head. She turned on Hamp. "What was I thinking, slaving for you all day? That you would take me out to dinner, buy me wine, shag me afterwards?"

Hamp pivoted on his boot heels, the boots she'd polished over and over this afternoon. They were dusty. "You think I like this?" he asked savagely. "Marina's my student now and she'll be paying my bills. Maybe I can help her. Maybe not. But she's got money to burn. Me, not a lot."

"Oh." Dear God, Lexy felt so small. Short on cash, she understood. "Then go for it."

"I'm too tired to fuck Penelope Cruz tonight, if that's what's got your breeches in a twist. But Marina—" He let out a harsh breath. "You don't get it, do you?"

"Evidently not." She lifted her chin, trying to salvage a shred of self-respect.

He sat on the step to the tack compartment of his used but serviceable trailer. He must be in hock for thirty, forty grand. Plus the truck, double that.

"I thought you were different."

"Different how?" She felt at sea.

He ran his fingers through his spiked black hair. "To most of them, I'm a notch on their bedposts. Let's check out the noble savage. You know, does he have hair on his chest? A bigger cock? Does he make love in Navaho?" His green gaze searched hers, wounded. "I don't do performance sex for rich girls any more."

Mortification swept her. "That never occurred to me."

His gaze warmed. "That's what I like about you."

"Really?" After all she'd said, and not said?

"Yeah." And he held out his hand with its sturdy bones and callused copper skin and twined her fingers in with his. "Nobody but Brenda helped me like you did today, and she was paid. The rest—they drop by to hang out with the halfbreed."

"That sucks."

He shrugged, looking embarrassed. "Hey. My mother's alive, and she adores me." He picked up a stack of empty buckets, the last thing they had to load. "Let's get these ponies home."

He drove her back in a tired but easy silence through Aberdeen, bypassing Pinehurst and Southern Pines on the left to Youngs Road on the right, to Hawks Nest Farm. He pulled his rig into the big circular drive, turned to her from his captain's seat, leaving the engine on.

"Can you get off tomorrow night?"

"Think so."

"Good. Dinner at my place. I'm cooking."

"I'd like that," she said. "A lot."

"Seven?"

She grinned. "If seven's good enough for Marina, it's good enough for me."

"Witch," he said, pulled her to him for the deep steamy kiss she'd wanted from him all week. Tongue and teeth and sweet hot breath, and her arms around his iron-hard body. By the time they stopped, desire had heated her, but he pulled away, heavy lidded, serious.

"Don't worry about the Whiskey Queen, okay? That's business."

"Right." She rubbed her aching wrist. She'd just worry about Parker who couldn't decide whether he wanted to fuck her or drive her crazy. Because she'd just won and he'd lost big time. He was bound to make another move. "Tomorrow."

# Part Three. Watch List

## *October*

In the days of the Military Games, three-day riders were officers or enlisted men—young, brash, daring, and when at peace, bored.

After mess, cavalry men amused themselves by setting up a line of chairs from the refectory outside and jumping their horses over the flimsy, spooky obstacles.

From chairs, they graduated to hand-held crossed swords, and their horses cleared them too.

*A History of the U. S. Army Olympic Equestrian Team (1912-1948)*
By Colonel Jacob McRae, USA Maj. Ret.

# Twenty-three

Two weeks passed, and Fair Hill International Horse Trials in Maryland had come up faster than Lexy had expected, no texts, no attacks, no solid proof. Was Parker planning to waylay her at the competition? Or was her soft-hands theory so much rot? He'd been pestering her for another "date" like some rocker bloke who believed no woman was immune to his charm. For her, Parker's charm was gone, and a sense of lunacy settling in. His, or hers, she wasn't sure. She'd not been remotely tempted to give in to his pressure, but she dreaded the sight of him for fear of what he'd say next. Today, she finished her dressage test in a pelting rain and left the arena, shivering.

"Coulda been worse," said Colonel. "Your test, not the weather."

He handed her a slicker. She shrugged into it, spread a waterproof quarter sheet over Bo's hindquarters, and wiped wet glop from her face. The arena had a state-of-the-art surface of sand, tiny chunks of rubber and shredded carpeting, but the going had been sloppy.

"A monsoon could have been worse. How did you survive your army days?"

"We were tough, ma'am." Mounting his ATV, he grinned up at her under his rain hat, the grand old man of eventing with deep lines of dignity bracketing his smile. Even in the rain, people eavesdropped on him, as if to pick up some nugget of wisdom.

"Where's Jordan?" she asked.

"The mud's too deep for the rental cart, and I told her not to hoof it. You, on the other hand—" he shifted seamlessly "—got a great extended walk out of Bo just now. I'd score it a nine."

"Why, Colonel," she said, in the Southern belle accent she'd picked up from the boarders, "that's about the nicest thing anybody ever said to me." She shifted to her own accent. "But I muffed the rein back. He pinned his ears and reared."

"Don't worry about it. Best monsoon test I ever saw. Put him up, and we'll walk the course at two, rain or shine."

She scanned the heavy skies, no letup in sight, and groaned. "You got a hot line to the weather gods?"

"Parker's on his laptop, checked it out on radar. Should blow past by evening. You in?"

"I'll be there."

He drove off.

She was itching to hear his strategy for tackling the thirty-five enormous solid obstacles she and Bo would face Saturday, itching to get round safe and sound. After a hasty lunch, she was bedding Bo's stall when Colonel's ATV churned through the mire. He offered her a ride. Honored, she mounted behind him. He handed her his stainless steel cane with a top that flipped into a seat. Mud sucked at the chunky vehicle's wheels and splattered the undercarriage. Near the start box, in the rain, Parker and Marina stood next to her ATV. It was fancier than Colonel's, but like his, clumped with gobbets of wet red clay.

"What took you guys so long? We're drowning here," Parker complained. His gaze raked Lexy's form-fitting riding clothes beneath her open slicker.

She snapped the slicker closed.

Colonel seemed to miss that and shot back at Parker, "'Fraid you'll melt?"

"No, sir," Parker said. "'Fraid you're not up to it."

"Hmmph," Colonel grunted. "My wand, Miss Imbriani," he added with a twinkle for her eyes only. She handed him the cane, and he pointed it ahead like a wizard, or an explorer setting off to chart an exotic plain. "Okay, folks. Talk me through the course."

Lexy gritted her teeth. She'd hoped to have her mentor to herself and dreaded a three-and-a-half mile trek in the company of the playboy of international eventing, with the Whiskey Queen horning in. Wasn't Hamp her coach now, anyway? Double dipping—the thought just made her boil. Get a grip, she scolded. She would learn everything she could from the three of them, then do what she did best—ride hell-for-leather over daunting courses, go clean and make the time.

"Ladies first," Colonel said, urging them onto the course. "Marina, darlin', your plan for the first four obstacles."

They were straightforward galloping jumps, a typical start, inviting the horse to find its pace and settle in, Marina explained. She didn't see a problem. Colonel did, and tweaked her analysis, reminding her that the fourth jump sat beneath a shed. Savannah hated running under anything.

Marina sniffed. "I fixed that."

Colonel turned to Lexy. "Your plan for the coops?"

"They're angled. I'd take them straight on," she said.

Colonel agreed. But on their way to the next fence, Parker sidled up to her, saying *sotto voce*, "I'd take you straight on anytime, Imbriani, like, say, tonight back at the RV."

"Stuff it, dude," she said, deploying her best new American slang.

"Is that an invitation?"

She didn't dignify that with a retort, but Colonel glared at them.

"Your turn, son," he said, officer in charge.

Parker complied, giving a textbook analysis of the tricky double corners. His words and manner made him a dead ringer for the father who'd coached him from his lead-line days. The rain pelted them. "This is fucking miserable, Colonel," he concluded.

His tone and language struck Lexy as disrespectful, but she slogged on without a word.

"Buck up, buddyroe," Colonel said. "War's worse, if you'd ever been in one."

Parker rolled his eyes, but Lexy saw a glint of anger.

"This is nonsense, Dad. This weather front moves out tonight. We can do this in the morning."

"You civilians go on back. I'm not walking this course but once."

Parker fell in line, and they kept walking. Between Parker's come-on's and his griping, she had to concentrate to get the benefit of Colonel's wisdom, but his youthful pace impressed her. She planned at least three more walks, two on Friday, one with Hamp and one alone, and the third early Saturday before warm up.

She wished she'd had a moment to talk with Hamp. She studied the lay of the galloping lanes but couldn't stop thoughts of him, pelting her like this cold autumn rain. She knew he was competing six horses in three different divisions again this weekend, but she wanted him around, needed him to buffer Parker.

If Parker were truly out to destroy her and Bo, he wouldn't keep after her for sex, would he? Near the end of walking the course, Parker bumped a shoulder into hers, more sexual tease than buddy nudge.

"Come on, luv. Gimme a chance. It's not like you got an exclusive on ol' Hamp."

"You think I don't know that," she snapped, and instantly regretted any sign of jealousy or possessiveness, but she couldn't help how she felt. Flocks of women on two continents dropped their jaws when Hamp Gambrell walked by.

"So… you know about Nikki? She's in love with him."

She hadn't known that, and her breath hitched. "Way to score points, Romeo," she managed.

"Hey," he said, doing the hang-dog thing again. "I'm just trying to get laid."

She almost laughed, his act was so unrelenting. Could he be an uber-letch and a sociopath too? Let it go, she upbraided herself. Because nothing was more pressing now than her need to know, dead on, the risky course she'd be riding Saturday. It had to be her total focus. She concentrated on the final few obstacles.

At last, Colonel's walk done, she hitched a ride with him to the stables, brooding—no, re-riding the big course in her mind and weighing her chances. She'd had a brilliant ride at Badminton which had greater crowds, a longer course, and risky obstacles that demanded more skill and daring. And now, here, she had more experience and Bo was healed, rehabbed, going better every workout.

She just had to show up on the day, rested, ready.

# Twenty-four

Friday morning before daybreak, black clouds rolled across the sky, but crevasses of gray hinted at the rising sun. In the permanent stabling, Lexy was mucking out Bo's stall, double-checking for Parker. But he wasn't a morning person, and she saw no sign of him amongst the dozen other early risers on her row prepping their horses for day two of dressage.

Bo was awake too, eyes brighter than at home and watching her, a human in her rightful place slaving away for him.

The door chain clinked. "You ready to walk that course?"

It was Hamp, delivering on the promise he'd texted yesterday.

"Madmen and Englishwomen," she tried to joke, but in truth she was relieved. She'd been prickly about Marina, and she knew it.

She locked the heavy-duty mesh screen that was Bo's stall door when they left him in a stall at an event and hopped behind Hamp on his scooter to ride the half mile to the course. He smelled of something spicy and exotic she suspected Grandpop had sent him for his harmony, and she put her arms around his lean torso. He probably had a body-fat percentage of, oh, say, nine. She thought of his dark, smooth skin and the desire he'd shown for her in bed, and swore to say nothing about Parker's harassment. She had to handle him by herself.

Hamp's scooter fishtailed through a puddle, fanning muddy water in their wake.

"No groupies this morning?" she asked, half an eye out for Nikki who was competing here this weekend. After Parker's taunt, Lexy had learned Hamp's student had big Olympic dreams but was stuck at Preliminary, not able to square her ability with her ambition.

"Students, Lexy," he said. *"Paying* students."

They hit a rut, and her curiosity got the best of her. "Nikki's in love with you."

He groaned. "I can't tell you how much that improves her riding."

Lexy couldn't press for more. She had to clear her mind to walk the course, Hamp style. Near the start box, he took off his boots and socks like last time, and she did too, but carried her boots along. He jogged barefoot three times a week. Her feet wouldn't last the course. The galloping lanes were firmer than yesterday, the turf being old and well tended, and the ground beneath it doubtless originally worked with some elaborate combination of gravel, sand, and rock screenings underneath the overlying sod to maximize drainage.

"The take-offs and landings will get sticky tomorrow," Hamp said. "Even if the rain stops now."

Out so early, they had the course to themselves, and he pulled her to the far side of a huge pile of cordwood—obstacle nineteen—that butted against the trunk of a giant oak tree. He backed her up to it and wrapped her in his arms. His instant hard-on flashed through her like lightning, and his stormy kiss answered a great yawning gap of need in her. She melted into him, desire drenching her.

"A novel approach to course walking." Parker emerged from behind the tree.

"Son of a bitch," Hamp growled and lunged at Parker.

"No, don't," she cried, catching Hamp's arm and restraining him with every ounce of her strength. She feared his flashpoint temper more than Parker's.

Parker grinned, obviously enjoying Hamp's fury and her misery. "I was right, telling Colonel to wait to walk the course. Much more educational this morning."

"Parker, you're a bloody wanker."

"That something we can do together?"

"You son of a bitch," Hamp said, rigid with anger.

"Why don't you two go on doing what you're doing?" Parker said.

"We're walking the course, mate," she said in her most off-putting British accent. "I suggest you do the same, backwards."

He gave a mocking grin and strolled away.

Hamp's stiffness eased against her. "Thanks," he said wryly. "If anybody saw me kill him, they'd kick me out of the competition."

*More than,* she thought, but said, "You scare the hell out of me when you go off like that."

"Sometimes I scare myself," he said, but a slash of the once-clouded sun crossed his face, and he withdrew her clenched hands from his arm. "You go on to the next one, and give me a coupla minutes."

"Can I—"

"I'll catch up to you. I need a few minutes alone."

She walked on, scanning the lane ahead and the woods on either side. Parker could come back. Some trees were big enough for him to hide behind.

Then she heard Hamp's voice, quietly chanting in Navaho. He must be saying his people's morning blessing at the rising of the sun. She was touched he'd let her this close to anything so private. Holy, even. By the time she'd assured herself Parker was not lurking in another clump of trees or behind the next obstacle, Hamp caught up to her, his harmony apparently restored.

"Sorry I let him get to me, sorrier you saw it. Sometimes I lose track of who I am."

"At least you've got your prayers. I admire that."

"Thanks for seeing it that way." He gave her a quick but passionate kiss. "Let's get to work." Taking her hand he launched into a discussion of how to approach the next obstacle, a big farm wagon covered with bales of bright yellow straw. She summoned her competition focus, the bubble of concentration she lived in on course. They got round in record time and skidded to the stables on his scooter through the mire, passing riders warming up for Friday's round of dressage tests that started at eight a.m. Near Bo's row of stalls, Hamp took her hand and pressed her knuckles to his mouth.

"Chip's got me stopping in Virginia to try out a prospect Monday, but I can free up Monday night."

"You sure?"

"I'll call you from the road if I'm gonna be late, okay?"

"I'll be there."

His green gaze bore in on her. "Be bold out there tomorrow. Beat everybody."

"Even you?"

He blinked, then his eyes twinkled. "Dang. You're up against me and Ax. All right. Try to keep up with us. Beat the heck out of everybody else." And he disappeared into the rows of handsome permanent stabling with his own horses to warm up, students to coach, and a temper to manage.

# Twenty-five

By Saturday, cross-country day, the drenching rain had ended. Lexy should have been primed to pilot Bo around, but Parker's nasty intrusion yesterday had poisoned her weekend. How had he known she and Hamp were walking the course at daylight? He went clubbing till the wee small hours. And what did he hope to gain by horning in on them? She still couldn't prove he'd sabotaged Orsino, sent the text, or mugged her, but now she'd have to clear her thoughts of him to ride her best and get strongly round the course.

Luckily, the skies were clear, the lanes were drying, and the footing better than she could have hoped, having jogged the course an hour ago to study the play of sunlight and shadows on the obstacles as near as possible to her riding time.

But warm up had been a disaster. A couple of times, Bo had skidded sideways, shying at perfectly ordinary fences, the kind they'd cleared dozens of times in their two months together.

Then he'd flung himself at a simple schooling coop, overjumping it by two feet. Twelve minutes before their start time, he was a basket case, wild-eyed, drenched in nervous sweat, as freaked as the day he'd catapulted off the trailer.

"You okay, Two-Sixty-Four?" The warm-up steward called Lexy by her number as she jigged past on Bo. No touchy-feely, already-knew-her-name stuff like at the Horse Park last month, but still with real concern.

The short answer was no. "A spot of anticipation anxiety," she told the steward.

Bo's, and hers, she thought, but surely he'd settle down on course.

She had to as well.

Hamp, warming up Ax, trotted over. "What's with Bo?"

"Dunno. It's like somebody shot him up with go-juice."

Hamp's eyes darkened beneath the brim of his safety helmet. "You serious?"

"Of course not. He's just keen." Or so she hoped.

"Try a hand-gallop in that big field."

Galloping revved Bo up. Her nerves were bad enough with Parker going after her and Hamp, and yesterday in front of Colonel. Was he after Bo now? How low would he sink? He could have drugged him with some quick-acting OTC concoction to make him hot. She'd heard of that in England. But how had he gotten to her horse?

Bo's night stall door was solid wood below with an iron grill top, and they'd locked it.

Had Parker put a burr beneath his saddle? No, Bo wasn't bucking.

Besides, when saddling him, she and Jordan had double-checked everything—saddle pads, saddle, billets, buckles, girth. Bridle, breastplate, boots.

Then what the devil was the matter? Sweat trickled down her ribcage under the ASTM-certified safety vest that now did not feel safe.

Horses *died* eventing. People too.

Near the start box, Jordan speared her cane into the still-damp ground. Colonel stood beside her, fingers steepled at his chin.

"I don't know what's gotten into him," Lexy told them, unable to hide her concern.

Colonel's hands parted, lifted. "Stallion. You check the mares?"

"They finished, the four of them."

"Spectators," Jordan suggested, and gestured at the distractions.

Fair Hill's big international event was called "Family Festival." Bo had sidled past a giant vendors' tent with pointed spires, snorted at dogs darting through agility trials. He'd skittered away from shrieking kids running through a straw-bale maze. Here and there, bundles of corn stalks with pumpkins piled at their bases rose out of the ground like ghouls. He'd balked. Years ago in France, Lexy had seen Bo sail around the course at Pau with a bigger crowd than this, afraid of nothing.

Today, he trotted in place, executing a near-perfect Grand Prix-level piaffe—not what she was asking for—and Lexy felt him ready to explode. She put him on a small walk circle to calm him, but he crow-hopped underneath her.

"Okay. That's not good," Colonel said, his tone practical, neutral.

Jordan, using her cane, lifted the white plastic tape around the warm-up area and came to Bo's side, touching his neck. He flinched away. "You can withdraw, no harm, no foul." Doubt clouded Jordan's eyes, and Lexy fought doubts too.

No risk, no opportunity. She should be cool, calm and collected. She should forget Parker. "He'll settle on course."

Jordan studied her stallion, who jigged in place. "I'm not so sure."

Colonel's mouth curved into a wicked grin. "He just needs to gallop."

"Three minutes, Two-Sixty-Four," the steward said.

"Righto," Lexy said, wishing she had Colonel's confidence. But would he have it if he knew about Parker?

Jordan's mouth crimped but she nodded, and they followed Bo and Lexy to the start box. Bo danced alongside as if it held a pit of writhing rattlesnakes striking at his fetlocks. Once, in London at Wembly Stadium, she'd seen an exhibition rodeo, and a bareback bronc had reared in the chute before it opened.

This felt like that, terrifying, with her throat locked and her blood pounding behind her eyeballs. But in a moment, the business of simply staying on three-quarters of a ton of lit explosives overrode her panic.

*Ten, nine…two, one. Go and good luck.*

Bo plunged from the box, setting his jaw against her hand, running away. It was one-hundred-twelve meters to the first obstacle, a stair-step effect with sprays of evergreens on the sides and cheery fall chrysanthemums arrayed along the top coming up so fast it took her breath away. Bo sailed over the flowers, but she felt him spook beneath her in midair, trying to look down to make sure the mum-monsters weren't reaching up to rip off his heels.

But she got the feel of his mouth on the bit and let him set his pace for the next fence, seeing a blur of brightly clad spectators lining the galloping lane. Its white tapes fluttered in the breeze, but mostly she saw the fence ahead, its take-off zone freshly laid with dry gray screenings.

*Don't micromanage him,* she thought as they flashed past everything. Let the incline slow him down.

It did, minutely, and the second obstacle—a gray stone wall with a low-pitched dark green roof called The Springhouse— came up fast, but it was as straightforward and inviting as a big fence could be. Bo sucked back for a millisecond, but cleared it with air to spare. She got her breathing rhythm back. He took the third the same way, and the fourth, and then barreled onwards to a trakehner, a foot-round log set high and at an angle above a deep, wide ditch.

Two strides out, he went squirrelly underneath her. Before her fast reflexes caught up with his faster ones, he ran out to the left, passing the obstacle but barely slowing.

Damn it. A run-out counted as a refusal, their first ever on cross-country, whether schooling or competing. And Bo had lost it. *She'd* lost it. She'd let Parker—if it was Parker—get to her. No way would she retire Bo now. Shifting her crop to the side he'd run out to, she organized him and presented him to the obstacle again, then felt his micro-impulse to refuse. Tightening her legs, she popped him with the crop. He surged over the log, landed smoothly and was instantly up to speed.

"Well done, my friend," she said, and galloped away, slapping his neck in approval.

One refusal did not disqualify them.

He stayed with her for the next three obstacles then headed for the ninth one, a combination brush fence and drop to a sunken road followed by a skinny, a diabolically narrow jump that tested the horse's obedience and the rider's control. Colonel had drilled her on it, and she'd paced it every walk thereafter and confirmed the spot she'd aim for.

Bo cleared the brush, but as he dropped six feet to the ground, his big body panicked underneath her. His front hooves landed on grass, and he lunged across the bright gray gravel screenings of the Sunken Road. Unnerved by the crunchy footing, he spooked, zigging right.

Thrown left, she grabbed a hunk of his short mane for balance, yanked him back on course, and gunned up the bank to the skinny a stride away.

He bolted over it, but snapped the left standard. He landed bucking at a gallop. She kept her seat and gripped the reins, fiercely focused, but Bo veered toward a cluster of spectators lounging on the grass a dozen strides away, ten, eight, and terrified people scrambled.

A toddler screamed. Its hoodie-clad mother stood frozen, as if unsure how to escape the charging horse. Lexy grabbed mane and flung herself off between Bo and the mother, half pulled half pulling on the reins, running alongside till she diverted him from the mother and child and hauled him to a stop.

A fall within thirty meters of an obstacle meant elimination even if the rider landed on her feet, but she'd dismounted outside that zone and could continue. The jump judge rushed to check for injuries. Lexy touched the crop, still in her hand, to the brim of her helmet, signaling she was fine. But finished. Quitting.

"Tough luck," a man said from the crowd.

"Great save," said a woman.

Lexy was nodding and shaking and flooded with self-recrimination. But suddenly in front of her was the mom with her toddler clutched to her breasts, standing well clear of the devil stallion who'd nearly run them over. The child bawled in great gulping sobs. Wild eyed, Bo took no notice of it or its mother as his flared nostrils sniffed the air.

"We've been here since... I had no idea..." the woman blubbered, her pretty chubby face puckered in lines of horror.

"Are you sure you're okay?" Lexy asked.

Tears sprang to the woman's eyes. "Yes, thank you. I'm so sorry," she babbled. "We ruined your day."

"Oh no, ma'am," Lexy said, managing a small smile. "We did that by ourselves. Thank God, you're okay."

Still pumped, Bo trumpeted to Ax, already on course and headed toward them.

Lexy could tell the instant Hamp glimpsed Bo riderless and her beside him on her feet. *Keep your mind on the course,* she exhorted him. Ax cleared the brush and dropped to the graveled road unfazed. Hamp gave her the quickest worried glance. She held a thumbs-up, and then remarkably, Ben was at her side, walking behind Bo to check his leg where it had snapped the standard.

"Bad cut. Good you retired him," Ben said grimly.

She handed him the reins so she could check too. "Shit. Nasty gash above the stifle." Four inches across, half an inch deep, where his hind leg joined his flank.

"Which explains why he bolted."

"But nothing else."

"Yeah, I saw you guys in warm-up. He wasn't with you."

"I thought we'd work it out on course. So did Colonel."

"Too bad. I'll walk you back." Which was a particularly kind mark of attention, though little sacrifice to him. From here, he could see the action at a dozen fences and keep on evaluating his Olympic prospects. Any hopes Jordan might have had for them was shot to hell.

Three minutes after Hamp, Parker stormed by on Brad, spotting her and Bo, as Hamp had done, as a potential hazard.

"You okay?" he called out, as if he cared, as if he hadn't been driving her crazy.

"Yes," she said, which didn't begin to describe it. She felt an utter failure for losing control of the best stallion in eventing on the continent.

Parker galloped on, in sync with Brad. How competitive they must look to Ben, while Bo jigged at her side, still revved to run, but busted. He would have conquered that course, if only she'd been good enough. Calm enough. But she'd failed him. Three minutes later, Marina sped by on Tosca, not giving her a glance.

With Ben, Lexy ran into Colonel and Jordan near the start box. Roger and Chip walked over from the nearby finish line.

Jordan was livid, Colonel rigid.

"I told her she could withdraw," Jordan was saying. "But you dared her to go on."

Bo fidgeted beside Lexy, looking with keen interest at the course she hadn't let him finish. She loosened his girth and ran up his stirrups, appalled she'd forgotten this simple end-of-ride routine. "It wasn't a dare. I hadn't seen this side of him since I started riding him."

"He didn't used to *have* this side," said Jordan bleakly.

"But Lexy mostly worked him at home," Ben pointed out. "And the Horse Park where she won is practically his backyard. This was what—his first time at Fair Hill?"

"Third," Jordan bit off. "Those bastards ruined him."

Colonel's lined features darkened. "Have him checked out when we get home."

Chip stepped up with Roger, and a smile broke across Colonel's face at the sight of his best friend. "Buddy. Didn't expect to see you here."

"I flew us up for the day," Chip put in.

"In case I needed to look at any of his horses," Roger added, his gaze instantly dropping to Bo's hind leg. He scowled at Colonel. "Or yours." He walked round to Bo's off hind, inspected the injury and stepped back. "What the dickens happened?"

Lexy lifted her chin. "I lost control. My fault."

Ben shook his head. "No, honey. Jordan's right. It wasn't you. They ruined him. He's as dangerous as the day he came off the trailer, too untrustworthy to compete."

Jordan's face went red. "You're saying he's not rideable."

"He is," Lexy protested. "There's just something wrong with him today."

Roger shook his head. "Could be an underlying lameness. They can be hard to detect. Or he was abused, the way they rode or handled him. Or maybe the way they fed him led to a gastric ulcer. That can make 'em temperamental as all get out. You see any other signs of ulcers—lethargy, gone off his food?"

"No!" Lexy and Jordan said in unison.

"He gets plenty of hay, as much turnout as possible," Jordan said.

"Minimum grain for his level of competition. And no drugs," Lexy added, glad for the moment to be on the same page with Jordan. "I'd like to see a blood panel on him."

"Anything you're hoping to find out, darlin'?" Colonel asked.

"Anything, absolutely. That he's normal, that he's not. That somebody slipped in, in the night, and traded out good Bo for his evil twin Beelzebub."

Jordan's brow knotted. "A blood panel's another coupla hundred bucks."

"Yeah, but it would confirm ulcers. Or drugs," Roger said. "Come to think of it, he coulda been shot up with something, speed, or uppers off the street. They use 'em in off-track match races. It can really crank 'em up. So it'd be good to rule these things out."

"I'll find the money," Lexy said, still clenching her crop in her hand. "I need to know."

"I'll cover it," Ben said, his gaze now trained on the remaining horses tackling the course. Jordan protested, but he waved her off. "Syndicate. I got a share in Bo. But don't get your hopes up, either one of you. His behavior's bad news. It'll take a miracle to sort him out in time to even be considered for the Short List next summer."

"He won at the Horse Park, and he's been going great," Lexy protested.

"We don't have to decide today," Ben said.

"Don't blame him. I messed up big time."

"Don't be too hard on yourself. You gave it a game go."

Roger cleared his throat. "Let's clean the wound, folks, and draw that blood."

"Yeah, y'all go on," Ben said, even as he grunted approval seeing Marina fly over the final obstacle in classic form. "I got more horses to track."

Lexy watched in astonishment as he gave Jordan a gentle hug and a quick parting kiss on her lips, in front of Roger and the rest of the world. Then Lexy heard Ben murmur something about grabbing a bite for supper later, adding, "You stand by your rider. She's going to be suicidal on the way home."

He was wrong about that, Lexy thought.

Leading Bo back to the stables with nothing ahead but everyone else's brilliant stadium rounds tomorrow, she felt suicidal now.

# Twenty-six

**B**ack in their hotel room to change for the competitors'
party, Lexy lay on her bed waiting for Jordan to finish
showering. Roger had cleaned Bo's cut, stitched it up, and
pumped him with antibiotics. She felt miserable, lost in vivid
memories of Bo's terror at the Sunken Road, the snapping
standard, the scrambling crowd, and the toddler's wrenching
sobs. So she jerked up when her cell vibrated against her side
and flipped it open, hoping it would be Hamp and they could
talk it over.

It was not.

> **Congratulations 2 U,**
> **Congratulations 2 U,**
> **Congratulations my dear Ms Imbriani,**
> **U saved me a shitload of wrk.**

She launched to her feet and paced from the narrow passage
between their double beds to the curtained window and to the
door to make sure it was locked. Fear and fury flooded her.
Who was low enough to taunt her after what had happened?
And why now, when it was obvious she'd blown any chance
for Bo's success in the near future and probably forever? No,
no, she admonished herself. Pick yourself up, get back on, and
sort Bo out when you get home.

Jordan emerged from the bathroom with a big towel wrapped around her body, apparently unaware of the raw red scars that train-tracked down the outside of her left thigh.

"Your turn," she said brightly, as if she knew too well the misery of a failed ride and wouldn't add recriminations.

But she hadn't known this misery with Bo, Lexy was fairly certain. Jordan had piloted him flawlessly. Taking care to bring her cell phone with her, Lexy escaped into the shower, but the pounding hot water couldn't stop the shudders that besieged her as every line echoed in her mind.

She was out of contention, so why pour acid on her wounds?

Half an hour later she passed through the competitors' party, force-feeding herself on bitter grapes and chunks of not particularly interesting American cheese. Parker had been eliminated on cross country, she'd heard, and wasn't there to goad or cheer her. Hamp was at the stables, icing his horses' legs, he'd said when she called, and getting organized for tomorrow. She'd offered to help, but he'd insisted she be here tonight, game face on, stiff upper lip.

She refused anything to drink, afraid her hands would shake around a glass of wine or can of beer, and everyone would see how devastated she was. Every stranger. American strangers, people she did not know, talking louder and faster as more and more of the happy competitors who'd made it round the course showed up and more alcohol was consumed. The eventing community's vaunted camaraderie. She couldn't be the only one here who'd messed up today, could she? She looked around, she didn't know. But her game face wasn't working, and she'd left her stiff upper lip in England. She couldn't meet Jordan's gaze, both her failure on course and the new message weighing on her.

Stacy and Brittany, two lower level Junior Riders she'd met across the aisle in the temporary stables, found her. They were best friends, skinny blonds in pony tails and unapologetically electric pink and purple tees, their colors. Fair Hill was their big fall event, each one showing her only horse at Training Level. They were enthusiastic members of Nobilo the mighty stallion's fan club Jordan had warned her of.

Before the weekend had gone to hell in a handbasket, Lexy had shown him to them and let them feed him gingersnaps. Secretly she was proud he'd dazzled them.

"That was an awesome emergency dismount," Stacy said, eyes shining with approval.

"You saw us at the Sunken Road?" Lexy asked.

"We were following you around the course," Brittany explained.

"Really? It was an act of sheer desperation."

"But the bravest thing I've ever seen," Stacy added.

"So..." Lexy began, dying to know what they'd seen "...what did I do wrong?"

"Wrong?" Brittany sounded incredulous. "You risked your life to save that baby."

"No, I mean what did I miss? How could I have gotten him through that combination?"

Stacy set down her can of Coke. "I can't imagine. He looked terrified."

"Exactly," said Brittany. "Hats off to you for jumping off and stopping him. Is he okay?"

"He cut his stifle, but the vet says he'll heal fine."

"Wish he'd finished," Stacy said. "We were going to run down to the second water and see him go through."

Lexy was stunned. She'd just put in the worst ride of her life, and these girls still worshipped her horse and took her for a hero.

So why didn't she feel like one?

She held onto pleasantness by a thread. She ought to accept their approval and admiration, but wished she could see her actions as they did.

Rachel and Ann, Hawks Nest boarders and part of the weekend's convoy for the last big event of the season, extended commiserations too. They'd completed the Preliminary course before nine a.m. and would be done with stadium by ten-thirty Sunday morning.

"What happened, honey?" Ann asked. Lexy told her, and the diminutive rider's thin, lined faced crinkled into horror.

Rachel, with her frankly fire-plug of a masculine body, jammed her fingers into her jeans' back pockets and rocked from heel to toe. "Heard it was a dog off leash yapping at his heels."

"No," Ann said. "I heard a tinfoil wrapper picked up by the breeze."

Lexy lifted her shoulders in a helpless shrug. "Whichever. He just seemed terrified by the change of footing at the sunken road, or maybe by the dip. Or the sight of it...or breaking the standard at the skinny."

Ann shook her head with gentle sympathy. "If only they could talk."

Lexy choked up.

*If only.* If only she could talk it over with her mother.

She excused herself, went into the bathroom, closed herself in a stall, and for the first time that weekend, cried, choking back sounds in case anyone came in.

# Twenty-seven

How's Bo this morning?" Jordan asked stiffly on Sunday at the stables. She and Colonel got out of her electric rental cart.

Bo's wound had been long, ragged, at its worst a good inch deep. Roger had promised he'd be good to go within a month. When the season would be over.

"Bored out of his skull," Lexy said, trying to downplay yesterday's disaster.

"And how are you, darlin'?" Colonel asked warmly. He'd skipped the last night's party, and the legendary eventing guru's absence had been noted.

"Bummed."

Colonel slapped the cart's roof. "Join us for stadium."

*You fall off, you get back on. And never let them see you cry.*

She took the seat facing backwards, and they zoomed off in the crisp October air, so fresh, so clear it ought to cheer her up. But no. She felt suicidal, as Ben had predicted, re-riding every stride of warm-up and the first eight fences in her mind, lost in a swampy bog of self-doubt and suspicion. Was it lameness? Abuse? An ulcer? Amphetamines? Or the fact she'd let Parker get under her skin?

Colonel and Jordan talked about who'd made it to the final round—Hamp, Marina, and a slew of other top pairs who'd benefited from Ben's coaching at the USEF's High Performance Training Sessions. Not her.

Parker hadn't qualified either, which might well intensify his efforts to undermine her riding. But she refused to live in fear. Enrico Imbriani had bullied and abused her, but horses were her safe place, eventing her respite. She was damned if she'd let Parker take that away from her.

"You got a favorite, darlin'?" Colonel prodded, obviously to reel her back to the conversation.

"My money's on Hamp and Ax," she said brightly, glad to put her obsessions behind her, if only for a moment.

"Dutton, O'Connor, Martin, Springer—" Jordan said. "You can never count them out."

"And a host of others. At any rate, darlin'," Colonel said to Lexy, "it's a good chance for you to study the competition."

"*If* we compete Bo again," Jordan cautioned. "Roger was adamant last night. Ben too. Bo's not reliable or safe."

"Let's see what the blood work tells us," Colonel said, "before you give up on him."

Jordan parked the cart, and they clambered up the temporary bleachers, wearing hats against the harsh sunshine, with only Lexy putting on sunscreen.

She wanted a mask instead. She watched the riders still competing with a sick gut feeling of her dream flushed down the loo. Worse case, and she would never know, she'd failed to protect her horse from Jordan's brother, Colonel's son.

*Tell them,* her conscience kicked in. But no, Colonel would clap Parker in the brig if he had an inkling of her suspicions. Or her, if she had no proof.

Parker walked over from watching Marina warm up and slid across the metal seat to her. "Buck up, kiddo," he said in brotherly sympathy, as if he hadn't spent weeks trying to charm her out of her breeches…and sabotage her confidence.

"Back atcha," Lexy said, braving her new American slang, wishing she could believe his apparent compassion for her now was real. "What happened to you chaps on course yesterday?" she asked, she hoped, with sisterly concern. She couldn't let him beat her at his game.

"Just your average garden-variety jack-ass rider brain fart."

She nudged him reprovingly, but couldn't help admiring him. Parker did down-and-out with bravado. "Seriously."

"Surely you know." He looked down his nose and launched into a spot-on imitation of Marina's socialite drawl and nervous fidget. "They've got this silly ol' rule where we have to take every jump in the order it is numbered, no turning back if your horse skips one."

Lexy faked a gasp. "Oh my word, you didn't."

"It's *so* much harder on us elite riders," he confided, his breathy tone exactly like Marina's. "We have *so* many horses and *so* many different courses to keep track of. It's not fair."

"Oh, and it's hard to get good help these days."

"Bingo," Parker said, sounding himself again—mimic, clown, charmer, all rolled into one hot package of a playboy.

But not to her. She believed he'd put Bo in Orsino's paddock, sent the messages, drugged Bo only yesterday.

In the ring, Alison Springer put in a clean round, which kept her at fifth, and Philip Dutton was up next, in fourth. Lexy watched him finish clear with his usual textbook precision.

"The Whiskey Queen is next, tied for the lead. *Go, Marina,*" Parker called out with tepid enthusiasm.

Marina took out a rail over the one give-away fence on course, dropping from first to fourth and bumping Dutton to second.

"Arrgh," Parker grunted. "She'll be fun on the ride home."

Lexy whipped her head around. "You came with her?"

"You think I'm a masochist? No-o-o. I mean, fun for poor Greta."

Marina's groom. His sympathetic tone sounded almost sincere. The next rider pulled two rails and dropped to sixth.

It was Hamp's to lose. He and Ax pounded around the course, nailing their victory. The top six came back for the awards ceremony and accepted their plaques, ribbons, and vigorous applause from the largest audience she'd seen in America. Then they took their victory gallop. Hamp charged around the ring wearing his winning rosette and sashes with sterling modesty, dropping the reins and pointing at Ax, giving him full credit. She whistled and applauded, smiling from the inside out for the first time in days.

Parker sat forward, elbows on knees, inscrutable. "So the good guy wins, and he's already got the girl."

"He is the good guy." You chump.

He made a motion of surrender, then said, "You guys really think Bo was drugged?"

She was so not going to ask where the king of barn scuttlebutt had gleaned that nugget. "Roger's looking at a spectrum of possibilities."

"I heard he thinks amphetamines. They'd rev 'im up."

Wary, she said, "He's testing for any number of things."

"Man, if I was trying to sabotage a horse—not saying I am—" He winked provocatively. "I'd come up with something more original."

Warier still, she prodded, "Like what?"

"Dang, I dunno. Ask ol' Hamp. Bet he's got something in his medicine bag of tricks."

Stars of outrage danced before her eyes, but she said only, "You just don't know how to stop, do you?"

"Not over fences, luv. Or with women."

All she wanted was to ditch Parker and go give Hamp the hug he so richly deserved. Pasting a smile on her face, she said, "Better luck to both of us next time."

He managed to look bereft. "Righto. See you around the farm."

She threaded her way through a small throng of well-wishers clustered around Hamp and Ax. It included Ben, Jordan, Colonel. She touched Hamp's left boot, still lodged in its stirrup in perfect equitation position, and he smiled down, a private smile she recognized from between the sheets. Her weekend was ruined, but she was proud of him and secretly proud to be the one he'd be coming home to. He dismounted and they walked Ax back to cool him off and put away the ribbons and trophy. Along the way, men and women called out congratulations, the women divided between wishing him well and looking like they wanted to jump his bones.

But they gave her time to think about Parker's take on Roger's guesses.

*Amphetamines,* he'd said, where Roger had said street drugs, speed.

Why would Parker say specifically *amphetamines* unless he'd gotten something legal from a pharmacy? This might be her best chance to catch him, to find a sales receipt from a drugstore or an invoice on the laptop he kept tuned to the Weather Channel for everyone to consult.

Reluctantly, she excused herself from helping Hamp. He had only one of Chip's sales prospects left to ride and didn't really need her. She could see Parker bowing and scraping to help the Whiskey Queen organize her last two horses to present them in Hamp's division. Colonel and Jordan were watching Marina, and their other students, leaving the row where the Hawks Nests horses were stabled unattended.

She hurried back, slipped into the tack stall, and logged onto Parker's computer account from home, having learned his password when ordering barn supplies.

She scrolled down his emails for the last week, her spurt of indignant energy fading as she saw banality after banality—a dinner date, a client problem, attachments of sales horses, some racy videos forwarded by women. Someone was pressing him to pay a debt, and he was fobbing them off. He and Marina texted each other day and night in a rapid fire of one-liners. Lexy could only imagine how many texts they sent.

But she turned up nothing here, and misery swamped her. She'd been riding one of the top four-star horses in eventing, hadn't made it halfway round a three-star course, and had nothing to show for it but a swamp of suspicions she didn't know how to follow up on. And now, with Bo out of competition, she'd never felt farther from her dream, or more in danger.

# Twenty-eight

Packing to go home late that afternoon was utter drudgery—the saddle she'd jumped out of, the bridle that hadn't controlled her horse, leg wraps that hadn't protected him. Evidence she hadn't found. After the awards Colonel had flown back with Chip and Roger. Jordan had stayed to go to dinner with one of Bo's syndicate members to "explain" Bo's meltdown, not, after all, with Ben.

A shadow crossed the aisle, and there Ben was, scrubbing his hand across his mouth. "Is there somewhere we can sit?"

"Sure. In here," Lexy said, taken aback. He couldn't have seen her logged onto Parker's computer, poking around where she had no business. She led Ben to the tack stall where big tack boxes sat, packed and ready to be loaded. She took one, and he another an arm's length away.

"You may not be aware of a coach's duties."

"I couldn't begin to guess." And she couldn't like his tone, intimate and grave.

"When officials make a determination of dangerous riding with an Advanced rider, I'm the messenger."

The horror of those moments flooded her. "I could have killed that baby."

"No." He lifted a hand. "You saved that baby. No one has a quarrel with how you handled an enormously tricky, scary situation. The footing, the barking dog, the broken standard—"

"Barking dog?"

"Yeah. We do our research. It was enough to spook a saint. But for dangerous riding, there has to be a pattern, same rider, same horse. You may have won at Five Points last month, but you won with your horse running away—literally, in the eyes of some who saw you. You did not have control."

"I thought I did, didn't you?"

He gave a judicious frown. "I didn't see your entire ride. And it's not my decision although it's made with due deliberation. I'm just the Notifying Agent. But without question, Bo was not under your control for the eight fences you took at Fair Hill before he charged into the crowd."

A thin sweat trickled down her sides. "So I'm suspended?"

"No. But we're putting you on the Watch List."

"Meaning...?" She'd pored over the rules, but they changed constantly and she was still confusing fine points of difference between the U.S. and British systems.

"Meaning, we need to have this official talk. Make sure you're aware there's a problem with your riding. Make sure you're making an effort to fix it. Eyes will be on you."

"Whose eyes?"

"For now, only the Reporting Agent, the committee and me. It's confidential."

"You're not telling Jordan?"

"I don't have to."

Lexy felt relieved, and then ashamed. "She's his owner."

"So you might want to tell her."

No. She absolutely did not. Being on the Watch List was a big black blot on the imagined trajectory of her career. And, on top of yesterday's cross-country debacle, a humongous failure. "What would you advise?"

Ben glanced at the calendar on the wall, crowded with dates of competitions past. "You riding any other horses?"

"Three at home, sales horses. Jordan mentioned competing them, but nothing's scheduled yet."

"Bide your time then. She's got enough on her plate right now. But if you go tearing past on any of them, even Training Level, I'll be on your case before she is."

"Well, thanks. I think."

He cupped her hand resting on the box, his iceberg blue eyes warm. "You're a terrific rider, Lexy. Nobody wants you to get hurt."

"Bo either." A pang of sympathy washed down her legs at the thought of Bo's nasty gash. Had Parker been responsible for that?

"That's the spirit. The good of the horse," Ben said, and got up. "Anything I can do before I go?"

She stood too. "Thanks, no."

He squeezed her hands and kissed her, right cheek, left cheek, very European, very kind. "See you on course in the spring then."

And he left, carrying her secret. She didn't have to tell Jordan, not today, and no need to trouble Colonel either. Should she tell Hamp? She trusted him, but no, she was too ashamed. Secrets carried burdens of their own, though, and this indictment of her riding felt like a tight band around her chest.

She jammed used towels into a laundry bag and heaved it into the trailer's dressing room, almost done and no one to turn to. But there was an upside to this downside. She fervently believed Parker had somehow engineered Bo's meltdown on course and sent that second message. Now was her chance to prove it, and her spirits lifted as she formed a plan.

# Twenty-nine

Back home Tuesday, Lexy stomped around her tiny apartment, strategizing. Roger could get a quick-and-dirty blood panel on Bo overnight, but one that tested everything would take a week. In that time, Parker could destroy any evidence, and she wasn't about to just stand by. Her one hope to nail his ass was to search his flat. Moments ago, he and Marina left, going out to dinner. Lexy had to act, and fast, before dark, when the gates at Parker's condo locked.

She pulled on jeans, shrugged on a denim jacket, then laced on her trainers so she could run if things went wrong. She strapped on her pre-paid too. She'd been to Parker's only once. Her little Neon purred to a start as if ready for an adventure. Steeling herself, she nosed out of the driveway, enough light in late October not to need the headlamps, and arrived at Foxcroft Villas a quarter hour later. Her bright red tin-can of an economy car stood out among the sleek and subtly colored luxury cars and SUVs that lined the curbs. She took the first narrow side street she saw, parked beneath a weeping evergreen, and got out, heart pounding and palms damp. It was cool. She skulked behind the row of condos, aromas of supper wafting from kitchen vents—grilled steaks, yeast bread, an overpowering curry. A man jogged by with whippets on leashes. "Evenin'," he said as he passed by. Everyone else seemed to be inside.

The façade of Parker's condo had dark gray shingles, she remembered. In back, she found the sliding door that opened to admit that cat. She pushed it wider and slid in, letting her eyes adjust to the shadows, taking in a scent of aftershave and something floral. Gardenia. Wasted no time finding his next prey, the bloody wanker. She went straight to the jumble of old computers, keyboards, abandoned monitors and wires that made up his office, excavated down to the bare bones of a desk, and opened its top drawer. She hadn't known what to expect, but it held generic office supplies heavy on the computer-geeky side—thumbdrives, AA batteries, labeled and unlabeled CDs, and a couple of mice, not the live kind.

Something batted at her calf, then claws stuck in her jeans. "Troll," she gasped. She'd left the sliding door open. She bent to pet him. He purred and pushed his head into her hand. Would a man who tamed a wild stray cat to be this sweet plot to hurt her horse, Orsino too? She opened the top side drawer and found embossed stationary, a half-empty liter of Jack Daniels, shot glasses, a pipe, an unopened pack of smelly French cigarettes, unfiltered—a man cave in a drawer. She pulled out the next one and found three prepaids on top, still in packaging.

*Works on people 2* caromed through her, so visceral, so real, her throat went dry. *Steady. Think.* Nobody needed three unused prepaids, but they proved nothing.

Troll butted her leg again. She scratched behind his ears and pulled out the bottom drawer. Receipts were crammed inside. Fingers jittery, she flipped through them, looking for anything to do with drugs.

*This was taking too long.*

She dumped the drawer's contents on the one clear patch of floor. Out tumbled little bags of white powder and dried "herbs."

Bloody hell.

A key snicked in the lock.

"Hey, dude, kitty kitty…" came from the front door.

Parker. Shit. She raked the drugs and receipts into the drawer, shoved it closed, and dove into the knee hole, folding her body into a tight ball. He hadn't had time to finish dinner. Had the Whiskey Queen cancelled? Or had they had a fight?

Troll bounded out to meet him, footfalls thumping on the carpet heavy as a dog's. Parker made surprisingly mushy snorts, obviously snuggling with his cat. Keys clanked onto a counter and a can's top popped open. Beer? Then another can, and Troll meowed, ordering supper *now*. The condo was so quiet she could hear him slurping his food, hear Parker chugging beer, hear her pulse throbbing in her ears.

How to get the hell out?

She couldn't. She'd have to scrunch here unseen. Parker had to go to bed.

A decade passed, or maybe half an hour, and her knees ached and thighs trembled. Doubting she'd last, she shifted, and her head bumped the underside of the desk.

Troll prowled in, meowing bossily.

"'S'up, bud—" Parker talked to cats? "—you got a hairball?"

A light flicked on, and Parker followed his cat in. She scrunched in deeper, her back against the kick plate, but the bloody cat padded straight to her.

Parker saw, and a crooked smile spread across his face.

"Sexy Lexy," he hummed, confident as Casanova. "Knew you'd come around."

She crawled forward, stood, unfolded cramped arms and aching legs. "This isn't what it looks like."

He snorted. "*Looks* like you changed your mind."

"Not a chance."

His hot gaze raked her as if to say *my turf, my terms*. "It's not like you're a virgin."

"That's none of your business."

"It's my business why you broke into my house."

"Didn't. Door was open."

He moved closer, crowding her. "Not how, luv. *Why?*"

Not backing down, she scraped for a reason. "I lost my mother's necklace and couldn't find it anywhere." She lifted it from beneath her tee. "Came to get it. Your place was my last chance."

He raised a brow in doubt. "You coulda asked."

"Panicked. It's sentimental."

"That's a crock of shit," he growled, his sudden shift giving her the barest warning. His hand clamped her jaw and tilted her face toward him.

His hand was soft.

"Tell me the truth, sweethahdt." Imitation Bogart.

Fear galloped through her, but truth had sometimes worked on Imbriani. "I'm trying to find the speed you gave Bo at Fair Hill."

He gave a disgusted growl. "You've gone over to the dark side."

"I thought that was your bailiwick."

"No, Colonel, Jordan, Gwen, even Ruth—it's always my fault. Now you." He pinched her face so hard it hurt. "I didn't give Bo fucking anything. I had no idea what happened till I heard Roger trying to impress my sister with how much he knows."

She faced Parker's bitter anger with a deliberate shrug. "Somebody gave him something."

"You don't know that yet, and you blame me. Fuckin' a—. You and the rest of them always fucking blame me. Just get the fuck off my case."

"Okay, all right." She backed away, hands up. *Play the trust card, then run.* "I got my necklace. Thanks for keeping it safe. I'm going home now." She crossed the cluttered office, headed for the door.

He blocked her with his body, a horseman's smell of day's-end sweat radiating off him, sharp, sour. "S'long as you're here, luv," he purred with a mean tone, "we got unfinished business."

He scooped her up with steel-strong arms and clamped her to him.

"No!" she yelled. "Put me down." But it was hard to fight his unyielding leanness with her arm pinned to his chest. He stomped down the hall then marched upstairs, grunting when she hit him but laughing diabolically. She'd been sure she had the strength to fight him off, but he shut down, impervious to reason, protest, pain.

Upstairs, he dumped her on his rumpled bed, shucked her jacket halfway down her arms, trapping her as Hamp trapped him when they'd fought in the barn. Then Parker pulled down his pants, commando underneath, and leaned his weight across her chest on his left forearm while he jerked at the waistband of her jeans.

She did not want to see his dick. She kicked up but kneed his rigid abs.

"Bitch," he grunted, grinning savagely, eyes flared, possessed. "Little lady's serious. So am I."

"Stop, Parker, stop," she yelled, gasping for breath. "I'll report you to Gwen, swear to God." She flailed and kicked and writhed, but he kept working at her waistband, his thick erection lodged against her pubic bone, his body grinding her into the duvet now fluffed up around her, smothering her. She felt the heavy-duty snap give way, felt him jerk her zipper in short savage yanks. Heard the brash rasp of the metal as it gave way. He shucked off her jeans with both hands, but she shrugged her jacket onto her shoulders, reached for his face, and clawed his cheek.

"Stupid *cunt*." He shoved her back down. "I'll show you rough."

"Parker, this isn't rough. It's rape." She struggled to get up.

He kept her pinned but practically purred, "Hang on, luv, you'll like it like this."

In hell. With a surge of rancid terror, she thrust her palms into his chest, dislodging him. She was shouting, *No, no, stop,* pummeling his head, his arms, his torso, anything to break his hold.

Shielding his face, he suddenly stopped and plunked himself on the bed's edge, the down-filled duvet puffing up around him. She couldn't fathom this quicksilver change, but she had a new horrific measure of how far he'd go. Jordan's brother, Colonel's son, rapist, madman. Blood trickled down his high sharp cheekbone to his sculpted jaw.

He rubbed his wound then studied the blood smeared on his fingers.

"Thought you'd like it rough, Imbriani, the way old Hamp fights. Y'all gotta do it rough." He sounded truly puzzled.

"Is this how you win women over? Using force?"

"I can do romantic," he said, that hang-dog look again. "Trust me just this once."

"Are you freaking *nuts?*"

"I'd be nuts not to want you, honest. Friends, okay?" His drawl had never sounded sexier, but his sour smell was acrid now. Then he had the balls to slip an arm around her waist and nestle his face in the crook of her neck. "Stay. Please. Stay."

She shot up. "Not on your life. I'm leaving. Now." She pulled her jeans up and jerked her jacket closed, feeling slimed.

He captured her again.

She braced to slam his nose into his brain.

"Don't go," he pled, but gentler, as if her terror was nothing more than a slight misunderstanding. Then in another dizzying shift, he added, "Otherwise, ya know, *I* can go to Gwen. I caught you cold, breaking and entering. Sex for silence, silence for sex."

She held up her fingers, his skin scrapings beneath her nails. Unlike the night she believed he'd mugged her, this time she had evidence—the broken zipper, a dark spot of precome that stained her jeans. His DNA.

"I've got you for assault and attempted rape."

He didn't deny it, but for a moment his clawed face went so steely cold and distant she feared he might kill her. Jordan's *brother*, murderer.

"I don't know what you're so uptight about," he said. "After that fiasco, Jordan's retiring Bo to stud."

Hot blood and icy shivers warred within her. His shifts were so bizarre. But she latched onto talk of Bo to focus him on anything but her.

"Who told you that?"

"I heard Jordan talking to Roger. Colonel was there. Ben. So it's over for you."

Parker might as well have thrown her body in the pond she'd feared the night he'd brought her here. She couldn't give up. "So leave me alone."

"Long as you stay quiet about tonight."

"Deal," she said, stepping away. But he snagged her hand and touched the scratches on his face.

"How'm I gonna explain these?"

Asshole. She should have gouged his eyes out. Colonel's son's eyes. She'd never felt so trapped, so cross-pressured, damned if she told because she'd broken in, damned if she didn't tell and left him free to attack her again. She shivered, desperate to get away, but afraid if she ran he'd flip and come after her again.

"Just don't say I did it, okay? I'm leaving now." She stood on trembling legs, forced one foot before the other, walking away, alive, holding her ruined jeans to her waist, insanity behind her.

"You got everything?" he called after her.

The necklace on its silver chain had withstood his assault. Then she heard heavy footsteps on the stairs. She dared not look back lest he mistake a glance for a change of heart. She grabbed her purse off his office floor. He caught up to her and escorted her to the door, solicitous as if they were longtime lovers who'd just enjoyed an evening of companionable sex, and he was letting her go home because she had to show up at work in the morning. She was leaving intact, physically unharmed, but inside she felt raped.

She'd risked all, proved nothing, but discovered Parker was more slippery, more volatile, crazier than her worst fears.

Outside, streetlamps softly lit the curbed lane and cut lawns. Parker's world looked safe. The moment she cleared the nearest cone of light, she fled. Her pathetic little economy car crouched like a goofy tropical frog under the prickly evergreen. She eased her shivering body in, jabbed the key at the ignition till it seated, and turned the engine on to mask great gulping sobs. She banged her fist against the steering wheel, trying to stop the tears, then remembered. Waking. Wanting water. Padding with her teddy across the atrium of the villa to her parent's forbidden bedroom. Seeing her father on top, hearing her mother pleading *Stop, Rico, stop,* in a broken, rasping voice, seeing them wrestle, his big bare bottom pumping up and down.

Oh God. How had she forgotten that terrifying night? Her father had raped her mother, God knew how many other nights. Had her mother confided in Pookie about his violence too? Lexy would never know, but knew her mother had moved to England to protect herself and her daughter from his rages.

Because no one would have believed their life with him. In public, he was well liked. In private, too, except when—it had been like flipping a switch from agreeable and charming to crazy, violent.

Like Parker. Was she the only one who saw?

Locking the doors of her little car, she hurtled down the tranquil streets, braked for the gate to open, to let her out, to leave him in.

Back at the dark, deserted barn, horses nickered at her, ever ready for a hay snack.

She turned the wash stall water on as hot as she could stand it, stripped to her shirt, and stood under the pelting spray, praying it would wash away the humiliation and his sour smell.

Finally her skin puckered. She mopped it dry with a barn towel. Memories flooded back, her father's voice, her mother's, and Parker's face, distorted with rage and lust, then shame, then bland and blank as if he'd done nothing.

Unable to bear the thought of putting those clothes back on, she went into Bo's stall door, wearing only that wet shirt. She flung her arms around his neck, sunk her face into his mute, stalwart strength, and wept.

# Part Four. Dangerous Riding

## *Late October–January*

Cross-country has always been the heart of three-day competitions. In the days of the Military Games, cross-country simulated the dangerous, daring rides across terrain a courier might traverse in battle conditions, transporting strategic messages from one division of the army to another, rain or shine, day or night, hell or high water. A great rock wall, a prickly hedge, a chicken coop, a fallen tree—all were obstacles to be cleared and put behind him.

If a courier were careless or unlucky, he might stumble upon an enemy encampment. An enemy soldier might pursue him or a sharp-shooter stop him in his tracks.

In modern competitive eventing, the enemy is the clock. To face that enemy requires the horse and rider's highest level of fitness and skill, and the steadiest of nerves.

*A History of the U. S. Army Olympic*
*Equestrian Team (1912–1948)*
By Colonel Jacob McRae, USA Maj. Ret.

# Thirty

No, I'm not free tomorrow night," Lexy said when Hamp called to bail on their date for dinner Tuesday night. She'd been eliminated at Fair Hill Saturday, put on the Watch List Sunday, and Parker had nearly raped her in his flat on Monday night. His assault had haunted her all day. She'd counted on Hamp's harmony to erase those images. Not that she'd risk telling him what happened. It would be hard enough to rise above the disaster at Fair Hill and tell him about the Watch List.

"I gotta help Marina," he explained.

"Help her what?" she asked, feeling threatened. Jealous.

"She dropped Jordan."

*Bitch.* She'd already dumped Colonel. "She'll turn on you too, the next time she's knocked down a few places."

He reminded her how difficult Marina's brilliant mare Tosca was. He didn't have to say how broke he was.

"Chestnut mare syndrome," she said, trying to give him slack.

"Right. But more, Jordan can't get on and school the horse. I'll probably spend more time in the saddle than coaching from the ground."

She couldn't be jealous of that, but hated Marina's hold on him. "I'm sure you'd do the same for me."

"Faster," he said. "Happier. How about later in the week?"

"Booked," she said on impulse, and instantly regretted it but couldn't bring herself to take it back. The thought of him with Marina—

"Okay." He sound puzzled, and rang off.

She curled on her bed, arms wrapped around her like last night, shaking with silent sobs. This wasn't about Marina. It was about Bo's meltdown, the Watch List, Parker's assault. And his saying Jordan was retiring Bo. She was gutted. If she lost the best two males to ever come along in her life—Hamp and Bo—she might as well go back to England, crawl under a mossy rock, and take up with the local trolls.

She couldn't. She plugged her cell into its charger, dressed in jeans and a plain yellow Oxford-cloth man's shirt, and headed for the house to confront her boss.

In the kitchen, Hawks Nest's inner sanctum, she found Jordan sitting at an old harvest table with Colonel. Judging from the food on their plates, they were almost finished. At the counter, Ruth was washing up.

"Is it true you're retiring Bo?" Lexy asked Jordan.

She exchanged a glance with Colonel and nodded gravely. "We're seriously considering it, depending on Roger's test results."

So it wasn't final. That bastard Parker had just been jerking her chain. "I have to believe Fair Hill was an aberration."

"We don't know that yet, darlin'." Colonel waved her to a chair. "Come, sit, eat," he added quietly. "Ruth, a plate for Lexy." Then he turned wise, tired eyes on her. "We can't have you getting killed on that horse. It would break our hearts."

"But Bo—" She almost blundered and said that Bo was her only horse, but said instead, "He's too young, too fit, too… amazing to put out to pasture."

"Here, honey. You need to keep your strength up." Ruth set down a plate of food she'd ladled from pots and skillets on the stove—home-fried chicken, mashed potatoes, beans and corn, and a tall sweating glass of iced tea. Lexy took a sip but stared at the beans and corn, not remotely hungry.

"No, not out to pasture," Jordan said, and Lexy couldn't help noticing Ruth at the sink, able to hear everything. "We'll stand him at stud."

"People will want to breed to him after what he did?" *After what I let happen.*

"Jordan picked up a coupla more bookings at Fair Hill," Colonel said.

Jordan broke off a big piece of a biscuit and sopped gravy off her plate. "His bloodlines are phenomenal."

"And he already has some exciting youngsters on the ground," Colonel said. "Several going great at Training level."

"Dana's gelding started Preliminary this fall."

"Does this mean I'll have to find another job?" Lexy asked, clamping down on doubt and dread. She'd only just begun here, and she couldn't leave Hamp.

Jordan shook her head. "You've been great with Bo, Fair Hill notwithstanding. He'll still need you for hand walking, riding under supervision."

"And we need somebody we trust to compete our sale horses." Colonel tore off a last golden chunk of fried drumstick with his bare teeth, chewed it with relish, then said, "They're not Bo, but they're a nice bunch. If you can stay—"

Lexy's thoughts exploded. She'd lost, she'd won, she had a job, a ride.

*Rides.* "You don't blame me for Fair Hill?"

"Darlin', we don't know what to blame, or who. You're at the bottom of our list."

"But at the Sunken Road, I—"

"You stayed with him," he said.

"And averted a disaster. We'd trust you with anybody." Jordan took her plate to the kitchen sink. "I put a call in to Roger today about that blood sample. It'll be next week before a full panel comes in, but in the meantime, Bo's on stall rest with that leg. Tomorrow I'll start you on his six-year-old brother."

"You mean Marcus?" The young stallion had immense potential, Lexy had heard, having swept Young Event Horse classes as a four- and five-year-old before Jordan's injury. "Who's been riding him?" Parker? Again the inner shudder.

"Tyrone. But he doesn't compete. You do."

"I can compete him?" she asked.

"We'd like to work him up to Preliminary next year with a view to his first Intermediate next fall. Think you can do that?"

"Well, yes."

"And the sales horses."

"For real?"

Colonel thumped the table with the handle of his knife. "Your skill and quick thinking prevented a disaster at Fair Hill."

"Thank you," Lexy said, gobsmacked. She hadn't thought about it that way. But what about Parker? Would he back off Bo, or take his quarrel with his family to Marcus?

"One change," Colonel interjected. "Until we get a handle on Bo's problems, I'm riding with you."

Was he mad? He was eighty-five. "On who?" Lexy asked.

"Curtis," Colonel said.

"He's U.S. Calvary retired from duty in D.C.," Jordan added, shockingly supportive of her father. "He did crowds, parades, the works. He's bombproof, so he'll help steady Bo."

"And we'll both be schooling you on Marcus and the sale horses," said Colonel. "Redford, Shamrock, and Gossip, that off-the-track-Thoroughbred rescue project, I think you remember."

"Super," she said which didn't begin to describe how fast her battered self-esteem shot up. Parker could just go fuck himself. She hacked off a slice of plump fried chicken breast, put it in her mouth, and chewed. Food tasted good again. "I'm thrilled."

# Thirty-one

It was not that easy. Overnight, she was frantically busy riding four horses a day and rehabbing Bo, but Hamp stopped calling.

She called him from the privacy of her little room upstairs.

"Yes?" he answered. "Oh. Lexy." He did not sound overjoyed.

"How's Ax?" she plunged in, determined to make a go of it.

"He's great, I'm great. Crazy busy. You?"

"Bo's healing fast, and I'm loving schooling Jordan's other horses. Marcus is a gem, and Gossip's surprisingly quick to learn." She was babbling. Thank God he couldn't see her chin tremble.

"Good—Excellent," he said, as if remembering how supportive he used to be.

"I miss you," she ventured what she'd called to say.

"Miss you too," he muttered.

"I'm sorry," she tried one last time.

"Me too. See you soon," he said, and they hung up. He didn't invite her to his hunt box, not even after her apology. She sunk into the thin mattress on her bed. It wasn't the same without him.

It wasn't the same with Parker either, who acted as if nothing had happened. She ricocheted from panic at the sight of him to outrage and revulsion.

How did he fake normal? Had he done it all his life?

Now, the American Halloween was at hand, and a dramatic, ghoulish afternoon it was, Lexy thought, with a hurricane attacking the coast of North Carolina over a hundred miles away. Inland, even as far as Southern Pines, rain sheeted down, the gusting winds driving it horizontal.

"Hurricanes never hit the Sandhills, and never the coast this late," Parker said, clicking off the Weather Channel in disgust. "They're just beefing up their ratings, and I'm running a Halloween charity event at the country club with Marina. Not cancelled yet." He drove off with her in his old Porsche, windshield wipers slapping at the torrential rain.

Here, the boarders had abandoned ship. Lexy worried about Hamp. Was he at Chip's? She didn't know. She was texting him when Jordan strode in, raingear head to toe. Seeing her, Eduardo juttered out something about *un huracán del monstruo*, his three little *niñas* and wife *aterrorizada*.

"You go on home," she told him. The groom sped off in his battered brown Chevy S10 pickup. "He lives in a trailer house," she explained to Lexy. "His wife barely speaks English. And his girls are one and three and four."

"We'll manage," Lexy said.

But how? Tyrone was at some funeral in South Carolina—his and Ruth's extended family. Lexy was the only able-bodied person left. Colonel charged up on his ATV, water streaming off his slicker.

"Let's get those horses in."

"Too rough for you out here," Jordan said.

"With Tyrone and Ruth out of town, I'm the best help you've got."

"Not in this madness, Daddy. We need you to set up feed."

"Bullroar. I'm army-tough, my whole life."

Jordan bit her lip. "Feed *and* hay. Somebody's got to do it."

"Please stay out of the weather, Colonel, for safety's sake," Lexy said, impressed by his resolve to save his horses.

"See, Daddy," Jordan said. "Two against one. You stay."

He stalked toward the stallion wing, muttering.

Jordan sighed. "Lexy, I'll get the boarders' and sales horses from the near paddocks. You get the broodmares and yearlings from the pastures."

Lexy threw on a slicker, slung half a dozen halters and lead lines over her shoulders and raced out into the rain. Twigs and limbs and God knew what flew through the air. An empty feed sack flapped past and a tarp took loft.

She trotted in with the first pair of mares, running as fast as she could. Their nursing foals cantered alongside on knobby knees, pinning their fuzzy ears against the rain. She made two trips, then managed the yearlings four at a time to give them the courage of each other's company. Nearing the barns, stainless-steel dog dishes clattered off the back porch and pinged down the flagstone steps. Rain sluiced down the roofs like waterfalls, overshooting burdened gutters.

Gasping for breath, she could see that Jordan had emptied the near paddocks of the boarders' horses. She was bringing the sales guys down the aisle. Lexy put Marcus and Gossip in their stalls while Jordan managed Redford and Shamrock. The smell of wet horse pervaded the barn.

"Where's Colonel?" Lexy asked.

Jordan panted for breath too. "I caught him trying to handle Bo and Marcus by himself. I told him he was a stubborn old coot to put himself in danger with no one here but you and me. What would we do if he got hurt? He left for the house in a first-class snit."

"At least he's okay," Lexy said.

Jordan helped fill water buckets and feed hay, then grain and supplements. "If you can finish closing, I'll check on Daddy and warm the supper Ruth left. Join us."

Jordan headed for the house. Lexy battened down the stall windows and rolled the heavy aisle doors closed in every wing to protect the horses from objects flying in the night. She was turning off the tack room lights when they flickered and went out.

She rifled blindly in the utility drawer for flashlights and emergency candles, cursing herself for not setting them out earlier. She should have remembered. Jordan had drilled boarders and staff for emergencies.

Just how bad was this?

She turned on the battery-powered radio, dialing from a country-and-western station to the weather. Contrary to Parker's skepticism, a late-season hurricane had made landfall at Cape Fear. High winds and heavy rains were swirling counterclockwise over Raleigh, a hundred miles farther inland than predicted, and were now sweeping south to Pittsboro, Sanford, Pinehurst, bearing down on Hawks Nest.

Leaning into ripping winds, she trailed her flashlight's beam to the barn generator outside and pressed the toggle switch to *on*. The motor fired, sputtered, died. She pressed again. Nothing. Had she been supposed to prime it? Not sure, she struggled across the yard leaning nearly forty-five degrees into a monster headwind, rain drenching her beneath her heavy yellow slicker, and burst into the lea side of the house. Wet strands of hair stuck to her face, and water streamed onto the threadbare Persian runner.

She slammed the door behind her and called into the darkened hall, "Jordan! Colonel! Jor—*dan!*"

"Coming," she yelled from the kitchen.

"Generator's dead," Lexy yelled back.

Outside, wind buffeted the house, whistling through the windows of the historic old structure. A huge tree crashed in the yard, ripping limbs off its neighbor, shaking the house when it hit the ground, and sending shivers of dread through her.

From the kitchen a flashlight lit the hall.

It was Jordan. "I was just calling Daddy to supper. *Daddy*," she shouted, "supper's ready."

Lexy met her at the kitchen door. "Surely he didn't go out."

"He's probably hiding out in the den, still pissed. Daddy!" she cried again. No answer. "Something's wrong." She sprinted for the den, forgetting her cane, her limp, the pain she must be in from running with the mares and foals. Lexy swept off her slicker, kicked off her boots and followed, wet feet slapping the wooden floor.

They found him in his recliner, his body tilted left, drool spilling from a corner of his mouth, and vomit on his shirt and the worn upholstered arm of his favorite chair. The fingers of his right hand scrabbled at his left arm, which lay limp at his side.

"Oh God, Daddy. Don't leave us," Jordan cried.

"He's not leaving," Lexy said, and hunkered down in front of him. "Look at me, Colonel. *Sir.*"

"I 'nt 'et up," he mumbled through slack lips.

"He can't get up," Jordan translated, her face pale.

"Colonel. Look at me, and smile," Lexy ordered.

His glazed eyes couldn't focus, but the right corner of his mouth crooked up. But not the left. Not good.

"Lift your arms, sir. Please."

The right arm rose, the left one didn't move.

"Stroke, like my grandfather's," Lexy whispered, her heart constricting as the memory buffeted her. "Call nine-one-one."

"In this storm?" Jordan snapped, but found her cell and punched in the numbers. "Oh no. Static. Try yours."

Lexy patted her jeans' pockets and pulled it out. Her call went through. A woman, speaking fast and sounding frazzled, asked her name, location, problem. Pushing back her fears, Lexy gave the information slowly, clearly. "Eighty-five year old male, vomited, can barely speak, can't move his left side. It's a stroke. I'm ninety-nine percent positive."

"You a nurse?"

"No. But my grandfather had one. Major McRae needs help now."

"Ma'am, I will put you on the list," the dispatcher said briskly. "But a Category Four hurricane has just reached Moore County. It's toppled trees and taken out power lines all over. Most two-lane roads are blocked. Can you get to U.S. One?"

"We can try."

Jordan's eyes begged to know what was going on.

Lexy put a finger over the mouthpiece. "Trees down, everywhere. They can't get to us."

"Our crews are working to keep the four-lane highways clear," the dispatcher went on. "Is the major awake, alert? If you'll hold on, somebody can talk you through this."

"I'll call you back. I only have one phone to round up help."

Lexy rang Hamp, didn't even get voice mail. Were the towers down? She sat holding Colonel's hand while Jordan hurried into the kitchen and returned with towels. His gaze was bleary, but one steely eyebrow knotted at the sight of her laboring over the mess he'd made.

"'El Ooth thorry," he mumbled as if he had a gag in his mouth.

*Sorry,* Lexy heard. Of course he would apologize. How mortifying for a man who always turned out at his regimental neatest.

"It's okay, Daddy. You just got sick. I'm cleaning up."

He grabbed her arm with his good hand, his chestnut eyes blackening with effort, and mumbled slower, punching each word with his indomitable will. *"'ell 'Ooth mm thorry, damn it. Verr thorry."*

"Ruth won't mind," Jordan said. "You had a little accident."

*"Te' huh,"* he said, so fiercely he must think he was dying. He sank into his chair, darting arrows at Jordan but looking so old and vulnerable Lexy wanted to go and comfort him.

She tried Hamp again, dead air. "Cell towers must be down. I'm going to Chip's."

"You're *what?*"

"We need a truck, men, chainsaws. Every minute counts with a stroke this bad."

"But you can't—"

"Trust me. I'm going to find Hamp and bring him back with any other able-bodied man or woman I can round up."

"How do you plan to get there if nobody can get here?"

"On Bo. He'll clear anything." She knelt in front of Colonel's chair and briefed him as if he had his mental faculties about him.

He shifted his good shoulder toward her and eked out, "Hemmt." He struggled for the next word, his lower lip flapping like a tired old horse's. "Vesh."

Lexy's eyes burned with tears, and she covered his old freckled hand with her tanned one.

"I won't forget my helmet, sir, and you betcha I'll wear my vest. Overgirth, chaps, the works. Gotta go."

Still bleary-eyed, Colonel gave a crooked smile, but Lexy's heart twisted to see the magnificent old gentleman—the legend—frail and shockingly shrunken, hewn down by a full-blown stroke.

Jordan chased her to the door, and Lexy pressed the cell in her hand. "Use this. Nine-one-one can tell you what to do."

Then Lexy flipped a switch, but the porch lights didn't come on. Of course. Son of a bitch. Trees down, lights out, Colonel possibly dying, the poor man alone in the night with no one but his crippled daughter. Jordan took the best care of her horses, but did she know what to do for an old man who'd had a stroke?

"Offer him water, get a blanket, keep him warm. I'll be back with help."

"Be careful," she ordered Lexy.

Lexy nodded, thinking instead, *Be fast.*

Out in the dark night, it was a battlefield, and the trees were losing. With the wind thrashing her back, she flew across the yard and slammed into the barn door. The wind pinned it fast. She tugged to no avail, then adrenalin kicked in and with a desperate surge, she found the strength to crack it open and squeeze inside. She dashed upstairs for her vest and helmet. Downstairs, hands icy from the wet and stress, she saddled Bo and lashed on her safety gear, wishing she could have guaranteed Jordan they'd be back soon. By the time she and Bo thundered down the trail to Chip's, the storm had... *passed?*

Could that be?

Yes. The winds died down. The rain subsided to a drizzle and then stopped. A half moon shone in a starlit sky. If the hurricane had moved inland, she must be in the eye of the storm. But how long before the lashing winds resumed?

She didn't know, and the desperation of her mission gripped her.

Ahead of her, wind had felled shallow-rooted pines, a danger to her and her horse, but Colonel's book and coaching, and her experience, had prepared her for it. Without hesitating, she put her big fit stallion to the test like a military courier of old, facing a life-or-death mission that competitions only mimicked—huge solid obstacles she'd never seen, not certified by the USEA Technical Delegate as meeting safety standards.

Did she have the nerve? The guts?

A light, restless breeze picked up. Thank God, no river lay between them, no crucial bridge the storm could have washed out. The inches-deep stream they normally splashed through raged high as Bo's broad chest. He plunged into the water, snorting through with a primal will to conquer it that awed her. On a clear day, without the fallen trees, a good gallop at cross-country speed would have gotten them to Chip's in six, seven minutes.

It might take a quarter hour now—if they got through at all.

Lexy felt the press of every second and urged Bo on as fast as she dared, but a jumble of logs made her pull up. Pines spilled across the trail like an angry giant had flung down pick-up sticks, too many to clear in a single leap, but none so high Bo couldn't step over them. He torqued his head and studied the strangest obstacle his puzzling humans had ever put him to.

She didn't push. He was smart, thinking his way through.

Then as if it were old hat to him, he high-stepped over the splintered trees, then came to a dead halt before a giant old pine too massive to step over, no space behind to get a running start.

She patted his neck with a believing hand and legged him. He leapt it from a standstill and cantered on.

"Good man," she said, kneading his lathered neck. A clear stretch lay before them, and she urged him back to speed. The sandy soil had soaked up the afternoon's torrential rains, and they galloped down the thickly needled path. Nearing Chip's, she heard the grinding whine of a big electric generator, maybe two, ravaging the unnatural calm of the storm's eye. Bo snorted but only, it seemed, to warn her of new danger, the Bo she'd recovered and believed in.

"You're fine, my friend," she murmured, and squeezed his side lightly with her calf. Boldly, he galloped toward the light glowing in the distance, no trace of the spooky, squirrelly horse she'd ridden at Fair Hill.

Chip's farm had every luxury, and he kept his generators in proper working order. In the yard under battery-powered service lights lay a yearling with someone sitting on his head. She made out the forms of three other men working on it. Trotting closer, she could identify the emergency team—Chip, Roger, Ben and Hamp.

Hamp ran to her and grabbed Bo's bridle, clothes clinging to his whipcord leanness, sopping wet and smeared with dirt and blood.

"Are you fricking insane coming out in this?" They'd barely spoken in two weeks, and she didn't like his tone.

Bo slowed to a walk and she slipped off, pulse pumping. "What's with the colt?"

"Filly," he bit off. "Tree landed on her, she tore up her legs struggling to get free. Roger's about stopped the bleeding."

But Hamp didn't take his eyes off her, and then Ben Holt was at their side, arms crossed, his blue eyes searching hers, perplexed and challenging.

"Wild night for a joy ride, Lexy."

"Colonel had a stroke. Land lines and cells are dead, and secondary roads are blocked. It's up to us to get him to the hospital."

"Jesus," Ben said. "And Jordan?"

"She's with him, alone." Lexy wiped her face, hiding her emotion.

"I'll fix that." Ben pivoted on his heel. "Roger, you finished? We need that Hummer."

Roger looked up, baffled, his gloved hands and official tan coveralls red with gore. "I need my stuff."

"Your friend Colonel's had a stroke. We need a truck with a big-ass winch, plus a crew to clear the roads." Ben turned to his former boss. "Chip, round up a couple of chain saws, and the rubber trailer chocks—anything wood or rubber we can use for insulation to get past downed power lines."

"My truck drives over live wires," Roger snapped without looking up, and stitched up the last of the filly's wounds.

Chip passed the order on to Hamp, who clamped a hand on Lexy's shoulder, and muttered, "Don't go, I'll be back," and ran for an outside storage shed.

Roger tied off the last suture, dressed and wrapped the wounds, stripped off his bloody gloves, and stood. "OK. Done," he said to Ben, then rallied a couple of Chip's staff. "When she starts waking up, sit on her head until she's alert enough to get up safely." Then he turned to Lexy, all earnest concern and medical frankness, "Colonel conscious?"

"Yes, trying to talk," she answered briskly. "It affected his left side."

He threw equipment into his medical kit. Hamp emerged from the utility shed with two big Stihl chainsaws, dumped them in the Hummer, and ducked into the barns. He came back with ropes, chains, and another couple of Chip's staff, a short plump guy and wiry gal. They piled into the Hummer, but Ben strode over to Lexy still waiting there with Bo.

"Put him up here and come with us."

"I'm going back the way I came. I'll get there faster."

"We've got one huge problem on our hands. We don't need another."

"Bo was steady as a rock. Steadier." She vaulted on and galloped off.

She got home fast, put Bo up, and half an hour later, met the rescuers at the door—Roger, Ben, Hamp and Chip's employees. The rain had started again.

"In the den." She pointed the way.

"Vital signs?" Roger asked. Vet kit in hand, he pushed ahead of everyone to see his friend, looking genuinely worried, Ben close behind.

"His pulse is racing," Lexy called after them. "And his breathing's shallow, just like when I left."

He belonged to them now, and she could do nothing more. She found Hamp waiting for her on the dark porch.

"You got through okay. How's Bo?"

"Another double clear. He's fine. I put him up."

"Crazy woman," Hamp muttered and clutched her to his chest with an intensity that stunned her.

"Crazy for you," she whispered back, throwing her heart into the fire.

# Thirty-two

Ben and Roger carried Colonel out, Jordan lighting their way with a giant torch. It made ghastly shadows of them tucking his floppy body in the passenger seat and strapping him in. Ben and Jordan crammed in back with Chip's two grooms, and Roger gunned his make-shift ambulance down the drive under the avenue of oaks still standing.

"God, I hope they make to the hospital," Lexy said to Hamp. She watched the Hummer's lights disappear and turned on her emergency lantern. Pine cones, broken limbs, and ripped-off twigs were strewn across the yard, more falling with each new blast of wind. "And thank God, you're here," she added to him. She was running on adrenaline and had much to do. "I have to check everybody, make sure no one's hurt, and do night hay, and—"

"In a minute." Hamp's fingers gently pressed her lips, shushing her. "I need to know you're okay."

His kiss was urgent, deep and searching, sending spirals of desire into her. It went on and on, his arousal pushing against her, his arms enfolding her, his hands roaming her back, his tongue tracing her lips, touching her teeth, probing her mouth as if to make sure all of her had come through safe. Then he pulled away enough to speak.

"God damn it to hell, Lexy, the next time you take it in your head to pull a dumb-ass stunt like that, call me instead, okay? You scared the bejeezus out of me, showing up in the middle of the storm, then taking off again. What were you thinking? Trying to be a hero? I wouldn't be impressed one whit if you ended up puffing on a straw to push your wheelchair across a room for the rest of your life. Or dead."

After weeks of doubt and distance, she let him berate her, basking in every angry, loving word. "I did call you," she said rationally. "No cell."

With a grunt, he stepped away, spun around, came back and glared at her. "Well, calling didn't fricking work, did it? So you show up at Chip's, then tear off back here alone. What if the storm had started up again? Lightning again? The winds. A tree fall on you like that filly."

"Bo kept us safe," she said. "I never doubted him."

"Don't pull that crap on me." Hamp snapped, putting up a warning hand. "You saddle the one bona fide whack job of a horse in Colonel McRae's stable and entrust your life to him on the most dangerous night in our goddamn universe."

"Hamp, I'm safe," she said, cupping his jaw in her hands to calm him down. "Bo got me there and back. And Colonel's on his way to the hospital."

"You could not have known that this would work."

"You don't know, do you?"

"Know what?"

"How great Bo's been doing lately."

"I know how great you've been *telling* me he's been doing."

Which was the problem and the point. In a flash, her anger ratcheted up to the level of his. "You'd know if you weren't always at Chip's hiding behind a string of horses and sucking up to Marina and ignoring me."

Under the lantern's light, his green eyes shut down and she couldn't imagine what he was thinking.

"I'm not ignoring you."

"Then what the bloody hell would you call the silent treatment?"

"I'm staying away from you."

His flat assertion stabbed her like a knife.

"Why?" she croaked.

Marina, she thought. She had her talons in him deep.

Hamp shook his head. "This isn't working, you and me."

Lexy's stomach plummeted. "What did I do?"

Hamp took her hand in his and led her to the swing, a genuine old-fashioned white wooden porch swing with carved slats for the back. The wind had twisted the chains that fastened it to the ceiling, and he straightened them. He sat, and she sat beside him, her pulse pounding.

"It's not what you did. It's what you do to me."

"Sorry I scared you, showing up on Bo tonight."

He torqued his head as Bo did before new obstacles, then gave a crooked grin a horse could not. "Not that. I want us to be together."

She swallowed hard. "Pardon me?"

"My place."

"There's nothing I want more but…"

"But what?"

"I'm needed here."

"What if I need you?"

She looked into his steady open gaze, astonished. "You?" she croaked. "You're the strongest, most independent person I know."

"So…?"

"I'm flattered. Pleased. Thrilled."

"Is that a no?"

"I have a commitment."

"Jordan's retiring Bo. You won't be competing him. He doesn't need you like before."

"Maybe, maybe not. And what if it's not over—the messages, the pranks?"

"Even if you're one hundred percent right about Parker, he has no motive to continue."

"He could expect the ride on Marcus?"

"Marcus isn't going Preliminary. Parker's about glamour. He wants a four-star ride."

A mighty gust set the swing bobbing on its chains.

The hurricane winds were back.

"This isn't about Parker," Hamp said. "He'll do what he's gonna do no matter where you live."

"And I should be here to prevent the damage."

"Which still doesn't answer my question." Hamp had to raise his voice over the rising roar. "I don't like playing games. It messes with my harmony. So tell me."

She laced her fingers into his hand, and he didn't pull away. "I want to live with you more than anything, but I can't, not the way things are."

He scowled at her. "Is this about Marina? Because I do not *like* the woman, but I feel sorry for her. I can make her a better rider. But I do not enjoy time spent in her company."

"I guess I know that, but she's playing for you."

"Or for Parker, or any other upper level rider of the heterosexual persuasion."

"Until Mr. Moneybags comes along to meet her on her level," Lexy added, seeing that for the first time.

"Exactly. And for the record, I know Nikki's in love with me. It's an occupational hazard. I'm not even flattered. It gets in the way."

She hated feeling she'd pushed him into a corner, but was pleased with what he'd said. "I want us to be lovers, nobody on the side."

"No jealousy, no—Shit, no teenage crap. I'm thirty years old. Most of my business is women. Middle-aged women and boy-crazy girls. My fantasy is you."

Lexy let out an involuntary *Oh* of astonishment and felt her blood pool in her belly with a throb of sweet desire.

"You kept that a secret," she said lightly, not sure he could even hear her.

"No," he said firmly. He twisted her chin toward him so she had to look into his eyes. "No teasing on this subject, not tonight. If you don't feel it, tell me and I'll go."

"I feel it," she said, also feeling stripped bare and vulnerable.

"Good." His tone lightened, but the wind rose and the rain came at them sideways. "Tell me about it. When you knew."

It was almost humiliating, like the teenage crap he said he didn't want. But this was her chance to tell the truth. "At Pau, in France, four years ago. When we met. When I was nineteen."

"Yeah?" His bowed mouth curved into a sexy grin. "Before we kissed, or after?"

Ohmigod. She wanted to cover her face. "Before. You were in Ax's stall, sitting on him bareback, backwards, massaging his hindquarters. You said you didn't want him to think it was all work every time you got on his back. I thought it was sweet."

"Hah! I knew it," he shouted, smiling under the porch's light, his bronzed face wet with rain. "You liked me. Grandpop told me I didn't make this up."

Embarrassment, squared. "You told your grandfather about me?"

He lifted a shoulder. "Wouldn't you? No, scratch that. Of course you wouldn't. Trust me, you'll love him. He loves you already."

Which led to another kiss, a deeper kiss, a mad dash to her quarters in the drenching rain, to her clean but narrow bed, where she could put the past behind her. Parker behind her. She lit the last candle she had left from England, and its sweetly floral scent, so un-American, filled the room.

They stretched out side by side, and he said, "You with me now?"

"Yes, but I can't move in with you."

He shot her a sideways glance. "You holding out for marriage? Because if you are—"

She covered his mouth with her hand. She didn't want to hear what he might say. "I'm not saying, 'No, never.' But I signed on with Jordan, and she'll need me after the storm, with Colonel in God knows what kind of shape, and the farm in turmoil..."

He lay back on the pillow, hands behind his head. "Damn. Sexy, and responsible. You're not making this easy."

She grinned, with the wind and rain swirling overhead. She needed to check for injuries, put out night hay, and refill water buckets, and Hamp would help but first... The only thing that disturbed their lovemaking was the storm—land lines were down, cell phone towers had toppled, and there would be no word of Colonel's condition until who knew when.

Afterwards, armed with flashlights, they went from stall to stall. Apart from nerves and a few bumps and scrapes, every single mare, foal, colt, filly, and gelding was okay, the boarders' horses too. In the stallion barn, Bo, Marcus, the sales horses, and Parker's geldings were nervous but unharmed.

But back upstairs, crowded with Hamp in her narrow bed, Lexy slept fitfully.

Wind rattled tin roofs overhead and roared through cracks around the barn's doors and windows. Then a prolonged gust would come howling through, and she'd hear another tree creak and crash to the ground.

After a spate of crashes, Hamp pulled her into his arms. By daybreak, the storm had passed. They got up, shoved into their damp, dirty clothes, and Hamp took her hand as they walked outside to survey the damage.

Two massive oaks had toppled, but into the yard, not across the driveway. Hurricane force winds had wrenched great limbs off other big old trees. Twisted patio chairs, upturned buckets, dog pans, and trash littered the yard and pastures. A rusted hood from a neighbor's vehicle stood upright like a sculpture, driven into the loamy soil in Ruth's garden.

"Jesus." Hamp shaded his eyes from the cheerful sun.

Except for the wreckage, it was a perfect day, the air washed clean. Birds chirped joyfully. Bright yellow butterflies Lexy had never noticed fluttered about. Spider webs spanned trees still standing, intact despite the wind.

But the generator was still dead. "Wouldn't start last night," she complained.

"Here, let me." Hamp kicked it, jiggled a toggle switch, and it clicked on, its grinding whine powering the lights and well pump. He helped her dole out morning feed and supplements and water. Then they found a chainsaw and a bucket of tools, piled them on the back of Colonel's ATV, and zoomed around the farm. Fences had been kept clear of trees, but here and there a limb had tumbled across a field and blown onto one. In the woods, downed trees lay across the trails, many more than she and Bo had encountered on their harrowing ride.

Chainsaw droning, Hamp cut the trunks to fit the fireplace, and Lexy dragged them to the sides of the trails, working in harmony. She couldn't repress a heart-tugging wish that this was their farm, that they were a team like the O'Connors or the Fredericks, but starting out, working toward a common goal, training and competing. She quashed that girly fantasy as if it were a nasty fly feasting on a horse's life-blood. Once they'd moved the horses to their pastures, he went back to the Center, saying Chip was short-handed too, and Lexy had to let him go.

His job was there. And hers was here.

After noon, Roger pulled up in his Hummer, sweaty and disheveled in last night's coveralls. He, Ben, and Chip's guy and gal had been stuck in the hospital cafeteria till morning, he explained. Coming back, they'd chain sawed through dozens of more trees downed by the second wave of hurricane-force winds.

"Where were the road crews?" Lexy asked.

"Working like the rest of us," Ben said. "Anybody who owns a chainsaw is out clearing roads, but it's not enough."

Tyrone drove in with Ruth, swearing when he surveyed the devastation. "We couldn't get through last night. Stuck in a effing Wal-Mart parking lot in Charlotte."

"You missed the worst," Lexy said, and told them about Colonel.

Tyrone's face twisted, but Ruth collapsed against her son.

"Don't worry, Miz Gantt," Roger said. "He's stable, grumpy, but responding to the drugs." Then he gave details of Colonel's paralysis, delivering grim medical news in a practiced, reassuring tone.

Ruth wrung her strong, thin hands.

Ben took them in his. "The doctors aren't sure how long he'll be there, Miss Ruth. But he's out of danger and lobbying to come home."

"He can't be ready," Lexy put in.

Ben shrugged. "The doctors don't have a prognosis. But Jordan won't leave his side."

"Can he have visitors?" Ruth asked.

"Family, I'm sure," Ben said.

"I can take you, Ruth," Lexy said gently. "I'd like to see him if they'll let me in."

"Y'all go on into town," Roger said. "My calls are backing up, and I gotta take Chip's folks back. You coming, Ben?"

"Yeah, I gotta check my place. Unless you need me, Lexy?"

She gestured at the chaos all around them. "This? Piece of cake."

He laughed and hopped in Roger's Hummer. They sped off, taking Chip's staff.

Tyrone ushered Ruth inside, their carry-on bags over his broad shoulders.

Alone at last, the horses safe, Lexy retreated to her shower, everything upturned by what she'd done and what she'd seen. Bo had been the hero of the night, redeeming himself for the Fair Hill disaster. Had it been her fault, her *nerves*, worrying about those stupid messages? Or had Parker drugged him?

# Thirty-three

Hospitals were all the same, Lexy thought a couple of weeks later, whether in England, Italy or America. Whether the patient was her nonno or her hero, Colonel.

She crept into his room. He was staring out his window onto a landscaped pond. Ducks bobbed on the water, and weeping willows draped their limbs along its sides.

"Top of the morning, sir," she said cheerfully.

"What fuckin' mornin'?" he growled.

Whoa. This was a big change. "Saturday, sir, two weeks after your stroke. You had any company?"

He frowned, as if trying to remember. "Gwen and the girls, I think. Her boys were at some thissy thoccer practice."

He'd feel better if she talked back. "It's not sissy in Europe. Where's Jordan?"

"I tol' her I wass fine. Get outta my hair."

"Anybody else come by?"

Another scowl. "Parker did a duty visit, cracked a joke, 'n left."

"Sounds like him," she said neutrally, relieved she'd missed him.

"Thank God, it was only family. I'd rather die than thudents thee me like this."

"You're not going to die, but you gave us a good scare."

He jerked at his hospital gown with his good hand. "I can' thave yet, and I can' find a nurth at this prison tha' gifs a shit."

Nonno's complaint exactly. "I wield a mean razor, if you'd like."

"Fuck that. This sucks. My jailors won't let me take a pith without a goddamn catheter."

Fuck that indeed, she thought. He was bored out of his skull. So she pulled a chair to his bed and said, "Tell me about your cross-country ride in 'forty-eight."

"You're jus' tryin' to make me pra-tiss talkin'," he grumbled.

"I am indeed," she said, giving him her most posh, stuffy accent.

"Therapiss wore me out," he complained.

"Thera-*pist*," she corrected. "Say *therapist*. I hear she wants you to work on your *t's.*"

"Thera-*pissed*," he said deliberately.

"Olympics," she shot back.

"You'r's ba' as Yord'n. Okay, 'lympics. We had clear roun's. Double clear. Frank Henry and Thwing Low won In-dividle Thilver. Team won gold. End of story. Power back on home?"

"Yes, a few days ago. Jordan didn't tell you?"

He looked aside, jaw clenched. He must not remember. Lexy could only hope some memory would come back, but she knew better than to offer empty promises. She leaned forward, giving him no quarter. "Tell me about your round. Every obstacle."

He snorted and scrunched his face. "Ancient history."

"That's what I want. It was the Army's last Olympic competition before everybody went civilian. Right?" She touched his left shoulder, to urge him on.

"Thartin' to feel thuff there," he muttered, but began his story, taking her from the hospital's green walls and slatted blinds to describe Tweseldown Racecourse outside London on a cool, rare sparkling August day, to roads and tracks, the steeplechase, and then the daunting course.

He struggled to piece so many sentences together, but she was rapt.

He'd been the junior officer, and after months of drill, it had been his first chance to compete at the highest level. The natural wooden obstacles had been heart-stoppingly enormous, no gaudy decorations like those today, or frangible pins so obstacles could break away. The ride had been all thrills and chills.

By the time he finished, Ruth had arrived, driven into town by an obsessively attentive Jordan. Together, the two women had sneaked in a whopping serving of Ruth's best chicken casserole and an oversized wedge of her blackberry pie.

"Picked last summer from bushes along Hawks Creek," Ruth said.

"Wanna go 'ome," Colonel said.

"My, my," said Ruth, constitutionally unable not to fluff his pillow. "If grumpiness is any measure, we are getting better by the day."

"Goddamn drugs."

"They saved your life, Daddy," Jordan said with admirable sickbed patience.

Colonel skipped over her for Ruth. "I'm lobbying my jailors for Early Release."

"Now Daddy..."

"Now Yord'n," he drawled back. "They're not doing a goddamn thing here we can't do at home. With better food, comp'ny, view."

"The view's not better yet. We lost a lot of pines along the creek, some oaks and cedars in the yard. It's amazing Lexy got through."

He pushed up on an elbow, wincing when the IV shunt pinched him. "Got through what?"

"Got through to Chip's, to get help for you, in the middle of the storm."

He'd been wolfing the chicken casserole, using his good hand, but he put down his fork and glared at Lexy. "You di'nt mention this."

"Did too."

"Humph. Mention it again."

She gave a tree-by-tree account of her night ride, including Bo's bold swim across the risen creek. Then she described how he'd studied the pile of pines before stepping through them.

Colonel pushed away his tray and sat up. "Tha's our old Bo, Yord'n."

"Yep," she said. "Reading the course, studying the jumps."

"I could practically hear him thinking," Lexy put in, reliving Bo's amazing performance that scary night.

"Fair Hill never made sense to me," Jordan said. "He never blew up like that."

Colonel agreed. "Not for no reason."

"That night," Lexy said, "maybe he knew you were in trouble."

Ruth put a piece of pie in front of Colonel and pressed a fork into his good hand. "Maybe Bo just likes the dark."

"Tha's it!" Colonel said, as if the fog had cleared from his befuddled brain.

"That's what?" Jordan asked.

All heads bobbed around to look at him.

"The dark. Bo wath never inconthithtent," Colonel said, still struggling with words.

"Until now," said Jordan.

Lexy banged the heel of her hand against her forehead, memories flashing back like lightning. "But now he's inconsistent when the sun is out, like the day he arrived, the day he had the meltdown, and any day he's been difficult to school."

"How did we miss that? Sheesh."

"We're idiots," Colonel said.

"It must be his vision," Lexy said.

"We work him on sunny days," Jordan said.

"Mostly in the mornings when the light's low." Lexy drummed her fingers on the metal railing of Colonel's bed. "At first because of the heat, then because he was scheduled early."

Colonel looked at his daughter. "Yord'n?"

A line between her eyebrows was becoming a permanent scowl. "Roger did a thorough work-up after Fair Hill. Said his eyes were fine." Her scowl deepened. "This warrants a second opinion."

Colonel bridled. "Roger's my friend. He knows what he's doing."

"I'm taking Bo to the vet school's ophthalmologists."

"Won't you need a referral?" Lexy asked.

"Roger will refer you," Colonel said. "But if he said his eyes were fine, the vet school won't find anything either."

"We don't know what they might find, Daddy."

"It's worth a try, sir," Lexy said, hope rising. "Bo was a different horse that night, bold and sure of himself. Like when he won Five Points at the Horse Park on a cloudy day, except that night the obstacles were a hell of a lot harder."

Colonel stuffed the last big bite of pie in his mouth and finished it with relish. "Tha's one vet exam I'd hate to miss. 'Nother reason for y'all to thpring me from this joint."

Jordan sighed. "Daddy, you can barely walk."

"I'm workin' on it." He lifted his left arm as far as it would go, pushed the table away, then drew up his left leg until his knee was bent and his foot flat on the bed. "Get me tha' damn walker."

Jordan's jaw dropped. "They tell me you'll walk again, but don't rush it."

"Rushing it would be hiking the Appalachian Trail. Get me the goddamn walker."

Ruth rolled it over, and Lexy held the gait belt around his waist to steady him as he struggled out of bed. But he took the handles on his walker as if it was his beloved ATV, filled his lungs with air, and hobbled across the room. Lexy pushed the stainless steel IV pole behind him, worrying.

His left leg dragged but he could pick it up and put it down, as his therapist had assured them. Could he turn around?

He could.

Left foot, right foot, balance head and heart and soul. He executed a one-eighty and turned back to bed, looking exhausted from the effort but exhilarated. Ruth and Jordan looked astonished and relieved. Lexy exhaled.

"So go ahead and make that vet thchool 'pointment, darlin's," he told them, grinning. "Give an old coot thomething to look forward to."

# Thirty-four

Lexy perched on the flat back seat of Jordan's truck, bracing as her boss braked the three-ton rig down to fifteen miles an hour. The exit ramp nearest the vet school was a diabolically short tight turn, and Bo would fight the pressure. He'd been wiggy in the sunlit morning, but with patience and gingersnaps, she'd enticed him onto the trailer.

Colonel's doctors had reluctantly released him to make the trip. He sat in the captain's chair beside Jordan, grimly clutching the shoulder strap of his seat belt. Ruth had come to manage him and rode in back with Lexy. He'd grumpily agreed to use his walker but refused the gait belt.

*Insulting,* he'd said. *I'll be fine.*

At least, Tyrone had fixed the on-board camera. Lexy could see Bo in his narrow stall anxiously snatching the odd bite of timothy-alfalfa mix from his hay rack. So far so good, no thanks to Roger who still swore nothing was wrong with Bo and tried to talk Jordan out of spending money on a fix that wouldn't work. But Lexy had insisted something was wrong, and Roger had grudgingly referred them to the vet school. Now Lexy was steering clear of Jordan's offended vet, but her first loyalty was to Bo.

Jordan wheeled the rig in at the brick sign—North Carolina State University College of Veterinary Medicine. Bo's career was on the line, Lexy's too, and nervous anticipation zinged through her. To say nothing of her hope of recovering the brilliant athlete who'd chewed up tough cross-country courses under Jordan like a champion. To the right, sheep and cattle dotted acres of rolling pastures at the edge of Raleigh. On the left, smaller paddocks held horses and a pair of llamas.

They passed all that and stopped at the entrance to the large-animal hospital. A morning sun now blaring glinted off an industrial-strength, woven-wire metal gate. It opened automatically. Jordan threaded the big rig onto the asphalt receiving area past half a dozen others—economy stock trailers with open-slatted sides for cows and pigs, and a luxury rig bigger than theirs.

Lexy had barely stepped out of the truck when a couple of vet students in short white lab coats crowded in on them with questions. Jordan gave her name and Bo's appointment time, and handed them the required copy of the Coggins test signifying he was clear of a fatal infectious disease. Then she started signing papers—releases, ownership, referring vet. Who, at that instant, drove through the automatic gate.

"What's Roger doing here?" Jordan asked Colonel.

"I told him he had a closed mind and dared him to come learn something."

"I'm tense enough, Daddy. He's the last person I want nosing in on this."

"Friend's a friend, darlin'. He did give you the referral."

Behind them, Ruth had Colonel's walker ready and helped him from the truck. He met his friend and scolded him for leaving the dogs behind.

Lexy opened the rear trailer doors, hoping she could handle Bo alone. He scrambled out, hooves thudding on the mats and the asphalt, then trumpeted to unseen mares, sides heaving like bellows. Lexy led him to a patch of tempting grass, but he was on patrol, too absorbed in new smells and strange activity to lower his head and take a nibble.

"You're here about the eye problem," the taller student said, her gaze assessing Bo's behavior. "I'll go get Dr. Klinepeter."

The shorter student grilled Jordan about Bo's history and then asked Lexy how his symptoms manifested.

"He spooks at shadows in bright sunshine," Lexy said.

"Like now," Roger said, his tone disapproving, "when she unloaded him."

The student jotted notes on an aluminum clipboard, unfazed by Bo's behavior. Roger placed himself next to Lexy as if Bo belonged to him. The student asked about the scars on Bo's face. She made a note that the wound had healed without complications. "Anything else we need to know?"

"He's standing at stud this spring," Jordan told her.

The student took in his conformation with frank approval. "Very good."

Roger escorted Ruth and Colonel to a metal picnic table and came back. Lexy wanted him to butt out and wished Ben were here instead. She'd trust his take on the situation.

Shortly, a pale, slim fellow about Jordan's age ambled up. Dr. Oren Klinepeter wore a blue Oxford-cloth shirt and khakis and a stethoscope like the students' around his neck. He had a trimmed goatee and unassuming manner. He nodded at Roger, then Jordan, and stuck out his hand. You must be Jordan McRae."

"Yes."

"So this is our candidate?" He caressed Bo's neck by way of introducing himself to the stallion, then looked in his right eye and the left. "Yep. Problem worsens in bright light. The iris shuts down, narrows his field of vision. It's not so bright in barns, so his irises will open. Let's see if he calms down there."

Bo pirouetted alongside Lexy, horseshoes thunking on asphalt, then clattering on the concrete floor inside.

Klinepeter studied the live wire dancing alongside of her. "Pretty spooky feller, eh?"

Lexy described the Fair Hill debacle, then Bo's rock steady midnight ride.

Klinepeter seemed to file that away, led them into a darkened stall, and shone a pin light in Bo's eyes again.

"Bilateral." He grunted. "Pretty advanced." He directed the two vet students to examine him as well, corrected one of their angles on the pin light, and invited Jordan and Lexy to take a good look, Roger too. Colonel trailed in with Ruth, and Klinepeter greeted him with a warm handshake. Everyone knew who Colonel was. "I'm sure you'd like to see this too, sir."

"Yeth," Colonel said firmly. His speech was a work in progress.

The medical man took note of Colonel's walker and weakened state and, shielding him from the horse, led him close enough to look into Bo's eyes. With great respect, he explained what they were seeing.

Roger hovered, protective too, but with an eyebrow raised in doubt.

Colonel studied Bo's eyes intensely, Lexy thought, the man before the stroke.

"In'res'ing," he said, slurring the words. "Coulda use' this in da ol' days."

"No kidding." Klinepeter still held on to Colonel's elbow, but said to Jordan and Lexy, "Y'all agree the problem's affecting the horse's work?"

Lexy defended him, blaming herself for not keeping him in hand.

"Don't be too hard on yourself," Klinepeter said to her, and then to the entire party, "Bo's unpredictability is pretty typical. Our failure to make the connection between bright sun and bad behavior is common too. What do you know about cystic corpora nigra?"

"It has a *name?*" Jordan's voice cracked.

"Yep," he said, then went clinical. "It's a rare but operable eye condition. Horses have small growths called *corpora nigra* along the top rim of their lozenge-shaped irises. Black bodies, smaller than peppercorns."

Lexy prided herself on her internship with Simon, so how had she missed this? "Sorry, I never noticed."

Roger drew himself up. "That's normal. You see it all the time."

"We sure do," Klinepeter said blandly. "But we only recently figured out how it affects the horse." He addressed Jordan. "In the normal eye, we think they act like tiny umbrellas to protect the retina from the sun's glare. Your horse's hypertrophied, or overgrew. His irises contract in sunlight normally, but he loses eighty, ninety percent of his vision in the center of his eye, and—" he shrugged. "Oh, man. Who knows what the world looks like to him? It's gotta be scary. Put two fingers in front of your eyes, and walk back to your truck."

Jordan shook her head, but Lexy tried and took a few steps. "Good God. I can barely see. That's why he tilts his head and arches his neck and snorts at fences, jumps, and puddles. He's trying to see them."

"Yes. He may compensate better at home where he knows the jumps and the lay of the land."

"But tackling a cross-country course he's never seen is a perfect storm," Jordan said.

"A simple outpatient laser surgery will shrink them to normal."

"And you think that will fix him?" Roger's underlying tone of skepticism struck Lexy as unprofessional.

Jordan winced and shifted topics. "How does this relate to his behavior?"

"The surgery? He may need time to overcome any misbehaviors he learned with his previous owners or to get over his last experience."

"What's the recovery time?" Lexy asked, itching to ride again.

"Theoretically, you could put him to work tomorrow, but I'd give him a coupla days off."

"And he'll be his old self?" Jordan asked.

"That's been our experience."

"What's the complication rate?" Roger put in, still skeptical.

"Negligible, especially with a healthy horse this age." Klinepeter launched into a geeky medical treatise, citing records they'd kept on horses over the twenty years he'd been refining the procedure.

At last, Roger didn't have a comeback.

"Do they grow back?" Lexy pressed.

"Short answer, no," he concluded. "Not all our patients' owners report back. We hope that means success, but clinically speaking, no news is just no news."

Lexy hung onto Bo's lead line, frowning. "Will it hurt him?"

"Nope. Day op. Can do today. Mild sedative, and a local anesthetic cream to the cornea so we can press the laser on it.

"I'd like to observe," Roger said, to Lexy's exasperation.

"Naturally," Klinepeter said, totally professional. "Not much to it though, goes by pretty fast. By the time the drugs wear off, he'll be seeing normally." He turned again to Jordan. "You want your good horse back?"

"Big time," Jordan said. "But could it be this easy?"

It was. They'd pulled in before eight-thirty and had paid up and signed out before noon. Bo's sedative wore off, and he loaded like the pro Jordan said he used to be. From the truck's cab, the camera showed him munching hay, oblivious to speed, or stops and starts, or the roar of trucks and semis passing by.

Roger sped off ahead of them. Good riddance, Lexy thought, glad to see his bumper pulling away from them on this otherwise fine morning. Because Bo was going to be okay. She felt it in her bones, and in the hope and relief that washed through her.

At home Jordan hung over his stall door, watching his every move in crisp clean shavings up to his fetlocks. "So he gets tomorrow off. We can assess him then, like Dr. Klinepeter recommends. Lunge him maybe, ride the next day, depending."

Lexy stood guard beside her, not yet daring to dream her dreams. "He seems normal," she volunteered as ten minutes slipped into twenty.

Jordan nodded. "I'm afraid to believe what I see, but he's more relaxed than he's been in years."

"Could the corpora nigra have been enlarged when you were riding him?"

"Thoroughbred." Jordan grinned with pride, and Lexy thought she glimpsed the competitive woman she'd once been. "He always had his *whee* moments."

"At home too?"

"More at competitions. I thought of them as his fifth leg, his extra gas."

"I'm thinking if he already had the condition, he was okay with you away from home because of the trust you'd built."

"I never said he was pushbutton."

"But with a new rider, less than one-hundred percent confident?"

"Yes, and his trainer put on heavy hardware, adding to his resistance."

"You mean...?"

"The severest bit the rule book allows. Then when he sold him to that hot-shot amateur—" Jordan bit her lip. "God, it makes me sick. At least, Bo scared the hell out of that kid before he killed them both. I've got to hope Bo'll go better now that he can see."

"I can't wait to take him out," Lexy whispered.

"Yeah," said Jordan unconvinced. "Don't know how I'll face another setback if Klinepeter's off the mark."

# Thirty-five

On Thanksgiving, Lexy rode Bo out with Jordan on Jazz for a holiday hack before the family feast. Ben surprised them coming round the corner, and Lexy couldn't help noticing how pleased Jordan seemed to see him. And how pleased she was too.

"Bo better?" he asked her after catching up. He was looking for signs of the injury to his leg.

"All healed, thank you."

Then his eyes narrowed. "You're riding him in a snaffle?"

She couldn't repress a smile and gave Jordan a pleading glance. "Tell him?"

Jordan told him about the surgery, the return of the old original Bo. They had half an hour of companionable, quiet, obedient trotting and galloping on the trail, then Lexy popped the stallion over a few fences. Ben was impressed. He tried to beg off dinner, but Jordan dragooned him into staying.

At the Thanksgiving table, Jordan sat by Colonel, who'd been sprung from the hospital he still called a prison for a special day at home. Jordan's older sister Gwen, the sheriff, had pulled her absentee spouse David out of the woodwork, and descended on the old farmhouse with their four kids. The preteen and three teenagers were installed at the harvest table in the kitchen. Roger had been invited too, and Parker was there, of course. It was Lexy's first time compelled to be in his presence for longer than it took to give a curt nod and run. The scratches where she'd marked his face a month ago had healed, but her wounds lingered in the panic that flooded her if he caught her by surprise.

She forced herself to make eye contact with him and show no fear.

"You do the honors, son," said Colonel from the head of the table.

At the opposite end, Parker rubbed his hands together and picked up the carving knife with a flourish, all charm. "Turkey day," he said, and sawed at an enormous bird roasted to a rich, perfect bronze. Juices spurted from it.

Everybody ate—cornbread dressing, green beans and corn, cranberry sauce, giblet gravy in a china boat—and conversation flagged until Jordan passed second helpings.

"What I want to know, Ben—" Colonel said "—is what did you think of Bo on course this morning?"

Parker paused, gravy boat in mid-air. "You were jumping him?"

Lexy poked her sweet potatoes, hating the tension between father and son.

"He looked good. Great," Ben said, taking the boat from Parker and ladling Ruth's rich gravy over everything.

"Makes him a more attractive stud prospect," Roger said to Jordan.

Lexy glanced up. "Yes, but we're putting him back in work. He's doing super."

Parker's carving knife clinked on the platter. "I fucking don't believe you people." Lexy shifted in her seat. This was shades of the Parker who'd caught her in his condo, genial then belligerent.

"Hold on, buddyroe," Colonel said.

"No, you hold on," Parker snapped. "He almost killed a kid at Fair Hill, and you're giving Lexy a second shot? Dad. Jordan. I want this ride. I've earned it."

"I recommend against it, even for you, Parker," Roger said. "Let alone her."

Jordan's chin jutted out. "They're in the Pipe-Opener in January at the Horse Park."

Roger raised a brow at her. "A good morning at home cross-country doesn't mean he'll go well there even if he did have that surgery."

"Surgery for what?" Parker demanded.

Jordan pressed her lips together, then sighed. "Oren Klinepeter operated on his eyes, Parker. Simple laser surgery, outpatient, cheap. Bo's corpora nigra had enlarged so much he had trouble seeing in bright light. Fixed him, a miracle."

"If he's fixed, I should have the ride," Parker insisted.

Jordan crossed her silver on her plate, finished. "Lexy's done the hard work, Parker."

"And if anybody's going to keep on doing it, it ought to be her," Ben said. "You can see their bond."

Inside, Lexy felt a spurt of pride. That bond had only strengthened with Bo's new confidence.

"I like the girl's chances, Parker," Colonel said in a tone that killed further argument.

Gwen's youngest, Brianna, came in and snuggled under her mother's arm. The rest of Gwen's brood had crowded in to scavenge leftovers from the grownups' table. Roger teased them like an indulgent uncle, and Ben asked each one about their favorite sports. Lexy was amused by Roger's teasing and touched by Ben's interest. Unlike the no-nonsense coach she'd come to know, he seemed an instant uncle too. Ruth whistled the teens back to the kitchen for pumpkin or mincemeat pie, topped with whipped cream or vanilla ice cream, their choice. They'd barely finished when Gwen took a call from dispatch and ordered her family to their van. They mustered like troops going to war.

Colonel headed for the barn with Roger, Parker storming after, but Ben signaled Lexy to join him on the front porch. He gestured her to sit in a rattan chair that had survived the hurricane. He sat across from her. The late fall afternoon was warm.

"So you decided not to tell Jordan about the Watch List."

"Doesn't the surgery change my status?"

"Not till you've proved yourself. You have a record, so to speak. We still need to address that."

"Address what?" Jordan came around the corner of the house carrying a compost bucket she'd emptied out back.

Lexy clenched the arms of her porch chair.

Ben offered his chair to Jordan and braced a shoulder against a column of the porch.

"Your call," he said to Lexy.

Jordan set the bucket down, climbed the steps, and took a seat, her eyes narrowing.

Lexy met her gaze. "If you're entering us in the Pipe-Opener, there's something you need to know."

"Okay. Shoot."

"Since Fair Hill, I'm on the Watch List for losing control of Bo."

Jordan crossed her arms and looked out over the sweeping lawn. Almost a month after the hurricane, limbs and twigs and detritus had finally been removed.

"I wish you'd been upfront with me."

Lexy winced. "You were retiring him to stud. I didn't see the need."

"I entered you in the Pipe-Opener unaware of that."

"Yes, ma'am, but you only mentioned that today. I'm not sure what difference it makes."

"For starters, for the next six competitions, all eyes are on you and Bo."

"Not all eyes," Ben said. "A handful of people know, including me. A couple of them will be there. Me, for sure."

"I don't see how this won't get out," Jordan said. "I see another train wreck on the on-line forums."

"The association takes confidentiality seriously."

Her fingers tightened on her arms. "The whole eventing world took my suspension seriously. With Bo on the Watch List, the 'we-told-you-so's' about a stallion would hit the forums overnight."

"Apples and oranges," Ben said. "Suspensions are public knowledge. The Watch List was never intended to be. It's the least invasive thing we can throw up at a rider who appears to be in trouble on her horse."

"Speaking as the rider," Lexy put in, "I feel invaded. Watched, so to speak."

Ben gave her a kind look. "Honest, honey. It's a yellow flag. It has no teeth. It's new, but the few times we've invoked it, we've seen excellent results. Parents, coaches, riders—all have taken it well. Straightened out. We know you will too."

Jordan turned to Ben. "After the way you saw him go this morning, do you see a problem with giving it a go in January?"

Ben scrubbed a hand across his mouth. "My role is to advise the rider. How about I give Lexy a lesson before I go to Florida, and look at them again when I get back in January?"

"As the Olympic coach?" Jordan asked.

"As owner," he said. "Friend."

"Then they can do the Pipe-Opener?"

"Danny, whatever I advise, whether we do a lesson or not, even with them on the Watch List, you are free to enter them."

Jordan pushed up from her seat, arms tight across her breasts.

Lexy stood too, eager to reassure both of Bo's owners. "I'd love to have a shot at the Pipe-Opener." Then she looked at Ben. "And any advice... I'd be grateful, honored. Fair Hill was hell. I never, ever want to see another infant in our path."

"Then that's settled," Ben said, with a twinkle in his eye for Jordan. "Are you too full to show me how you're doing with Jasmine? Or did you have too much champagne?"

"Is this a challenge?" she asked.

"Try invitation," he said warmly.

"I'm good for twenty minutes, maybe half an hour."

Lexy was surprised by their quick shift to intimacy. They'd hidden it all day. But she wanted to see her boss ride. "Mind if I watch?"

"Watch? We'll put you to work," Ben said.

She was glad to. She helped groom and tack the mare, then moved the portable mounting block for Jordan to get on. Under the arching roof of the cold, dusty arena, Jordan warmed Jasmine at a walk, Lexy watching alongside Ben.

"How do we look?" Jordan asked when she passed in front of them again.

"You've lost your beautiful picture. Bring your leg back a bit. There. Now grow up and down. Good, *that's* vertical," Ben said. He was professional, remote, but right, because the moment Jordan did what he suggested Lexy could see Jazz's back round and her hindquarters engage. The mare reached for the bit, and her stride lengthened.

Jordan beamed. "This feels terrific."

Ben coached her for twenty minutes, asking for relaxation more than perfection. They ended with two big loopy circuits of loose, rangy trot around the arena.

Jordan dismounted awkwardly but unaided, the soles of her boots digging into the sandy surface. She was winded, but a rare grin lit her face. "That's five minutes longer than I've gone before."

"You're coming back," Lexy said.

"You are indeed," Ben said, and then as if he and Jordan were alone, he pulled her to him and kissed her, her mare's reins dangling from her fingers. Finally, Ben lifted his head and said, "How about another lesson a week from Saturday when I get back, then dinner again in town?"

"I'd like that."

~ 251 ~

"And Lexy, lesson for you too. Be ready." And he gave her a holiday hug and a jaunty wave as he walked on.

Jordan looked as surprised as Lexy felt. Were they getting serious? Then Lexy saw Parker was standing in the gateway, arms crossed, eyes glaring.

# Thirty-six

A month later, and Lexy had had two solid lessons with Ben, and Jordan had coached her every day, with Colonel observing as he gained strength. Today Jordan had invited her to join her and the men for a Christmas morning hack. Quiet grey clouds lowered over the cool December morning, lending a misty briskness to it that threw Lexy back to foxhunting days in England with her mother. She should be beyond tears by now, shouldn't she? She wiped them off. She and Bo were less than a month away from the Pipe-Opener. Despite the fact that Bo was listed on the Horse Park's Entry Status page for everyone to see, there'd been no text messages or attacks.

"Where the hell is Parker?" Colonel groused, riding Curtis. Ben rode alongside on Marcus, taking his turn for the older man's safety. This morning, Colonel was riding outdoors for the first time since his stroke. Lexy worried. Under protest, the old campaigner had let them kit him out in a safety helmet, an inflatable vest, a deep-seated dressage saddle with breakaway stirrups, and a grab strap to boot.

"Parker's flying in today from Florida, Daddy," Jordan reminded him patiently.

"Fuck Florida. Who does he think we are, the Kennedys?"

"He's helping Marina move there for the winter, remember?"

He didn't, Lexy realized. His mind was sharp, and he retained details from the past as her grandfather had done. But Colonel's short-term memory, like Nonno's, was still spotty. Equally as distressing, the stroke had wiped out some social censors in the mind of the uber-correct Southern gentleman, and he now swore like a sailor.

"And Gwen and the kids," he grumbled. "Where the hell are they? Shit, I used to have a family."

"You still do," Jordan called back. "Gwen's crew was with us Thanksgiving. Christmas is David's family's turn so they've gone to Boone."

"What the devil was she thinking, marrying somebody from Boone?"

"Boone's a respectable town, and David's from a respectable family." Jordan raised her voice over the squeak of saddle leathers.

"Bullshit," Colonel said. "Boone's in the fucking mountains. She could have married someone from here, a neighbor."

Scowling, Jordan twisted in the saddle. "Like who, Daddy? Roger?"

"No," Colonel shot back. "*You* should marry Roger. Or this Ben fellow riding on my ass."

"Oh, for Pete's sake," Jordan cried, bristling. She swung Jasmine to a sideways halt, blocking Ben and Colonel.

Lexy stopped too, wishing she could run away.

"Stop meddling in my life," Jordan said to Colonel.

Ben tapped his helmet in a half-salute. "Besides, sir. Once a wet-behind-the-ears redneck, always a wet-behind-the-ears redneck." He looked at Jordan. "That's what he said when I asked him for your hand in marriage."

Jordan's face flushed. "When was that?"

Ben shrugged. "I wasn't good enough for you then anyway. No money, no family, no future. Right, Colonel? So why now?"

"Don't think I haven't seen what's going on between you two."

"Daddy!" Jordan scolded.

"Still think you didn't do right by Roger, but if you're serious about Ben, don't let him get away this time."

Her knuckles tightened on her crop's handle. "You said he'd break my heart."

"So sue me. I was wrong."

Jordan made a face of shocked surprise. "That's a first."

Colonel turned to Ben. "You turned out all right."

"Thanks," Ben said with a wry grin.

But Jasmine fidgeted under Jordan's tension. "You didn't help me then, Daddy," Jordan said, "and I don't want help now."

"She's right, Colonel," Ben went on in his forthright way. "If and when Jordan and I get together, I'll do my own proposing."

"At your ages, you shouldn't waste time."

Ben laughed. "Does that mean I have your permission to ask for your daughter's hand in marriage?"

"What the fuck else could it mean?"

Jordan's brown eyes flamed. "You two stop it. I'm over forty, and it's the twenty-first century."

Ben winked at her but went on talking to Colonel. "Could mean you think we should start dating first. We probably changed since that summer, need to get reacquainted. Or maybe you think we should set up house."

"Marriage first, then house," said Colonel. "And you live here. Plenty of room."

Lexy pressed her lips together to keep her mouth from gaping. What a tyrant the old man could be—shades of her ex-father.

"Ben Holt," Jordan snapped. "I absolutely forbid you to discuss our past, present, or future with my father. You and Lexy go ride while I try to talk some sense into him."

Ben's eyes glittered with amusement. "No problem," he said, then to Lexy. "Let's do some jumps in the meadow over there. Show me how Bo's going for you."

Ride for the Olympic coach on the spur of the moment on Christmas day to escape a family altercation? She gulped. "Super."

He gave her a huge, dare-you grin. "Take that line down by the woods. I'll follow with my critique."

"What about them?" She glanced at Jordan and Colonel, going head to head.

"Looks like they're having a genuine McRae family knock-down, drag-out fight."

"Ouch."

He shrugged. "You can love somebody too much."

She started Bo over a coop, a rounded, inviting obstacle on the practice course. For a good ten minutes, they jumped obstacles scattered about the meadow. Ben had her work on adjusting Bo's speed.

By their final time around, Jordon and a stone-faced Colonel had stopped speaking, and Lexy rode over to them with Ben.

"Settle things to your satisfaction?" he asked wryly.

Colonel glowered. "No. See if you can handle her. I'm tired of being bossed around. If I've got to have a minder, I'd rather it be someone young and pretty like Miss Imbriani here anyhoo."

"Can you manage him, Lexy?" Jordan asked grimly, her holiday mood gone.

"Yes, do go on. I'll get your father home, one way or the other."

Ben and Jordan cantered away, leaving Lexy in charge of the stubborn old man who seemed intent on getting well and running his family's lives again. She blinked at him, still shocked by his uncensored intrusion into Jordan's love life.

And now by her unexpected responsibility for him.

His chestnut eyes twinkled. "That ought to flush them out of the duck blind. She wouldn't let on if they're screwing yet. You reckon they are?"

Lexy's face burned with embarrassment. They were her boss and coach, and Colonel was the last person she wanted to talk with about their sex life. Colonel pushed Curtis into a walk, and she caught up to him on Bo. "I didn't know they were an item."

"They were always an item, darlin'. Even when they hated one another."

Sworn enemies, she'd always heard. "They don't seem to hate each other now."

"They broke each other's hearts, and because of—" He clamped his mouth shut as if he'd finally found his inner censor.

Lexy was dying to know. "Because of what?"

"I don't know," he said cagily. "With me it was always some other woman."

Oh no. Way too much information, Lexy thought.

"You can't be too careful," he went on. "That hothead Gambrell's got a reputation for the women too. Looks like I was flapping my jaws in the breeze."

"He's not a hothead, except when Parker goads him."

"Course I do love to see talent marry talent, Ben and my daughter, you and Gambrell. Something I never quite pulled off," he rambled on in his wild new way. "You'd be safer with a man at your side."

"I appreciate your concern." Their horses walked on, their hoof falls in a pleasing syncopation.

"Jordan would be safer too. With a husband, I mean, not an old fart of a father who can barely zip his pants. Are you in love with the halfbreed?"

The insult to Hamp flamed through her, but she could control her tongue if Colonel couldn't. "I'm sorry you see him that way, sir. Hamp's an honorable man."

"Half breed's a fact. Indian father, white mother, vice versa, whichever. Are you in love with him?" he repeated, his memory not so short that he'd forgotten her evasion.

~ 257 ~

"Are you being nosy, or do you really care?"

He grinned, and the age lines that bracketed his mouth deepened. "Well, both, since you put it that way. You ride better than my grandchildren, as good as my daughter at her best, and I'm officially adopting you. Are you in love with him? Simple question."

Her face heated. "Am I that obvious?"

"To an old coot like me, you bet. Been there, broke some hearts. Broke my own, but that don't count when you're the one spreading the misery. Love's a good thing though. Don't let a woman come between you and Gambrell like Ben and Jordan did."

"We talked about that. He's into fidelity."

He blinked, as if she'd turned the tables on him, then said, "Let's go eat. Race you to the stables." He wheeled Curtis toward the barn.

"Don't you dare!" she cried, fear for his life shafting through her.

"Darlin', if I'm not daring, I might as well be dead." And he was off, urging Curtis forward, signs of his old Olympic form still there. Curtis struck off boldly.

"At least hang onto your grab strap!" she yelled after Colonel, pacing Bo who wanted to race too.

By the time she caught up to them, Colonel had dismounted, his face flushed with the same joy she felt when she did something daring.

"Don't be afraid of surprising people, darlin'. Make 'em keep up with you."

Easier done, she thought, when he'd been young and healthy, and no recipe for safety now. But she said nothing rather than provoke more alarming actions.

Whatever else she thought of Parker, she had to admit he came by his reckless charm naturally.

# Thirty-seven

Without Gwen's family, Christmas dinner that afternoon had been a quiet affair—too quiet. Ben and Jordan had sat in strained silence, passing bowls and platters, poking at food, forcing a word here and there. This morning Colonel had spoiled everything with his talk of marriage. After the meal, Ben followed Lexy to the barn to help with chores, still preoccupied. Tyrone and Eduardo had a rare day off, so Ben helped with the broodmares, the boarders, and the stallions.

Halfway through, finished with dinner dishes, Jordan came and pitched in.

Chores done, horses crunched their grain. Occasionally one snorted, content in his safe space. Horse heaven, except for Ben and Jordan's mood.

Perhaps, Lexy thought, the champagne she'd stashed upstairs would cheer them. She'd practiced a toast, borrowed flutes from the house, and now brought the bottle down.

Mustering a smile, Ben moved three plastic stacking chairs into the aisle, popped the cork, filled the flutes, and passed them around. The champagne was pale as straw, and bubbles climbed the flutes. Its sharp tang rose above the scents of hay, molasses-flavored grain, and pine shavings in freshly bedded stalls.

Then Ben took a chair, still not looking at either of them.

Determined to recover the spirit of the season, Lexy downed the champagne and held out her flute for more, her cheeks warming in the cool still night.

"I'd like to make a toast. To us—the luckiest people in the world," she said. "To be here, Christmas day with these magnificent horses and you. Mom would be so happy for me, and I thank you for your support."

Ben gulped his glass, then Jordan tilted her head at him as if to say, *Go on.*

"I'm sure she would have been," Ben said quietly. "You know, I knew her."

"Honest?" Lexy asked, then remembered. "Right. Jordan said she'd been here. What was she like?"

Ben cleared his throat. "When she was on, she was the best rider of us."

She felt a spurt of pride. "That sounds like her. But you were all here?"

"Yes. Jordan lived here of course, but your mom and I were working students. Colonel was a fierce taskmaster."

"She never mentioned that."

"Maybe your mother never mentioned that summer because she and I had an affair." Ben set his flute on the rubber pavers, pressed his lips together, then looked straight into her eyes. "Maybe because she knew…well, Lexy, I'm your father."

Lexy's heart stuck. "What are you saying?"

"I'm so sorry, honey. I know it's a shock. I'm your biological father."

Her hands fluttered like the wings of a dove shot down from the sky. "How could it—You're joking."

"I've never been more serious in my life."

She shook her head violently, her Christmas-tree earrings jangling. "She should have told me it was you."

"For what it's worth, she didn't tell me either."

Jordan scowled. "Maybe she didn't tell you to protect you. Or maybe she wasn't positive herself."

"She knew enough to write a letter to someone years ago about my real father." She couldn't stop the trembling of her lower lip or the anger boiling up inside. "Imbriani found it in her effects in a safety deposit box. That's when he kicked me out."

"A letter to who?" Ben asked.

"'Dear Pookie.' Do you know who the hell *Dear Pookie* was?"

"No," Ben said. "But your mother nicknamed everybody. I was Benjy, after that stupid movie dog. And Jordan—she was Danny to us both."

"I don't understand," Jordan put in. "Why would she make a copy of a letter she wrote to someone else?"

"She never sent the original. After she died, he read it to me, then said he'd thrash me to a pulp if I'd known." The words felt like acid on Lexy's tongue. "If I'd used him for his money like my lying, not so dearly departed mother."

"Honey..." Ben reached to touch her shoulder but she shrugged him off.

"As if he'd not used us, to bolster his reputation. Then he said if he ever found out who that asshole was who'd fucked his wife, he'd rip out his balls and shove them down his throat. And make me watch."

"Son of a bitch. I am so terribly—"

"Sorry? *Sorry?* How long have you known?"

"Jordan told me today after you and Colonel left us out on course."

"*She* told *you?*" Lexy wheeled on Jordan, champagne splashing from her crystal flute. "You were Pookie."

"No. Never."

"Then how did you know? And when did you find out?"

"When you showed me your medical card, I saw your mother's name and your birth date."

"Which doesn't prove a bloody thing."

"You look like Ben. I saw it the instant I made the connection. Look at the slant of his brows, the way his fingers taper."

"So you *knew* all this time, and didn't tell me?"

"I had no idea if Ben knew or wanted you to know. You've had so much dumped on you—losing your mother, moving here, being new, Bo being so difficult, and then the messages, the Watch List. There was always the possibility you knew and wanted it kept secret. I couldn't know what was best."

Lexy suddenly felt all alone. "I deserved to know as soon as you did—whether he cared or not."

Ben leaned toward her. "Lexy, I'm proud to call you my daughter."

"Jesus, who are you two? Jordan, you kept this from me— lied—while you—" she looked Ben up and down "—*damn* you—while you condemned my mother to a life of hell with my ex-father."

"And then you too," Ben said, as if it had just struck him. "Lexy, I honestly had no idea. I wish to God I'd had."

Anger at him jetted through her, all the hurt and wasted years. "And you would have done exactly what?"

"Intervened. Stolen you away," he said. "Whatever the courts would have permitted, or your mother would have allowed. Although who knows what that would have been? She was wild, scattered."

"Pardon me," Lexy said, torn between her mother's betrayal and the love and support she'd given her until the day she died. "My mother was my rock and my best friend. She devoted her life to me."

"I'm sure she changed. I did. I wish I could have been there for you, honey."

"I am not your honey. And I don't have to deal with this today." She turned and headed out.

"Lexy, wait. Let me make this right."

"How can you right twenty-three years of wrong?" She tossed back the rest of her champagne and slammed the crystal flute against the feed room door, shards of sparkling glass clinking on the floor, her new-found capacity for violence startling her.

"Oh shit." Appalled to lose control, she darted into the tack room, dragged out the shop vac, and noisily sucked up the mess she'd made. When she'd cleared the last of the shattered crystal, she pointed the roaring wand at him. "You can't make this right, and I don't need another father. My first one was a brute, and I can make it on my own."

She dove into the tack room, grabbed a saddle and bridle, turning anger into purpose as she walked into Bo's stall, rage and turmoil whipping through her. If she moved calmly, she would be calm, she told herself. She breathed into the center of her being as Ulrich had taught her, and Bo lowered his head into her chest in that ever-ready empathy the best horses always offered. She tacked him up slowly, carefully so as not to startle him. When she led him out, saddled and bridled and quiet at her side, Ben and Jordan were waiting.

Ben walked toward her, palms out, offering…

"Don't," she said, hands up to fend him off. "I need to be alone."

And she was never alone on a horse. In spite of how much she hated her new father at the moment, somehow she knew he understood. People failed her, horses never. She trotted off on Bo, too good a horsewoman to gallop off on a horse not yet warmed up. Deep in the woods, leaves crackled underfoot, assaulting her nerves like gunshots.

She slipped from the saddle to the ground and cried great gulping sobs.

If her mother had set out to find her a perfect father, wouldn't Ben Holt have been the man? He'd been nothing but kind to her, and he was brilliant, so brilliant, at everything he did in the one world she knew and loved. But how could her mother have lied to her? Betrayed herself? Subjected both of them to Imbriani's cruelty?

How could Ben not have known?

And how to treat him now? She didn't know what to say, think, feel. Do. Whether to tell anyone, even Hamp. That Jordan knew seemed a horrid violation of her privacy.

Still throbbing with pain and anger, she climbed back in the saddle. Bo craned his head around and nibbled the toe of her worn paddock boot.

"Good horse." She swiped at tears that leaked from the corners of her eyes and turned him toward the barn, his rhythmic, steady hoof falls telling her she'd be all right, all right, all right. Under the setting sun, winter birds chirped, going to roost as if everything was normal. But Ben and Jordan stood in the barn's big open door, concern on both their faces. She got off, new anger surging through her.

"I don't need you two babysitting me."

Ben folded his arms across his chest as if her words had pierced him. "Maybe, but we're not done."

"I don't think five minutes of fucking my mother or however long you had it up while you deposited your sperm inside her makes you anything to me."

She hadn't fully grasped how angry and betrayed she felt until those ugly words escaped her.

"Fair enough, but it would mean more than I can say if you'd give me a chance."

"Did it take five minutes, ten? Or did you go on all night?"

"Look, I'm not liking myself a lot right now. Let's go over this again. Your mother died in a car accident. The man you thought was your father sold your horses out from under you and tossed you out of the EU. And then I turn up."

"My *real* father," she said. "Who finally after all these years is proud of me."

"Not just that. Is prepared to get to know you better, to support you...to love you."

"That's rich," she spit out, still in shock and disbelief.

"You don't have to love me back," he said with such transparent anguish she regretted every spiteful word she said.

A mortifying blush burned her throat, her cheeks, her ears. "I already—" she broke off "—quite liked you—but—This is impossible. I'll have to move. Find another position. How long do you think it'll take me to get work in Canada?"

Ben exchanged a glance with Jordan. "Why Canada?"

"Jordan needs a rider who has a shot at the Olympic team with Bo. But my new father's the Olympic coach. You'd be accused of nepotism. All hell would break loose."

"Possibly," Jordan said, sounding reasonable.

"It might be awkward," Ben agreed. "But I can't think of anything in the rule book on nepotism."

"It isn't the done thing," Lexy said. "Plus you own a share of the horse."

"I can sell it." He clamped his hands together as if to stop himself from reaching out to her. "Look, sweetie, I only just found you. I don't want to lose you."

A catch in his voice bowled her over. She looked at Jordan. "You want me to stay?"

"Yes." Jordan nodded at Bo. "He wants you to stay too."

Lexy turned to Ben, chin up. "On one condition. Don't expect me to be your little girl. I'm way past old enough to immigrate to America on my own, buy a car, hold down a job. Next election, I'm registering to vote."

"Well, then, how about a friend and a coach?"

"You want me to keep working Bo and Marcus? Take lessons with you?"

"Yes. And I won't say another word about this embarrassing father business."

She drew herself up. "I have to think about it," she said. "Horses I trust. Fathers, not so much."

# Part Five. Road Warriors

## *January–April*

The Military Games were always dangerous, often deadly. But the sport reached its nadir in the highly politicized atmosphere of the Berlin Olympics in 1936. After dressage, the Germans went into cross-country with a slight lead over the Americans who had won gold in 1932.

Obstacle Four, a jump over a three-rail fence into water three feet deep, was no extraordinary challenge for the elite forty-eight athletes from eighteen different countries. Most chose the obvious shorter course to the right only to find the water deeper than expected with sucking mud at the bottom.

Twenty-eight horses fell, three so badly injured they had to be destroyed. Only fifteen horses negotiated the obstacle with ease, including the four Germans, who took the long, safe route to the left.

*A History of the U. S. Army Olympic*
*Equestrian Team (1912–1948)*
By Colonel Jacob McRae, USA Maj. Ret.

# Thirty-eight

G ood work today, Lexy," Ben said. It was two-thirty in the afternoon at the Horse Park's January Pipe-Opener, Bo's first public outing since his surgery. Today's competition had had only two phases, dressage and then stadium jumping, no solid cross-country obstacles. Marcus had been a trooper, and Bo had proved his hurricane heroics hadn't been an aberration.

"Thanks." Lexy turned the latch to lock the trailer and blew hot breath onto her frozen fingers. The sun was bright, but it glanced off patches of snow left from a two-inch dusting a couple of days ago, now followed by an Arctic blast from Canada. "Was this a Watch List event for me?" Being watched had preyed on her.

"Counts in my book." Ben made notes on his program, no hurry to leave, no pressure to talk.

"So how'd we do?"

"Bo's a different horse, apparently stable, safe. That's what I'll report." He gave her that kind smile he gave his regular students.

Not sure how she felt about that, she said, "One down, five to go."

"You're going to be fine."

Fine? If she ever thawed out. Despite a thermal top, good gloves, and wool socks under her boots, she felt frozen to the bone. She pulled on her insulated coveralls. "I need a bracing cup of English tea, steeped in a china pot under a tea cozy for five minutes at the very least."

"Don't think they've got that at the Coffee Hound here, but let's go see."

She kept up with his fast pace. Today, she could see her resemblance to him in his long stride, lanky body, and the set of his chin, but she'd persuaded herself that didn't change a thing. She was getting beyond her initial shock, but could she trust a man who'd fucked her mother in a one-night stand? And if he was her real father, so what?

She wanted to manage her own life and never be on the receiving end of anything that smacked of favoritism from him. After her Christmas evening declaration of independence, he'd hardly smothered her. In fact, he'd barnstormed the East Coast and flown to California to hold winter training sessions for the teams' A and B List riders, which included Hamp and Marina.

But on Ben's rare days home, he'd not failed to come to Hawks Nest to work with her on Marcus and then Bo.

At the Coffee Hound they looked over the chalked-in menu. "No tea," Ben said.

"Dang," she said in her best new local vernacular. "Hot chocolate it is then."

He ordered a cup for her and coffee for himself straight up, *leaded,* as some said here, when Parker strolled up. He had on a worn but stylish winter riding parka, mountain boots, insulated gloves and showed no signs of having competed.

"Coach," he drawled congenially. "How long you back for?"

"Florida tomorrow."

"Wish I was coming with you."

Ben studied him. "Get any of your new guys ready for Advanced next year, and we'll take a look at them."

"What about Sailor?"

Ben shrugged. "He ready for Rolex?" The only four-star course in America.

Before Parker could answer, the server plopped their hot drinks on the counter.

Ignoring Ben's question, Parker slid in and stuck out a crisp twenty.

"On me," he said to the girl, then, "I'll have hot chocolate like the little lady."

Lexy's head fizzed with indignation. She didn't want Parker paying for her hot chocolate, taking away from rare time with her father, or hanging around her as if she should forget he'd harassed and assaulted her. Even in this bitter cold, his play of innocence was chilling. And she still hadn't figured out what to tell Colonel or Jordan. After their year from hell, shouldn't she leave them in peace?

Excusing herself to go take Bo and Marcus home, she dumped Parker's hot chocolate in the first trash bin she passed. The horses loaded without a hitch, and she stuck the key in the ignition when she saw Ben halfway down the shed row, headed for his truck.

She rolled down her window and called after him.

He stopped and returned with a concerned expression that made her feel protected. "Yes?"

"Thanks for your help with Bo and Marcus."

The corners of his eyes crinkled. "Owner. Comes with the territory."

No. He was giving her special treatment, after all, and her resolve to resist him folded. "Cross-country schooling in last week's miserable weather was more than I expected."

He shrugged. "Too rough for Colonel to be out. I was glad to do it."

"Then thanks again."

"My privilege. You're on your own this spring though. Don't know when I'll get back or how much time I'll have. You firmed up your schedule?"

"Starting in Florida at Red Hills, Intermediate, then Poplar Place in Georgia, then here in March at Advanced, then The Fork CIC three-star before Rolex."

He nodded. "Makes sense."

"Jordan thinks so."

"I'll be at each one. Be sure to look me up."

"I will."

"Have a safe drive home." He slapped the truck's hood and walked away, other horses, other students, other responsibilities. While she'd been in that first roaring state of anger that her real father had turned out to be the Olympic coach, she'd demanded that he and Jordan not tell anyone. If that had hurt him, then or now, she couldn't tell from the kind look in his ice-blue eyes. But his attention made her feel he cared for her without her having done one thing to deserve it.

What would he do if he found out Parker was after her?

# Thirty-nine

On an early April Sunday morning at The Fork Stables east of Charlotte, the sky cleared after days of drenching rain. Lexy had campaigned the new Bo through three grueling spring competitions to qualify him for the Rolex Kentucky three-day four-star event at the end of April. She'd braced to fight for her horse's life, but there'd been no messages, no incidents and no more attacks.

So what was Parker up to besides hanging out with the Whiskey Queen?

She wouldn't give in to fear. She lost herself in the morning ritual of mucking out and steered a loaded wheelbarrow to Bo's stall in The Fork's temporary stabling. Hamp was lounging in the doorway, his dark copper features set off by a desert tan polo shirt.

"Don't you have a bunch of rides today?" she asked, but the cut of his tight taupe breeches made her think of last night in the darkened crew cab of his truck.

His slight smile said he read her thoughts. "I scratched Chip's sales prospects. He's pissed, but one has an old suspensory injury, and the other had stifle issues a few months ago. The footing would be hell on them."

The footing sucked. The Fork's massive green and yellow John Deere tractor rumbled past, hauling another big rig from the nearby mud pit that was Day Parking. This weekend everything was primitive.

"I'd pay for a toilet that flushes," she told Hamp.

"You could use Marina's," he deadpanned, and nodded at the Whisky Queen's posh forty-eight-foot long trailer with luxury living quarters. Somehow she'd managed to park it above the muddy lot.

"Not invited. You have access, don't you?"

"Command performances. The hired help has to take his boots off to enter the inner sanctum so she can show me off to friends. And get snapped at by Minx."

Lexy laughed. "But your coaching helps her."

"Yep," he said with a hint of pride. "She's got a serious shot at the Short List this summer."

Lexy topped off the wheelbarrow with a final forkful of wet shavings. "Whereas, you're a shoo-in."

"Don't say that," he hissed. "Bad luck."

He pushed her wheelbarrow to the muck pile while she chose good fat studs for grip and screwed them into Bo's shoes, seating each one tight. Their safety, perhaps their lives, depended on good traction. All around them, horses went out for cross-country and came back, charged with adrenalin.

Bo pawed, clearly eager for his turn.

Saturday, they'd done stadium. It was usually scheduled on Sundays, but the event's directors had switched days, hoping the rain would stop and the cross-country course would be navigable by something other than a boat. Since dawn, when she'd walked the course again, smaller green tractors with front loaders had raced down access lanes, dumping grit and screenings on take-off and landing points to make them safer.

The Preliminary division, starting at eight, had gone well, and so had Intermediate, next up. For Advanced, the Technical Director and Ground Jury had eliminated three obstacles in a low area too boggy from the rain.

Hamp came back and propped the wheelbarrow on the canvas wall at the end of the stall row. "Have they posted changes for us this afternoon?"

"Promised, any moment."

Then she saw riders streaming toward the bulletin boards at the far end of the stables—Olympians like Severson and O'Connor, and other upper level riders she now knew by name, having competed against them all spring up the Eastern Seaboard.

She and Hamp studied it and marked the changes on their original course maps. "Looks like a two-star course," she said.

Hamp's fingers drummed his thigh as if he were galloping it on Ax. "It'll ride like a three-star. But man, it'll mess up start times. When do you go?"

"Early."

"Ax is early too, Trapper, late. God knows when, with all the withdrawals. I may move Trapper up. In between, I'm coaching Queenie through warm up." Queenie was his irreverent nickname for the Whisky Queen. "She's in the middle of the pack."

"Lucky you." Lexy was sorry he had to bow and scrape to her, but she finally understood. Money talked. "I'll wave as we paddle by."

He walked Lexy away from the other riders and squeezed her shoulders. "Pace yourself. Remember the soil here is clay. The galloping lanes could be slick. They're not treating them."

"I'll remember," she said, more confident of Bo than ever. This was their final competition under the Watch List.

"Excellent," he said sincerely, then frowned. "You got a message yet?"

"No, none." Parker hadn't sent a message since Fair Hill in the fall, hadn't made a snide remark, not even after she and Bo had finished well up in the standings in the three biggest competitions so far this spring. She flipped her cell open, just to show Hamp.

"Don't tempt fate," he warned, but a new message flashed on the display.

**Step on a crack**
**Break your horse's back.**
**Or your own.**

Oh God. Parker was back. She had no doubt he'd sent it, sly fox that he was, biding his time, catching her before she went out to ride a slippery, tricky course that had been revised. She hadn't walked the final route.

In the past, his messages had hit *after* the disaster with Orsino, at Fair Hill, and she couldn't forget the mugging. Then HORSE KILLER on Jordan's clinic flyer flashed through her. Each time, she'd known Parker could have done it, and now this latest message would corrode her focus on the course.

The hell it would, she thought. She clenched her teeth and shoved the screen at Hamp. "Better rhyme this time, but the meter's off."

"Be serious, for Christ's sake, and report that bastard."

She read it again, clicked off, and clipped the cell to her waistband. "To whom?"

"The TD. The Ground Jury. The sheriff of what-the-hell-ever county we're in this weekend."

"I will not let him intimidate me."

Hamp flicked a hand in anger. "You are so in denial."

Perhaps, but she knew Parker's day was jammed with running Brad and George at Intermediate and Sailor at Advanced. Before she tackled the course, she had just enough time to see if he'd left any tracks behind him in Marina's RV.

She kissed Hamp's cheek. The kiss felt natural, easy, except for the fact that she wasn't confiding in him about her plan. He would go ballistic. "You're such a mother hen," she said.

"And you're one stubborn goose."

"I'll text it to Gwen for her record. OK?"

"That's my girl," he said. "See you after."

# Forty

Portapotty," Lexy whispered to Jordan near the start gate to cross-country half an hour before Marina's scheduled time, eleven thirty-two. Lexy had watched her warming up Savannah and knew her big rig would be unattended. Unless she'd left Minx to guard it. With luck, the obnoxious yappy little dog was hanging out with Greta.

Lexy slipped through the spectators, nerves firing from the risk she'd chosen.

Back at the muddy stables, she snaked past the temporary quarters, then past the smaller rigs to the dinosaur-sized ones with living quarters. Marina's luxury RV and trailer combo was amongst the largest, wedged side by side, shielding Lexy from passersby. The main door would be locked, but she could climb in through a window.

She lifted the main door's latch, and it was open. She prized off her muddy barn boots, hid them beneath the trailer's chassis and tiptoed in, on alert. No Marina, no yapping, biting dog. Her stockinged feet sank into the posh pile carpet. The living room and kitchen reminded Lexy of yachts she'd been on with her parents as a child, luxury everywhere—granite countertops, walnut cabinetry, gleaming stainless steel. The sofa in the slide-out was tufted leather with brass nailhead trim. Over an unlit gas fireplace, a plasma TV screen ran a loop of Marina competing Tosca and Savannah.

Lexy hurried past a wine cooler that held a dozen fine wines into a bedroom with a wall of drawers and closets. The furry bedcover looked like mink.

Marina's ever-present BlackBerry had to be with her or Greta.

But an iPhone lay in plain sight on a vanity. Lexy checked its memory for her number, but no. She texted herself its number, then scrabbled through drawers, this time trying to return things where she'd found them. Then she opened the nearest closet, looking for overnight bags, hoping to find… what? Digging deeper into a leather duffle, she found expensive perfume, fancy underwear, a luxurious silk robe.

Didn't make Marina guilty of anything but self-indulgence.

With a thud of defeat, Lexy set the luggage back in place and turned to leave when she heard laughter, then a man and woman arguing—Marina, and… Parker? Bugger. Had they both scratched a horse? Or been eliminated? No, right, she remembered, with so many changes to the schedule they could have ridden early.

The main door swung out. Clipping her cell to her waistband, Lexy ran on tiptoes through the marble and glass bathroom to a narrow door that opened into the tack compartment beyond.

"Did you bring the stuff?" Marina asked.

*Stuff?* Lexy froze. Looking back, she saw Marina reflected in mirrors that seemed to be everywhere. And then Parker, who handed her a red box like the Cadbury chocolates Lexy's mother used to give her to celebrate a win. Marina opened a storage cabinet in the bedroom and unlocked a safe.

Whoa. Nobody stored chocolates in a safe.

Had to be drugs. She'd seen drugs at Parker's, but was he Marina's dealer? In the mirror, the outline of their bodies merged. His attack flashed through her, and her yuck factor hit the stratosphere. She fumbled with the flat latch of the back door to the trailer but it wouldn't open. She swore. Surely Marina wouldn't lock it inside the living quarters. Must be jammed. Desperate, she scrunched what felt like her enormous gangly body into a corner of the bathroom. Her knee bumped the stainless toilet paper holder, and she fell across the toilet. The holder clanged on the marble floor, and she scrambled to get up.

Marina stormed in, in boot socks and mud-splattered breeches, shirt clean after she removed her safety vest. She grabbed Lexy's arms, twisted her hands behind her and hauled her, off balance, onto the deep-piled carpet in the living room.

"Well well well," Parker rumbled, still sweaty from cross-country. "Lookee who we've got here."

Marina released Lexy's hands and whipped out her BlackBerry. "I'm calling event security."

"Er. Um." Parker nodded at the safe.

Marina looked down at Lexy. "You stupid little bitch."

*Villgiachia*. Imbriani's taunt of choice. Lexy flushed.

"'Fess up, luv," Parker leaned in, threatening her with a hardness she'd never seen. "You need money? Looking for some weed? Something more exotic?"

"I'm looking for the phone you used to text me."

"That's preposterous," Marina said. "You broke into my RV. I can have you arrested."

"Or not." Lexy fixed on Marina's sculpted face. "I saw you guys with drugs. Authorities will be very interested."

"How dare you," Marina said.

Parker laughed. "Don't worry about her, babe. She's losing it."

"Oh no. She knows exactly what she's doing." Marina's lips thinned. "She's a conniving fraud who snowed Colonel and Jordan into giving her a free ride on the best horse in the country. And now she's got Ben Holt in her hip pocket. What are you doing for him, honey?"

Everything Lexy knew of anger from Imbriani flooded her. "Whereas you use people like Greta and Hamp to do the hard work so you can play the star."

Fast as a viper, Marina slapped Lexy's face.

The blow ramped her anger into rage. She jabbed the heels of her hands into Marina's chest, and she toppled to the floor.

"Yee-haw! Girl fight!" Parker cried, stepping out of the way. From nowhere, Minx chimed in, yapping furiously, and he scooped her up.

Lexy turned from them, revolted by the venom that consumed her, and offered Marina a hand up. "I am so, so sorry."

Marina launched to her feet and flailed at Lexy's face and chest. Grunting in pain and renewed fury, Lexy landed a defensive blow, but Marina grabbed her hair and jerked her off balance. Lexy stumbled and fell on the carpet. Marina fell on her, scratching, punching, swearing.

Parker ditched the dog and ploughed between them, pulled Marina off, and wrapped her in his arms. She bucked against him.

"Hey, luv, chill," he drawled. "She's just the hired help."

Shaken, shaking, Lexy pushed off the carpet and stood, wiping her mouth and tasting blood.

"My daddy would be so disappointed in you ladies," Parker scolded, then shook his head and said to Lexy with concern, "You okay?"

"She *broke* into my *trailer*," Marina reminded him.

"It was unlocked," Lexy said.

Parker's eyes glittered. "Ya gotta stop making a habit of this, Imbriani. Somebody's gonna get hurt."

*Not me,* she vowed, and stumbled out the door, face and body burning.

"Don't come snooping here again," Marina called after her.

Bloody hell, that was close. Still Marina couldn't tell a soul. She may have caught Lexy dead to rights, but Lexy had the scoop on her, and Parker.

He wasn't just her lover but her dealer.

Dazed, she snagged her boots, stuck them on, and stumbled through the sucking mud, illogically desperate to get back to the barn and find Bo safe. At the far end of the row, Greta was scraping Savannah dry. She gave Lexy a hostile once over. Even Tyrone, hosing Brad after Parker's ride, raised a brow at Lexy's rumpled state.

Bo was restless, up for action. So was she. She brushed mud off her boots and set out Bo's tack, glad she'd told no one but Hamp about the ugly new test message. But she'd promised Gwen to keep her posted, for the record. So she punched in her personal number to tell her, but not about the fight or drugs. Not yet.

She got shunted into voice mail and had to leave a message.

# Forty-one

At the stables, Bo was on his toes, keen to run the course his buddies were coming back from. She couldn't rush through tacking him up, or through warm up either. She couldn't let him down. This time, he was the professional, unflappable.

As she should be. At the start gate, she checked her cell.

No word from Gwen.

No new messages from Parker.

Colonel, whose doctors had okayed the weekend away, took her cell, which wasn't allowed on course. Bo was buzzed, but he felt solid. He hadn't been wiggy all spring despite the sunny weather at Red Hills in Florida, at Poplar Place in Georgia, following the spring schedule up the eastern seaboard to Carolina Horse Park. His surgery had held.

Jordan double-checked the girth, bridle, breastplate, stirrups. Lexy felt, as they said in America, good to go. But moments before her final countdown, Ben strolled by. As Olympic coach, he seemed to be everywhere, checking everyone. He looked up, one hand on the knee roll of her saddle.

"Bo's been carrying you around these courses. Don't expect that today."

"You said don't micromanage him," she shot back.

"That still goes, but don't be a passenger either. By all reports, it's tough out there," Ben said, walking beside her to keep Bo moving.

"You mean slick?"

"I mean the going's spotty. Keep your eyes on the lane, your mind on your job."

She didn't need beginner fundamentals, she thought. Bo hadn't been carrying her.

But perhaps Ben had. How many times had he shown up, despite his many duties, with warm support and the exact advice she needed.

Countdown started, and she entered the box.

"Go, and good luck," the starter said, and Lexy launched her stallion into their toughest test yet. The course flew by, fewer spectators than at other courses, kept away by rain and the last-minute switch to Sunday.

As Hamp had predicted, the takeoff and landing spots were superb, and the footing in the galloping lanes was decent.

*Break your horse's back.* The message popped into her mind. Damn Parker.

She jerked her attention to her task, finding her fierce focus.

Focused too, Bo dug in his toes, motoring over the ditch and brush, down to a tricky corner of the Turtle Pond, hooking over to a trakehner—a big log set high over a deep, wide ditch—and then on to splash through the Goose Pond over a gaily-painted giant carved wooden goose, its body bigger than his.

She was in the bubble, brain in gear, body alert, balanced, strong.

Bo was too, no limit to what they could do together.

Three quarters through, she bypassed the canceled jumps and headed up a long grade, demanding at the end of even this shortened course. She was in rhythm with Bo, feeling his every move, her senses alert for the next obstacle, thinking ahead—

half-halts stride by stride down the hill before the steeper drop into the Turtle Pond.

At the top of the hill, Bo arced over an enormous oxer, landed at an angle, and in a sickening second, his hindquarters dropped beneath her. She sank her weight into her stirrups but the left one gave way and was gone. Bo lurched up, flinging her out of the saddle and onto his neck, then stopped.

She grabbed for mane and hooked her right heel on the cantle at the back of the saddle, scrabbling to hang on, one moment her body parallel to Bo's, the next her legs flinging for purchase on the saddle. One leg almost touched the ground, no time to think, but she kicked up under Bo's belly, making herself a human pendulum, trying to get on her horse at the apex of another kick. With her left hand, she grappled for the reins and hooked her left heel in front of the saddle, all of her dangling upside down. She dropped her right leg under Bo's belly and kicked for impulsion, scrambling to climb on, struggling not to touch the ground and be eliminated.

Confused, Bo pinned his ears but nobly stood for her.

Then she glimpsed some stupid spectator heading up the hill to save her.

"No help!" she yelled. Help would disqualify them when they were almost home.

She blanked him out, and with a final massive thrust, she was sideways above the saddle, then dropped onto it, regained her seat and gathered Bo's reins. From the hilltop, a whistle shrilled, the jump judge warning that idiot to clear the lane.

Then Lexy saw the idiot was Ben, obviously ready to rip her off the horse, tuck her under his arm and take her home.

She looked him in the eye. *"No help."*

Her left stirrup was gone, but she found the right one and gunned Bo past him, aiming for the water complex. Bo cleared the brush jump before the water, then bounced the log at the water's edge and cleanly dropped six feet into the pond. He took three splashing strides, and she saw his ears prick forward, felt him fix on the massive carved wooden turtle in the water, felt his resolve in her body and her heart.

*Her hero.* He popped over the big odd obstacle as if it were an ordinary schooling fence.

She checked herself. With only one stirrup she'd have to use all the strength she had left to keep her balance. Driving out of the pond, she faced him to the skinny corner, the kind of jump he'd run out on at Fair Hill.

Trusting his new confidence, she asked him for the tricky short route.

He powered over the skinny. She galloped him the few short strides onto a sunken road and two big strides up a muddy bank made slick by dozens of rivals who'd preceded them. Then on to the final jump, a replica of the handsome stables that were The Fork's pride. The long wide obstacle was inviting to tired horses at the end of the grueling run.

Bo soared over it, nothing ahead but finish line. Lexy let out a war whoop and, in sync with Bo, legged him up to racing speed for the final hundred meters, past the timer and the steward. Bo was trotting when she leapt off to relieve him of the burden on his back.

Her knees buckled when she landed, and she saw Ben charging up the access road, something dangling from his hand.

Jordan, Colonel, and Tyrone—her team—swarmed to her side with water buckets, a halter and a sweat sheet. She loosened the girth, Jordan took the saddle, Colonel threw on the sheet, and Tyrone swapped the bridle for a halter.

Steam rose off Bo's flanks, but his eyes sparkled.

Colonel thumped Lexy's back. "Well *done*, darlin'. *Well* done."

"Did you see that? We almost fell," Lexy said, bracing her hands on her knees and gulping air, the horror of what almost happened catching up to her.

"Save of the decade," Jordan said, "if not the century." She took the lead line from Tyrone.

Lexy didn't need praise, she needed to check her horse. She walked round him, eyeballing every inch of his sweat-slicked body, then running her fingers up and down his steel-strong legs. He'd made it. They'd made it together.

At the start box directly opposite, Hamp was giving Marina last-minute advice before she put Tosca to the course, unaware of Lexy's ordeal. Before she could wave to him that she'd come in clear, Kim Legris, the Technical Delegate again this weekend, raced up the access road in her official Land Rover, her salt-and-pepper hair bristling. Another official braked behind her and got out of her SUV, wearing a vest labeled Safety Delegate over ample breasts.

Kim flipped open a notepad. "Are you hurt?"

"No, my horse was awesome." *Saved my life*.

"What exactly happened?" Kim asked.

Lexy described how Bo had slipped, how she'd scrambled to stay on.

"Did you touch the ground?" Kim asked.

"She didn't," Ben put in, just arriving, his expression grim. "I saw the whole thing, from the start to her spectacular save. But—" He held a stirrup and its broken leather up for everyone to see. "She finished on one stirrup."

"That's not illegal," Kim said.

"Is your horse okay?" The Safety Delegate scribbled furiously.

"He seems to be. We'll know more at Trot Up in the morning. Can I go ice him now?"

"Sounds like a plan," the woman said, her grim expression easing. "I'll write this up. *Horse slipped but did not fall, rider finished on one stirrup*. Congratulations."

She and Kim stepped aside to confer, then got in their vehicles and sped off on separate access roads. Lexy turned for a closer look at Bo's hind legs. Catching her breath, she probed every inch of stifle, gaskin, hock, cannon, fetlock, and pastern, searching for any injury he might have sustained in his struggle to stay on his feet.

Hamp came round behind the horse with Ben.

"You should have pulled up," Ben said, his face livid. "Jumping three-star obstacles without a stirrup was a damned fool stupid thing to do."

She hadn't told Hamp and Colonel who she was to Ben, but couldn't let him get away with this.

"Are you saying that as my father or the Olympic coach?"

Hamp went stone still and Colonel arched a shaggy brow.

"As your father, I believe." Jordan touched Ben's arm. "For Pete's sake, Ben, Andrew Nicholson went round Burghley four-star on one stirrup a few years ago. It's what we train for."

"Andrew Nicholson is one of the top riders in the world."

Lexy looked Ben in the eye. "So am I, and younger."

"You tell 'im, darlin'," Colonel said.

"Besides," she went on, "if you're thinking dangerous riding, he was under control. The wet ground made him slip, not his speed, and he protected me. He's genuine, smart, the horse Jordan says he used to be."

"You risked your lives to prove that."

"Bullcrap," Colonel said. "This sport used to be for men, not chicken-shits."

"I just did my job. And he did his," said Lexy.

"For now, you're ahead of us," Hamp said wryly, obviously trying to get Ben to lighten up.

With a humph of protest, Ben ran his fingers over the broken stirrup leather and held it up to Lexy where everyone could see. "You didn't check your tack."

"I always check my tack."

"I saw," said Jordan. "And I checked after her."

"Somebody missed something."

"Let me see." Jordan took the leather from him, studied it, and handed it to Colonel.

He poked its edges with ridged, blunt-cut fingernails. "Ben's right. Some sonabitch did something."

Lexy leaned in to see. Stitches that had attached the leather to the buckle had frayed and given way. "I should have noticed this."

Hamp shook his head. "Not necessarily. The buckle's hidden under the saddle flap."

"Or," said Jordan, "they could have wiped the excess off."

"Whoever did it, it happened at home," Colonel said. "So tell Gwen. She's been on the case from the get-go."

"Don't know what good it'll do, but worth a try," Jordan said.

"I have to cool Bo down," Lexy said stiffly, and took his reins.

"I'll walk you back. Ax isn't up for another hour," Hamp said.

She strode off with him, leaving Ben and the leather behind.

But not her sharp new fear. Parker had hit a new low, she didn't know when or how. But he'd gone past messing with her mind. He didn't care if he killed her, and she had no idea how to stop him, short of throwing in the towel and never competing Bo again.

Not an option. Still, terror she'd never felt flying over giant obstacles, or even with Imbriani, lashed her, but she walked on, plotting furiously to ransack everything Parker owned when she got home, looking for—what?

Her shoulders sagged. She had no idea.

Beside them, Bo clopped happily along in his rangy walk, endorphins flooding his system after his grand run. The temporary stabling came into view.

"Maybe you should lay off competitions till we catch him," Hamp said.

"Hell, no. No way."

"He could kill Bo too."

"I'll camp outside his stall."

"You did that before. Parker's only gotten more devious."

She turned on Hamp. "What do you want me to do? Let him dictate my life?"

Hamp punched a memory number in his cell and handed it to her.

"You tell Gwen."

"I already bothered her about the message."

He glared at Lexy. "Bother her about this."

She took the cell but had to leave another message.

Lexy secured the last Velcro strap on Bo's final shipping boot, and stood. He craned his head around and nudged her back, telling her he was in charge. But he wasn't, and fear for his life lashed her. She squared off in front of him, her hands on his halter, and gazed into his bright eyes, all trust and liquid chocolate. "No matter what, I won't let him hurt you."

She led him off and he took comical exaggerated steps, adjusting to the thick wraps. Tyrone cranked the truck, and Bo gave an impatient whinny, sleek sides heaving, all stallion, tall on his toes and looking over the world he thought he owned.

"Never, ever, buddy boy," she whispered, and walked him on the trailer.

An hour and a half later, Tyrone wheeled them into Hawks Nest. The seventy-mile drive had been fast, the truck's passengers mostly silent. Everyone piled out of the club cab, Ruth coming to help Tyrone with Colonel, Jordan propping on her cane, obviously more done in than usual by long hours on her feet. Ben supported her free arm, his tender attention touching Lexy's heart.

Gwen met them at the barn door in her off-hours uniform —a windbreaker with *Sheriff* embroidered on the back and *Moore County* in a half-moon above it, plain polo shirt and cargo pants beneath. She'd pinned her badge at her hip pocket. "So, you're alive," she said to Lexy grimly.

Lexy gave her the stirrup leather. "You wanted to see this."

Gwen inspected it, then looked at her sister and her father. "Don't suppose we're lucky enough nobody touched it."

"Only us." Ben swept his hand around, including everybody.

"Right now, I want to talk to Lexy. Privately."

"I told you on the phone."

Gwen scowled. "Really? I think you're holding back on me."

"Sweetheart," Ben urged. "Tell her everything you know. Because it looks to me like someone's after you."

"That's all I can say."

Gwen hissed through her teeth. "It's bad enough when the bad guys lie, but when the good guys hold back, I can't do my job. And my job tonight is to protect my father and my sister. You too, in spite of yourself."

"She's not the problem, Gwennie," Colonel said. "Somewhere on my farm, in my neighborhood, there's a traitor, liar and cheat who's plotting to harm this pretty young woman and my best horse. What are you going to do about it?"

Gwen bit her lip, then said with obvious control, "I can expedite the lab tests, Daddy, but I don't know what we're looking for. I'll have something Tuesday. Tomorrow if we're lucky."

They were lucky, more or less. Monday at Hawks Nest, late in the afternoon, Lexy was finishing half an hour of quiet, lovely flatwork on Marcus. He was light but bold beneath her, soft in his mouth, on his way to being the star his winning record as a four- and five-year-old had promised.

She should be elated. But Gwen in uniform crossed the arena to her, thwacking rolled-up sheets of paper against her palm. She looked at Lexy with her father's piercing chestnut eyes.

"Any reason you use muriatic acid on your stirrup leathers?"

Lexy dismounted, jarred by the shift from her blissful ride to Gwen's stern scrutiny. "I don't even know what it does."

"Clean things, sterilize them? Rot the stitching?"

Blimey. "Where would he get it?"

*"He,"* Gwen repeated in her dry, ironic way. "You think it's a man."

Jesus. She'd have to watch herself. "I don't suspect a woman." *Of the sabotage, just doing drugs.*

Gwen scanned the report and gave a wry grin. "Sorry. My lab guys can't test for the perp's sex."

"But where would anyone get acid?"

"Swimming pool supply store, any home or commercial pool's storage shed containing chemicals."

"You mean, like Chip's pool?"

"Exactly. Or the country club's."

"What does the acid do?" Lexy forged on.

"Lowers PH in pools. In people it burns skin on contact, eats away at fibers. Nasty stuff. On your saddle leather's stitching, it was injected with a syringe. Different gauge needles, interestingly. Eighteen, twenty, twenty-two. Like an experiment to see what would work."

"Crazy."

"Yeah. Look, I gotta go tell Jordan. Daddy—he doesn't need to know this yet. So don't bring it up with him." Then Gwen peered into her eyes. "But you're on notice. I need you to come clean. Tell me anything you know."

Lexy hadn't known about the acid, and everything else she'd found out about Parker would break his family's heart.

"I'll do my best." If it was new, if it offered proof.

Jordan kept a medicine cabinet on the wall filled with first aid and emergency supplies. She was fastidious about sanitation, which Lexy respected from what she'd learned working for Simon. Riffling through the cabinet, Lexy found half a dozen syringes in cellophane, unopened, ready for their first use. There were needles of several sizes, all in safety caps, seals unbroken, none hooked up to a syringe.

Which proved nothing.

She needed to find one in Parker's keeping.

The next afternoon, Lexy got luckier. Parker and Marina finished schooling their horses before dinner, then headed for Virginia in Marina's Range Rover to look at, Parker said, a dynamite sales prospect for her. Lexy couldn't get into Marina's RV, which she now made much of keeping locked. But Parker had left his tack box unsecured and the Porsche in the drive. This time, he couldn't possibly get back early and surprise her. She'd check the tack box first, then the car, then, if she had to, his condo again.

Because it was Parker she suspected of the acid. He had daily access to Bo's saddles in the family tack room where he kept his too. It would make sense for him to keep needles and syringes handy in his tack box, the one place she'd not searched last fall. But the acid wouldn't have been there then before the sabotage. Checking for it should be a simple matter now, but she was shaking. That ruined stirrup leather could have killed her, and he knew it. If he found out she was zeroing in on him, God knew what he'd do to save himself. Or get even.

Finally the boarders left, and lights went out at the house. Lexy looked out back at Tyrone's trailer. The blue aura of a TV flickered. She hoped to God he'd fallen asleep.

The stuff in Parker's tack and storage boxes looked like the post-apocalyptic chaos of his office in his condo, but nothing incriminated him. Crushed, she headed for his Porsche. She didn't know how to pick locks, but cocky psychopath he was turning out to be, he'd left it open. She scrunched into the driver's seat, her heart in her throat. Programs and results from the spring's events littered the passenger's seat.

She checked the glove box. Nothing there but a much-thumbed Porsche user manual and the car's current registration. She scrabbled deeper into the litter on the passenger's seat and, amongst programs and orders of go from the spring's events, found a half-full water bottle and an unopened beer. Beneath the jumble, her fingers bumped into a digital camera.

She clicked through the pictures and saw herself on Bo in the arena, over jumps, on Hawks Nest's trails and practice course. With Hamp, about to start cross-country at The Fork. With Hamp that early morning, in the sensual embrace Parker had interrupted.

Pervert. They were all of her.

She sucked in harsh breaths, feeling violated. Would he put the photos up on Facebook, Pinterest? Were videos on YouTube next?

She called Gwen.

Gwen turned into the driveway in ten minutes, headlamps off under a crescent moon, straight from home in cutoffs and a denim jacket, no badge. Without a word she took the camera and flicked from shot to shot, disappearing behind a shield of detached professionalism. It occurred to Lexy this was the first time anything she'd reported to Gwen had definitively pointed to her brother, and she was giving nothing away.

Finally she spoke. "Thought you said you were looking for syringes."

"I didn't find any, just the pictures. They give me the creeps."

"They're, ah, interesting, not probative, not illegal—I mean, it's a free country. But—honest, I don't know what to do about them. Add them to the pile."

"You mean take the camera?"

"God no. Wipe it off and put it back. Keep an eye out."

"For what?"

"Honey, I love my brother, but I know for a fact the shrinks threw up their hands on helping him by the time he got to high school. Under all that charm, he's like one button shy of a nuclear blast."

"And you're telling me this now?"

Gwen winced. "I just never saw him hurt anybody but himself."

"What about women—girlfriends?"

"He's the original rolling stone—I thought they all knew the risk."

And now, so did she.

"I'm glad you called," Gwen went on, her tone softer, personal. "I mean, not glad to find this out. But you did the right thing. You got a gun?"

She shrugged. "My trusty Swiss army knife, everywhere I go."

"Not enough."

"Please. Don't tell Jordan. Or Colonel." They had enough on their minds.

Gwen cocked her head, thinking. "I can talk to Parker."

"God, no." That would just drive him deeper in.

"Okay. I'll ask Tyrone to keep an eye out."

"And he'll come running to my side."

"Yeah. Maybe."

"Then thanks."

Gwen squeezed Lexy's shoulder. "Be careful, sweetie. I don't have a legal leg to stand on, and I can't predict where my brother's going."

# Forty-two

For the next three weeks, Parker avoided her, which was no reassurance whatsoever. Her spring schedule was intense, but she stuck to her plan to camp out at Bo's stall. She and Hamp squeezed in time to be together prepping their lower-level mounts for local events but she missed his touch. Missed sex.

Still what mattered most for now was fine-tuning Bo and Ax for Rolex in Lexington, Kentucky. It was one of only six elite four-star competitions in the world, and the only one in North America—no lower level divisions competing, just the crème de la crème of four-star horses.

At last on a late April Tuesday after midnight, the Hawks Nest Farm and McRae Center convoy was underway.

"Thank goodness," Jordan said to Lexy a few hours later. They entered the blue-hazed mounds of the Great Smoky Mountains, heading to Tennessee, routed to hook north to Kentucky. "They cleared the rock slide on I-40 so we didn't have to go by West Virginia."

Lexy was driving the big rig, caravanning with Marina and Parker in front and Hamp and Ben behind them in Chip's rig, each with all their four-star horses. She and Jordan had Bo and a couple of four-star horses from neighbors in the area.

The pre-dawn hours of the drive had felt slow and arduous. Now the sun rose behind them. Lexy wanted to get to a gas plaza and hand over the wheel to Jordan. They hadn't stopped for gas since leaving the farm at three a.m., and were running on the back tank.

"What does the GPS say now?" Lexy asked Jordan.

"We just passed Black Mountain, and Asheville's coming up in twenty minutes. Oh crap," she added. "Morning rush hour in the mountains on the interstate."

Lexy glanced at the clock on the cab's console. It was seven-thirty, and they were driving into heavy traffic. Hauling horses was plain hard work, requiring no end of vigilance. Ninety-eight percent of the drivers on the road in the U.S. as well as Europe zigzagged in and out around a four-ton rig, oblivious to the fact that in an emergency it could not stop fast. The two percent who understood drove semis and fought this battle every day.

"We're making good time, though, right?" Lexy asked, psyched to be on the way.

"We'll get to Lexington by three, find their stalls, set up for the night, stretch our legs, eat."

Lexy laughed. "Collapse. If I weren't so excited. My first four-star on Bo. Blimey. Who'd have thought? I can't wait."

Jordan sighed, folded the map one fold, placed it on the floorboard, and laid her head on the head rest. "Me either. You guys couldn't be more ready."

Suddenly Lexy heard a loud *ka-pow* beneath the right front side of the engine. The cab wrenched violently right too, almost jerking the steering wheel from her hand.

*Don't flip, don't fishtail, and get off the road,* flashed through her brain, and she clutched the steering wheel for dear life, her chest on fire. She heard the harrowing flappety-flap of a blown-out tire tread and steel belt banging the wheel well and the rat-a-tat-tat of rubber bits of tire carcass striking the underbelly of the cab. She steadied it to the left and tapped the brake pedal to engage the trailer's brakes as well.

But the truck's cab bucked beneath her, and the trailer fishtailed into the vehicles overtaking her. As a last resort, she touched the manual brakes to bring the trailer into line. Heaven help Hamp, coming up behind, if he was not on his toes. The tires crossed the grinding washboard of the rumble strip. It vibrated through the steering wheel and up her arms. The steel barrier along the road was coming at her fast, and she hung on to the wheel, no time to pray. The cab's right front fender hit the barrier at an angle. She straightened the wheels, but the rear axle whipped into it, metal screeching on metal. She braked, and braked, and softly braked again.

Stopped. From the blowout to full stop took mere seconds, but it felt like forever.

Irate drivers zoomed past, pounding their horns as if she'd endangered them on purpose. She checked the rearview mirror. The end of the trailer poked into the right-hand lane. Gingerly she steered left, away from the barrier, and the truck limped ahead far enough to bring the trailer in line, the whole rig now safely on the emergency lane. Thank God, it was a straight stretch of road, but every cell inside her quaked, and hot tears streamed down her face.

"Honey?" Jordan touched her forearm with trembling fingers. "Are you okay?"

"There were no barriers where Mom went in the lake."

"Oh sweetheart, I'm so sorry."

Alarm replaced her tears. "Ohmigod, the horses." She checked upcoming traffic in the undamaged mirror on the driver's side. At the first break, she threw open her door and got out. Jordan tried the passenger's door, but it was crumpled shut, so she scrambled over the console between them, threaded her legs under the steering wheel, and got out too.

Lexy dashed to the trailer, Jordan behind her, as Ben and Hamp pulled in, emergency lights flashing. They burst out of their truck, slammed doors, raced up.

"What do you need?" Ben shouted above the roar of tires and engines, cell in hand. "EMTs, wrecker? What happened?"

"Wrecker. Blow out, right front tire. Hit the wall hard at an angle," said Jordan.

"Probably bent the frame," Lexy added. *Totaled*. Jinxed. Unlike the truck, the trailer hadn't hit the guard rail. She opened its escape door, and three pairs of luminous equine eyes blinked into the slanting morning light. *Where's our hay?*

Lexy's knees buckled with relief. They were safe—the horses, Jordan and herself. Lexy checked Bo, stem to stern, and Jordan checked the boarders.

Ben stepped in. "Wrecker'll be at least half an hour. EMTs say soon."

"We don't need medical," Lexy protested but her voice cracked.

"They always send them anyway," he said. "Horses okay?"

"They're troopers," she said, and gave him a weak smile. "*That was different. Fun.*"

Ben grinned, obviously relieved too. "Eventers. You gotta love them."

"Adrenaline junkies," Hamp said, and she knew he was right. He wove between them to Lexy and wrapped her in an embrace. Ben hugged Jordan too, phone in hand, and then walked up front to check the damage. He came back with flaps of rubber in his hand, his face grim.

"Sidewall disintegrated. Wonder how they did it?"

"How who did what?" Jordan asked.

"Whoever did the stirrup leathers."

"It's a blowout," Lexy said, not wanting Ben to know she suspected Parker, who she wanted roasting on a spit. How the hell had he pulled this off? And how the hell could she prove it?

"You think this nut case is going to stop?" Ben asked.

"Honestly," Jordan said. "Blowouts happen. But how do we get to Rolex now?"

"There's room for one horse in Chip's trailer," Hamp said from the door.

"Marina's got room for two," Lexy pointed out.

"So who wants to make that call?" Jordan said with an ironic smile.

"Marina does not share," Hamp said.

"And she'll have to turn round," Lexy said, and suddenly everyone but Ben was laughing. They'd survived and were back to mundane matters, like the Whiskey Queen and how the world revolved around her, her wishes and desires.

Hamp nodded at Ben. "She's not apt to turn you down. You know—What's in it for me if I do the coach a favor?"

Ben rolled his eyes, but Hamp gave him her number. Ben walked away to call as the EMTs pulled in.

"You folks need help?" a burly fellow asked.

"We're fine," Jordan told them. "So are the horses."

The EMTs and the North Carolina Highway Patrol filed reports, and the EMTs pulled away. One patrolman stayed behind to direct traffic when the wrecker came. Arriving half an hour later, Marina pulled off the road in her luxury liner, looking supremely inconvenienced. "It took ten minutes to find a cloverleaf large enough to safely get off the interstate and another twenty to get here," she complained.

Parker climbed down from the high cab of her semi, trotted to see Jordan's crumpled truck, and returned with wildly inappropriate cheer. "Man, sis, tough luck. You got that rig insured?"

"Naturally," Jordan said stiffly, then added to Marina, "Thanks for coming. I knew I could count on you."

Marina glanced at the truck then Jordan with a shudder. "Oh, my dear. This is a disaster."

"It's a delay all right. Luckily, only the truck was damaged."

"Well then, let's get this show on the road," Marina said in best-friend, good-sport mode which Lexy suspected was to impress both Jordan and the Olympic coach.

"Great," Jordan said mildly. "We'll have to transfer the tack and supplies, and then the horses."

"Sorry," Marina said sweetly. "No way that stallion's coming with my mares."

"No, of course not," Ben put in. "We need you to take the geldings."

Marina pursed her lips. "I'm not insured for commercial towing."

"Then do it for free, luv," Parker said cavalierly. "It's not like you can't afford to."

All six people bustled about, moving tack and supplies into the two already packed trailers while keeping an eye on the traffic zooming by. Marina oversaw that every piece of equipment and supplies did not touch her stuff. Parker ran interference for her, relentlessly upbeat.

Lexy flipped from suspicion to conviction.

He was too happy, as if he'd won again.

Then they unloaded the horses one by one, Bo first into Ben and Hamp's trailer, and the others into Marina's fancy rig.

Meanwhile, a big Kenworth heavy-duty wrecker drove up. The driver got out, crouched on his hands and knees, and checked the chassis of the damaged truck.

"There's a good outfit south of town can look at this," the driver drawled in mountain-ese, "but the frame looks bent. I'm guessing that truck's a goner."

"I know," Jordan said stoically, then cleaned out the cab of her truck and signed the papers.

Thank God, Lexy thought. The truck was the only fatality. But how had Parker done it? Damn Ben, for planting that idea. Not knowing—and not knowing what was next—would prey on her and make a difficult weekend hell.

Which was no doubt Parker's intention. She'd be damned if she'd fold now.

The wrecker guy hooked clanking chains to the chassis of the disabled truck when Ben came up to Jordan. "I'm gonna miss that rig," she told him.

"You got everything out?"

Lexy forced a smile. "Luggage, snacks, papers, log books, health certificates."

Everything but peace of mind.

Ben picked up their bags and started walking away. "No, wait. Let's take that tire to Gwen." And before Lexy could react, he turned to the wrecker guy. "Can you take that tire off, buddy?"

With a "whatever" kind of shrug, the chap loosened the lug nuts, pulled it off, and set it in Ben's truck bed. He motioned to its spare.

"No need to put that thing on where this wreck's going."

"Right," Ben said.

The wrecker drove off, Jordan's giant rig hobbling along behind it, broken now, like her.

"Hey," Lexy heard Ben say to her. "We'll get you another one. Let's hit the road."

Marina had climbed into her cab. Parker stood outside. "She's got space for another passenger, but the mood's a little dicey. So here's my recommendation. The two young lovebirds in Chip's back seat, and the two old ones up front."

Lexy wanted to smack him.

"Fine by me," Hamp said, putting a possessive arm around her waist.

Ben held the doors for Jordan to get up front with him, and Lexy behind. Lexy climbed in and caught his gaze. "If I'm stuck with you for the next five hours, no lectures and no smothering."

"Oh ho," said Parker, hands up to shield himself. "So that's the way the wind blows. I am so outta here." And he turned, climbed into Marina's big diesel, consulted with her and called back. "We'll lead. Meet you at the next gas plaza." The highway patrolman cleared rush-hour traffic from the right lane, and they rolled out.

Hamp climbed in after Lexy, and Ben grinned at them through the rearview mirror. "As long as I can't see you guys necking, I'm cool."

"Snogging, Coach," Hamp shot back. "In England, it's called snogging."

Lexy gave a self-conscious laugh but pressed her fists into her roiling stomach. Parker couldn't have known the tire would blow out on a straight stretch of road instead on a tight curve in the Smokies with nothing but a steep cliff dropping down.

And he hadn't given a flying fuck whether they'd survived.

# Forty-three

**Y**ou can sleep in," Hamp murmured in Lexy's ear in the throaty night-time voice she loved waking up to. They were sharing the motel room Jordan had reserved months ago to share with Lexy, but Jordan was with Ben tonight.

"Three-thirty," he went on. "I gotta get up."

"Mummmph," she muttered, seeking his heat. It was Thursday. Trot-up had been Wednesday, and their guys had passed in fine form. Her dressage test was today, but she still ached from Tuesday's crash. She'd lain awake beside Hamp reliving the speed, the grinding crash, the bruising impact. Images of the last moments of her mother's life assaulted her, fresh and agonizing as last summer.

*But we go on,* her mother would have said.

To go on, Lexy needed Hamp and being held and making love. She wiggled up to him, hoping he'd have time for a reassuring quickie.

They did it in the shower, fast and hot and soapy, then rinsed off, dressed and headed out. She stretched her stride to keep up with his longer one, climbed into the truck, and took out her cell to text Jordan that she'd meet her at the stables.

**Red rover red rover
It's time it's over
The next one's on you**

"Son of a *bitch*," she shrieked, and held the display for Hamp to read.

He stuck it on top of the steering wheel and scanned it, not slowing.

"Bastard," he ground out, taking the ramp onto I-75 and gunning it to interstate speed. Bluegrass farms sprawled quietly along either side, ghostly in the pearly light that edged the eastern horizon. A sunshiny day was coming up, as Parker had predicted yesterday after consulting the laptop weather gods. He'd had the gall to look her up and say he hoped she was okay.

"Asshole's taking credit for Tuesday's blowout," Hamp added.

Lexy clenched her fists in vengeful fury, digging her nails into her flesh. "It's evidence he was there, not proof."

Hamp cut her a warning look. "Do not leave my side, or Ben's, or Jordan's. Do not go this alone."

"Not remotely tempted."

"And you tell Ben the minute he gets here. Jordan too."

She agreed to. She'd spent yesterday on the prowl for Parker and Marina, but they'd retreated into her RV with their drugs and pre-paids and their plan. Or was it only his? Had Marina had anything to do with the blowout or the message?

"There's our exit," she said to Hamp at Iron Works Pike. "Sorry to add my problems to your weekend. You have enough on your mind."

He pressed her hand on his rock-hard thigh. "No, babe, I'm signed on for this."

They drove into the Horse Park in silence. It was easy to get lost on the twisting, turning roads, confusing to make out which led to the competition complex, the museum, the polo fields. At the barns, grooms and riders bustled around, mucking stalls, putting out morning hay, grain and water. One of the ninety-seven equine entrants kicked its stall wall. Another gave a leisurely snort. An anxious whinny demanded grain. Bo was stabled far from any mares. Lexy looked for his head over his stall door but did not see him.

*The next one's on you* inched through her mind like an earworm.

Don't race to him and spook the other horses, she told herself.

Don't let anyone see how freaked you are.

She found him lying down, his mahogany coat dotted with shavings, showing he'd rolled. She panicked. Horses rolled when they colicked and their bellies hurt, then lay down after they'd given up. Summoning everything she'd learned from Ulrich and Simon, she slipped into the stall and dropped to her knees alongside Bo.

He lifted his head, blinked with curiosity.

"Buddy boy," she whispered, running her hands over him.

With a grunt, he got up and shook, creating a mini-blizzard of pale shavings. She jumped out of his way. He nuzzled her, seeking a treat. He wouldn't ask for food if he was colicking.

She was getting paranoid. But the message said her tormentor wasn't through.

"Hamp said you wanted to see me," Ben said from the door.

She handed him her cell.

"Oh honey, that's low," he said. "Okay. One of us will be with you all the time, Hamp or me or Jordan. Tyrone. Roger, in a pinch." On Wednesday, Chip had flown Roger and Colonel here in his private plane and brought Tyrone for added security.

She nodded, dazed. The U. S. Olympic coach had appointed himself her protector.

"I know what this competition means to you," he said. "But you know you could scratch. Whoever it is will leave you alone."

*No.* "That's caving. Besides, it's not your call."

"I wish it was, but do what you gotta do." He hugged her shoulders under the arc of a strong arm, and his compassion

broke her. Tears spilled down her face. "I worked so hard—"
She sobbed, gulping words "—to get on my feet after Mom—
died."

He wrapped his arms around her, rubbing circles on her
back, and she leaned into his strength. Never once had Imbriani
comforted her like this, but she'd longed for him to care.

Finally Ben pulled away. "I'm here for you, okay?"

She looked at him, embarrassed. "I—Thank you."

"As your father." He glanced heavenward, vulnerable and
almost shy. "Your real father. This may be terrible timing, but
I have to tell you something. Your mother left me a letter."

Her stomach clenched. "She wrote you?" And Pookie and
everyone in the universe...except her only daughter.

"Just once. Her letter came last summer when I took up
the coaching post." He looked down, a tinge of red flushing
his high cheekbones. "London postmark, no return address,
you know the way they do it over there. I figured some broker
trying to sell me a horse and chucked it in the backlog pile. Ran
across it last month doing taxes, and sat on it. Didn't want to
distract you from the spring competition."

"My mother wrote you before she died?"

"Years ago," Ben said. "To be delivered to me after her..."
Death. "She *knew*?"

"She'd put Imbriani on your birth certificate, but it was
me, she swore it. She apologized for deceiving me, and you.
She was terrified you'd be alone and hoped I'd find it in my
heart to, ah, to—her words—help you out. With horses."

"I'm glad she told you," she said at last. If she'd had any
doubts about what Ben had known, this put them to rest.

"Me too," he said. "And proud of you."

She lowered her head, embarrassed to be so pleased, then
met his gaze. "I'd like to see the letter."

"Done."

"I—I don't—know what to call you."

His smile was warm, accepting and approving. "We got through the hard parts, sweetie. I'm sure we can figure this one out."

His confidence bolstered her, and she vowed not to let Parker defeat her before Rolex even began. She would be the keen, honed rider she'd been at Badminton last year when it had been spring and her mother had been at her side. But now she had a year's more experience, the best coaches in the world, and the best horse she'd ever ridden.

That afternoon, an hour before her test, she groomed Bo and tacked up under Jordan's careful scrutiny. Earlier Lexy had shown her the latest message and told her she suspected Parker. Jordan had groaned in helpless anger and turned away.

"Show him up today," she now said firmly, then was considerately silent as Lexy went through her pre-performance ritual, fighting the earworm of the warning, and then riding to the warm-up ring, outwardly calm, inwardly trying to be.

Twenty minutes into warm-up, Bo broke stride twice during extensions. Ben motioned her to the one-board fence surrounding the area. "You need to forget that message, honey. Bo can only be as loose as you are."

"In other words," she said gamely, "ommm."

"You got it, and lay off that inside rein. Get him coming through behind."

"I can do that."

"Counting on you," he said, and softly squeezed her knee.

Bo did the test with such ease and precision, she didn't pick up her score sheet till after lunch. They'd come in at an incredibly respectable thirty-two and, for the moment, were in the lead. At Rolex.

# Forty-four

The next morning, Parker hadn't sent another message, and Lexy rode her stallion down the roped-off lane to their first four-star cross-country challenge. Bo had placed well at Pau, and she'd aced Badminton, but the enormity of this venue's challenge was sinking in. Kentucky Horse Park might not have the stately homes and ancient grounds of the top European competitions, but the course was relentlessly world class, its bright spring bluegrass and huge old greening trees beautiful and deceptively inviting.

At warm up, just minutes before her ride, Lexy saw Jordan standing by, fist clenched on Bo's spare halter. Colonel looked ready to chew the golf cap on his grizzled head. Ben was working his way back and forth between warm-up and the finish line, saying a word to his Olympic team contenders before they started, then meeting them as they came off the course. She could see their respect for him as they took his debriefings with a smile, and she held her secret knowledge of his confidence in her to her heart. Not only was he her mentor, but he was a sterling example of the best in the sport.

After she'd distrusted and resented him, he still wanted to be her father, to coach her and just bloody well love her. He kept a keen eye out for her too, something she'd lost when her mother died, something Hamp wouldn't have time to give her here.

Inside, a weight shifted, and her heart opened to the love he'd freely given her from the day he'd learned she was his daughter.

She'd ride Bo to hell and back to prove she was worthy.

Without a word about yesterday, Ben put her and Bo through their paces, making sure she focused, lengthening and shortening Bo's stride to the different practice fences. Two months ago, even one, Ben's intervention might have put her off, but today she was simply grateful. He saw everything and was so bloody confident in her. He patted Bo's neck and walked them away from the crowd. "You two look great. Feel ready?"

"We're good to go," she said.

"I know, but this course is the devil. Don't forget to fight for it."

"I fight for everything."

His iceberg eyes warmed once again. "So you do."

She counted down the seconds in the start box, and Bo launched onto the course, his life in her hands, simply trusting her. She trusted *him*, and the wreck and Parker's latest message disappeared as they tackled skinnies, oxers, coffins, trakehners, a ditch and brush, and splashed through the goose and turtle pond.

They finished with a double clear, no refusals and no time faults. Their partnership felt so solid and harmonious she didn't care if they were fifth or tenth, or twentieth, but in fact because of Bo's stellar dressage test, they were in seventh. She looked for Ben to share the glory, but he had other riders to attend to. Hamp was still on course. She checked her watch. He must be halfway round.

Walking back to the stalls, Tyrone took Bo's reins and Jordan shooed her off. "Colonel and Ben are at the Head of the Lake. Go watch."

"I'm staying to guard my horse."

Tyrone crossed his burly arms. "Go. I'm bigger, stronger, meaner. They expect you."

She found Ben and Colonel at the Head of the Lake, spectators everywhere.

Colonel kissed her cheek. "Brilliant, darlin'."

"You bobbled the brush and ditch," Ben said, but hugged her to his side. For now, he could give no stronger praise than an honest evaluation and that hug.

A couple of tired horses, first timers at Rolex, spooked at the giant carved wooden duck, a tricky obstacle set on an angle in the foot-and-a-half deep waters. Another rider's horse slipped, and the rider took a bath. The horse bolted into the spectators but was quickly caught. His rider trudged through the pond, water pouring off her. Closing in, Marina came through on Savannah, her ride efficient, clean. But Lexy shuddered at the woman's duplicity. The pure pros came next— Dutton, O'Connor, Springer, Law, and Davidson all vying for the lead.

"Textbook," Lexy said to Ben after they'd gone through.

"Been a great afternoon," he said.

Hamp splashed through flawlessly, a primer of harmony between man and horse. Lexy watched, impressed. A few minutes later Parker plunged into the lake on Brad, his top horse. The gelding tossed his head, looking unusually winded.

"More leg, less hand," Ben coached though Parker couldn't hear.

The pair was out of sync, Parker riding as Lexy had never seen him. Brad shortened stride as Parker pointed him at the giant duck. At the last instant, Brad ran out, dunking Parker in the frigid water. The crowd gasped. Brad galloped toward the stables, reins and stirrups flapping. A few brave bystanders spread their arms as if mere mortals could stop a train. Others darted ahead, hoping to cut him off.

Parker leapt up, water streaming off his vest and helmet.

*Fuck,* he mouthed, then caught his balance, turned, and did a double-take, seeming to realize he'd crashed in front of V.I.P.s and possibly the Olympic coach.

A grin spread across his face. Instantly assuming the easy charm he'd shown the day Lexy first met him, he lifted his helmet off his head, pointed a booted toe, bent his torso forward, and swept his arm behind his back, bowing like a cavalier.

The crowd answered with laughter, wolf whistles, and wild applause.

"Damn," Ben said beside her. "Wish the rest of his work measured up to that."

Lexy felt nauseous. Beneath Parker's charm and gutsy recovery was a man plotting to hurt her horse. And her. Would he be more determined to ruin them now, after his fall and her success?

That night back at the hotel, Hamp slept beside her like a man who had no inner demons. She slept in fits and starts, not allowed to guard Bo in the competition barn as she could have done at home. She got up, paced, and checked her phone. No texts. So what would it be this time? A rein, a martingale, a dog breaking free and flying between Bo's legs when they galloped past?

But she couldn't control random elements—babies, backfires, blowouts. What would Parker think of next?

Her nerves jangled. Only Hamp, Dutton, Law, Marina and a couple of others stood ahead of her. If everyone had a perfect ride, she had a shot at seventh at the worst. If anyone fell short, she could inch up the leader board. She lay with her eyes wide open, text messages flashing across her mind. She didn't need sleep to have a kick-ass round.

Just nerves of steel.

# Forty-five

Shortly after two Sunday afternoon, Lexy trotted into the stadium on a revved-up stallion. She was revved too but not in a good way. Parker had let her alone on cross-country and done nothing in the night. He had to make a move today. Her body throbbed with the usual aches after yesterday's tough ride and deeper soreness from the wreck, and she wished she'd gotten a good night's sleep. Or any sleep at all.

Her gaze swept the grandstands on all four sides. They held twenty thousand people, Colonel had estimated. And Parker could be anywhere, plotting anything. He had to know by now she wouldn't fold.

*Never let up, ride every stride,* Ben's words came back to her. She prepared by reviewing the enormous jumps inside—colorful replicas of equestrian landmarks in Kentucky, the twin spires of Churchill Downs, the cupolas of Claiborne Farms, others she did not know the names of. Trotting in, she merged into Bo's rhythm. Her hero was on task, ears up and haunches gathered. He pounded around the course he'd never seen as if he could read the course map in her mind. Cutting the corner into the final combination, she felt only his forward movement and saw only the red, white and blue striped poles before her.

A flash of light blinded her. She flinched, refocused on the center of the jump, but Bo felt her hesitation. He chipped in half a stride, and launched them up and over, but his left hind nicked the top pole. The crowd groaned, a distant murmur. The pole rocked, wood creaking on the metal jump cup.

She trained her sights on the final element, but a split second later, the pole boinked behind her onto the textured surface, one end then the other, as Bo gathered for their final fence. Ears pinned, he cleared it vengefully and galloped past the electronic timer, under time, she was sure of it.

But the pole cost them four faults and moved them down in the standings.

Bo didn't keep score but hated rails down. She gave a consoling pat below his braided mane and swore in anger. Because, as she trotted Bo from the arena, she was sure Parker was behind the flash, but how? The crowd applauded as if she'd won. Forcing a big grin, she gave a jaunty wave of thanks. Outside, she signed off with the ring official, then all was over but the waiting.

Adrenalin leached from her, and she collapsed inside, shattered by the wreck, the fight, the sleepless nights, and now defeat.

Ben stood by the gate, and she dismounted into his fierce hug.

"Almost perfect, honey. I'm so proud of you," he muttered, loyal and steadfast.

She choked back a sob. "We had it, too, till that flash blinded me."

He held her away and looked into her eyes. "*Blinded* you?"

"Three strides out, like sunlight off a mirror. I flinched, which put Bo off stride and we—"

"I'll kill him," Ben ground out. "When I find out who did it."

"It had to come from the main grandstand, the one in the sun."

"Same thing happened to Jordan on Rosie. I'm reporting it to the TD." He stalked off before she could stop him. Tyrone materialized and offered to walk Bo while she watched the final rounds. Feeling very much alone, she scanned the grandstand for another flash. Sun glinted off cameras everywhere, so it could have been anybody, not aimed at her. But she didn't believe in coincidence. Marina dropped a rail and went from fifth to sixth. O'Conner held her own, and so did Davidson and Law. Then Dutton dropped a rail and Hamp did a double clear, putting him in first. He punched air with his arm, dropped his reins and pointed down at Ax, giving him full credit. They'd been flawless.

To Lexy's astonishment, in spite of everything, she and Bo had squeaked into eighth place of ninety-five competitors, last in the ribbons and the money. It was only a few thousand dollars but her first contribution to the Hawks Nest team. Tyrone brought Bo back, and she trotted her horse into the vast arena for the awards ceremony.

It gave her chills to *be* there, almost a winner, but also a target. Not even Hamp could make her feel safe. She had to speak to him, but Marina swung Tosca into her path, cutting her off.

*Stand down,* Lexy told herself. Forget the fight, the insults, the disdain.

Hamp loved her and was riding home with her.

Her eighth-place rosette was a somber brown, but she pinned it to the hip pocket of her breeches with a deep sense of accomplishment. The crowd applauded, and she pointed to the sky, hoping her mom was one new bright star, looking down on her.

A brass band struck up, and the top eight finishers galloped two laps round, the Olympians' red jackets lighting the arena in brave patriotic splotches. Everyone stopped for Hamp to take a final solitary lap, and the crowd cheered. Lexy cheered too, thrilled for him. The good guy finished first, and he'd earned it, quietly, consistently. He'd worked so hard, always putting his horse's welfare first. He posed for pictures with event officials and the Kentucky governor as the money, the trophy, and the winner's watch were awarded.

Celebration over, Lexy rode out. Ben stood at the gate with Kim Legris. Lexy went cold, though she'd done nothing wrong. Ben was standing up for her.

"You remember Kim from Fair Hill," he said. "She's ready to take your report."

Tyrone raised a brow but led Bo off. Kim's debriefing took only five minutes, but she grilled Lexy as if she'd willed the flash. Still, Kim assured her their talk was confidential. The FEI and the USEF didn't want an incident like this to get out before they'd drawn and quartered the person who'd done it. If it had been deliberate. If it could be proved.

"She's worse than Gwen," Lexy told Ben, watching her speed off to other duties.

"Tough lady," he agreed.

"I'm getting a reputation for trouble."

"No. She has to be impartial. No room for error."

Her fault. "No room for stupid, squeamish riders."

"Where the hell did you get that idea?" he asked, earnest, concerned.

She caved inside. "I was supposed to be perfect."

"You mean Imbriani."

She nodded through a glaze of tears, and her new father pulled her to him. "Honey, I'm so sorry."

"I'd have won, you know."

"Sorry 'bout that too."

Then a reporter from *Eventing Nation* nabbed him for a post-competition analysis. Jordan arrived with Colonel. "Congratulations, Top Rider under twenty-five," Jordan offered as consolation. "Huge accomplishment."

Colonel winked. "Must have a hell of a coach."

Parker showed up in time to hear their praise and self-congratulations, and crimson anger blotched his face. "You two are out of your minds. Your protégé absolutely fucking blew it."

Lexy gasped, horrified by the flip-flop return of the madman who'd almost raped her, and here, in the public ebb and flow of people streaming out of the grandstands.

Jordan looked heavenward as if for patience. "Chill, bro. Let's not spoil a good day."

"It was crap. I could have gotten Bo around that course."

Colonel bristled. "If you ever took responsibility for anything, you might get good enough to ride that horse. This gal brought him back from hell."

"You're just hankering for a piece of young fresh meat, but the best you can do is give her your prize stallion."

Lexy cringed at Parker's insult to Colonel, but her mentor drew himself up, still imposing despite his weak left side.

"Apologize to Miss Imbriani, son."

Parker fisted his hands as if to stop himself from striking his father then turned on Lexy, bitterness spewing from him. "You stupid bitch, I shoulda called the sheriff when I caught you at my house."

Flamed, she shrugged. "I could tell them about your stash."

"Go a-fucking-head. I got nothing to lose."

Colonel growled. "Free board, unpaid loans, for starters if you keep carrying on like this, and what the hell are you two going on about?"

"Business, Pop."

"Business, bullroar. You lost this weekend, buddyroe. Just tuck your tail between your legs and drag your whiny ass back home."

"Go to hell, you old cocksucker," he said.

Colonel gave a steely glare. "I'll see you two in my office eight a.m. Monday morning."

Parker snorted like a horse mad at the whole wide world, but Lexy didn't have a hope he could be reclaimed. He stalked off to God knew where and left her shaking.

Somewhere between the blowout, his fall, and her success, Parker had gone stark staring mad.

# Forty-six

Back at the stalls, Tyrone and Greta had driven Chip's and Marina's trailers between the shed rows and loaded tack and supplies to make an early getaway.

Lexy was desperate to get out of here, away from Parker's madness. She wasn't up for a long haul home worrying how he'd managed the flash that killed her chances, but at least she'd be with Hamp.

Chip ambled up, holding out a chubby fist to shake Hamp's hand.

"Next year, win it on one of mine," he said with a smarmy smile. A shadow crossed Hamp's face, but Chip added, "Naw, man, seriously. Congrats. Huge win. The three of you, Marina and Lexy too. Happy to be part of the McRae family enterprise. Ready, Colonel? Tyrone? My plane's waiting across town."

"Room for me too?" Parker showed up out of nowhere, mask on, the public row with his father apparently forgotten. "Day job, you know."

Chip rolled his eyes. "You people think I'm the family taxi service."

"You love it, dude," the good Parker said, then went to get his things.

Jordan put a hand on her cousin's arm. "Daddy won't admit it, Chip, but he's bushed. You'll get him home in four hours where the drive takes nine."

Marina stalked after Parker, Minx pressed under her arm, and Lexy heard her whispery tone go sharp.

"You promised to drive *me.*"

In another dizzying shift, Parker cranked up the full-wattage smile of a man used to getting his own way. "Greta's a great driver, she can spell you. Or Hamp. Yeah. Go get Gambrell, and ride home with the winner."

"I'll do just that." Marina whirled and headed down the shed row after Hamp. He was folding Ax's new embroidered stable sheet, a prize for the win. Lexy could see her run her fingers up Hamp's shoulder and clamped down on an urge to wrench her arm out of its socket.

Then he nodded way too fast, and Marina walked off.

Lexy caught up to him, stomach churning. "You were riding with us."

*With me.*

He blinked as if he had forgotten. "Sorry, I was, but now I'm not."

"You can't. There are drugs in her RV."

He scowled. "How the hell do you know that?"

"Because I broke into it at The Fork, looking for evidence, and then—"

"Whoa. You broke into her trailer?"

"I was looking for evidence for Gwen. Then Marina and Parker came and he gave her some drugs."

His scowl deepened. "She's using drugs at competitions? She must be insane."

"Didn't see her using."

"Shit." He walked off, walked back. "You didn't tell me."

"Didn't think you'd approve of what I was doing."

"I don't." He took a breath, calmed. "Sweetheart. Breaking in was nuts."

"Driving her home would be nuts too." She took his hand. He didn't have to know about the fight. "Please. Don't go."

"Winning hasn't made me rich."

"She uses people—Jordan, Parker, Chip. Men. You."

His green eyes blazed. "I know that. And I'm using her. Do you have any idea how much she's paying me?"

"No. It's none of my business. Sorry."

He kissed her on the cheek. "Have a safe ride home. Get some rest."

But nothing about when he'd see her again.

What was it about men? But she was way too frazzled to figure it out this evening.

Nine and a half hours and four hundred plus miles later, Lexy woke as they pulled into Hawks Nest. It was after three a.m. That last hour, Hamp and Marina must have abandoned the convoy and sped ahead because there was no sign of them.

Of him. Crushed, Lexy palmed a gingersnap for Bo. He snuffled her hand and gobbled his treat and nuzzled her chest for more. She loved her stalwart friend more than any fickle man because he came by his quirks honestly. She found another cookie and held it high. He nipped it from her fingers. She held another low, and his knees buckled as he bent to snare it.

"Clown," she said, cheered despite Hamp's dumping her for a paying client.

Bo had given her the ride of her life at Rolex.

Her father was on her side.

She couldn't be luckier, happier, could she?

She tucked Bo in his stall and helped Ben and Jordan put other horses up. Then she climbed the stairs and peeled off her jeans and dirty shirt, her moment of cheer subsiding. She sucked at relationships. She slipped into the powder blue cotton sweat suit she always slept in and collapsed on the bed, hoping Hamp was home safe too.


She couldn't sleep. She couldn't let go of the best, worst weekend of her life. She warmed a can of black beans, cheaper than soup and full of protein, and stood at the tiny counter, jabbing them with a fork. Hamp had had every right to drive back with Marina. Chances they'd have been stopped, drugs found, and him arrested had been infinitesimal.

But the chance that Lexy's possessiveness had driven him off was not.

She picked up her cell to apologize. He'd been her rock, her foundation here. If he were awake, his phone would be on, but he did not answer.

She fretted what to say and finally texted,

**No harmony without you.**
**Ride tomorrow?**

Then she crawled into her narrow bed and slept.

# Forty-seven

She woke to the *wrank wrank wrank* of the commuter geese. Were they leaving the pond to go to work, or did she have—a hangover? If the geese were headed out, it must be after dawn, but she felt so confused. Was she in Kentucky? On the road? At home? She couldn't see, she couldn't think, and her head throbbed. She struggled to sit but couldn't move her arms and legs. A wave of nausea struck her, and the beans rose in her gorge as she tugged against—Ropes? Her arms were tied.

What the hell? Had she been drugged?

No, blast it, her fuzzed brain thought, she'd left the hot plate on.

But it was too early for the geese. She'd set her alarm for six. Then she caught an acrid smell, like smoke. Could the honking be the smoke alarm?

The barn on fire?

God no, oh Bo, he and Marcus were trapped in their stalls.

At least she'd turned Parker's guys out for the night.

Fire safety, drilled into her since Pony Club, kicked in. The stallion wing had a metal roof and frame, but the rest would torch like kindling—hay set out for morning, rubberized bricks that lined the aisle, dry pine shavings used for bedding, even the manure. Flames would flash along cobwebs on the rafters. Tyrone had scheduled spring cleaning for next week to brush them down. But the horses wore sheets to protect their clipped coats from dirt and chill—please God, let them be cotton.

Synthetics would melt into their skins.

She jerked her arms against the narrow cords that bound her wrists. They bit into her flesh and felt like baling twine.

Her brain felt like scrambled eggs.

She had to find her Swiss army knife, but where'd she put it? Blindly she patted the sheets, fear and desperation locking her breath in her ribcage. Try her breeches. Last night she'd peeled them off and tossed them to the foot of her bed. Nauseous, she rocked upright, smoke burning her eyes.

Hurry, hurry. Knees up, ankles bound, she kicked off the covers and scooted toward her breeches. Her toes found their suede seat, then she grappled with fingers that were numb where the twine had cut off circulation. Working her crossed hands against each other, she forced her fingers up the pants' leg to a seam, then felt a smallish, narrow lump. Thank God, the knife.

Jerking at the small zippered pocket, she opened the blade then sawed at the rough twine, jabbing herself in haste and crying out in pain. But the twine gave way, and she tugged her wrists apart. In the dark, she crumpled over and cut her legs free. On hands and knees, she patted up her bed to the headboard. A small perpetual-battery flashlight—Colonel had insisted—dangled there. She shook it for thirty endless seconds, felt for the switch, and turned it on.

Smoke swirled in its blue beam from the middle to upper reaches of her slanted loft ceiling. Jabbing her light into the murk, she found her cell charging on top of the dresser, unplugged it, then dropped to the floor to escape the smoke.

She flipped on the cell and saw another message.

**sayonara btch**

Parker. She gagged on bile that rose in her throat. He'd been here? Knocked her out? Set a fire? Left a message to mock her only if she woke before she roasted?

Could he be that far gone?

*Call nine-nine-nine—No, nine-one-one.* This was America, not England. Clamping the cell to her ear, she plunged down the steep stairs. Toxic smoke billowed around her. A dispatcher answered, and his drawl and distant calm made her feel homicidal. She gave him Hawks Nest's address.

A crescendo of terrified whinnies rose around her, more than Bo and Marcus could produce. She raced past the stalls and saw Brad, George, Sailor, Timmy, all of Parker's geldings in them, pacing, whirling, panicked.

What were they doing up? She'd turned them out.

Who the hell had put them in?

At least they were on their feet, but she had only minutes. The smoke would destroy them before the flames.

Fingers shaking almost uncontrollably, she called Jordan, then Tyrone. *Fire in barn. Barn in flames. Hurry, help. Help on the way.*

Hamp did not answer.

*Get wet, stay wet.* She found the hose and blasted it at the hay, fingers of flame hissing like angry geese, subsiding slightly. Next, she doused her hair, her clothes, and grabbed a stack of grooming towels to throw over her shoulders and the horses' sheets. She left the sprayer on the hose trained full bore on the hay.

She raced from stall to stall, opening doors so they could get out if they would. The heart of the fire threatened Marcus first, but it was Bo she thought she could handle. She haltered him, then Marcus, hoping to lead them out together.

Marcus planted his forelegs, terrified.

His fear invaded Bo, who reared and retreated to a corner of his stall. Praying he'd come out on his own, she threw wet towels on him, her heart shredding to leave him behind.

But Marcus would die if she didn't get him at once.

Outside, the younger stallion reared and twirled, panicking to be separated from his herd. Lexy made the soothing, whirring noises she'd learned from Ulrich, softened her grip on the lead, and raced him to safety as fast as she could run beside him. At the arena, she stripped his blindfold off and let him go. He tore away in a frenzied gallop. She closed the gate and raced back for Bo, the fire hotter, smoke thicker. He paced his stall, wild-eyed, frantic. But she hooked the lead line to his halter and set out at a dead run down the aisle, flames licking at the wet towels still clinging to his sheet. He struck out in stride with her, miraculously following her, head high and body surging down the bricks into the night toward the arena.

Across the yard, yellow porch lights flared. She spotted Ben sprinting toward the barn, Jordan stumping behind, shouting into her cell. Eduardo's battered truck wheeled in, and he dashed for Tyrone, speaking so fast in Spanish Lexy couldn't make out a word, but the two men came out with Brad and Sailor.

Hamp skidded in on his motorcycle, his face contorted.

A distant siren wailed.

*Too far away, too late,* Lexy thought. She had Bo, Marcus, Brad and Sailor safe in the arena, but George and Timmy were dying in the fire.

Far away, a second siren wailed.

Then Lexy saw Ben disappear into the hot red lashing flames, and her heart seized. She plunged after him, terrified of losing him, only to feel Hamp wrap his arms around her, his breath hot at her neck.

"No way you go in."

"Ben's gone after George and Timmy," she cried, bucking against Hamp.

Ruth came out with Colonel, yelling she wouldn't let him kill himself.

"Take her," Hamp said savagely, passing Lexy off to them. "She's suicidal. I'm going for the horses."

"No-o-o," Lexy cried, clutching the one wrist she could. He tore from her grip, ran for the barn, and black smoke engulfed him too.

"Let me *go,*" she screamed at Ruth, but the woman's wiry arms were strong, and Colonel joined his arms with hers. Lexy couldn't risk hurting him. Yielding, she let them lead her to Eduardo's truck and sit her on the hood, useless and defeated.

Interminable seconds hurtled past. Fire trucks wheeled in. Firemen unfurled hoses and pumped pond water into the snapping flames. Hamp burst through the smoke, clinging to a lead line attached to a thoroughly freaked-out Timmy who spun, reared and whinnied frantically for his mates.

Hamp braced to stop him from plunging back in.

Lexy wanted to rush to his aid, but Ruth and Colonel held her to them tight.

Ben came out last with George. The gelding was crazed, fighting every step, and then she saw patches on his bare neck burned to raw muscle. Embers had rained on the high-tech stable sheets Parker had splurged on, and they'd melted into the flesh along his topline and hindquarters.

Timmy settled enough for Hamp to coax him to the arena. Tyrone left his charges there and ran to help Ben with George, who flailed about, insane with pain. Finally they released the wounded geldings into the great sheltering space and closed the gate.

Then Ben, his charred clothes in tatters, saw her, and his fierce look melted into sheer relief. She slipped free of her minders and flew into his arms, sobs wracking her seared lungs. Ben winced and drew away.

"Ohmigod, you're burnt," she said.

Red blisters splotched his hands and streaked his forearms.

"Your hair…" he rasped.

Lanky tendrils, singed to bristles, crumbled in her fingers. She had less hair left than he. He touched her with light fingers as if she were porcelain, inspecting her face for injuries. "Dear

God, sweetie, are you okay?" He was choking from the smoke, but his love filtered through.

"Yes," she croaked. "But the horses?"

"Not good," he said, tilting his head at her. "You up to this?"

No, never. "I saw burns in England."

Roger's Hummer skidded into the drive, and he yelled for Jordan out his open window. She gestured at the arena and ran ahead to hurry him, her limp growing more pronounced as the ordeal took its toll.

Roger braked at the gate, got out, slammed the door, and charged inside.

Parker's old black Porsche screeched to a halt behind a fire truck, his rear wheels doing a U-ie on the gravel. He took one look at the inferno of the barn and marched toward it.

"Arena!" Ben cried. "We got them out."

"Got who out?" Parker shouted.

"Bo, Marcus," Lexy yelled. "Your guys."

"What the hell were they doing in the barn? They're on night turn out."

"We just saved them, asshole. Barely."

Parker towered over her, shaking with instant rage. "Night turn out was your job."

"And one I carried through on," she shot back.

"So who the hell—ah fuck it," he said, flicking his hands down as if to shake off her very presence, and he tore after Roger, desperate now as the full horror of it all sank in.

The sky glowed angry orange as the barn burned on, flames shooting through arcs of water in a demonic dance. One fireman turned his hose on the nearest wing to keep the fire from spreading. But the stallion barn was lost. Against the rising sun, Eduardo and Tyrone evacuated the boarders' and the sales horses from the other barns and ran them to far paddocks. It all went so fast. Lexy couldn't fathom what Parker might have done, or how. How could he have done it with his own horses in the barn?

But she had to see how badly Bo was burned. Ben hurried her to the arena. Ruth and Colonel followed fast as they could manage. Lexy moved toward Bo quietly, dread pumping through her. Chunks of his short mane and long thick tail were seared away, and it gutted her to see burns from flying embers splotching his face and neck. First-degree burns, maybe second there, but her wet towels and his old-fashioned cotton stable sheet had spared him worse.

Still, he had to be in pain. She reached for Roger's arm.

"Later," Roger brushed her off. "The others need me more."

Last out, George and Timmy had the most horrific burns, and Roger injected them with Banamine. Parker paced around them, his face a rigor of agony. He reached out to them, pulled back, desperate to help, able to do nothing.

Less severely burned, Brad and Sailor quieted enough for Hamp to turn them over to Ruth and Colonel. Jordan commandeered the medical kit.

"Okay, folks," Roger said. "This is gonna be ugly. We gotta get those sheets off."

Hamp held George while Parker held Timmy, Parker mired in revulsion and despair as he saw the extent of their injuries and their pain.

But Lexy still felt the ties around her wrist, still heard the smoke alarm, still felt her struggle to get downstairs and save the horses from the fire.

Why had Parker shown up now? Anyone she'd alerted could have called him, but how had he known to send the message?

*He'd sent the message because he'd set the fire.*

And in that moment she wanted to throw him on the pyre.

Across from her, Ben worked steadily on Brad and Sailor, his jaw clenched. She joined him, and they peeled the geldings' blankets off their tortured backs. The acrid smells of grilled flesh and burnt synthetics curled into her nostrils. From their withers to the docks of their tails and halfway down their sides, charred hide peeled off with the melted fabric like layers of an onion. Here and there, they were burned down to raw muscle.

Third degree. She fought to stand on watery knees, nausea rising in her throat. Damn Parker's corrupt soul.

Stone-faced, Roger injected all four geldings with another dose of Banamine.

She was about to insist he give Bo another injection when he barked, "Someone get a God-damned trailer over here. These two go to Raleigh."

George and Timmy, to the vet school, Lexy understood, to be saved or euthanized. It could take weeks to know, or with George they might know by evening.

"Calling Chip," Jordan answered Roger. "He's got the nearest working truck and trailer." While she auto-dialed him, Lexy could hear Roger alerting the vet school that two bad burn cases were on the way.

Standing helpless beside his once handsome youngsters, Parker vomited. Chip arrived in minutes in yesterday's wrinkled clothes. Parker collected himself enough to lead George onto the trailer, tears streaming down his ravaged face as if he were the victim and actually loved his horses.

She couldn't prove he'd done it.

She helped Ben load Timmy, the next worst injured gelding with swathes of raw flesh on his back. His drugged, glazed eyes did not hide his pain.

Chip cranked the truck, and Parker jumped on the running board.

Colonel grasped his arm. "No way, son. I want Gwen to hear your story."

"That's deranged," Parker exploded. "I gotta be there, sign things."

"Chip can sign for you. There's not a damn thing you can do up there but barf your guts out. Gwen's gonna want to see you."

Colonel gave Chip a thumbs-up to leave. His rig lumbered out the driveway, passing Marina, who zoomed in in her BMW roadster. She slotted it under a mimosa tree wilting from the heat of the fire and raced to Parker's side.

Gwen's official SUV roared in next. She got out, took in the burning barn, and dashed into the arena, unable to hide her horror when she saw the horses. "Okay, folks. Listen up. I need to confirm where everybody was last night."

Lexy told Gwen she'd been in her apartment. Jordan and Ben had been in bed. Chip had been at home with his wife Sloan. Ruth had seen Colonel to his room and helped him change into his pajamas, then gone upstairs. Tyrone had slept in his trailer.

"I was in fucking town," said Parker, still bereft, but angrier.

Gwen looked over her reading glasses from person to person as if reevaluating what each one had said, then said, "Anybody see anything out of order when you got back? Anything irregular?"

"How about something regular?" Parker handed Sailor off to Eduardo and pointed at Tyrone, who was calming Marcus. Ty's wet clothes clung to him, and a ghostly film of ash lightened his dark complexion. *"He's* always here."

"Jesus, Parker," Jordan said. "He's our brother."

"That's a damned good motive, isn't it? Getting diddly from Father who gave us everything. Not that he gave me what he gave you."

"Bullroar, son. I loved your whiney, ne'er-do-well ass no matter what, so help me God."

"Like you loved my mother? You drove her to drugs and drink," Parker raved.

Tiny Ruth, a full foot shorter, stepped up to him. "Parker McRae, your mother drove up with a bottle of Jack Daniels in her hand before you were even born. Your daddy tried to save her."

Parker's face contorted. "I would call that one of your more spectacular failures then, sir," he said, fury foaming at the

~ 329 ~

corners of his mouth. "You failed, old man, didn't you? Her and Ty and me."

"You got it all twisted, Parker," Ruth put in. "You have no idea how hard he tried… how hard we all tried to keep you on track."

He glanced at his horses, lost in rage, and pivoted to Colonel. "But you play favorites, don't you? Your favorite daughter's crippled now. I may be a bastard, you philandering old goat, but I'm yours too. Bo should have always been my ride. Not some too-young, hot-shot interloper," Parker said, and stomped over to Roger.

He was still treating Brad and Sailor. Up close, he looked devastated by the gruesome burns he was debriding, blood and gore smearing his hands and coveralls.

Glancing Lexy's way, he tossed her the key to his Portavet. "The Banamine compartment—left front center drawer—is locked. It's the smallest key. I need four more and some lactated Ringer's solution. That's in the—in the—*shit*—the right side cabinet."

She was hurrying into the arena with bags of IV fluids hugged to her breasts when from deep within, she heard Ben shouting, then a banshee Rebel yell.

It was Parker bareback on Bo, galloping him across the arena with nothing for control but a halter and a lead line. Her mind froze, then adrenalin kicked in. She ditched the fluids and spread her arms, making a human fence. Parker urged Bo forward faster, flapping his arms and kicking his sides, bearing down on her.

At the last moment, she lurched out of the way. Bo thundered past, overjumping the metal gate, Parker crying, "I'll show you motherfuckers."

He was headed for the cross-country field.

# Forty-eight

"No-oo!" Colonel cried.

Parker's yell echoed across the farm, startling a red-tailed hawk who lifted off a high pine, spread her wings in the morning sun, and banked a rising current. Then the only sounds were the tattoo of galloping hooves and the hawk's high scolding *shree, shreeee*. Lexy ran into the wing that had survived the fire, grabbed a bridle near the tack-room door, found Jazz milling in a paddock, and flung the reins around her neck.

The mare was Lexy's only hope to catch Parker, tackle him off Bo, and beat him to a bloody pulp.

Jazz took the bit and Lexy secured the headstall, sidled her up to a three-board fence, climbed it and threw herself on. Jazz was keen to escape the chaos, and Lexy urged her with her knees and calves and heels, the mare seeming not to mind a bony butt digging into her back. Racing like the wind was in her Thoroughbred DNA, and she was fresh where Bo had just come off a four-star course.

Thank God, Parker wasn't headed for the jumps.

Oh, no, Lexy realized a quarter mile farther on. He'd targeted a distant obstacle, the newest, scariest one at Hawks Nest, a massive trunk of a giant old oak toppled by the hurricane, so high she couldn't see over it. A leader root stuck up at one end. Parker had dubbed the obstacle "God's Thumb."

"No, stop!" she shouted. "You'll hurt Bo and kill yourself."
But Jazz's speed whipped her words away.

Kicking Bo, Parker charged toward it.

"Parker! Please! Stop," she screamed, burning with fear that
he'd kill himself and Bo. They galloped on. She was catching
them when, to her shock, he pulled a gun and fired over his
shoulder, not even looking back. Jazz bolted, and Lexy let her
go, flattening against the mare's neck as best she could, praying
she could cut Bo off before Parker put him to the jump.

Even injured, tired, Bo was too fast for Jazz.

Reining her in, Lexy watched, despairing, as Parker,
bareback, drove Bo on, the stallion's ears up, primed, as ever,
for his next thrilling leap. It was too soon after Rolex to ask for
such an effort, but she felt him gather to hurdle yet another
obstacle he'd never seen with all the courage of his noble heart.
He bunched his powerful haunches, rocked off his hocks, and
launched in a split second of perfect form and pure desire.

Parker, not used to Bo's raw power, grabbed for mane and
missed, yanking the lead line. Bo's forelegs smashed against the
tree. In sickening slow motion, Parker tumbled over it, and Bo
cartwheeled after him. They disappeared behind the tree. She
heard a light thud and a heavy one and wrenching grunts from
deep within both horse and man.

Bo's head popped up a moment later.

For an instant, Lexy felt relief. Bo scrambled to his feet,
then tore off at a gallop, bucking angrily as the lead line
whipped his flank. Her heart buckled. If he'd incurred a hairline
fracture, that pounding could shatter his leg.

Behind the tree, Parker made no sound. She slid off Jazz,
looped the reins over her left shoulder to keep the mare from
tearing after Bo, and crept round the tree trunk, hoping Parker
had survived, worrying he still had the gun. She peeked around
the trunk, heart thumping in dread. Parker staggered to his feet
with vacant eyes. His handgun lay on the ground several yards
away. Dragging Jazz, she dove for it.

"Don't shoot, luv." He raised his arms like an outlaw in the old West, but yelped in pain and lowered them. "I'm shure my shisters will do it for you. Whersh Bo?"

She flipped the safety on and slid his gun into her hoodie's pocket. "He ran off." She looked at him more closely and shuddered. His hair and face were scraped and smudged with grass and dirt.

"'S'matter, luv? Never seen a man take a fall before?"

"You shouldn't have gotten up, and you'd better sit down now."

Ominously compliant, he stretched a hand out to the tree, stumbled toward its great spreading roots, and collapsed, moaning. Large and small, the roots entwined him, Lexy thought, like a mother's arms.

Lexy heard Hamp's motorcycle roar up. Ben shouted, "Lexy! Parker!"

Shaking, she rounded the sawed-off end of the big trunk. Ben leapt from behind Hamp who dropped his bike on the sandy turf and ran to her, bypassing Ben and yelling, "We heard shots."

"They missed. He's hurt."

"How bad?" Ben asked.

"Rotational fall."

Both men groaned.

"But I couldn't see them land. Then, when I went round the trunk, he was on his feet, talking, crazy."

Still hanging on to Jazz's reins, she led Ben and Hamp to Parker. He was sitting on the tree's giant root, as if at home on the old porch swing, blood still dribbling from his mouth onto his shirt.

Even so, he rose drunkenly to meet them.

"You need to sit, my friend," Ben said.

"Naw, man. I'm okay. Shoulda seen my stallion. Sucker can jump the moon."

"Listen to Ben, please. Sit," Lexy urged.

He scowled. "Sitting's for sissies, that's what Pops would say."

Just then Gwen pulled up in her SUV, skidded to a stop, and hurried over. Jordan, Ruth and Colonel followed fast as they could move.

Gwen looked at Parker, and her face crumpled. She took his hand as if he were a child, led him back to the spreading roots that made a perfect seat, and said, "Parker, honey, you have to sit down now. This is Gwen, your sister, and you're hurt."

Parker blinked, bewildered, then patted down to find the trunk and sat.

"Did Bo fall on you?" she asked gently.

"No way. We fell together, roly poly." He rolled fist over fist like tumbleweeds.

Lexy turned away, nauseous at this image of what she'd only heard.

Nauseous too that he must have set the fire. Gwen must suspect this too now, but she'd left Parker with Jordan and Colonel and was barking orders into her mobile.

"Yes, this is the sheriff—" Forced to wait, she hissed impatiently. "I *know* you sent fire trucks, Bonnie. I ordered them. Now I need the EMTs." Gwen listened, chewing her lower lip. "Somebody'll meet them at the gate and show them to the field we're in—" More listening, then Gwen said, "Yes, it's like Armageddon out here—Thanks."

"Jordan," she said after she clicked off, "tell Tyrone to stay at the barns to direct the EMTs. I'm calling Archie." She rang another number, and Lexy chafed. She needed to tell Gwen what she suspected. "Chief, if your men can handle the fire, we got a bad fall here needs your evaluation." Gwen listened for a moment. "Yes, Archie, the key's in Colonel's ATV... Yes, we're over the rise. Due north of the burning barn."

Lexy crossed her arms around her body, horrified by Parker's injuries and the burden of everything she knew. Ben slipped an arm over her shoulder, holding her to his side as if he could shield her. His short blond hair was singed in splotches to his scalp, and ashes smudged his high cheekbones. He captured her gaze, more vulnerable and loving than she'd thought possible. "Couldn't have borne to lose you."

She dropped her head on his broad shoulder and circled an arm around his waist to stop her body's quaking. "Me too, you."

Hamp stood at her other side. "I shoulda killed the bastard."

She took his hand with her free one. "Please, no anger now."

"Not anger. Fear."

Finishing her calls, Gwen knelt at Parker's feet. The family hovered around her, powerless to help.

"What have you gotten yourself into this time, buddy boy?" she asked, so sad, so soft Lexy could barely hear.

"My horses were on night turn out," he said dully, then seemed to come to life. He blasted a bleary glare at Lexy. "'S'all your fault. Why'd ya hafta bring 'em in?"

All heads turned to her. "I went straight to sleep," she rasped, her throat so raw she choked on a whisper.

To her surprise, Ruth knelt too and put her fingertips to Parker's as if she was afraid she'd hurt him. "We had a lightnin' storm, honey, don't you remember? Ty always brings them in for storms."

"So what if they were in or out?" Colonel bored in on Parker. "Did you set the fire?" Then he clutched his chest as if in agony.

"Daddy, are you okay?" Jordan cried, at his side in an instant.

He waved her off with his stronger arm, his attention riveted on Parker. "How'd you do it?"

Parker gave his head a shake but grunted from the pain.

Gwen joined her father. "What are you thinking, Daddy?"

~ 335 ~

"That Parker knows what happened tonight. Tell us, son." *Son*, with obvious contempt. "This has the marks of your work."

"Di'n't mean—Sir," Parker mumbled, blood bubbling up between his lips.

"Didn't mean to what?" Hamp demanded.

Archie Snow wheeled up on Colonel's ATV, still in his orange- and silver-striped protective fireman's regalia, with Marina perched on its cargo rack.

"My partner in crime," Parker greeted her, bright again.

"No, Parker!" She leaped off the ATV and sprinted for him, crying, "It was a game. Tell them. Only a game."

Freeing herself from Ben and Hamp, Lexy lurched to confront her. "Burning the barn, rigging my saddle and the tire was a *game?*"

Parker laughed like a man who'd gone quite mad. "It was just a smoke bomb. You know, to smoke Lexy out. Show them. She's careless. She doesn't deserve Bo."

"Neither do you," Hamp said, sinews straining as he clenched his fists to control himself. Together Lexy and Ben pulled him to the side, and the fire chief waded through the small, bunched crowd. He was tall with a balding dome shaved clean.

"Give us some room here, folks," Archie said with the calm of one used to disaster.

Colonel and Marina did not move, but everyone else stepped back, forming a ragged circle around Parker so the chief could check him out. Archie took Parker's vitals, asked him the day, the month, the year, the President of the United States, then pressed a stethoscope to Parker's ribcage and flicked on his mobile.

"Dispatch Air Care," he ordered, and paused to listen. "Yes, we're in Vass, off Youngs Road. Gwen, can you give coordinates from your SUV?"

Gwen called out latitude and longitude. The chief gave Dispatch the numbers, repeated them, and then turned from the McRaes and spoke softly into his mobile. *Looks bad,* Lexy heard. Parker's vitals, no doubt. Coming back, the chief spoke louder. "Yes. Destination, Chapel Hill."

"No, Citadel," Parker mumbled, lost in the past, clearly thinking of his college, not the university hospital. "I go to— Citadel."

Gwen and Jordan shared a grim, shocked glance.

"Air Care's ten minutes out, max," the chief said with practiced calm.

"But Archie. My son…" Colonel pled.

Archie's ash-streaked face was a mask. "I'm sorry, sir. Best guess, we got a TBI—traumatic brain injury, probable collapsed lung, sternum fracture, cracked ribs."

Jordan gasped. "You mean Bo rolled on him."

"He means pray," Gwen said.

"Both," said Archie.

Lexy's pulse flailed. Badly as Parker had treated her, she couldn't imagine, couldn't want, to see him dead.

But Bo was in danger too now, loose in the field, and maybe injured. A monster helicopter landing near could launch him into the next county. She thrust Jazz's reins into Ben's hands. "I gotta get my horse."

Frantic, she ran toward where she'd last seen Bo, sucking soft April air into her smoke-damaged lungs.

Hamp caught up to her, coughing too. "Need backup?"

"God, yes," she rasped, hearing the drone of a distant engine in the sky.

They made it to a rise, and there, at the bottom of a grassy slope, Bo grazed greedily on lush Bermuda grass. She picked up the lead line trailing on the ground, handed it to Hamp and inspected her stallion for injuries. She found none.

"It's a miracle," she said, stroking his neck to comfort him, to reassure herself. "What about the helicopter?"

Hamp scanned the field. "I'm guessing we're a couple of hundred yards from where they'll land. So he should be okay."

*Okay.* That was all that registered—that, and then the chopper's whomp, whomp, whomp, soon a roar as it cleared the pines, its blades thrashing overhead. Bo flicked an ear but kept grazing the rich grass.

In the distance, by the tree trunk, Air Care touched down on slender skids. Tiny human forms popped out, ducking the rotors and pushing a gurney as they raced to Parker, placed him on the bed and wheeled him into the chopper. It lifted off and she and Hamp walked back to the site with Bo.

Ben met them halfway down the hill. Everyone had gathered around Gwen and a fuming Marina in handcuffs.

"My lawyer will sue for false arrest."

"You can lawyer up all you want," Gwen said. "But the words of a dying man are incredibly convincing to a jury. So I repeat, partner in *what* crime? Did you help him set off that smoke bomb and start the fire?"

"I know nothing," she said as if from a lofty throne, but her voice trembled.

Gwen shot Lexy a probing glance. "Or maybe you're ready to tell us what you know. Something to jog Marina's memory. Lexy?"

Lexy choked. She didn't know what Marina had confessed to or Gwen suspected.

"You've kept things to yourself long enough, sweetie," Ben said quietly. "Tell us what you know."

Lexy looked from him to Jordan, Colonel, Gwen. Their faces were drawn and pale with shock.

"Not much," she said. "Everyone knows about the stirrup and the blow out. What I didn't say was after our first win, someone mugged me behind the barn."

"Mugged?" Ben asked. "You mean—"

"Grabbed from behind, threatened."

"Were you hurt?"

"I fought him off, but he pushed me to the ground. Landed on my wrist." She stopped, confused. Who had she told what, and what should she tell now?

"There were messages," Gwen prompted her.

"Yes, always anonymous and, as you said, 'hard to trace, harder to prosecute.' Meant to shake me up at competitions. They did."

"You shouldn't have carried on alone," Jordan berated her, but gently, too shattered to press for more.

"I suspected Parker. I went out to dinner with him once, hoping to trip him up. He took me to his condo, but all I learned was he has a very friendly cat."

"You broke into my trailer," Marina said, still glowering in her cuffs. "I should have charged you."

"She couldn't," Lexy said, to Gwen. "I saw drugs in Parker's condo, and he brought some to Marina at The Fork that day."

Colonel was sitting where Parker had sat, on the giant root of the old tree. He rose slowly, Ruth supporting him. "I knew my son was a scoundrel. Didn't know he was an idiot."

"Shhh." Ruth took his pale hand in her dark one. "He's going to need us now. Let's just get to the hospital."

The fire chief had left long ago. They all trailed back to the barn—Jordan, Colonel and Ruth in Gwen's SUV with Marina in custody. The family planned a bedside vigil by Parker in Chapel Hill, and Gwen would transport her suspect to the sheriff's office. Hamp followed on his motorcycle, quiet as could be. Lexy and Ben led Bo behind them all in the saddest procession she had ever been a part of.

# Forty-nine

Pretty damn sad when the bad guys die young," Lexy overheard Chip drawl. He propped an arm on the mantelpiece in Hawks Nest's parlor, still in his funeral clothes, like all the mourners who'd followed them back to the farm.

"Zip it, cuz." Gwen, in black, gave him her official glare. "Daddy and Jordan are devastated."

"Hey." He lifted his glass. "Parker was young. And bad. I'm sad."

"Show some respect. I'm devastated too."

Lexy shivered. She'd been a block of ice since word came that Parker hadn't made it. She watched Chip chug three fingers of Jack Daniels neat. Spirits—wine, beer, and good bourbon—flowed, and the crowd ricocheted from laughter over another Parker story to hushed whispers about what really happened.

Parker had died in a coma the day after his horrific fall.

Sympathies had poured in from around the world, for him, the horses, even the old barn. The condolence book on the Hawks Nest website, managed by him no more, was getting a hundred hits an hour. Jordan and Colonel kept the lurid details to themselves, but speculation ran wild on the forums.

After a dignified service at the First Presbyterian Church of Southern Pines, family, friends, horsemen and horsewomen, farriers, vets, business associates of Parker's—a well-heeled bunch of doctors, lawyers, realtors whose websites he'd maintained—descended on Hawks Nest Farm. Parker's fans, a stream of bottle blondes and streaked brunettes, packed the parlor. Lexy couldn't help wondering if the ones with red-rimmed, swollen eyes had been his lovers, wannabees, or victims. Had he forced them too, or charmed their breeches off? She shuddered, trying to shake the memory. She'd had to fight him. She hadn't wished him dead for that.

But to risk her horse's life, and hers, repeatedly, then tie her up to die with the horses in the burning barn…

Bastard. Psychopath. She'd never gotten a fix on the good Parker or the bad one—the divided self his family had dealt with for years.

And she'd never know how he'd pulled off everything. Just yesterday Gwen announced her lab guys had confirmed that chloroform had caused the blowout. As the tire had heated on the road, the chemical had degraded the lining, making the tire explode. Easy to order off the Internet, she said. Then he'd used what he had left to knock her out before he tied her up.

If Marina had been in on anything beyond the first text message in the fall, she'd obeyed her lawyer's injunction and admitted nothing. Gwen wasn't pushing Lexy to press charges. The family didn't want to put her through anything more after what Parker had done. And they didn't want to pile dirt on their dead brother's name. Let him lie in peace, and let them get on with their lives. Within an hour of Parker's death on Thursday, Jordan had given Marina walking papers. Greta had packed her stuff and moved her out, but not before Marina blasted Jordan for betraying their friendship, destroying her life and, oh, yes, having a tight-assed, country bumpkin sheriff for a sister.

Lexy wandered in a daze from the parlor to the den. Colonel sat in his good desk chair turned inward from the window to face his visitors. Jordan commanded his strong side, and Ruth protected his weak flank. He received neighbors and friends, even Parker's clients he'd never met, with military dignity, but Lexy could see his soul stripped bare for all to see. He'd loved his wayward son.

She stood in line until she got to the front where she could kiss his cheek and murmur that she loved him. Then she moved on to the kitchen in search of Hamp. Rachel and Ann had trapped him against an antique breakfront. Ever polite, he excused himself and hurried to her.

"You okay, sweetheart?"

No. She ran her fingers through her hair, after the fire a short cropped fuzz. She could have burnt to death, and she was at her second funeral in a year. Her mother had died, and Parker too, and she was freezing.

Hamp took her cold hands in his warm ones, and the miserable guilt she'd been trying to deny erupted.

"I couldn't stop him," she choked out, her throat still raw.

"Sweetheart, no. He brought it on himself."

"Even so—" she protested.

He cupped his calloused hand around her elbow. "It's thick in here. C'mon. Let's get some air." He escorted her through the crowd, down the hall into the soft sweet air of the early May evening. A blur of people thronged the front porch waiting to get in. Others clumped in bunches on the lawn, having given their respects to Jordan, to Colonel most of all, and Hawks Nest's history, tradition.

The full moon made shadows sharp as daytime beneath the surviving oaks and etched the sharp edges of Hamp's face. He gripped her shoulders and said earnestly, "Parker didn't care if he killed you or Bo any more than if he killed himself."

"But I saw them take that jump. I heard them..."

*Crash. Grunt. Groan.*

Saw Parker lying on the ground, broken.

"I should despise him," she said.

Hamp folded her in his arms. "You're not like that," he murmured, his warm breath at her neck.

She pressed a hand to her mouth to hold back sobs. "I thought he'd make it. Reform. He was so damn—"

"Crazy."

"No. Alive." It hurt to breathe when someone she knew couldn't. "Despite what he did, I couldn't help liking him."

"Everybody liked the good Parker."

"But he's dead, and my mother's dead, and poor innocent George," she said, and let go her tears.

Hamp pressed her to him, his slow steady breathing not quite a consolation.

"What do I do with my life now?"

"Dunno," he said, glancing past her shoulder. "Ask him."

It was her father. He'd had to miss the service, called away to the High Performance committee to select the Short List horses and riders. He'd had his burnt hair shorn into a buzz cut. More clearly than ever, she saw herself in the planes and angles of his face.

She swiped tears from her eyes but not before he saw them.

"Aw, honey." Ben patted her back awkwardly. "You'll be okay."

She wasn't sure, but she and Hamp filled him in on what had happened since he'd left—details of Parker's death, Gwen's test results, Marina's dismissal.

He asked probing questions, which they answered, then said, "Don't know when I'll get back again. I need to talk to you both."

"Of course," she said, but her heart stalled.

"Sure," Hamp said, in rock monument mode.

Her father was the coach, their future in his hands.

He shuttled them toward the paddocks, away from the guests and the charred remnants of the barn.

Bo whickered, recognizing she was near.

Ben gave Hamp a handshake and a hearty hug. "You made the Short List, man. Congratulations on a great season with a gritty horse."

Hamp's impassive crag broke into a grin.

Ben went on. "The Selection Committee has great expectations for you at the Mandatory Outing." An Advanced competition, Lexy knew, where the dozen or so short listed horse-and-rider teams would be evaluated for soundness and fitness for final team selection.

Her heart swelled with love for Hamp and a jig of wistfulness he'd made the cut and she had not.

Ben gave her a big smile. "Sweetie, you made the Short List too."

"I what?—How—?" she stammered, her cold blood flooding her with sudden heat. "I mean... I blew Rolex. You mean, we're..."

Ben's iceberg eyes seemed warmer, proud. "Yeah."

Lexy clutched. She desperately wanted this to work. "That's nepotism."

"I can vote, but where there's a clear conflict of interest, I can withdraw from the discussion. As your father, I withdrew."

"It's your team."

"I got the people I wanted—some old, some new, some East Coast, a couple of super folks from the West." He sobered. "Tough times here at Hawks Nest, but you two—enjoy this moment. The hard work starts tomorrow."

She just wanted to get away from sadness and mourners and put her arms around her horse. She and Bo had met all tests, and she had a bona fide shot at the Olympic team. She flipped from grief to hope and back again.

"Told you so," Hamp said after Ben went inside. He pulled her into a lusty kiss, and she was instantly on fire.

"We can't do it here."

"Just warming up..." he said, and kept kissing her, nothing stopping them but clothes until Hamp drew away and grew serious. "There's a hitch."

"Yes?"

"If I make the team, I was planning to ask you to come and groom for me."

"Cool," she said, then saw the problem. "If we both make it, we both need grooms."

"So instead," he said, his green eyes soft and more intense than she'd ever seen them, "I hope you'll do me the honor of going as my wife."

Speechless, she covered her mouth with her hands and searched his gaze for affirmation. With his stark black hair and copper skin and shocking clear green eyes, he'd never looked more beautiful, or vulnerable. She dropped her hand away.

"You mean it?"

"Lying messes with my harmony." Then he grinned, a cocky grin, sexy as all get out. "Getting turned down would mess with it too."

"Then yes, of course, yes, nothing would make me happier. Bloody hell, marry you? You mean, forever?"

He dug his fingers into the fuzz of her regrown hair and steadied her head to make her look at him. "Forever, and a farm, with at least fourteen horses, four babies, four dogs and four cats. A sheep or goat or two. I draw the line at llamas and pet snakes."

She leapt into his arms, cinched her legs around his hips, and together they tumbled onto the grass for a private celebration of their future.

## Acknowledgments

Many readers imagine us writers spending our time alone, fingers flying across the keyboard as we channel our stories from the ionosphere. On some glorious days that's true. But a story like this one requires a cavalry of supporters. I salute the horses who inspired me and the many wonderful readers who joined my campaign—spies, soldiers, and the folks back home.

My brilliant production team was committed to preserving this novel as a horse story. Carol Hay introduced me to horse whispering. She brought her sensitivity to every draft and her keen proofreader's eye to the final version. Tashery Shannon, novelist and devoted volunteer at Old Friends retirement facility for Thoroughbred stallions, edited and designed the beautiful book you have in your hands or are reading off your Kindle or Nook.

Samantha Clark, reporter at www.EventingNation.com, and Alison Springer, short-listed for our Olympic team, generously gave their permission to use Samantha's dynamic photo of Alison and her long-time partner Arthur on their way to their stellar win in the Advanced C division at The Fork this year. Lucky me, I was there and saw them clear this tricky corner. I am deeply grateful to Scott Osborne for permission to reproduce on the back cover "Autumn Afternoon," by his father J.L. Osborne, Jr. It's Hawks Nest house.

Several horses inspired Bo. First and always, my beloved, tireless, quirky Winston. For twenty-three years until his peaceful death at the age of thirty-two, we galloped over the countryside, splashed through creeks and rivers, charged up and down the steepest hills. Blackjack, Carol Hay's rescue off-the-track Thoroughbred, lived his last years at my farm and taught me so much about the sensitivity and tact we need to deal with the breed. His big heart and floating trot are Bo's. Dana and Manny Diemer's Cold Harbor, currently ridden by Boyd Martin at Advanced, inspired Bo's name and has his flash and dash. Special thanks to Steuart Pittman of Dodon Farm, Maryland, for answering questions about the ups and downs of eventing stallions. Salute the Truth, his gorgeous chestnut stallion now standing at stud, successfully competed at Advanced. Like Bo, "Willie" has a fan club.

Many writer friends helped me hone my story while learning perhaps more than they ever wanted to know about horses—Gayle Feyrer (Yves Fey), Susan Sipal, Wendy Lindstrom, Maree Anderson, Nancy Northcott, Lynn Coddington, and Alicia Rasley. Google them. They all have wonderful books and Maree a TV series! Bill and Gloria King and Bob Aldridge advised me on all things vehicular and airborne and spared me errors. Robin Gurlitz test drove Stallion in doctors' waiting rooms and couldn't put it down. Dennis Forbes encouraged me to keep on keeping on.

I thank the horsemen and horsewomen—some writers, all readers—who helped me nail down details to the last blade of grass used in pastures in the Sandhills. Nate Chambers, Kelly Clement, Dana Diemer, Sarah Dunn, Stacey Neil, Tiff Teeter, Don Warren—bless you all for reading one or more drafts of this book. But more, for inspiring me with your devotion to horses' welfare and for sharing your intimate knowledge of them and our noble, historic sport. Kelly invited me to shadow her as she directed a spring schooling event, managing the myriad details from ribbons to snacks to announcers to order of go.

Max Corcoran, Karen O'Connor's gal Friday, welcomed me to chat as she gracefully performed the day-in, day-out nitty gritty tasks of grooming Karen's horses and supporting her at competitions. Holly Hudspeth welcomed me to follow her for a day of coaching at her farm just north of Southern Pines. Sally Ike at the USEF graciously answered questions about the Watch List and other technicalities. Shauna Spurlock of Spurlock Equine Associates sent me up-to-date information about surgical procedures and medical treatments. Chatham County Sheriff Richard Webster kindly talked me through the use of prepaids and the legal issues of harassing text messages.

Finally, Nate, bless you, for being my go-to guy for insider information about jumps, saddles, bits, libations, and so much more. I'm thrilled to participate in your four-star aspirations with Rolling Stone II ("Rolly") and our new horses Satisfaction ("Simon") and Winsome.

Dana Diemer, your warm welcome to Carolina Horse Park at the very beginning of my journey with this novel was the making of its authentic horse world. You introduced me to upper-level riders, technical and safety directors, jump judges, volunteer coordinators, score runners—to so many of the competitors and staff it takes to make our complex, daunting sport so compelling. You made it possible for me to spend an entire day learning from Kathy Rowse as she scored upper-level dressage tests. You gave me access to the office and announcer's booth, but best of all you and Manny gave me a ring-side seat to observe your competence, vigilance, and the commitment it takes to stage a three-day event.

In my years working on this novel, I can never forget all I learned from meeting and watching our talented, generous, and courageous United States and Canadian four-star riders—Olympians, Pan-Am team members, and medalists at the World Equestrian Games. Friends of my heart, I may not have talked to you, but here and there you may glimpse a moment that reminds you of something you said or did.

I especially acknowledge Karen O'Connor, Boyd Martin, Philip Dutton, and Michael Pollard, gifted and fearless riders all. Your courage in adversity and loss is a sterling example to us all. Kim Severson, John Williams, and Nate Chambers kindly let me tag along on course walks. I learned so much at schooling shows on Denny Emerson's Tamarack Hill Farm South on Youngs Road in Vass, NC. Yes, Youngs Road exists. Hawks Nest Farm is NOT Denny's, but an amalgam of eventing stables I've known in several states over the years.

My understanding of the discipline of eventing deepened after I re-read the legendary James C. Wofford's books then audited his two-day clinic at Adrienne Claussen's farm, Wit's End Eventing, in Elkin, NC. Everyone knows there's no better clinician, rider, writer or gentleman in the eventing world.

With deepest appreciation to all my sources, any errors that remain are mine.

My husband Peter Harkins keeps my computers running when I'm home and then cleans the kitties' litter boxes and mucks out after my horses for days on end when I'm gallivanting around the country having way too much fun!

I wouldn't have gotten us into nearly such a fix without the inspiration of my daddy Clyde Phillips and my granddaddy Colonel (his given name) Jacob Smith, horse traders who lived for the next good deal.

Ann Pope Stanley, my dear childhood friend, read every draft and always wanted more. When we were nine and so horse crazy that our teachers turned us loose at recess all by ourselves alone to play horse and make up their stories in our wild free way, how could we have known we'd still be best friends and still crazy about horses and their stories.

Photo by Carol Makemie Hay

Author of four historical novels and RITA finalist, Judith Stanton first imagined equestrian triumphs on her grand-daddy's persnickety black Shetland pony and balky donkey, her daddy's mule, even the milk cows. At nine, riding bareback with only a halter, she taught her pinto Blaze to jump hay bales. During a career as a scholar, professor, technical writer and fiction editor, she kept fit riding three-day eventers. She now celebrates her favorite sport in fiction, doing her most daring riding ever on the page. Judith lives in North Carolina, where she and her husband tend to her elderly equine friends and a steady stream of rescued cats. She's a proud owner of Satisfaction ("Simon"), a fancy young eventing prospect ridden by Nate Chambers.

Made in the USA
San Bernardino, CA
16 April 2014